continued ...

"*Valentine's Exile* isn't an average vampire novel.... The vampires and their soul-sucking Lovecraftian masters are like Dr. Moreau on steroids. This is nicely drawn horror: not gross, not psychologically terrifying, but very creepy.... E. E. Knight is a master of his craft. His prose is controlled but interesting, and his characters are fully formed and come to life. The point of view is tight and rigidly maintained, and the transitions are beautifully handled from scene to scene. The novel maintains a sense of place, with touches of sound and taste keeping each setting vivid and acute. Consistent tone and voice and excellent pacing keep the reader glued to the action and adventure. Even the futuristic touches are drawn with just the right tweaks of reality: never overdone, no R2-D2 types, no *Trek* guys. E. E. Knight's work is creative, and the voice is his own."   —*Science Fiction Weekly*

"Knight gives us a thrill ride through a world ruled by the vampiric Kurians and filled with engaging characters and grand schemes, and promises more to come."   —*Booklist*

"The Valentine series is still going strong. Each book reveals new secrets concerning the world which expose new levels of complexity.... I'm looking forward to more."   —*SFRevu*

"The latest addition to Knight's popular alternate-Earth series maintains the high quality of its predecessors, combining fast-paced action/adventure with the ever-popular vampiric threat."   —*Library Journal*

"The Vampire Earth series just keeps getting better and better.... A fantastic work of science fiction in the vein of Wells' *War of the Worlds*."   —*Midwest Book Review*

Praise for the Novels of *The Vampire Earth*

"I have no doubt that E. E. Knight is going to be a household name in the genre."   —*Silver Oak Book Reviews*

"A winner. If you're going to read only one more postapocalyptic novel, make it this one."
    —Fred Saberhagen, author of the Berserker series

"Knight is a master of description and tension.... Character-driven speculative-fiction adventure at its very best."
    —*Black Gate*

Novels by E. E. Knight

The Vampire Earth

Way of the Wolf
Choice of the Cat
Tale of the Thunderbolt
Valentine's Rising
Valentine's Exile
Valentine's Resolve
Fall with Honor

The Age of Fire

Dragon Champion
Dragon Avenger
Dragon Outcast

VALENTINE'S RESOLVE

A NOVEL OF THE VAMPIRE EARTH

E. E. KNIGHT

A ROC BOOK

ROC
Published by New American Library, a division of
Penguin Group (USA) Inc., 375 Hudson Street,
New York, New York 10014, USA
Penguin Group (Canada), 90 Eglinton Avenue East, Suite 700, Toronto,
Ontario M4P 2Y3, Canada (a division of Pearson Penguin Canada Inc.)
Penguin Books Ltd., 80 Strand, London WC2R 0RL, England
Penguin Ireland, 25 St. Stephen's Green, Dublin 2,
Ireland (a division of Penguin Books Ltd.)
Penguin Group (Australia), 250 Camberwell Road, Camberwell, Victoria 3124,
Australia (a division of Pearson Australia Group Pty. Ltd.)
Penguin Books India Pvt. Ltd., 11 Community Centre, Panchsheel Park,
New Delhi - 110 017, India
Penguin Group (NZ), 67 Apollo Drive, Rosedale, North Shore 0632,
New Zealand (a division of Pearson New Zealand Ltd.)
Penguin Books (South Africa) (Pty.) Ltd., 24 Sturdee Avenue,
Rosebank, Johannesburg 2196, South Africa

Penguin Books Ltd., Registered Offices:
80 Strand, London WC2R 0RL, England

Published by Roc, an imprint of New American Library, a division of Penguin
Group (USA) Inc. Previously published in a Roc hardcover edition.

First Roc Mass Market Printing, July 2008
10 9 8 7 6 5 4 3 2 1

In memory of Don and Rita,
who always had smiles on their faces, jokes on their lips,
and a cold beer in their fridge.

ACKNOWLEDGMENTS

Liz for her patience and understanding; John for his guidance; Howard for his perception; Mike for his research, ideas, and experience earned in Laos; my parents for the family vacations to Washington; and Stephanie for her love.

There are some remedies worse than the disease.

—PUBLILIUS SYRUS,
MAXIM 301

CHAPTER ONE

Weathercut Manse, Iowa, November, the fifty-second year of the Kurian Order: A Hawkeye from the first quarter of the twenty-first century would hardly recognize his state in the snow-dusted fall of that year. The corn and soybeans, yes, the birches and willows claiming soggy land rimming the streams and lakes, and the majestic oaks, elms, and cottonwoods, the slopes and crests of the low rolling hills around the river basins, certainly.

The beef cattle in the fields give some hint that times have changed. They are undersized compared with the big steers of better times. A few cough; others have the strained look of an animal who has picked up a bit of wire or a piece of a can.

It's the architecture that's changed most, the roads and bridges and little towns in between. A well-traveled or imaginative Iowan might think himself in some quiet stretch of French or English countryside.

Instead of four-lane towns surrounded by farms with frame homes, barns, and silos rising nearby, or sometimes the newer Wal-Mart blisters girdled by parking lots and fast-food stops and sprawling exurb, the new centers of public life are the Great Homes.

Like the French villas and English manses of old, the Kurian Order Great Homes are built to impress. Some are vaguely Alpine, with high-peaked roofs, elaborate woodwork on the overhangs, and two or three stories of glass window broken only by balconies; others mimic the heavy beams and plasters of Tudor dignity; a few seem to be almost brick-by-brick re-creations out of a Jane Austen movie. But the most popular style might be called French modern.

Weathercut Manse is an example of the last style. A big, bold front of limestone and picture windows, shielded from the elements by a tall slate roof, grows a stablelike garage looking out over the gravel turnaround to the right, and a turret like a miniature castle keep to the left. The off-balance arrangement is pleasing in the daylight, when the sun lights the flower bed in the center of the turnaround, so that the manse seems to be reaching out to embrace visitors and present a bouquet in the day. However, at night the lanes resemble the arms of a boxer dropping into a defensive stance.

Around behind is a smallish patio, reached by French doors, flanked by the glassy refuge of the marbled indoor spa, and topped by a private balcony outside the master's bedroom, and the aviary-greenhouse locally famous for its lemons and year-round supply of plum tomatoes.

Gardens, wilder woods, and a nine-hole golf course surround the house. It is only once you get beyond the thick hedge to the east, the three rails of white fencing to the west, or the stone wall with iron gate running the road to the south that you reach the working part of the estate, a seventy-acre horse farm. There's housing on the grounds for the pigs and chickens, and a New Universal Church parsonage. A thick wood separates the Kurian churchman from a little square of prefabricated trailer homes, a repair garage, and a gas pump.

The Mansion is the pleasant face of the estate, the parsonage its conscience, and the barns and tenant homes its muscle. But next to the gate, built into that dignified wall, are a small stone house and garage that are the lizard brain of the estate, the security center. The workers check in here each day and pick up a radiolocator watch that can be fixed to a beltloop; all traffic into or out of the estate must first pass through security, a sodium-vapor-lit double-basketball-court-sized stretch of pavement *surrounded by chain-link fencing, where vehicles can be parked while their contents are searched and inspected.*

The guards walk with a bit of a swagger in their camouflage and winter fur hats (in the summer they wear black pith helmets), carbines with telescopic sights and bayonets mounted as if to warn visitors that they are ready to deal with trouble, either at a distance or up close and personal. They defer only to the master with his brass ring, and the parson with his white clerical collar, as they patrol the grounds on ATVs or, for the romantically minded security chief, an ox-eyed Arab gelding and a silver-tipped riding crop that he uses as a pointer.

Not that there's much trouble in this quiet corner of northeastern Iowa, far from the troublesome Grogs of the Missouri valley or the noisome guerrilla band that has recently sprung up in the Indian-head territory of Wisconsin. The security guards can joust on their ATVs with cattle prods—also used as nonlethal inducements for the tramps and "mexicretins" to move on down the road without applying for work or largesse at the manse.

Just that morning, as a new wind came along to kick up the remains of the previous night's snow, the security team rousted a tramp from his shelter in the rusted, weed-grown hulk of a sport utility, tire-less remains in the woods where it had broken down in 2022. They woke him with a cattle prod and sent him on his way, after a cursory search of the grubby little odds and ends he shouldered in edge-worn bags. He carried a Wisconsin work card indicating that he'd last been employed a year ago, and swore he planned to return to his home province of Eau Claire. A request for food brought the cattle prod up again and instructions on how to reach the nearest New Universal Church hostel eighteen miles away—the manse parsonage serving only the Weathercut grounds and its tenants.

Now the tramp hobbles down the road in that toe-in, footsore fashion of a man who has gone too far on bad shoes. He wears a buttonless shirt held shut with stock twine wound round his waist crisscrossing his chest. His face, under a greasy thatch of tangled black hair, has a thick layer of dirt in permanent residence, and little can be read in his brown eyes, permanently downcast. It's a face that has seen its share of hardship; an old scar runs down from the right eye, and the jaw is a little off-kilter, though it gives his face a humorous set, as though he's turning up the corner of his mouth at a private joke.

The only piece of gear on him that might attract interest is his short walking stick, used to help mitigate the effects of his obvious limp. The twisting wood has a good steel cap where it strikes the road, a leather wrist loop, and a short handle projecting out of the knobby top.

One of the guards who questioned him looked like he was thinking of confiscating it, but the tramp told a convincing story of it being awarded to him after he was wounded fighting for the TMCC in Little Rock during Solon's brief tenure. The back of his ID card did have a half-peeled old shining service star—the sort of thing elementary school teachers used to put on spelling tests— and a discharge stamp, and at a glare from the senior guard, himself a TMCC veteran, the stick was returned.

The road wanders up a little treelined hill—only a technically minded surveyor would call it a ridge—as it reaches the edge of Weathercut's lands, then down and over a stream.

The tramp checks a litter-filled hole in the bridge's armpit—the bundle is still there, and the little piece of paper set to dislodge if it's moved is still pinned to the bridge's concrete by the pack—and then takes a long drink from the stream, lowering his face to the water as though he were one of the manse's horses, before settling down for a nap.

Had one of the guards followed to observe the tramp until he was off the grounds, he would have thought the last very strange. Travelers, especially vagrants, take care to travel only during daylight and hide deep and dark once the sun sets. Kurian Towers are few and far between in this part of Iowa, but their avatar Reapers use the roads as they go about their affairs, and are only too

*happy to remove a human mote like the tramp from the
picturesque dells of this corner of Iowa.*

David Valentine didn't rest under the bridge long. He
got to his feet again well before dark, but not before he
exchanged the flap-heeled road shoes for a pair of soft
buckskin moccasins.

He was tempted to take one or two of the weapons
from the cache under the bridge, but there was still
a chance that he'd be observed sneaking through the
estate's orchards. He could talk his way around a few
pilfered late apples, but not a pistol.

Valentine carefully cut upstream toward the manse.

This was not his first visit to Weathercut Manse; he'd
been on and off the lands a dozen or more times that
November, getting a feel for the rhythms of the estate
and its personnel. Taking your time with this sort of
thing made the results exponentially surer.

This being a Wednesday, F. A. James, late of the
TMCC but now enjoying a comfortable sinecure courtesy of Crossfire Security and the Ringwearer of Weathercut, would be on the east side of the grounds from
eight to twelve, after which he'd put in four more hours
at the gatehouse, then sixteen in ready reserve in the
security apartments next to the utility garage.

Not that Valentine intended for him to finish the
shift.

Sometimes the captain or one of the older hands
would accompany F. A. James on the field patrols, but
tonight would be cold. He'd probably be alone, driving
his ATV from point to point, possibly with a dog riding
in the back, as he checked the fields and fencing, warming his hands over the engine whenever he paused.

Valentine had picked out the spot a week ago, spent
two long cold nights, one watching it to get the lie of the
ground and the guard routine down, especially where
the headlights of the ATV would shine.

The east side of the estate ran down into a soggy
streambed, rough and dimpled and thick with birches

and poplars and a drowned oak that had fallen. The estate fence ran down into the bottom, probably to protect the pheasants that nested there.

The fence wasn't very formidable at this point: a chain-link barrier with razor wire strung atop in a Slinky-like tangle, a final fence for the estate's livestock and a serious warning to anyone else. But whoever had built it didn't account for smaller-animal activity, or simply didn't care. Prowling raccoons had dug under it and a dog or two might have expanded it, chasing the raccoons, for all Valentine knew. He'd opened it still farther on one of his scouts.

He looked at the fence one more time, and checked the distinctly nontrampish timepiece he kept in a tobacco pouch in his pocket. Made of steel thick enough to cause sparks if struck against flint, it was a soldier's wristwatch long bereft of band; it had a magnified bezel so the big white-painted numerals and hands could be easily read at night.

Stalking makes one feel alive and focused, yet it is oddly calming in the stretches of idleness. This night provided a little extra frisson of excitement for Valentine. F. A. James would be the last. He didn't know what he'd do after this one.

Tomorrow would take care of itself.

He took a breath and extracted the red balloon he'd found near Carbondale, Illinois, and carried around knowing he'd find a use for it sooner or later. He'd slipped a rolled-up piece of paper into a tiny white-capped orange plastic container, the kind Kurian-issued aphrodisiacs and fertility enhancers usually came in, and attached it to the lip of the balloon with a bit of wire. He put just enough breath in it to make it look like it was on its last legs, then added a knot in the bottom. Then he reached up to hang it on the razor wire where he was sure the ATV's light would hit it as James turned along the path.

He examined the ground around the thick oak on the manse side of the fence, picked up a few twigs, and tossed them back over the fence. No telling just where he'd have to drop and how far he might have to run.

Valentine patted the small knife in the sleeve sheath on his forearm and gripped the legworm-leather handle of his hatchet-pick. It was a handy little tool of stainless steel used by the legworm riders of Kentucky to mount their forty-foot-long beasts. This one had a pry blade at the other end of the slightly curved pick with its nasty fishhook barb, great for popping small locks and a hundred other uses, urban and rural.

Including lifting yourself up into an oak.

Valentine hooked a limb and swung his legs up, crossed his ankles around the branch, and was in the leaves and branches as neatly as a retreating cat. In his last scout he'd even found the branch he wanted to rest upon.

He passed the time thinking about Mary Carlson with her currycomb, or giggling at the dinner table.

He didn't doze, but fell into a mental state that lowered his lifesign, a form of self-hypnosis. He doubted there would be any Reapers prowling the estate; they were scarce in this bit of brass-ring-thick Iowa outside the bigger towns, but it was still good to stay in practice. Even if the fleas and ticks on his body helped obscure the signal humans gave off.

The blat of the ATV lifted him half out of his trance, the way a mouse's tread might cause a rattler to open an eye even as the rest of it remained quiescent.

Valentine tensed. There was always the chance that F. A. James wouldn't see the balloon. Then he'd have to drop off the tree and knock him from the saddle with a body blow, and that could be chancy if James was alert.

No dog in the back of the minibed. A bit of his neck relaxed. He hated killing dogs, even when famished.

James directed his ATV slowly along the fence. Part of his job was to check its condition. Cattle rustling was not unheard of in Iowa even among the estates; an ambitious young Grog could easily lope off with a couple of prime calves or a young bull tied across his shoulders and paddle them back to the Missouri valley in a canoe.

And at the back of the estate owner's mind there would be old sins, walled out of the manse but still lurking there like Poe's telltale heart. Most Ringwearers had made enemies on their way up. The fence was Weathercut Manse's outermost layer of skin protecting the vitals at the great house.

Unfortunately for F. A. James, the skin could be easily gouged if that's all an intruder wanted. He was protecting the house and its lands. Nothing but a handlebar-hung shotgun and a cattle prod at his waist protected James.

F. A. James must have seen the balloon as soon as his headlights hit it. He slowed and then stopped his ATV.

He turned off the motor and Valentine silently swore. The idling engine would have covered his footsteps. James warmed his hands on the engine and climbed off.

F. A. James' fur hat, its security badge at the front glowing dully like a third eye, tilted upward as he examined the balloon. A message in a tiny plastic jar—the old prescription label had been stripped off so the paper curled within could be more easily read—would be tempting. It was traditional in Iowa for brides and grooms to loose balloons on their wedding day, usually with messages of good wishes—"sky cheer" was the phrase—but it was always customary to send one off with a large-denomination bill inside.

What's given up to the world is returned hundredfold, read the New Universal Church bible.

For the past two years Valentine had been in the karma business. After tonight he'd close up shop.

He tightened his grip on the hatchet-pick.

Valentine dropped out of the tree when he saw James yank on the pill container, popping the balloon not quite at the moment his feet hit the ground. Valentine softened the landing with a roll, came lightly to his feet, and took two quick steps to the ATV's saddle.

The shotgun was locked to its bracket, so he sprang

up on the saddle and used it to vault toward James, who'd finally reacted to the noise behind and turned to be struck across the head with the blunt side of Valentine's climbing pick.

Valentine cuffed his prey and gagged him with a bit of his hat, so that this quiet corner of Iowa might remain so.

He checked the stout laces on F. A. James' tall combat boots and wondered how best to secure his captive to the cargo basket of the ATV.

Empty silos are not difficult to find in Iowa.

Empty, of course, as in "not containing corn or feed." Nature abhors a vacuum, especially when that vacuum cuts the wind and keeps out the snow, so the silo Valentine had chosen a week ago contained a good many creepers, spiders who ate the creepers, mice who ate the spiders, and barn owls who ate the mice.

And bats. Their guano added a fragrant decoupage atop the rusting chute gear and old feed sacks at the base of the silo.

F. A. James hung upside down by a single line of nylon cord, dangling from rigging far above in the black top of the silo. His slightest movement caused him to swing extravagantly, like the pendulum in a grandfather clock.

Valentine squatted atop the rusty mechanical rubbish, sharpening a short, thick, curved blade with a sturdy handle.

The security man's features were hidden under a white pillowcase, tightened about his head with a bit of the same nylon cord. Inked-in eyes and mouth made him look as though he were wearing an abbreviated Halloween costume. The effect was more for those who would find the body than for the benefit of the pair in the silo.

"Gate codes," F. A. James said, his voice stressed and cracking. "Is that what you want?"

Valentine kept sharpening the knife.

"There's a spare back-door key—"

"I don't want access to Weathercut," Valentine said, deciding the knife was sharp enough. "I wanted you out of it, Franklin."

"But I'm nobody important," F. A. James squeaked. "I don't even have my own room."

"That's the problem with being a Nobody Important. Someone might decide you're disposable. Kind of like that teenage girl back in Arkansas. The one you, Bernardo Guittierez, Tom Cray, and Sergeant Heath Hopkins raped and then killed."

Valentine smelled urine leaking.

"No! I mean, you've got the wrong guy."

Valentine was a little relieved that F. A. James kept talking. He hated the ones who just blubbered at the end. Cray had spent the last five minutes screaming for his mother.

"Her name was Mary Carlson. Ever catch her name? Bother to remember it? You must remember her face. What did it look like at the end? Now, I figure four guys, maybe ten minutes each—that was a long forty minutes at the end of her life. About as long as the next forty minutes are going to be for you."

James was panting now, and the pillowcase went in and out of his mouth like a flutter valve.

"Mary was into horses. Loved them to death—good at taking care of them too, once she learned what was expected."

Valentine drew the blade across the whetstone. The sound echoed off the cobweb-strung walls of the silo like a cat spitting. "This is a hoof knife," Valentine explained. "Horse hooves are tough to cut, and you need a short, strong blade to get through them. Hoof is way tougher than, say . . . the cartilage in your nose and ears, Franklin."

James spoke again from beneath the ghost mask: "Captain Coltrane over in Yaseda, he's got a whole jar full of ring fingers off of girls he collected for the Reapers. You should be going after him."

"I never knew the owners of those fingers."

"I didn't even come. I just did it 'cause the others did, and Hop killed her before I knew he'd drawn his pistol."

F. A. James' story didn't quite jibe with what the others had said. According to Guittierez, the corporal had demanded that the girl be "flipped over" to escape the indignity of "sloppy seconds," then made her—

But Valentine didn't care about the details anymore. The investigation and hunt were over. Now there was just duty to Mary Carlson.

"You see a white collar? The time to confess passed with the investigation. I read the documents. Consul Solon, for all his faults, didn't like civilians mistreated. You could have admitted it. You would have gone to prison, probably, but you wouldn't be hanging here now."

Valentine selected a spot for the first knife cut.

"This is just to scare me, right? You're done—I'm scared. What do you want? What do you *want*?"

Valentine never remembered much else that F. A. James said during his final moments, cut short, as they always were, because the screaming got to him. Part of him was distracted, puzzled by that last question.

CHAPTER TWO

Hobarth's Truckstart and Trading Post, Missouri, February, the fifty-third year of the Kurian Order: The days of long-haul trucking are all but over.

Nevertheless a few overland "runs" still exist. The Atlanta-Chattanooga-Nashville artery still trickles, as does the old interstate between Baltimore and Boston. The Vegas-Phoenix–Los Angeles triangle is the scene of the yearly "Diamondback Run," where supercharged muscle cars roar from the coast to Vegas, where the crews switch to off-road vehicles for a trip to Phoenix, then make a final leg in tractor-trailers running loads back to Los Angeles, something of an indulgence for certain wealthy or engine-obsessed Quislings.

Dashboard cameras record the experience, and sometimes the final words of the drivers.

But the longest of the "hauls" still in existence is that from Chicago to Los Angeles, much of which runs along the old lines of fabled Route 66, even if the end point at the Sunset Strip meets the ocean rather more abruptly than it did a century ago.

The veterans of the "Devil's Dietary Tract," as the route is known, make fortunes hauling art, rare firearms, expensive clothing, and particularly electronics from point to point, liquor and consumables flowing west, finished products imported from the rest of the Pacific Rim back east. The Kurian Order shrugs at such baubles for their human herds, or perhaps believes that physical and mental energy expended acquiring a Picasso, a pristine set of golf clubs, or a vintage Remington 700 is activity that isn't being spent resisting the regime. Black marketers are given a wrist slap in most instances. The security services of the great rail companies make sure nothing that can't be hidden in a purse or backpack moves cross-country on the rails—at least without a substantial bribe. That leaves internal combustion engine or pack animal for the traders and smugglers who want to move larger loads.

Some say that the "independents"—as the nonrail transportation companies are known—are riddled with Kurian informers. Any firm that helps the burgeoning resistance is quickly seized, its durable goods auctioned and personnel packed off to the Reapers.

Trucks need fuel, tires, and spare parts to run, and of course the crews need food and rest. So on the fringes of the Kurian Order, or within Grog-held territory, there are "starts," where men and machines can be reconditioned for the next leg of the run.

Hobarth's is a typical example of a fortress truckstart, encircled by wire and then an inner wall of broken tires wired together and filled with dirt, a tiny human settlement deep within the Grog territory of mid-Missouri. There's a substantial warehouse devoted to trade with the Grogs, cavernous aluminum barns for the repair of vehicles and the storage of spares. Behind it rusts a junkyard covering a dozen-odd acres guarded by rifles and half-savage dogs. The penalty for unauthorized scavenging is a bullet.

But for the tired, broken-down, and road-weary there's safety within. Even for those without the price of a cup of coffee, the Hobarth staff will feed, wash, and accommodate the most destitute—"three days of a month, three months of a year." "Christian duty," the staff calls it.

Others are welcome to buy, sell, or trade at Hobarth's store or the stalls of mechanics and craftsmen. There's even a small jeweler under the old three-orb sign, who also acts as a currency exchange, able to deal in most of the Kurian scrips of the Midwest. The local Grogs have become adept at extracting and reconditioning every-thing from wheel rims to timing belts and spark plugs, bringing them in to trade for bullets or sealable plastic storage containers, which the Grogs prize for a well-appointed, bug-free hut.

Three high-clearance flatbed tow trucks, armored and armed with machine guns, compose the toughest salvage team an overnight drive in any direction. Two of the team, the front one prowed in such a way that it resembles a vehicular battering ram, fling gravel as they turn in to the main gate, bringing in a rusted cab-over. Once inside the compound and behind the main building, long and flat as Dakota prairie, the crews elbow one another and point at a smallish legworm contentedly pulling up leaf-less kudzu near the tire wall. A steel-framed ergonomic office chair, complete with ottoman, folding umbrella, and movable windscreen, sits stapled and chained to its spongy, segmented back.

"Argent's in," the green-hatted driver of the battering-ram wrecker announces, opening a tow truck door with DRIVER CARRIES NO CASH, LOTS OF LEAD *stenciled on the side.*

David Valentine, reading a book as he drank his coffee in the four-table "café," recognized Tim Hobarth's step behind—the tow truck driver wore steel-heeled boots, which rapped distinctively on the boarding.

"What's the crawl, Max?" Hobarth asked.

Valentine, who'd left his name in the shambles of a wrecked career in the United Free Republic, drew his cup and book a little closer, making room for the big driver. He'd just as soon continue reading his book with the brew, though the bitter mélange that the Kurians labeled coffee insulted the palate of someone who'd had the real stuff in Jamaica.

"Omaha's getting set for a fight," Valentine said. To the families who worked Hobarth's, he was just a wandering Grog trader blessed with unusual luck in avoiding the Reapers. Valentine had stopped and visited the Golden Ones, in the fading hope that his old friend Ahn-Kha had wandered home with an epic story of escapades from the Kentucky foothills to Nebraska's far horizons.

"Kur needs those rail lines out of Omaha badly, now that so much south of Missouri is cut and Tulsa's been burned to the ground. The Golden Ones are great fighters, but if they put some big guns into Council Bluffs . . ."

"Poor dumb Grogs," Hobarth said. The sympathy in his voice belied his words.

Valentine liked Hobarth. He possessed some feeling for the creatures Kur had brought from other worlds to help subjugate humanity. Some of the tribes found themselves in wrecked and poisoned lands after the fighting was over, and a few, like the Golden Ones, had turned against the Kurians.

"The Golden Ones are a long way from dumb," Valentine said. "And they know engineering. They've got a network of tunnels under Omaha you wouldn't believe if you didn't see it, and they've rigged a few likely buildings to collapse. I wouldn't want to be part of the Omaha garrison, assuming the Iowa Guard takes it. They're recruiting out of the scrub-country clans again, looking for tribal support. Doubt they'll get it."

"How's business otherwise?" Hobarth asked.

"Lean. Omaha just wants optics and precision tools." It had been so long since he'd talked to another man that Valentine felt his mouth running on of its own accord. "Those are tough to come by, especially when they don't offer much in return. Leatherwork I can sometimes sell, but pottery? Oh, that reminds me. I might have a connection in Springfield for you for tires. That Grog molasses tobacco is getting popular in Chicago."

"Wonderful. Hey, I talked to Gramps again about you. He's upped the offer to a full family share if you join up."

"I told you before: I'm a crap driver."

"You'll learn, Argent. We could use you and that freaky hair of yours." Valentine had once explained that a nearby Reaper had caused his hair to stand on end. "The spring run to the coast is gearing up. See the world, you know?"

"Tourism through scratched-up goggles at the trigger ring? Not my way to see the country."

"Oh, I'm not talking hired-gun stuff. Scout salvage. You have a knack for getting in and out of places none of our clan come within a Reaper's run of."

Hobarth's was a great place to take respite, but Valentine wondered about settling down there. If he joined up, the next thing they'd expect was for him to marry—and there were a couple of widows near his age attached to the truckstart. Lora, who worked in the garage, never failed to do her hair and put on her best when he visited. Problem was, her conversation was limited to engine blocks, fuel injection, and ethanol when she wasn't parroting the New Universal Church propaganda she'd learned as a child.

"I'll think about it. Promise," Valentine said.

Hobarth was canny. He knew "Max Argent" well enough to know that if he wanted something, he jumped at a chance, whether it was a night on clean sheets or a volume in the little library that existed in the Hobarth attic.

"Reading again? *Confed*..." Hobarth knew parts manuals and truck manufacturers, but preferred the pool table and old pinball machines of the family rec room when it came time to unwind.

"Confederacy of Dunces," Valentine supplied.

"Sounds like the ministers in Kansas City. I hear there's cholera. Both sides of the river."

Kansas was bleeding again, and much on the mind of the whole Hobarth clan. She had broken into warring factions, supported by the UFR in the east and the powerful Kurians of the Southwest on the other side of the Arkansas River. "Route 666" had become tougher than ever.

Valentine contemplated his tea. "One of them will get bled. The Kurians don't like people dying without orders and proper processing."

Hobarth stiffened a little. It didn't do to say such things, even deep in the relatively neutral Grog lands.

Valentine changed the subject. "I'm about done with this. Can I get up in the book attic? I want to look up an item or two."

"Look something up? It's not an archive. It's a paper junk heap. Most of the stuff's falling apart."

"I saw a book there last trip. I just want to read up on it a little more."

"Wonderful. Do us a favor and clean up a few cobwebs while you're up there, okay?"

"Gladly."

"You accommodated?"

"Yes. Don't worry, the Dragon Lady's charging contractor rates. I had some Iowa scrip I wanted to dump anyway."

Hobarth smiled at the use of his aunt's nickname. "I'll tell everyone to be extra nice. You staying long?"

"Maybe a week. My worm needs a few days of feeding."

"You could use all that in-wall time to take a bath, you know. You could read in the tub."

"What, and lose my camouflage? The critters confuse the Reapers, you know."

"Wonderful. Something about you's just a bit out of alignment, you know that, Argent? And I don't mean that busted-up face of yours either."

Valentine didn't enjoy exercise. He'd rather heat his muscles chopping wood, or even digging a latrine ditch or picking apples, so something might be gained out of the calorie loss. He looked on exercise as a routine maintenance activity, like adjusting straps, darning socks, or sharpening and oiling a blade. It was not an end unto itself, but preparation so his body would be ready when called upon.

But he could combine it with a more interesting activity, like fishing.

So during his stay at the truckstart, every morning he'd sling his tackle on the legworm's harness and goad it out to one of the ponds or creeks, provided there wasn't a winter fog or cold rain. The Reapers sometimes prowled in daylight if the overcast was heavy enough.

So with a clear morning and in hope of a torpid catfish he'd prod his legworm out, where it could pull up bush in peace while he fished. On the way there and back he jogged from one side of the legworm to the other, practiced leaping on its back or mounting it using low tree limbs to swing himself up, until his breath came hard and fast and his bad leg ached. If the fish weren't biting, he'd practice with his battle rifle—a few cartridges now and again could be replaced, and there was no such thing as a wasted shot if it kept you in practice. The time might come when being able to eat, or draw one more breath, would depend on a single bullet.

Besides, the women at the truckstart believed the smell of gun smoke to be an improvement.

Evenings he'd spend in the attic library, unless a truck came in. Then he'd join the rest of the Hobarth's gang and listen to the latest news, reports of road conditions, and shortages, always shortages. Valentine would borrow any kind of printed material—even Kurian leaflets sometimes carried clues as to the progress of the UFR. He read them with the mixed emotions of an estranged relative catching up on family events.

He lingered at the truckstart until he found a driver Tim Hobarth recommended who was heading south into the UFR. He entrusted the woman, a wispy-haired piece of leather who went sleeveless even on a cold day and drove an ancient diesel pickup pulling a high-clearance trailer, with a letter and coin for postage. He'd addressed the wax-paper packet to "William and Gail Post."

Post would make sure his information about the Iowa Guard's movements got into the right hands. A few Bear teams and some Wolves inserted into Omaha would make a world of difference.

Valentine spent the rest of the afternoon and evening moody and anxious to be off. He'd staved off the empty feeling by composing his letter to Southern Command and seeing it sent on. With that done, the guilty memories marched right back into his forebrain and set up residence. Finishing with Mary Carlson's murderers had left him empty and with too much time to think. Now free to get back to St. Louis, conscience partially cleared by his plea for help for the Golden Ones . . .

He spent his last evening at Hobarth's wandering the acres filled with wrecks, getting glimpses of the old world through faded bumper and window stickers and business information printed on car doors and rear windows.

WARNING: FREQUENT STOPS AT GARAGE SALES
GET ANY CLOSER AND YOU'D BETTER
BE WEARING A CONDOM
IN THE EVENT OF RAPTURE THIS VEHICLE
WILL BE EMPTY

It was empty, unless you counted mice and spiders.

They weren't all pre-2022. Valentine saw one that he'd been told was popular in the early years of the Kurian Order. A smooth-sided luxury sedan with the half-sun, half-moon logo of the short-lived New World Fiber Network sat there, slowly hollowing like a rotten tooth as pieces fell away. Its rear-door sticker placed it firmly in the post-'22 generation:

I DON'T FEAR THE REAPER

Valentine heard a dull growl and turned, expecting to see one of the Hobarth dog pack. One good stare and they usually calmed down enough to make friends, animal to animal.

But he saw a quivering black-and-tan dog standing

between the rows of creeper-covered cars, looking through the gap toward the next row. Valentine had time to see a barrel move before he heard a quick hiss and felt a firm tap just behind the neck.

He started to crouch, but the world turned gummy, and his defensive stance loosened into a kneel. Then he felt grass against his cheek and dirt in his eye, but that didn't matter. A pleasant, dark warmth beckoned and he gladly slid down the hill toward it.

Motion, and the smell of corn.

The corn came from fabric covering his face, probably a feed sack over his eyes. A cloying, wet mess in his pants. He tried to rise, but handcuffs held his wrists together behind him. *Fight it fight it fight it.*

"Hey, he's coming out of it already," a husky voice said. The words were being bent and twisted in his ear, where a surflike roar fought with a deep thrumming reminiscent of the old *Thunderbolt*'s engines at high revolutions.

A little higher-pitched whine: "The doc said out for twelve hours for sure. Nothing like that, nothing near."

"Knowing his system, he probably just had a nice nap," a female voice added. She cleared her throat. "Get him inside and sit him up. I'll get the others."

Nice nap, indeed. Valentine flexed, tried to clear the creosote someone had substituted for blood in his limbs. They settled him into a chair and he felt a distasteful squish in his underwear.

A needle went into his arm. This time he stayed awake.

Sort of.

Hard to tell if time was passing or not. He swore, but it came out as a dry-throated moan. It seemed the first part of his brain that was willing to try to work his mouth had a vocabulary limited to profanity.

More words, but they didn't make sense.

Then he was awake, only now the fabric over his face was wet; so were his chest and shoulders.

"Up and at 'em, Valentine," the husky voice said, more intelligibly this time.

They know my name. This can't be good.

Husky voice again: "You reading me?"

Valentine needed time to think, but more water came.

"Anyone want to work him over with a bar of soap? He really needs it," a faraway female voice said. Hard to tell if it was the same one he'd heard before; the earlier conversation came back vague as a dream.

Another voice, female, nearer: "David S. Valentine, former major with Southern Command, we meet at last."

"Mutfurker," Valentine croaked.

"I suppose you know you've made a lot of powerful enemies. Someone gets to be too big a thorn, it gets pulled out and snapped." A throat clearing followed by a soft cough. This voice was the same as the one in the car.

"Death teams, man," the husky voice said. "You got death teams on your ass. Just like the one that got your folks. Just like the one that has you now."

"He's awake now, I saw his head jerk," the faraway female voice said.

So that's it, Valentine thought. *I wonder if they'll leave me strung up like F. A. James in Iowa. No, some Kurian will get me.*

Husky voice: "Big reward. All we have to do is take you north of the Missouri. We'll all be rich."

"Spend it right away, you pricks," Valentine said. The words were slurred but sounded intelligible enough to him. "There's some Bears and a Cat who'll get you in turn."

Valentine heard light footsteps and the bag came off his face—a little painfully, it took a scab on his chin with it.

Alessa Duvalier stood in front of him, holding the feed sack. Her freckles had faded with the season and she had a fresh bandage on her hand. A long, tattered coat hung off her thin shoulders. "If I'm s'posed to be the Cat, I wouldn't be so sure, Val," she said. "I still remember the tap you gave me in St. Louis. The cut inside my mouth took forever to heal."

Confused relief flooded Valentine. He tried to form words, but they wouldn't come. His eyes went wet.

"Get him some water, Roberts," a woman in uniform said from the other side of the room. The air smelled like mold and termites. She had her back to him, and was studying a series of wedding pictures on the wall. It had peeling paper and old, dust-covered fixtures that at one time had thrown light on the pictures. A few pieces of furniture with the cushions long removed had been pushed against the walls, and Valentine noted that he sat at one end of an oval dinner table, once a fine piece of work but now scratched and water warped. A single fat white candle leaned at the center of the table, providing the only illumination in the room.

A short, wiry man with horn-rimmed glasses in a Southern Command uniform offered the mouth of a canteen. Valentine noticed a corporal's chevron on his arm. "Just water," he said, in a surprisingly deep voice for his slender frame. Valentine drank, marking another man in Wolf leathers snoring on the bare spring bed of a sofa, oblivious to the conversation.

"So I've been recaptured by Southern Command?" Valentine said.

"For the record: name, place of birth, most recent rank?" the female with her back to him said.

"David Stuart Valentine, unincorporated Minnesota, major," Valentine supplied.

"He's sensible enough," Duvalier said. "Hungry, Valentine?"

"I'll eat." Valentine was shocked to see Moira Styachowski step in from another room. His artillery officer from the fight for Big Rock Hill on the banks of the Arkansas had put on a little weight since last he saw her, but her face still looked pale and her eyes tired.

"Quite a reunion," Valentine said as Duvalier slid

flatbread and a jar that smelled like fatted bean paste across the table.

"More than you know," the woman studying the photos said. She turned. A trim, neatly attired woman with a colonel's bird on her tightly buttoned collar regarded him with sparkling eyes.

Valentine felt a little like a hog at a county fair set before a judge. Sharp chin to match the eyes . . .

"Dots," Valentine said.

"For my sins, Colonel Lambert now," she said, her words cold and hard.

"Excuse me for not saluting," Valentine said. "I'm cuffed."

"Val, don't be difficult," Duvalier said.

"It's a private joke, Smoke," Lambert said. "I remember he once told me that he'd be saluting me someday, back when he was at the War College."

Duvalier, now sitting at the table, raised an intrigued eyebrow at him and he shook his head.

"Can I clean myself up?" Valentine asked.

"Please," Duvalier said.

"Roberts, take off the cuffs and show him his things," Lambert said.

The corporal led him to what had once been the house's kitchen. A ten-gallon jug of water sat on the counter; soap, towel, razor, and washcloth rested in a bucket.

Valentine saw packs and a duffel. The corporal extracted a set of Southern Command fatigues from one of them. Valentine recognized his old cammies from his stint as operations officer in the ad hoc regiment known as the Razors. His nose detected mothballs, though someone had made an effort to freshen up the uniform by packing it with acacia buds.

Valentine cleaned himself up, passed a forefinger over the thick fabric of the battle dress. Clever of Lambert. Once he was in uniform, sitting across the table from others in similar dress, old dutiful habits would naturally follow the way phrases come back when an adult who has long been in foreign lands speaks the language of home.

But Southern Command had made it amply clear that he was disposable. Valentine eschewed the uniform.

He heard a murmur from the other room and hardened his ears, but the exchange stopped almost as soon as it started. He returned to the table, the pleasant scent of clean women a welcome change in his nostrils.

Lambert watched him approach with steady eyes, a battered leather courier bag open in front of her. Styachowski was smearing peanut butter on a hard roll. Duvalier had taken off her duster and piled a small revolver, knives, and her old sword-cane on the seat next to her.

Valentine sat, the three women at the other end of the table making him feel like Macbeth looking across the cauldron at his witches.

"By the pricking of my thumbs, something wicked this way comes," he said.

Styachowski paused, the roll halfway to her mouth. Duvalier's nose twitched, but perhaps Lambert recognized the allusion. Her eyes warmed a trifle.

Valentine waited to hear it, playing with refusals ranging from polite to obscene.

"By now you've guessed we're not here to haul you back to the Nut," Styachowski said.

"I'll listen," Valentine said. "Right up until you slide the pardon across the table. I'm working up saliva."

"You can walk out that door, Valentine," Lambert said. "How long you can keep walking is the question you should ask yourself. The little drama we acted out could have been true. Kurian hit teams have you on their list. You do something traceable and they'll hunt you down."

"They just missed you in Iowa," Duvalier said. "I caught one of their sniffers drunk in a bar outside Garrison Nine."

"Suppose they do catch up. What's it to you?"

"You used to be one of the best young talents in Southern Command," Lambert said.

"I used to be a lot of things. Now I'm just tired."

Duvalier poked him with her toe. "Quit the burnout talk."

"You sure you want him, Moira?" Lambert asked.

Styachowski nodded.

"How's life treating you, Wildcard?" Valentine asked. "I never thanked you for visiting me in the Nut."

"Valentine, I need your help," Styachowski said. "I'm putting together a new unit."

"A force of condemned men for suicide missions, right? Not interested."

"You used to wait until you knew what you were talking about to open your mouth," Styachowski said, stiffening. "I liked that about you."

Lambert picked up her attaché. "Wasted flight."

"You flew here?" Valentine said.

"Once your old partner located you, yes," Lambert said. "Uncomfortable, cold, and loud."

Valentine knew that Southern Command had few air assets. Even generals traveled by train and car. Lambert must be a very big bug to have an airplane at her disposal.

"So Smoke tracks me down and Styachowski offers me the job. How do you fit in?"

Lambert tapped her courier bag. "I'm the answer girl, just like at the War College, Valentine."

"Young for a colonel," Valentine said.

"It looks better on the letterhead," Lambert said. "I had a staff position, really unimportant a few years back, 'cooperative commands operations director.' If something was happening in New England or Europe or South America that the staff needed to know about, I summarized and passed it on. Once in a great while we'd get a liaison visit from Denver or Quebec City and I'd arrange briefings.

"Then Archangel hit and suddenly we were plunged

into joint operations with the Texans. I had all the old responsibilities, but suddenly ten times the information was coming in, and we had to coordinate our movements with theirs, work out shared-supply issues, ad hoc attachments of Southern Command and Texas forces. Am I boring you, Valentine?"

Valentine looked up from his hands. "Not at all. I owe you a thank-you. You helped save the Razors."

"Texan enthusiasm saved the Razors. Once they started rolling I got out of their way. I just found them a few tugs."

The emotions of seeing the fleet of little boats come down the Arkansas River came back. Even the pain from the burns on his back and legs throbbed anew with the memory.

"What is my old friend General Martinez up to these days?"

Styachowski glanced at Lambert and shook her head, but Lambert spoke anyway: "Inspector general. It suits him. He keeps to the rear areas, getting expensive dinners and cigars as he makes his rounds. I can't deny he's popular. He sees to it that the food and comforts improve whenever he visits a post."

"Which reminds me," Duvalier said. "I've got a letter for you from Will and Gail. Over a year old now, but you haven't been leaving forwarding addresses." She dug in her duster and produced a wrinkled, grease-stained envelope. The letter smelled like turned bacon, but Valentine accepted it gratefully.

"So much for the past," Valentine said. "What do you have in mind for my future?"

"What I'm about to tell you is about as secret as anything can get, Valentine. Does your disenchantment with the Cause extend to materially hurting its efforts?"

"If anyone asks about this meeting, I'll assure them it was purely sexual."

Duvalier rolled her eyes. "Dream on, Valentine."

"C'mon, Major," Styachowski said.

"I don't have anyone to talk to, unless you count my

legworm. If Kur does get its hands on me, there's no keeping secrets from them." Valentine had been questioned under drugs before.

"This is more of a morale matter for our side. Our Lifeweavers have disappeared."

"Still?" Valentine remembered that after Solon's brief occupation of the Ozarks the Lifeweavers had fled, but he'd assumed they would return. *Assuming makes an ass out of—*

"Almost," Styachowski said. "Your Old Father Wolf has been located in the Sierras in Mexico. We're working on getting him back up here. Ryu and the Bearclaw are thought to be dead. There were a couple others in Southern Command, staff-level advisers, also gone. With no Lifeweavers . . ."

"No more Hunters," Valentine supplied, so lost in his thoughts that he brought up what was obvious to all of them.

"Our regulars are a match for theirs any day," Lambert said. "Unless they get the bulge on us with artillery. We can even handle the Grogs, most of the time. But when the Reapers show up—"

Valentine knew all this. "I'm supposed to locate some, right?"

"No, the locating's been done. We want you to get a message through to them. Maybe even try to bring a few back."

"They're not just across the Missouri somewhere, I take it."

"Seattle."

Valentine managed to blink.

"You got one out of the Zoo in Chicago," Styachowski said.

"His body, you mean. I came upon Rho by accident, and he died during the escape."

Lambert had clean nails. Valentine got a chance to examine them when she placed her hand, palm down, near his. "This isn't a case of going into a Kurian Zone and breaking one out. You'll simply travel to the resistance in the Cascades, meet one, and let it know our need."

"Simply? It must be fifteen hundred miles. One way."

"You've been traveling the Kurian Zone for years."

"You don't know that."

Three sets of eyeballs exchanged glances. "We just assumed—"

There was that word again.

Valentine let out a breath. "It's not worth arguing. I'm not interesting in slogging over who knows how many mountain ranges, sorry. Send a radiogram."

"You haven't heard what we're offering," Lambert said.

"Some kind of pardon."

"Not for you. You know that baby Reaper you brought out of Kentucky—"

"He has a name."

"How can you tell it's a he?" Duvalier asked. Reapers had no vulnerable reproductive organs sharing space with their simple elimination system.

"Calling him 'it' won't—"

"You've been good enough to let the researchers at the Miskatonic take a look at him a couple of times," Lambert interrupted.

"Until he broke two fingers and the wrist of the nurse subjecting him to ultrasonics," Duvalier said.

"They were hurting him," Valentine said, heating at the memory.

Lambert smiled. "The Kurians are very interested in your little Reaper. Their agents have offered substantial bribes for information up and down the Free Territory as to his whereabouts. They think we've got him in a lab someplace."

"Of course," Valentine said.

"Even I don't know where you've got him stashed, 'zactly," Duvalier said. "You always meet the Miskatonic people in the Groglands around St. Louis."

Lambert ignored her. "They think we've got him hidden in the deepest, darkest hole in the Ozarks and they're trying to find it. Sooner or later they'll learn the truth."

Valentine remained silent, waiting for it.

"Or," Lambert said, "I can make sure that every record, every test, every note, and every photograph disappears. We've mocked up a pretty convincing skeleton out of bits and pieces of other Reapers. He'll be listed as dead, killed during testing, the bones archived, some tissue samples dropped into formaldehyde, and everything but abstracts of the research will be destroyed."

How did they know the chink in his armor? Duvalier, probably. At times it seemed she knew him better than he knew himself. She was a sound judge, not just of risk, but of character, vulnerabilities—it made her a better assassin. Save for the bloodlust that sometimes came over her when a Quisling touched her—if she'd had an education beyond the sham of her early years in the Great Plains Gulag, she could have . . .

Keen judge of character. She picked you to train.

Valentine didn't know whether to hate the trio or admire them. He'd gotten careless with the last of Mary's murderers gone. Part of him was itching for something to do anyway. How much of his unwillingness was an act?

"There's got to be more to this," Valentine said. "Why not just contact the Pacific Northwest by regular channels? Southern Command must have some kind of communication route."

Styachowski suddenly became interested in a frayed cuff.

Lambert spoke again: "The Cause up there is in the hands of a genius. But like many geniuses, he's got his own ways."

"Friends and enemies both call him 'Mr. Adler,' " Styachowski said. "They say he came out of Seattle, originally. Didn't know one end of a gun from another when he showed up barefoot to volunteer, but he carried sixteen tons of grudge. He took a bunch of guerrillas starving in the mountains and fighting each other as much as they did the Kurians, and turned them into the Terrors of the Cascades. They appear and disappear like a fog, always somewhere the Quislings are weak. He's putting a headlock on the most powerful Kurian in the western half of the United States, Seattle himself. The Big Wheel."

"Him I've heard of," Valentine said. "Wasn't he trying to absorb the whole West Coast?"

"We were both at the War College then," Lambert said. "It was all the talk among the higher-ups, worries that Seattle would be running the whole coast, knock Denver out, then come after us. I suppose it could still happen, if the forces in the Cascades fall apart."

"All the more reason to set up liaisons," Valentine said.

Lambert shook her head. "It's been tried. One mission came back saying this Adler had no time for any war but the one he was waging against Seattle. The next mission we sent quit Southern Command and started singing his praises as the savior of the human race. The third never even made it there."

"Lifeweavers don't exactly advertise their whereabouts," Valentine said. "I don't see how I can find any without this genius' permission."

Styachowski opened her mouth to speak but lost her words in a cough.

"Ahh, but that's your specialty, Val," Duvalier said. "You're going to show up and volunteer."

Styachowski glared at her.

"Barefoot?" Valentine asked.

"I don't think that's necessary," Styachowski said. "You're talented. An ex-Cat of Southern Command. Hero of Big Rock Hill. You're bound to end up in Pacific Command's version of the Hunters."

Their faces stood out against the dark uniforms and the shadows beyond the table. Odd that all three were approximately the same height when seated. Three witches, telling him his future over a dirty table with finish bubbled and cracked.

"And if I make contact with a Lifeweaver?"

"Simple message. Southern Command needs their help. Badly. Or we're finished."

"That dicey, is it?"

"We're running out of Hunters," Lambert said. "The lieutenant I used to admire would have known what that meant, and been the first to volunteer. We've sent calls for help north, east, and south. We want you to be west."

The lieutenant Dots used to admire would have been so startled at the news of her admiration that he would have been able to think about little else. Valentine just noted it as an interesting detail.

Duvalier, eyes raised to heaven, and mouth like she'd just swallowed a spoonful of castor oil, muttered something about "Ghost" being the wrong clan nickname.

"Have you told me everything?"

"Everything," Styachowski said. "Trust me, Val. You did at one time."

"There is one more thing," Lambert said. "It's not an important detail. But it might mean something to you. The third mission, the one that disappeared, was led by your old CO from Zulu Company. LeHavre."

Lots of things could happen on the trail. Even to a man as experienced as LeHavre.

"I don't suppose Ahn-Kha has wandered in from across the Mississippi? He'd be invaluable."

"Sorry, Val," Duvalier said, her voice soft for the first time that evening. "He'd be sitting here if he had."

Styachowski smiled, but Lambert leaned forward. "Does that mean you're going?"

"I haven't spoken to a Lifeweaver in years," Valentine said. "I've gathered quite a list of questions."

"Great. We can get you as far as Denver," Styachowski said. "They can—"

"No. Sounds like your pipeline's got leaks, if Le-Havre couldn't get through. I'm going as David Valentine, ex–Southern Command. He'd have to figure out his own way there. I'll have to write up a list of gear I need, though. Gold will be on it."

"Give it to Moira," Lambert said, suddenly informal. "Where do you want it delivered?"

"Do you know Nancy's?"

"I know Nancy's," Duvalier said. "Used to be the best safe house between Kansas City and the Rockies. Practically in Free Territory these days."

"I'll meet you there in three weeks."

"Thanks for rejoining the team, Valentine," Lambert said.

Valentine felt a little warmth in the look they exchanged. A bad use of a football-coach metaphor made her fallible—and therefore human.

"Will I have a contact I can trust out there?" Valentine asked. "I might need backup. Supplies or gear."

"I'll catch up to you at Nancy's," Styachowski said.

"Good to see you again, Valentine," Lambert said. "From this day on, your little charge is history. On paper, anyway."

Duvalier was the last to leave and ran her tongue obscenely against her lips as they said good-bye. "Even Queen Balance Sheet folds at last," she said quietly. "I'll buy you a drink at Hob's to make up. I'm guessing that ego of yours needs some soothing after getting shaded by a woman half your size."

"I'll have to chit that. If I'm going to be back at Nancy's in twenty days, I have to get that list to Styachowski and get my worm rigged."

The corner of Duvalier's mouth went up, but she ignored the opportunity for another raunchy joke. "Be careful, sweet David. May flights of angels sing thee to thy rest."

First *Macbeth*, now *Hamlet*. He wondered where Duvalier had even picked up the line. He kissed her on the cheek. "I will."

CHAPTER THREE

St. Louis, Missouri: The mighty river-flanked city has again grown to be one of the most crowded civic centers in the Midwest, second only to Kurian-held Chicago, almost bursting at the bluffs when set against the mile-high vistas of the thinly populated Denver Freehold.

Except that the population is mostly nonhuman.

The Missouri River valley from St. Louis to Omaha belongs to the sentient bipeds—"Grogs" in the highly unspecific vernacular. In some of the Zones, they still serve their original purpose, acting as a military caste between the Kurian overlords and the human populace. Other Grog clans and tribes took land grants after their twelve-years service (Grog tradition holds that there are five twelve-year periods to a full life, and the Grog who makes it past his fifth age is revered indeed). The Kurians settled them as bulwarks against the few areas not under their control.

The reason the Kurians left such backwaters held by enemies or unreliable transplants is still a subject of no little debate.

Grog custom makes warfare a way of life and a path to status; theft entrepreneurship and slave-taking are the twenty-first-century version of human resource management. While the "Gray One" clans and tribes that inhabit the valley consider herding a noble and respectable duty, the dirt digging of agricultural work is left to their slaves of the human caste, not quite despised, but only rarely admitted into Grog homes on an equal basis.

Free humans live among the Grogs, wearing hatbands or wrist tokens that serve as proof that "foot pass" (as the term is translated) has been paid to the admitting tribe. "Looie" is a refuge from both the terror of the Reapers and the justice of the embattled United Free Republic to the south, and humanity there has carved out niches that many would consider enviable. They perform for Grog audiences under the Oriental decor of the Fox Theatre, sweep the streets of the Hill, operate specialized workshops, breweries, and distilleries in Carondelet, or keep trading posts stocked with goods imported from both Kurian Zone and Freehold. A small cadre of experienced arms men even teaches at the old City Museum. The best of the Grog child warriors are sent there by their tribes to improve their warcraftiness and learn from others.

Churches educate, heal, and minister to both human and the rare Grog desperate enough to seek succor outside his clan, under generous land grants from tribal leaders who otherwise would have fewer men to serve them. An entire human ghetto has grown up around the Basilica of St. Louis, catering to human needs, including that of a surprisingly well-equipped hospital and small school. The orderlies drink and the students study nearby at that eternal mark of urban culture: a café looking out on the sugar-beet gardens of the Jefferson National Expansion Memorial.

But everyone is careful to always have a foot-pass token on display: a red wooden bracelet with copper pennies inlaid for the Headstriker Tribe, a decoupage of old postage stamps set on a wooden tongue depressor for the Sharpeyes, a battered bit of embossed black leather with white stitching for the Startold....

David Valentine stepped out of the confessional, still able to sense the anxious sweat on the priest who remained in his stuffy little booth. The cathedral, lit by candles, arched overhead like a vast cave and echoed the noises of the few who remained after evening services. Janitors were putting out the oil lamps.

"Father Dahl might need a moment," he told the three people waiting. It had been a long and busy year since he'd last knelt next to a priest. The ritual always made him feel better, thanks to its tiny, tenuous connection to his upbringing in the schoolhouse of Father Max.

The priests and nuns also liked you to set an example. He'd happily swallow his doubts and buy some new rosary beads and show up for a few masses for Blake's sake.

He checked his tribal city pass as he left the church by the public side door. He wore it around his neck on a shoelace tether: a cardboard emblem the size of a bar coaster emblazoned with a two-color circle of blue and white copied from the BMW logo. The Grogs of the Waterway Guides had a knack for picking up on designs of deep spiritual significance. He shared a hobbyist's enthusiasm for fishing with a clan chief and they gave him his Looie foot pass at a steep discount.

The well-maintained shotgun formerly of F. A. James greased the transaction, of course. Offering up the weapons of a killed enemy transferred spiritual power to the Waterway. Valentine had been glad to be rid of its weight and associate memories.

Just across the corner from the cathedral was the dormitory and school. Even his limp became a little less pronounced as he bounced up the steps and signed in with the desk warden. She wore her foot pass in the form of an oversized earring, which swung as she pulled on a bell cord.

"He's still downstairs?" Valentine asked when Monsignor Cutcher welcomed him back.

"And thriving like a mushroom," the bristle-haired Jesuit said. He spoke with a faint accent, indefinite but distinctly European when compared with the usual Midwestern drawl of the Looies, and sometimes chose odd similes. Cutcher was the most well-traveled man Valentine had ever met, and had come all the way from Malta to assist with Blake, though he spoke of Cape Town and Kyushu with equal ease.

Cutcher took him to an alcove with a discreetly placed, heavy wooden door. "He gets the playground all to himself every night," Cutcher said. "We had a dark episode with a squirrel he'd been offering tidy-bits. He gained its trust and then attacked the poor rodent. Just like with the pigeons. He always obeys a warning for a few minutes but forgets unless frequently reminded. Tiresome."

"We may have to move him," Valentine said.

Cutcher paused at the bottom of the stairs. "Oh?"

"I've been informed that *they* are hunting him. The Freehold is going to fake his death in the documents. I'd like to make sure the trail dead-ends here at the same time."

"There is a small mission in La Crosse. But it may perhaps be easier to hide him somewhere else in this city. Strangers are noticed here—someone snooping around is sure to draw attention of the tribes."

They descended to what had probably once been preparation and scullery rooms for kitchens, judging from the number of sinks. Wooden partitions filled one whole wall, storage space and dormitories for the worst of the summer heat. Valentine's odds and ends filled one; the more permanent trunks of the Bloch brothers rested open in another. Behavioral biologists from the Miskatonic in Pine Bluff, they studied Blake's every intake and excrete, and gave him an occasional medical examination—and then only under supervision Valentine trusted. Getting Narcisse out of Southern Command had been easier than he'd thought: They'd put her to make-work in a convalescent home and treated her more like a patient than a skilled nurse or cook. Will Post had presented her with his offer and arranged to relocate her to a border town where they could be reunited.

Valentine looked forward to giving the Miskatonic fellows their walking papers. Their faces would drop lower than the muddy bottom of the nearby Mississippi.

Valentine smelled food cooking. The Blochs were

probably at breakfast. Blake was mostly nocturnal, and they'd adapted their schedules to his.

A squeak of rubber turning on linoleum sounded from the darkness of a corridor ahead.

"I heard your step on the stairs, Daveed," Narcisse said, coming into the dim light reflected from the dirty tile.

Valentine's old guide from Haiti smiled up at him from beneath one of her colorful bandannas. Her face had a few more lines, a few more liver-colored blotches.

"Hello, Sissy."

"You look tired. Rest and eat. Let me pour a bowl of soup for you. There is bread. Olive oil too, from some raid or other. It gives the gray folk the runs something terrible, so they give it to us."

"I'd like to see Blake first."

"Of course."

"I'll say good-bye to you two," Cutcher said. "Feel free to hop up and talk, David, if you have any concerns regarding Blake."

"Will do, Monsignor."

She led him down the hall. They'd mounted a first-aid kit the size of a briefcase on the wall since he'd last been there; Valentine wondered if there'd been worse trouble than with squirrels and pigeons. They entered the incinerator room that now served as the young Reaper's bedroom.

An aged nun with a face like a raisin watched him as he slept, a crack in the basement window admitting a shaft of sleep light.

"David Valentine, we see you again at last," she whispered as she hugged him. "Such a blessing."

Blake had grown like Iowa corn in a hot, thundery summer. Valentine felt the old pain, looked at his wrists, both of which still bore a faint track or two, like needle marks on the addicts he'd seen in Chicago's Zoo. He remembered the exhausting first months with Blake, shuffling him from Nomansland hole to Nomansland hole under cover of darkness, feeding him when there wasn't livestock to be had. He'd looked in a mirror once and thought he was staring at his own ghost.

"Blake," Valentine said from across the room. He could sometimes lash out like a wild animal if he was touched in sleep.

Yellow, slit-pupil eyes opened. The small figure sat up, wearing an old pajama top with characters that Valentine recognized as Ernie and Bert.

"papa," Blake said in his tiny, breathy voice. He sprang out of bed, crossing a meter or more in a clumsy jump.

"Jumping," Narcisse warned, and the obsidian-toothed mouth formed a regretful *"o."*

Valentine took Blake up, turned the child's head up and away from his breast—no sense taking chances, and besides, he wanted a good look at the growing face. He was shocked at the weight gain. At two years and three months, Blake was a good deal heavier than a human child his size, perhaps the weight of a five- or six-year-old. *"papa bek. papa bek see bwaykh!"*

"Yes, I'm back." Valentine's wary ears picked up a faint thump from beneath the cot and a little terrier mix appeared, wiggling as it scooted out.

"That's Wobble," Narcisse said. "Blake got heem as a puppy."

"wobbow not for eat," Blake informed Valentine, his blue-veined face going serious.

Wobble had a bare patch on his back and a tiny ridge of scar tissue, and a bit of a limp. Valentine wondered how many close calls Wobble had survived before Blake had finally learned.

"Of course he's not for eating," Valentine said, going down cross-legged—with a twinge from his bad left leg—so he could set Blake's formidable weight down and pet the squirmy dog. Of course when he'd run with Southern Command's Wolves he'd learned to dine on dog and had eaten them innumerable times since, but what was civilization but a lengthy set of agreed-upon tribal taboos?

Despite his change in size, Blake's grip on his arm and shoulder was a good deal more gentle than he remembered. What accidental pains Narcisse had suffered to her shattered body as Blake's nursemaid Valentine couldn't imagine.

Blake began to produce his favorite toys.

Which reminded Valentine. "I had a letter from Will and Gail. Ali tracked me down."

"A letter!" Narcisse said. The St. Louis Grogs weren't on any postal network. "What it said?"

Valentine handed her the grease-stained envelope, spiderwebbed with creases. "You can read it." Valentine went back to helping Blake work a spinning top made out of an old office-chair caster.

William Post, the former Quisling Coastal Marine who'd helped Valentine while crossing the Caribbean in the old *Thunderbolt*, had been given a sinecure with Southern Command. With some reading between the lines Valentine determined that Post had made himself indispensable with his usual efficient intelligence. He'd been given a minor position cataloging captured documentation from the Gulf Coast area and the Mississippi River valley, and had started making educated guesses based on everything from shipping manifests to maintenance logs.

His evaluations, thanks to his years of experience in the area, won him a position in the staff's Threat Assessment Bureau. TAB was charged with ensuring that Southern Command wouldn't get surprised again by the kind of coordinated attack that had allowed Consul Solon to roll up Missouri and Arkansas.

The news contained in the letter was good. Post knew that someone working the Kurian Zone would just as soon hear nothing but cheer. He and Gail were settled in Fort Scott, a trolley ride from his air-conditioned office. Hank Smalls was getting good marks in school and had a place as top starting pitcher on the academy's baseball team. His fastball was already attracting local fans.

Valentine could almost recite it word for word, especially one tantalizing paragraph:

I'm breaking security with this, Dave, but it's nothing the KZ isn't aware of anyway. Thought you'd like to know there's been a spike of action up and down the Appalachians, mostly in the Virginias and Kentucky. Only info on it is from secondary sources, but it's all the same story: guerrillas on legworms, popping in and out of valleys, and the K aren't having much luck with their whack-a-mole mallets. The coal mines are caught up in it, too. Here's the interesting bit: Supposedly some huge Grog's leading the revolt, bat ears and fur described as being either straw-colored or white. If we weren't SO short, we'd send a mission to help and I'd know for sure. It's been ugly.

Valentine had been tempted to tell Styachowski to let Mr. Adler remain mysterious and take the first slow barge up the Ohio. Post's mention that Southern Command was short on "Special Operations"—Wolves or Cats and Bears in the latest military parlance—put him back on the leash.

Of course, it wouldn't be above Moira Styachowski to ask Post to slip in a mention from someone Valentine trusted as a clincher. Styachowski and Post were both veterans of Big Rock Hill. She might ask a favor.

And so what if she had? They're your friends, man. Been in the Zone too much. They've given you a taxing but not particularly dangerous job to bring you back into the fold. Be grateful. And stop talking to yourself.

Narcisse waited until Blake was lost in the spinning, clattering, multicolored wheel from the old Life game to speak again.

"If Ali found you, that means they needed you to be found. Are you going off again?"

"Afraid so, Sissy," Valentine said. The wheel spun again and Blake pointed to the new number. Wobble chased his tail, imitating the whirling toy.

"You have so little time. He misses you, you know. He's human enough to pine. Too young to understand."

Valentine wondered how Narcisse had tipped to that. Of course he'd been interested in the challenge of the journey. But what was his absence doing to Blake? Was he cocking this up, along with everything else in his life? *Wait, Val, you made a bargain with the past four years ago. Let it be.* "Ten days. I'll stay here ten days. I need to fatten up on your cooking."

The wheel came off its mount. Blake picked up the wheel and offered it to Valentine. *"papa help bwaykh!"*

"You can do it yourself. See? Circle in the circle?"

Blake's bony features screwed up in thought. He put the spinner back in the little green dish of plastic. But he didn't align it and settle it on the pin. Valentine reached, but Blake gave it an experimental spin and sent it skittering across the floor.

"bwoke!" Blake said, smashing his fist onto the green cradle. The green plastic shattered and Wobble froze. Blake made a gurgling sound.

"Now it is," Valentine said. Narcisse stroked the back of Blake's neck with her intact hand.

"sowwy," Blake said in his faint, breathy voice. *"vewy sowwy, papa."*

Valentine picked him up again. "We'll make a new one." A piece of planking and a small, dulled nail would do. "Together."

Blake liked the sound of that. He showed all his fangs.

The days passed like the cars of a speed freight. Valentine contrived to take Blake on a fishing trip. Sufficient dirt, an oversized droopy boat hat, and some baggy clothes made him into a lean boy whose arms and legs were finishing up a growth spurt. The fish were biting, but any sort of motion, from a frog's leap to a rabbit's careful hop, made him drop his rod and investigate.

On his own, Valentine visited a little shrine near the old arch that he'd found on his first trip to the city.

Years ago his father had eliminated the Kurians from St. Louis—he learned this not from his father but from some men who had served with him—and the Grogs set up their form of memorial in the lobby of what had been an elevator to the top of the monument. Some bits and pieces laid out in an arch of parachute "silk" that imitated the one above—bullet casings, a canteen, a K-bar-style knife, a climbing glove, and some nylon rope he understood, but there was also a fox tail, a bunch of oddly shaped dice in a clear plastic tube, and a stoppered bottle of what looked like salad oil.

The mementos were meticulously dusted. Maybe at festivals a storyteller hopped up on the display (did the Grogs believe that putting the items behind glass detracted from their power?) and used the props. Or perhaps there were bodies buried behind the access door the heavy case blocked; the Grogs often put mementos outside grave sites. It wasn't even taboo for a Grog to take them up for a moment's examination or obeisance, provided they were returned when the task was done.

He was tempted to take the glove. Though it was larger than his own hand it still seemed small when compared with his memories of his father's huge, capable ones, but the aging Grogs clustered at the doorstep were already snorting and huffing when he bent too close to the display.

Cutcher took him up to the riverbank bluffs and showed him a house with a rambling basement cut into the limestone, lately occupied by a river trader who owned a wharf-side sawmill and a bone-wracking tubercular cough. In a fit of anxiety about his approaching death, he'd donated the property entire and its furnishings to the church.

"One last trade, this time with God," Cutcher chuckled. "May his bargain pay off."

They planned to move Blake as soon as the researchers from the Miskatonic did their last set of visual-acuity tests. He'd have room to explore up there, in the moonless darkness under the trees. Cutcher said that keeping up with him would be good for his cardiovascular health.

It felt wrong to say good-bye in a basement. Good-byes were for front yards, garden gates, train platforms, and bus pick-up corners, not shuttered basements that smelled like soaking diapers.

"If you need more money—," Valentine said to Narcisse.

"Monsignor Cutcher has ample sources. We want for nothing."

"Except the sight of one of those big palms."

"Royal palms," Narcisse said, nodding. "I do miss them, and the smell of morning wind off the sea."

"I want to thank you again for—"

She poked him in his good thigh. "Daveed, please. I am old, and have learned the difference between needed and used. Here I am needed. Here I talk long through the nights with our fine priest as we watch. A deep, kind man with the magic of the right hand. I have known only two or three others like him."

"I wish I'd had time to find Blake some blocks. And some early-reader books."

"I will find or paint some Scrabble pieces. Like the ratbits had. He will learn ABCs when he is ready. He learns, but his mind has not yet caught up to his body."

Valentine regretted the lost mah-jongg pieces. Blake would probably enjoy the colors and intricate designs. Valentine's last reminder of the good days with Malia Carrasca were in some prison warehouse deep in the Nut, probably.

Narcisse gave him a bag of dried-meat sticks, a bag of glazed biscuits, and some nuts mixed with oats and corn-bread crumbs—the Grog version of trail mix. He rolled one of the cheroot-sized tubes of meat and sniffed the greasy, peppery coating. Narcisse could make even the spongiest legworm flesh taste like tenderloin medallions in a sauce, but he suspected this was pork.

"You must not leave yet," she said. "I must press one last hug on you."

He knelt down so she could hug him. Those mauled limbs that had first met around his neck on a sunbaked Haitian street pressed at either temple, pressed hard, as though trying to meet somewhere in his corpus callosum. She closed her eyes and spoke in her Creole, sliding the words together so fast and low he didn't have a hope of understanding with his mother's Quebecois French. It went on for some moments and his pressed skin began to tingle.

Finally she stopped.

"What was that all about?" he asked.

"I asked heem to put honeycombs in your path, so your journey is sweet. There is too much bitter in you, Daveed, and it finds its way out."

Narcisse had a talent for cryptic expression that sometimes rivaled that of the Lifeweavers. Valentine wondered if he'd been cross with Blake, or the Bloch brothers from the Miskatonic when he gave them their marching orders. "If only you could add a little molasses to me, the way you do to the spoon bread."

Narcisse pursed her lips, then poked him in the breastbone with her maimed arm. "You already look better. Go now, or I cry some. Maybe I cry some anyway, but I don't want you around for that."

Valentine made Nancy's north of Tulsa in three days of round-the-clock legworm travel, arriving on the eve of the promised rendezvous. He'd made a deal with a driver from the Rabbit's Foot clan whom he silently called "Tic-tac" because the Grog's back-hide scars looked like a couple of drunks had started playing tic-tac-toe on it with hot knives.

Which wasn't out of the realm of possibility. Captured Grogs were sometimes cruelly treated to put the "fear of Man" in them before they were released. Of course captured men were often eaten when not enslaved, so cruelty was a matter of perspective.

They took turns driving the beast through day and night, skirting the UFR. Valentine hoped that the unofficial truce of the Missouri brush that had settled in when he'd first become a Cat was still holding, and that no wide-ranging patrols would risk a flare-up by potting what looked like a human small trader and his driver.

Difficulty showed itself in a six-man patrol. Three challenged him, and three more waited, kneeling in the brush. Five kids and a senior NCO. The kids were too young and the NCO was grizzled right to the hair growing out of his ears.

Valentine felt for the oldster, riding herd on a bunch of downy cheeks too young to know how easily they could die. But the Missouri bushwhack country would lend itself to giving the kids some experience without the risks that went with the swamps around New Orleans, the open plains to the west, or the alley between Crowley's Ridge and Memphis.

Valentine watched the rifles and picked out an escape route through the brush. If things looked bad, he'd topple off the legworm and run like a rabbit, twisting and turning across the mud through first spring flowers of the blackberry bramble.

"Hey, Freebies," Valentine called. "You boys looking for a little joy juice to keep out the nightly chill?"

"Check out that chair. Quite a ride he has on that legworm," one of the kids in the brush remarked to his fellows.

The NCO's rifle dangled in its sling, but the officer kept his hand hooked casually in his ALICE belt, close to the butt of his sidearm. "Just a friendly warning, Wally," the NCO said, using the Missouri slang for a trader who bartered with the Grogs. Valentine had been called worse. "You're about ten miles out of a UFR settlement. They'll panic at the sight of a worm and open up on you."

"Like a bunch of potato diggers could hit a legworm if it were on top of them," one of the kids in the brush said. The two backing up the NCO knew better than to add comment, but one kept swinging his rifle muzzle back and forth, making little figure eights in the air.

"Where you bound for?" the NCO asked, looking at the packs and accoutrements dangling from both sides of the legworm.

"South of Kansas City, Kansas."

"Top, he's traveling with a stoop—that puts him under suspicion," the twitchy kid said. "Stop and question."

"Question away, I'd like an excuse to get off this damn worm," Valentine said. "It's Tic-tac here who is on tribal-conference business. I just own the worm."

Tic-tac rocked nervously in his saddle, his anxiety evident, but kept his hands away from his long, single-shot varmint gun. Valentine doubted he even had any bullets for it. Instead he had a grip on his sharp-hooked worm goad. Valentine hoped Tic-tac wasn't getting any ideas about the worth of the kid's rifles and hair at the next tribal bragging session. If the kids knew just how quickly a Grog could throw a balanced utility ax like the one dangling from its leather thong on the saddle hook, they'd be back another ten yards or so.

Valentine tried to will the kid into slinging the gun and losing interest in the encounter, but the boy had either imagination or a grudge against men out of the Groglands.

"That's maybe a Kurian agent," the kid insisted. "He should be put under arrest."

"Not another word, Cadet," the NCO said. "If that Grog is a messenger, he'll die before he'll come out of that saddle. Then we'll have a feud with Rabbit's Foot and their allies."

Valentine's stomach sank. The kid was an officer candidate, looking to establish his record for initiative.

"Bury and buckle up, Top. C'mon," one of the kids quietly urged from the brush.

"And if he were a Kurian agent, we'd all be running to check out the sound of seventy legworms passing north of here, or shooting at each other," the NCO added.

Valentine felt a gurgle in his stomach, and took the

opportunity to lean to his right and bounce a loud fart off his chair.

"Never could handle those Grog mushrooms," he said.

The NCO chuckled and the quieter of his two charges laughed.

"Pass wind, friend," the NCO said, stepping aside and gesturing with his hand to the west. The cadet glared at him.

"Don't worry, we'll be out of UFR lands by nightfall," Valentine said as they goaded the legworm into its rippling motion again.

The NCO pulled the boys out of the way of the legworm's antennae and nodded to Valentine as they passed. Valentine considered that the peacefully concluded meeting was an example of the differences between the Free Territory and the Kurian Zone. In the Free Territory an NCO could use his judgment. In the KZ they'd be kept waiting while the NCO called his officer, who called a higher officer, who would order them searched and then, when they found nothing of interest, would call a higher officer still, who would ask "Why are you bothering me with this?" and order them released anyway, provided there wasn't a Reaper breathing down his neck with an appetite that made starting a feud with a Grog tribe over a single wanderer's aura worth it.

The kids who were covering from ambush stood up as they passed, and gaped.

There was a time when the whole check in the Nomansland between would have been done by Wolves, who would probably have just observed them from cover and tracked them to see what they were up to, unseen and unheard unless the patrol leader decided they constituted a threat. Then Tic-tac would have been dead and Valentine roped and cuffed in about the stopwatch time it takes a rodeo champ to bring down a calf.

It was a good thing for the UFR that Missouri was so quiet these days.

*   *   *

On the third day it took both of them together to keep their mount going—legworms had astonishing reserves, but eventually even the digging goads would have no effect.

Valentine let the Grog have his legworm and rig with many thanks and a swapping of Tic-tac's delicately carved ear-grooming stick for a half-empty tin of Valentine's foot powder. He felt no particular sympathy with Tic-tac, but if this wasn't the longest trip the Grog had ever been on, it was close, and he'd want something to point to when telling the story.

Valentine walked into Nancy's oddly peaked roofs—they always reminded him of old Pizza Huts—under his own steam, taking the first of many steps westward.

CHAPTER FOUR

Nancy's, March: David Valentine first learned of Nancy's from his old tent mate Lieutenant Caltagirone of Foxtrot Company.

Nancy's had been a retirement home for Tulsa's well-to-do who were unwilling to quit the rolling hill-country of eastern Oklahoma. Its single-story, vaguely Prairie-school architecture was spread out over several acres, with a central hub and an outbuilding or two. In the Kurian Zone people were "retired" in much the same manner as an old, worn-out tire, with the Reapers serving as mechanics, but its layout made it a convenient rehabilitation center for Quisling veterans. Nancy herself was something of a legend in the Nebraska Guard for her devotion to the maimed and shattered.

She kept her charges busy with arts and crafts, which she sold in Tulsa at Kurian patriotic festivals to buy a few luxuries. The "Nancy's" sticker became so famous that an art colony of sorts had sprung up in the area, with workers of metal, leather, wood, ceramics, and paint adding to the trade.

Nancy's also had the best food in three states. Kurian Order and New Universal Church dignitaries often spent long weekends visiting the "home" and enjoying the cuisine as they got their picture taken shaking hands with the more photogenic of the wounded.

It seemed the last place one would expect to be a warehouse for the resistance. When the Kurians heard the occasional whisper or screamed confession that Nancy's had been the place guerrillas got their explosives, they assumed that their prisoners had been coached into fingering the establishment in the hope that the whole staff would be swept up in a purge. The routine searches revealed nothing.

Of course, they didn't remove the wounded from their thick, comfortable, bleach-scented bedding, pillowcases lined with gleaming rows of decorations. Only the laundry staff, under careful supervision of senior nurses, ever changed the bedding.

Nancy's had grown since the last time Valentine visited, as a tired and hungry lieutenant trying to supply his men scouting the Kurian Zone.

The "Kurian Pillar" he remembered, breaking the horizon like a white needle, now had a cross openly displayed upon it, and the trees had spread their shade over the windows and doors. The vegetable gardens and stands of tomato vines had multiplied and spread to both sides of the road that met the old interstate a couple of miles south. New houses, mostly two- or three-room shotgun shacks built around a common well pump, circled the grounds like campers keeping warm at a fire. A red-painted market that Valentine had remembered being a livestock barn, promised FUEL * FOOD * LODGING thanks to a blue and white sign salvaged from the interstate. To the southwest, behind a small hill, birds circled the community trash heap. No distance seemed too great for gulls to travel in search of garbage.

A few hardy souls were out on the blustery day, mostly working in the vegetable patches or trying to dry laundry under the eaves. Some muddy kids and dogs chased one another through the culverts at the roadside.

Valentine paused at a roadside tap for water, tried to get some of the caked-up grime off his face and hands, and then turned up toward the main entrance of the hub.

WE'RE FULL

a repainted folding yellow caution sign told him.

Valentine ignored it and paused in the entry vestibule. A six-foot panel of plywood served as a local notice board. Along with advertisements for watchdogs ("Garanteed to bark at Hoods") and ironmongery and the weekly swap meet and different flavors of Bible study were dozens of messages giving names and destinations, probably of refugees from the destruction in Tulsa. Valentine scanned them until he found what he wanted.

Black—
I'm in Comfort 18.
*   —Red*

Ali had written their old nicknames from the trip across Tennessee and Kentucky. A faint pang of regret at their parting—she'd insisted he was crazy for harboring Blake. . . .

Jury's still out on that one.

Valentine stepped into the old reception area of the nursing home. The limestone of the outside gave way to cool, homey brick within. Two armed men wearing five-pointed stars played cards at a round wooden table, rifles and shotguns placed across a pair of ottomans with a snoring mutt between. A wide reception window looked out on the doors and waiting area, and behind it, a disarmingly young teenage girl sat writing on a pad.

Something about Valentine caused the security's antennae to twitch, and they gave him a long, careful look as he inquired of the girl. She directed Valentine to the appropriate room.

"Much obliged," Valentine said, and gave a friendly nod to the constabulary. He risked a glance back as he found the appropriate hall, and noted that they'd left their cards to watch him.

Valentine smelled barbecue and laundry soap and

disinfectants—sharp odors of chlorine and borax. A New Universal Church hostel smelled much the same, albeit with potatoes and cabbage substituted for the barbecue. Someone had brought in bluebonnets and redbud for the vases at the hallway intersections, adding color and aroma. He thought them a nice touch. Four-color propaganda posters provided the only color in NUC lodgings.

The halls were wide for the accommodation of hospital gurneys. Now spare cots stood in the halls and the little social rooms used by the patients. A TV or two blared old digital recordings in all their sound and spectacle—pre-'22 titles were much sought after, as the message-riddled Kurian productions had all the artistry and interest of an appliance manufacturer's instruction manual. More children played in the halls, racing toys on the smooth flooring or hard at work with blocks, LEGOs, and Tinkertoys.

Valentine found Duvalier's room. Its door stood open. He knocked at the bathroom just to be sure.

He heard a step in the hallway. A matronly woman in one of the cheery, embroidered staff aprons chewed on the inside of her cheek for a moment as she looked him over. He noted the frame of a cart behind. "The young ladies in this room are either at the clothes swap or the"—she lowered her voice—"bar. There's gaming and music and storytelling for those who like wasting good daylight."

"Thank you."

"They said a tall man with straight black hair would be coming. You shining on one of those gals, or are you already married up?" She fiddled with a scissors in her apron and Valentine wondered if he were being measured up for a trim.

"Not exactly."

The honey in her voice turned sticky. "Then there's something wrong with you. Sweet things. They shouldn't be unprotected."

If the other "sweet thing" was Moira Styachowski,

the pair needed as much protection as a pair of ornery wolverines.

"Thank you. Clothing swap—"

"The big green aluminum barn to the north," she supplied.

"Right. Or bar."

"It's not on Nancy's property. I never met a man who couldn't find a bar hissownself. The owner's name is Trumpet."

"Trumpet. Thank you, ma'am."

"You can thank me by handing me that water pitcher. The stuff from the tap is strictly wash water unless you're a local and used to it."

Valentine held it for her while she filled it from a set of big plastic jugs on her cart, and replaced it on its aluminum tray.

He wandered to the clothing swap first, and found the cavernous barn filled with odds and ends from darned socks to snappy but stained felt hats. A giant iron-bottomed laundry pot bubbled over charcoal and filled the whole barn with a faint smell of lye. More women and children sat on folding chairs or fruit boxes, talking and sewing.

"Offering, trading, or needing?" a bored teenage boy asked. He carried a plastic hamper.

"Looking," Valentine said.

He hadn't seen a bar coming into Nancy's, so he made for the other end of her property. Sure enough, some entrepreneur had taken an old buffet franchise resting just on the other side of the hill from the garbage pit and turned it into a sawdust-and-fat-lamp saloon. A tarnished trumpet hung from the sign outside. A few biodiesel pickups, several bicycles, and some wagon teams were arranged outside, with shade given to the animal transport and proximity to the door taken by the bikes. The pickup trucks were parked facing the road to give passersby a good look. One driver had even popped his hood to show off chrome exhaust pipes and a supercharger.

Valentine entered through the door cover, a carpet-remnant strip that acted as a windbreak.

Under the light of the front windows a guitar and banjo were keeping each other company, with bootheel syncopation as percussion.

Valentine smelled fryer oil and kidney-filtered beer. As soon as his eyes adjusted he picked out Duvalier in what would have been a crowd if everyone weren't spread out as though trying to keep out of one another's business. He walked past tables with cards and dominoes and guns being examined for trade or sale. A pair of women worked behind the bar, serving drinks and making sandwiches.

Lounging in a wooden, high-walled booth, Duvalier was in her usual earth-toned Free Territory clothing. Her knife-cut red hair dirty and disarranged, she'd put a good deal of effort into making herself look less attractive than she was, wrapped up in the duster that hid her body from the neck down. Valentine didn't recognize the young woman with her, noted only that she was blond with a longish face and nose. Duvalier pointed for the benefit of her companion, and Valentine took in the blonde's wide-set, steady eyes.

Then she blushed and dropped her gaze.

"Blackie, this is Jules. Be nice, she's like a sister to me."

Public code for another Cat. Valentine wondered what her real name was.

"Max Argent," Valentine said.

Duvalier waved over one of the bartenders and ordered three ciders.

"Bad news, looks like," Duvalier said. "Your shipment's delayed. Em is still getting it together."

Valentine wondered at that. Lambert could take a plane for a rendezvous with a potential operative, but they couldn't get a footlocker of gear to the edge of what amounted to the Free Territory?

United Free Republic, he reminded himself.

Jules spoke. "I hope you weren't planning to meet a

train." Valentine wondered at her voice; there was a bit of Eastern giddyup to it. She must not have operated in the KZ much or she would know to smother the accent; it attracted too much attention.

"No. I dropped word at Hobarth's that I'm looking to pass west."

"Not as driver, I hope," Duvalier said. Most of Valentine's efforts behind a wheel were ill-fated.

"Scout work, security, maintenance, whatever they need. There'll be westbound convoys for a month or two."

"I'll leave tonight to let Em know you've arrived," Duvalier said. "You can have my bed."

Valentine waited for a remark about staying in it; Duvalier treated his cocksmanship as something of a joke—which it was, considering the results.

"Traveling at night?" Valentine asked.

"It's almost as quiet as the Ozarks around here nowadays. Nearest organized Kurians are a hundred miles away west and north."

"Diddo-dish," Jules said, using Iowa slang for something easily accomplished.

In the last three years the Great Plains had been transformed into a bloody quilt of territories in revolt and those still under the Kurians. Grogs and mercenaries from as far away as inland China were holding on to North America's breadbasket.

The ciders came and Duvalier paid in cigarettes, one of the lower denominations in a ranking that went thus: gold, batteries, whiskey, ammunition, tobacco. Lesser necessities like darning thread, pens, gloves, and toothbrushes also served as unofficial currency in booze boxes from Kurian Zone to Freehold and back again, if someone was running short and could be talked into a swap.

Between songs, they made small talk about the weather and the food. When the guitar and banjo made enough noise to cover conversation, Valentine learned that Jules hailed from a privileged family in Iowa—her father owned an estate that sounded similar to the one he'd visited in search of F. A. James. She'd spent her teenage years "out East" at school and returned to the usual privileged child's choice of military, church, or management career. She ran away just in time to get caught up in Consul Solon's bid to put the Trans-Mississippi under the Kurians.

"I tried to join the guerrillas, but since I wasn't anybody's cousin or sister-in-law I couldn't find out anything about where they were hiding. When the 'strike' speech came," she said, "I didn't get to hear it but saw it on a leaflet—I didn't know what else to do, so I started a fire in a tire pile outside a TMCC garage. Some janitors were executed for it."

"Don't put it like that," Valentine said. "The Kurian Order executed them, not you."

Valentine waited for her mind to leave memories of strung-up bodies and return to Oklahoma. "I did a bunch of other stuff," she continued. "Punctured tires at night. I learned how to cut a hot electrical wire. Stuff where I could do a little damage quietly and then run away."

"A girl after my own heart," Duvalier said.

"I take it she never went through our little ceremony." Valentine looked at the scar on his palm, barely distinguishable from legworm-hook-hardened skin.

"No," Duvalier said, and Jules looked down, hiding under her hair. What did the girl have to be ashamed of? It wasn't her fault the Lifeweavers had disappeared.

For one awful second Valentine wondered if she was a Kurian agent, slowly digging her way into Southern Command. No, Duvalier was a good judge of character. You didn't walk up and apply to be a Cat; the Cats found you.

After the evening meal Duvalier disappeared. In all the time he'd known her she'd rarely been an initiator of good-byes—like a careful extra in a stage play she liked to make unobtrusive appearances and disappearances.

Probably why she still had blood in her veins after all these years in and out of the Kurian Zone.

Valentine explored Nancy's. It still housed dozens of crippled Quislings, pitiful objects limited to bed and wheelchair. They'd taught him in his Southern Command lectures that the Kurians consumed cripples, even those wounded in defense of their Order, save for a few to be trotted out at rallies and blood drives. Whether the soldiers still lived because of some shell game of Nancy's, or the sudden turnover of territory spared them, or he'd even been given a spoonful or two of medicinal propaganda, he didn't attempt to determine.

He saw Nancy herself, behind a wide nurses' counter, speaking to what looked like doctors. Her face drooped like a bulldog's. Hair that could be mistaken for a hawk's pole-top nest gave her a bit of a madwoman's air, but even the medical men listened to her speak.

As night fell people filtered back into the connected buildings and gathered around the tiny charcoal stoves on the grounds that provided heat for cooking and boiling laundry.

The talkative in the refuge discussed either Tulsa—when it would finally be cleared so people could return to see what was left of their lives—or the possibilities of finding work far from the fighting in Texas or Arkansas.

Then there were the doomsayers: "They'll be back," one man said, shirtless and with Kurian service pins on his suspenders. "No such thing as 'safe.' 'Scorched earth,' the order said, and just because the flame ain't touched you yet, doesn't mean it's not burning."

Even in the facility's new role as improvised refugee squat, Valentine had to admire the cleanliness of the rooms, painted in an institutional color he called "muted lime." The medicine cabinet in the shared bathroom held a couple of tonics for Duvalier's on-again, off-again stomach problems, antiseptic ointments, and a thermometer. The only disappointment was the ashy-tasting toothpaste.

They went to their individual beds with lights out—Nancy's had its own generators, but fuel for them had to be conserved. Valentine hid under a sheet, a little ashamed of the state of his underclothes. *Maybe a visit to the swap is in order after all.* Jules produced a bottle of Kurian rum and they passed it back and forth. Valentine refused more than two swigs.

"You need to be careful with alcohol in the KZ," Valentine said. "They say a little helps cut lifesign by relaxing you. Whether it's true or no, I'd rather be alert."

"This isn't the Kurian Zone. Not anymore."

Though she asked, he didn't want to talk about the rising in Little Rock. Instead he shifted the conversation to their childhoods. He told her a little about growing up in Minnesota—to an Iowan, nothing but hairy, thick-blooded barbarians lived north of Rochester—and in between swallows she painted a picture of the privileged life of a Ringwinner's daughter.

"I was supposed to go into the church," came the voice from the darkness. If anything, her diction became more precise as she drank. "I was a youth-vanguard leader, of course. Then it was army, church, or industry. Since Ving Junior went army, and Kirbee got her master's in production, we had that dried-up old prune of an priest sitting me down for improvement, effort, humility, care, and acceptance." Valentine's ears picked up movement in the darkness as she listed the church's virtues. You were supposed to touch forehead, right shoulder, right hip, left hip, and finally left shoulder as you said them. Her words faded as she spoke. "Man in his unnatural state. Spiritual recycle. Can't believe how much of that crap I remember. Didn't even try to learn it, but I can still recite the Truths word for word."

Valentine listened to her breathing until he too drifted away.

He woke, a little, when she got up to use the bathroom. He woke further when she returned and slipped into his bed. She nuzzled his ear.

"Object?" she asked.

Her clean-smelling skin enticed, and her hand knew what it was doing. He felt an erect nipple against his tricep. "Ask a silly question . . . ," he said.

She tested him with her grip. "Nice answer. Not a bit silly. Drop in."

He recognized another Iowaism, but one Valentine had never heard breathed in his ear, only secondhand from guy talk over beers.

"Not so fast," Valentine said, beginning a series of kisses down her neck. He hadn't touched a woman in over a year. Might as well enjoy the opportunity.

Spent, aroused, and spent again, he slept deep and hard in the sweat and slickness of their lovemaking after she retreated to her bed.

Gunfire and screams woke him. For three terrible seconds he was back on Big Rock Hill the night the Reapers dropped from the sky. *Waking from a dream, or waking into another nightmare?*

Jules sat up in her bed, the flush of lovemaking replaced by an awful pallor.

"Reapers!" came a shout from the hallway.

Her eyes, searchlights of fear, turned to him.

Valentine felt them. His old comrades in the Wolves called it the "Valentingle" and trusted it more than Valentine did. Sometimes he could detect a Reaper with pinpoint accuracy; other times he could walk right over one without sensing it. Now they seemed to fill his whole mental horizon, could be a dozen or more.

"Might mean nothing," he lied. "Every time there's confusion in the dark, someone shouts 'Reapers.' You have a weapon?"

"Beretta. Bag on the chair."

"Get it." She moved for her pants. "No, get it first, then get dressed."

Valentine retrieved his .45 ACP, the weight a calming comfort in his hand. Two more shots, this time from the front of the building where he'd passed the tin stars. "Drop lifesign and—"

"I don't know how!" she said, her words half-strangled with fear.

Jesus, Duvalier—

Reapers hunted using lifesign, an energy created by the vital aura their masters desired. Humans produced more than livestock; livestock produced more than crops. . . .

He checked the window, saw a family hightailing it across the fields, each holding a child over a shoulder as they ran, a dog keeping worried circles.

Over by the barn, a woman ran in the same direction. A shadow, moving so fast it seemed a trick of the eye, followed her across the field and engulfed her.

Or did it?

"Crouch, both hands on the floor," he told her, shutting and locking the doors to the hallway and shared bathroom. She complied quickly enough. He'd been told contact with the earth acted like the ground on a lightning rod, but he suspected it was bullshit. But it was a relaxing pose, you didn't feel as vulnerable as you would lying down, and there's the tendency to shift nervously when standing.

"Picture your whole life folding up, into a box," he said, hard ears searching the building. Still no destructive noises, but a lot of consternation in the halls, a confused babble.

"They'll locate. They sense pregnant women best!"

A beeping racket from a few crackly loudspeakers made her jump. "Emergency Alert Code Black Multiple. Code Black Multiple."

That doesn't sound good.

"What's that?" Jules said.

"Never mind. Fold up pictures of your family, friends, memories, whatever, and put it in a mental box," Valentine said.

The loudspeakers shrieked one final "Stop!" and went dead.

"I don't see—"

"Keep your eyes shut! What kind of flower do you like?"

"Flower?"

"Picture your favorite flower."

"Daisy," she said.

"Great, a daisy. There's just a daisy, nothing else, blackness and a daisy. It's a big one. You're keeping your eyes on the yellow center."

"Yes," she said, sounding a little better.

"Now it starts to spin slowly, like a windmill. Oh so slowly."

"Yes," she said.

Screams and a crash from the center of the building.

"Never mind that." Valentine lowered his own life-sign and tried to open the window. It had been painted recently and was sticky.

"Speed the daisy up. It's spinning faster now."

She didn't respond.

"Slow it down now. Slower and slower and slower." He lowered his voice. "Slower than that windmill, slower than a second hand on a watch, slow it so it's moving like a minute hand. You can barely see it, it's moving so slowly." More screams, this time female. The deep blast of a shotgun and running feet in the hall.

He unwrapped a souvenir from his time with the Kentucky worm riders. It was a short, stout hand ax, blade tapering into a legworm hook. He pulled on his pants and laced his boots.

For Valentine, lowering lifesign meant taking a big, bright blue ball that represented his consciousness and slowly shrinking it to a point like a star, which he watched with all the concentration of an astronomer at a telescope eyepiece.

"Keep watching the petals turn," he whispered. He reached up and gripped a chamois-wrapped handle from beneath his pillow and drew it close beside.

A heavy tread in the hall and she groped for his hand.

"Turning," he whispered.

A door torn open with a sharp metallic cry. Another scream.

"Turning," he repeated. He tried a fearful whining sound in his throat, trying to imitate a whimpering dog.

Something jiggled the doorknob.

More shots from the hall, and heavy, pounding footsteps as the Reaper ran toward the door ...

"Turning," Valentine whispered.

Five minutes later the noises faded into a last distant scream.

"Safe?" Jules asked.

"We are. They're not. . . ."

The old Cat Everready got to be an old Cat by hunting Reapers only in the daylight, when their connection to their master was weakest, or after they fed, when they, or more accurately the master Kurian animating them, got dopey from the aura feed.

The Valentingle weakened and diffused, throbbing on and off in his head like a bulb on fading current.

He stepped into the hall.

Carnage was the only word for it. Bodies, some still dripping and twitching, lay in the hallway, or had been flung across gurneys. Crushed necks and heads mostly. Some bore wet blossoms on their shirts from punches that had caved in rib cages.

Valentine followed the pointy, bloody boot prints down the hall, found the corpse of the person that had saved him with gunfire. The teenage girl who'd checked him in at the desk was folded around her broken ArmaLite, her auburn hair bound up with a cheerful, polka-dot scrunchie. She had a hole at the base of her throat, paying for the insult of her .223 shells with coin drawn straight from the aorta.

Valentine shut her glassy eyes, turned her on her back, and straightened her, tenderly placed her heels together and her palms at her side, put her riven weapon on her chest, and covered her with a bedsheet from one of the gurneys.

He walked out the exit door at the end of the hall. The walk turned into a trot, which turned into a run, which turned into a sprint, ax held like a runner's baton in his left hand, pistol in his right.

The cool night air hit him like a slap, and like a slap, it brought him out of the moment's madness.

These weren't "wild" Reapers, sometimes sent into the Free Territory to brutalize and maul, little dandelion seeds of chaos drifting where instinct took them. These Reapers had gone through Nancy's quickly and methodically, trying to cram as much death into a given number of minutes as possible.

Which probably meant they had a long trip back. Perhaps as far as Tulsa?

Valentine's cat-sharp eyes picked out motion at the outbuildings. A Reaper, moving south, hopping from rooftop to rooftop as it tried to sense if any beings hid within.

He pulled back the hammer on his gun, then dropped it and the pickax on the ground. He sank so his knees hid them.

"Why?" he bawled. Not much acting required for this. He searched the low spring clouds. "Why us?" He covered his eyes, decided not to sob—there was such a thing as overdoing it.

The Reaper didn't even bother to cut back so it could approach him from behind. It approached a little off kilter, shifting this way and that, reaching too far with its lower limbs stepping toward ten and two rather than straight ahead.

Valentine smelled the cordite on it. He hoped this particular one had killed the girl. Dots of blood decorated its face, a sticky pox. Old Father Wolf was proved right again: Enough hate and you felt no fear, just nervous anticipation.

It planted itself in front of him.

"some prayers are answered," it said, sibilants sliding out of its mouth like a snake's. *"look up and see."*

Valentine knew better than to meet its eyes. He

waited for the knees to bend and rolled sideways, shoved the gun almost into the folds of its robe, and fired.

Bullets wouldn't kill it, but the kinetic energy could sometimes stagger Reapers. Even with the powerful handgun cartridges slamming into it, it still reacted aggressively, swung at his head with a scooping motion that would have sent his skull spinning like a field goal kick.

Except Valentine was already behind it.

He buried the pick end of his hand ax into its upper back, where the nerve trunks gathered on their way to the armored brain case. He got lung instead, heard a sucking sound as flesh closed around the point.

It spun, jerking the handle of his pick out of his hands, and both opponents lurched off-balance. Its elbows clicked backward and its arms reversed themselves in a ghastly fashion as it sought the pick.

Valentine restored his equilibrium first, dropped, and sighted under the jawline. He put his remaining bullets into the underside of its chin.

The Reaper went mad, tore the pick free, and took off running, a blind flight with its hand held in front of it and the other holding its jaw on.

Valentine reloaded, retrieved his pickax, and trotted after it. It dived into the culvert beside the road and began to slither south at a pace he could just keep up with if he ran.

The Kurian clearly wanted his puppet back, even with a string or two cut. Had it been willing to sacrifice its avatar, it could have chased him down and killed him, hunting by heartbeat if nothing else. He paused in a tomato garden and calmed himself, tried to sense the emanations from the Reapers, caught a flicker off in the direction of the settlement garbage heap.

Valentine picked out a line of trees and used them as cover for an approach, hoping there wasn't a sniper or two guarding the gathering. He heard engines and movement, and risked a run.

He broke for the top of the low hill that kept the dump's sight and smell away from Nancy's, got up just in time to see a truck pulling a horse trailer, turning onto a brush-choked access road. A cut-down Humvee with a toothy brush cutter on the front and a winged Southern Command battle star painted on its side led it down the road.

You could pack a lot of Reapers in that trailer. An unpleasant surprise for the soldier who opened the door to check inside.

The vehicles, driving without lights—if they still worked—disappeared.

A roadblock would be helpful somewhere down that overgrown alley, but the false-flagged Hummer could just pull a disabled—

A blatting broke out from the garbage heap and Valentine saw a man in cammies with a scoped rifle slung across the handlebars of a dirt bike take off after the vehicles up the road. A cold wave passed over Valentine. Probably the sniper, tired and anxious after the operation and listening to the sounds of his buddies driving off, hadn't been searching the hill line or the trees in the direction of Nancy's through his night sight.

Had anyone in Nancy's called for help as the Reapers attacked?

They arrived within a couple of hours, a thin string of cavalry on horseback, followed by more troops on mountain bikes, riding in a pair of lines on either side of the road. He watched them the way a rancher might watch a cattle drive—making guesses as to health, morale, and training from everything from the condition of their bootheels to how they shaved their sideburns. Someone in Southern Command knew his business. Valentine guessed this to be a garrison from one of the supply depots supporting operations west of Tulsa.

He sent Jules over to tell the captain in charge. They could radio to scouts around Tulsa. Even if the vehicles couldn't be intercepted, the scouts might be able to track them to whatever hidey-hole they sought. The woman possessed an agile enough mind, and he could forgive a panic attack with a Reaper scratching at the door.

Valentine helped collect bodies. The Reapers had struck hard and fast, over a hundred deaths and a handful more wounded who would probably die in the coming hours from assorted traumas.

He mopped his brow after lifting one of the starred lawmen into an awning-draped wagon. He was happy to take part in the gory work; nothing quite took the spirit out of a man than having to pile the bodies of friends like cordwood, and as a stranger here he didn't know faces or names. The nasty business had to be taken care of both hastily and reverently.

Shadows on the road. Valentine looked up, saw the captain with a corporal and three soldiers trailing behind, Jules bringing up the rear, probably going inside to find Nancy. He lifted the camphor-dipped bandanna he kept over his face while moving bodies, and covered his features, wishing he'd grabbed a hat.

They turned for him. *The hell?*

Jules looked anxious. Was the captain going to get another paragraph added to his Q-file by bringing in an outlaw? Valentine went around to the other side of the cart and stuck a stiffened arm back under the awning.

"Excuse me, Mister," the captain said, a little Kansas twang in his voice. He smelled like horse sweat and service aftershave.

"Yes, Cap?" Valentine said.

"Major Valentine," a man with corporal stripes said, saluting. His hedgerow eyebrows had collected some road dust. "Sorry to disturb, I'm—"

"Tonley, from the Razors. Corporal Tonley now, by the look of it."

"Recognized your walk, sir. Saw you goin' up toward the buildings."

"Glad to see you again, and well. Or should I be?"

"No, Major," the captain cut in. "Nothing like that. I just wanted a chance to shake your hand."

Jules let out a deep breath.

"Glad it's that way." Valentine toweled off assorted flavors of filth and shook hands all around.

"Oh, you thought—," Tonley said.

"Hell no. Hell no, sir!" an unfamiliar private added. "Any sooner tries that, he'll have to walk back to the depot with his bike shoved up his ass."

"I beg your pardon," Valentine said. "Sooner?"

Tonley chuckled. "Oklahoma mounted. Mounted on bikes, that is. Get there sooner than the next guy and all that."

Tonley kept looking at his jaw as he explained the term and Valentine tapped the fracture point and said, "A nasty left hook." Unsaid was that the pugilist had been a Reaper, hunting him and Gail Post in the hills of Kentucky.

Valentine was invited to offer an opinion on tracking the Reaper-bearing vehicles, and the captain broke out his map. The party broke up within minutes, leaving Valentine with the feeling that he'd just got up from a long meal with old friends. Such was the nature of Southern Command's terrible, tasking comradeship.

"Sorry about that," Jules said. "I tried to tell them it was some big mistake, but they insisted on talking to you. They told me they just wanted to shake hands, but Duvalier said—"

"It turned out all right. But you needn't have worried, even if it hadn't. I would have gone quietly. They're Southern Command's boys."

"Meal break?"

"I won't feel like eating till tonight," Valentine said.

"Oh. Of course."

"Mind if I ask you something, though?"

She blanked her face, wary. "You bet."

"What was that about pregnancy last night? You're not expecting, are you?"

She glanced around, as though searching for an

escape. "I was scared. I had a close call a little while ago."

"If I'd known you weren't on the pill," Valentine said. "Dumb chance to take last night."

"It's a chance, all right," she said.

"I'm used to riddles from the Lifeweavers, or in the Kurian Zone. But not from fellow Cats."

Her shoulders sagged. "Can we go somewhere and talk?"

All the music and liveliness had vanished from the bar. Its door had been torn from the hinges. One of the bartender girls scrubbed a stain on the floor, and the other's eyes were downcast and red.

They had free Lemonclear, a sour concoction posing as lemonade, thanks to the soldiers. Southern Command's forces were departing, the bikers down the road and the horsemen cross-country. Before they'd left they'd put tabs of Lemonclear in five-gallon plastic jugs of the local water. The medicine both killed bacteria and water parasites and gave it a mild flavor.

They found a quiet corner out of hearing of the bartenders. Valentine skipped the polite talk. "Get it out. You'll feel better."

Jules' hands went to her kneecaps. "It's like this. You know we can't find the Lifeweavers, right?"

"I've heard rumors," Valentine said. No reason for her to know his mission.

"I feel like a creep. We should have just told you, but Ali said you'd have more fun the other way."

She expected a "Told me what?" so Valentine offered it.

"It's my way of, hopefully, becoming a Cat. I know the Lifeweavers do something to us, change our physical makeup somehow. They trigger a switch that's already inside us. That's the way it was explained to me, anyway."

"I don't think anyone really knows," Valentine said.

"Like blood from Bears, a transfusion heals stuff,

practically makes a miracle. Or the way a couple of Wolves have sex and their baby turns out able to smell really well. Seems like if Southern Command wants more Hunters, it's up to the Hunters to make them."

Jesus, we're being bred like foxhounds, Valentine thought.

"There's also the Dulcimet effect," Jules said.

"I've never heard of that," Valentine said.

"This doc, Dulcimet, with the Miskatonic discovered it. He did this study on a Cat from the Yazoo Delta who got a couple of teenage girls pregnant. Women make better Cats, generally, just like men make better Bears. It turns out that when a woman is carrying a Hunter's baby, sometimes it has an effect on the mother, since she and the baby sort of exchange blood while she's carrying. That's the Dulcimet effect."

"So the idea is, I get you pregnant, maybe you turn Cat, and Southern Command gets another potential Hunter in nine months. What do they do with the baby?"

"Secret. They have to guard them from the Kurians."

Valentine sighed. At least he'd had a choice when he became a Wolf. Or had he?

"Anyway," she continued. "There are only a couple of male Cats. They've been looking for you for a while now, hoping that you'd get one of the volunteers pregnant."

She laid the tiniest extra stress on the word "volunteer."

"Was it real volunteering, or are you being a good soldier?" Valentine asked.

"Oh, it was real. Ali had me meet Stykes . . . er, Major Styachowski. She painted quite a picture. Also, your rendezvous here was right for my cycle. They're keeping close track of that."

"I suppose they have to," Valentine said, feeling a bit like the butt of a cosmic joke.

"It's been almost a day. Maybe we should give it another go. The more sperm, the better."

They tried again. But Duvalier had been right: Knowing took a lot of the fun out of it.

Duvalier returned two days later with Styachowski and another fit-looking young woman wearing Southern Command Labor Corps fatigues and teardrop sunglasses. The last served as driver for a post-'22 flatbed, a high-axled transport vehicle made out of the odds and ends of other heavy-duty diesels. They were bringing a new generator and another radio set to replace equipment smashed in the Reaper raid.

A footlocker strapped to the rear seat held the gear Valentine requested. Styachowski carried a waterproof file folder with maps and basic information about his destination.

Duvalier hopped down from the webbing holding the generator, where she'd ridden, using the straps as a combination hammock and harness. She looked like a hungry, road-weary hitchhiker, but her eyes were as bright as ever.

"Heard about the trouble," she said.

"Jules and I came through for the team," Valentine said. In other circumstances he would have added an exaggerated wink, but Nancy's was almost a ghost town now. Many of the survivors of the raid had fled east after the dead were buried in their common grave. Some of those buried had been decorated Quislings, killed in some final fit of pique from the almost-vanquished Kurians of Tulsa.

Styachowski slicked back her moon white hair, impatient.

Duvalier twirled her sword-stick on its leather thong. "They think they've got it tracked down to central Tulsa. Storm sewers maybe. I'm going to go poke around a little. Be nice to get at least one before it has a chance to bolt."

The Kurians were near-legendary escape artists.

"When are you heading west, Val?" Styachowski asked.

"When the right convoy comes through."

"Spare me a couple more days?"

"Sure."

"Val, this is Darlene," Styachowski said, introducing the slim-hipped, curly-haired driver. "She's been selected as a potential, an aspirant for either Wolf or Cat. We were hoping you could find time to take her into the field for a couple of days, up toward the Zone but not in it. Teach her a little. Then we'd like your opinion."

" 'Lina' for short," Darlene said.

Valentine wondered what kind of eyes waited behind the driver's sunglasses, and if she'd been counting the days since the beginning of her last menstrual cycle. "Glad to be of service. As a favor to you and Ali."

CHAPTER FIVE

ϕ

*B*orders, Barters, and Bandits, April: *Because the Free Territory and Kurian Zone find their lands subject to change of ownership, and the occasional proposal to sit down and draw up peace plans meets only with ridicule, there are few well-defined borders. Even a widely acknowledged geographic obstacle such as the Mississippi River, serving as the unofficial eastern border of the UFR, is rather porous to penetration by small parties. David Valentine crossed it a number of times in the course of his duties as a Wolf or Cat.*

In the flats of the high, dry country around the Oklahoma Panhandle there's no such divider. Only a depopulated strip, perhaps fifty miles wide, where farming settlements emptied over the summer of 2074, once the locals learned that the UFR would advance no farther.

Some say the dry, flat plains unsettled soldiers used to bushwhacking their enemies from hilltop and timber. Others insist that the Kurians of the old USA's Southwest, one of the better-organized and more cooperative collections of the New Order, saw the coming threat and launched a Grog-led counterattack that sent the Texas and Ozark natives tumbling back. Still others say Southern Command ran out of plan and logistics, growing fearful at the decidedly mixed results of the revolts between the Platte and Red rivers, which their assault was supposed to support.

Historical bickering aside, the region between the Ku-

rian and UFR watch points is the home of rabbit, coyotes, and hawks, surveyed by high-flying Gargoyles during the day and aura-sensing Reapers at night. Remnants of the cash crops of the region—wheat, soy, sorghum, and barley—can still be found growing wild, sometimes grazed down by small herds of wild sheep and wily, testy goats.

The old interstate, shooting east-west through the flat with a bend here and there placed by engineers to keep motorists from growing hypnotized by the road, still sees a convoy every week or so. The Kurians allow the traffic so that their favored supporters might have luxuries brought in from far away, with the thrilling but harmless taint of black market goods, and the Free Territory needs the gear and medicines the inevitable smuggling compartments contain. The third winner in the arrangement is the road patrols, who inevitably take away a bottle of liquor or a carton of cigarettes as they carry out everything from fugitive searches to safety inspections on the road traffic.

David Valentine waited quietly in the backseat of the Land Rover, watching the checkpoint soldiers inspect the convoy behind.

The convoy had pulled off the road in the vast, empty plains at a watchtower-flanked checkpoint, the first and most important on their ride through the Southwest, according to the driver. A slight ridge, thick with spring prairie flowers, was noticeable only because the rest of the topography was so flat.

His "overwatch car" was the second of the string of nineteen vehicles in the convoy, not counting the motorcycles riding at the head and tail. Road Chief Lautenberg, a good friend of the Hobarth clan, signed on "Max Argent" when his convoy stopped for an overnight at Nancy's. The stolid Lautenberg, so phlegmatic he might be mistaken for one of the uniformed dummies that filled out the real warriors in the big army truck at the center of the convoy, had looked him up and down with his one good eye, and assigned him to one of the combat teams.

It had taken Valentine some weeks to find a ride, spending hours reading and waiting at Nancy's. Though he kept himself clean-shaven, his legworm leathers and their armored plates polished, and his boots beyond even a labor-corps fatigue sergeant's reproach, several smaller convoys weren't willing to take on a stranger.

When a big convoy finally arrived it was bound for Central America, and the second, riding in a series of converted school buses, gave him the willies. They purported to be musicians and dancers who sold protein powder and water filters during the day and performed for tips at night. Despite their promises of a substantial reward in the payout end of the trip in exchange for light guard work, Valentine wondered if they weren't "head-hunters," especially after he heard the quiet rattle of chains beneath the seats of their vehicles. A man could get rich bringing warm bodies to the Kurians, and Valentine guessed that the attractive slatterns who rode in the front minivan served as bait for the unwary. The whole group had a quiet, dangerous air that put him off.

The next had a desperate, last-chance feel to it, and the owner and all the drivers looked hungry. Valentine began to feel like Goldilocks, unable to find a convoy that was just right. Then Lautenberg came in like a thunderstorm of diesel exhaust and rubber.

At first Valentine rode guard with the "back team," a group of drivers in an armored minibus who slept or played cards while they waited to replace others when they came off shift. After he brought down a buck grazing in a field from 250 yards at dawn, Lautenberg transferred him to the overwatch "Rover."

The "Rover" was a high-clearance four-wheel drive, panels long since replaced by welded corrugated aluminum and old bulletproof vests. It had thick off-road tires, spotlights, a winch, and a cupola complete with bullet shield and a venerable heavy machine gun called the poker.

Its sights were made of carved Reaper teeth and wire.

Valentine patted his gun in its bracket on the back of the driver's seat. Styachowski had answered his request for a reliable, accurate, but not threatening-looking carbine with her usual precision. She'd shown up with a Steyr Scout "Viper," a deadly little killer with a forward-mounted 2.5× sight, flash suppressor, and eighteen-round minidrum feeding the oversized bolt action.

Valentine especially admired the scope. Your eye could wander to find the target, and then—as you aimed—your eye glided into the magnified image as if drawn there, with the weapon already lined up.

They'd supplied him with four boxes of ammunition for it, and a special little five-bullet leather holder. A note accompanied them, from a weapons researcher at the Miskatonic. He explained that the five shells were a new, experimental delivery method for Quickwood, suspending a distillate of the sap in a capsule that would be broken as the armor-piercing bullet fragmented, hopefully inside a Reaper. "Write me and let me know results, good or bad," the note ended.

Valentine wondered at that. If the results were bad, he probably wouldn't live to write the note.

New steel-tipped hiking boots, a hard-frame pack, thermal underwear, a bamboo sleeping mat, a thick wool scarf, leather gloves, mittens, a compass, and survival gear filled out the rest of the footlocker she'd brought. She also provided him with a thick nylon laborer's girdle that could be popped open to reveal two dozen gold coins. Resting in sawdust padding were six bottles of bourbon, and a minitelescope. Nothing had any tagging or labeling to identify it as originating with Southern Command. Even his ammunition was in Kansas City's Zeroload boxes, one of the biggest armorers in the Midwest.

Best of all, she'd found his sword. He'd asked for a similar blade to the one he'd carried on his first mission as a Cat, never expecting for his original to show up, sharpened and in a new stiffened black leather sheath.

Who knew what warehouse it had rested in since the day he, Duvalier, and Ahn-Kha left for his long mission into the Kurian Zone in search of a half-legendary weapon to defeat the Reapers that turned out to be Quickwood? Duvalier guessed that Dix Welles had buried it along with the other Cats' left possessions when Solon took over. The cache had evidently been recovered since then, and probably sat in some warehouse with his books and a few other personal items, a curiosity on some long inventory list.

Valentine watched the Quislings bearing ROAD RANGER patches on their shoulders conduct their inspection. Ostensibly the convoy carried pumping equipment, high-voltage cable, machine tools, and a dozen other industrial necessities. But behind the heavy equipment that required a forklift or crane rested cases of sealed black-label bourbon, boxes of chocolate, jewelry, furs, and precision optics.

The Quislings at the checkpoint wore dark khaki uniforms and bandannas. Most had cheap plastic sand-and-sun goggles. High observation towers and earthworks bristling with machine guns and 20mm cannon covered the inspection siding.

An officer with a red pillbox hat, thick with Kurian service pins, stuck his head in the window, examining Valentine's profile.

"I need that man out, please," Pillbox Hat told the driver. He pointed at Valentine. "Cuff him for now."

Valentine's back went clammy. Had a wanted poster made it into the Southwest? He could confuse the issue for a few days with his false IDs, but capture would mean—

"Okay, boss," the driver said as the man in the shotgun seat pressed a button three times on his belt walkietalkie. "Get out, Max. The girls here want to look into those pretty brown eyes."

Valentine complied, leaving his weapons in their

brackets, and as they snapped the cuffs on and patted him down, more Quislings gathered to watch.

"You ever go by the name David Valentine, chief?" Pillbox Hat asked.

Valentine just breathed, centering himself, pulling in lifesign. It kept the Reapers away, but it was also calming. "No, sir, don't know him."

"I didn't say if you knew him."

"Sorry, sir."

Lautenberg walked up, moving at a pace just short of a trot, his lead rig driver just behind. He approached the officer in the pillbox hat. "What now, Hopgood?"

"We're detaining one of your men so we can run some prints. He fits a description. Indianish, black hair, scarred, 'bout the right height and weight."

"Detain? How long's that going to take?"

"A day or two at most. You can move on."

"Argent, you wanted for something?" Lautenberg said.

"Some guy named Valentine," Valentine said, hoping he could still brazen it out. "All red man heap look alike, Road Chief."

Lautenberg planted his feet and crossed his arms. "This convoy isn't leaving a man behind."

A sergeant passed Valentine's papers over to Hopgood with a shrug.

"Up to you," Hopgood said. "Bring the wagon," he yelled across the gravel to his idling men. "We'll take him to Blackwater Holing."

"The hell you are," Lautenberg said. "Hopgood, I've been easy on you because you're new, and I don't like making enemies. But wouldn't it be kinda dumb for some fugitive to pass right through one spot he's sure to be looked at?"

"This guy's clever. He took out a whole regiment of TMCC and blew that big Mississippi Grog cannon into orbit."

"Be news to his mother," Lautenberg said. "Until she passed, Max here was taking care of her every day of his life. Kansas militia trusted him with a gun, I know that. My Ingrid's married to Tom Stormcloud over in Topeka. He's Stormcloud's cousin."

Valentine had no idea what spring this torrent of bullshit was coming from, but it fitted his faked papers like a jigsaw piece. Lautenberg had just glanced at them briefly back at Nancy's.

"Now, you can detain this kid," Lautenberg said. "I can wait here, getting madder and madder every hour. And when General Cox in Albuquerque runs out of black-label bourbon and has to listen to those three coochies of his bitch about how they're all outta lipstick and undies, well, I might just call you a bad name or two when he asks what was keeping me. You ever talked to Cox when he's bone-dry on whiskey?"

Hopgood looked from his thick sheaf of wanted posters at Valentine, then at Lautenberg, and back again.

Lautenberg patted his hip pocket. "Lord, Corporal Guadalco, you smoked three cigarettes with Max here last October. You showed him a picture of your kids."

"Oh yes, I remember, remember very well," a corporal in a nonregulation straw hat spoke up.

Hopgood wilted. "I'll cut him loose this time, Lautenberg. But your reputation's riding on this."

"My reputation's riding on about three hundred tires," Lautenberg said. "I just want them spinning again."

Valentine felt the cuffs come off, and showed his relief.

"Thank you, sir," he said to Hopgood.

"Smile, Hoppy, and have a cigar," Lautenberg said, extracting a gleaming silver case. "You road rangers know I'm just trying to get from A to B and back to A. Smuggling fugitives doesn't come between A and B. Or A and Z for that matter—it's a whole 'nother alphabet."

As the groups parted, Lautenberg offered Valentine a wink, and slipped something into Guadalco's hand as they shook.

And with that, the convoy got moving again. The scout cycles blatted out first, then the combat craft; the big tow trucks, capable of pulling a disabled truck or moving an unexpected obstacle with their thick cable winches; Lautenberg's Winnebago office on wheels; the "money trucks" with the tanker and "chuck wagon" RV guarded by a truck full of dummy soldiers; a few "gypsy" vans traveling with the convoy for protection like pilot fish hovering close to a shark; more cargo trucks; then the rear guard: the "remount" truck and more cycles.

"The Spikes must really have it in for that Valentine fella," the heavyset commander of the overwatch car said. By "Spikes" he meant the Kurians; their towers did look a little like spikes, glimpsed from a distance.

He had thoughtful eyes and a patchy beard. The rest of the car, Zuniga at the wheel and Swell at the ring gun, called their commander "Salsa." He spread hot sauce from an endless supply of tiny red bottles he kept in a machine-gun belt case on everything he ate, save fruit.

"Nice of the road chief to stand up for me. I was in a cell once before. Thought I'd cashed out."

"What were you in for?"

"Fighting and public drunkenness."

"That where you got your face rearranged?" Zuniga asked.

"Yes," Valentine said, which was almost true.

"What you guys talking about?" Swell called down from the ring gun. Swell loved riding in the wind, leaning on the canvas-covered poker, but always wanted details of in-cab conversations shouted up to him.

"We're talkin' about how your mother undercuts all the other whores," Salsa shouted up. Then to the others: "I swear to God, I should make him drive so he doesn't miss nuthin'."

"Except he bitches about how he feels cooped up in here," Zuniga said, leaning over to pass gas at a volume that rivaled that of the motorcycle sixty meters ahead.

"Phew, Max, I think this kid could drop a Hood with that," Salsa said.

"What's that?" Swell shouted.

Valentine winked at Salsa as he tied Swell's shoelaces together.

And with that, David Valentine passed out of Oklahoma.

Brief thunderstorms drenched the convoy.

"If you make this a habit, you'll learn that this is the best time of year Southwest," Salsa said.

Valentine had to agree. The forests, whose trees felt spaced out and airy compared with the thickets of the Ozarks, were cool and breezy and the dry grasses of the range country were bright with flowers, yellows and pinks and blues that attracted butterflies. Sadly, many of the latter ended up in gooey, colorful pieces on the windshield and grille of the 4×4.

Valentine, with little to do except watch the terrain roll under their wheels, enjoyed the trip. Except for train travel, this was the fastest he'd ever eaten miles.

There were stops, of course, for meals and refueling, and long detours around Kurian Zones or demolished bridges and culverts. He trotted around the vehicles, exercising his unused legs, marveling at the distance they'd come in a few short days.

At the overnights the convoy pulled off into lonely road stops, throwing a wide circle around Albuquerque, where Kurians who were at odds with the rest of the Aztlan Confederation were famous for letting strangers enter, but not leave. The road chief avoided towns as they crossed New Mexico. Towns brought local police to the vehicles like thirsty ticks looking for blood. New Universal Church missions and *monastis* provided safety of another sort, but the churchmen in their tube-steel clerical collars (grades of metal differentiated just what the ascetics had given up to more fully devote themselves to the betterment of mankind) were a more hygienic and annoying version of the lawmen. At least the lawmen didn't subject one to lectures about reproductive responsibilities as they took their graft.

"A tree must be rooted to grow strong in safety!" one wild-haired monk intoned as the maintenance teams replaced lost tires in the Cíbola foothills. He climbed a light pole to be better heard. His monastery had a patchwork look to it; this station was probably an exile for the head cases of the church. "Wandering seed is lost in the wind."

"Or lost in the joy girls in Los Angeles," a truck driver muttered to Valentine. He spit a mouthful of tobacco in the direction of the Easter Island–like Reaper-face set looking down on the monastery's wash well. "Ever hear about the Honeypot, pickup?" the driver asked.

"We have to get there first," Salsa said, interrupting. "Scouts are reporting some burned rigs in Holloweye Valley."

"We're too big for the Jaguars to try."

"I hope they know it as well as you," Salsa said. He turned and Valentine followed.

"Jaguars?"

"They wear bits of fur," Salsa said. "The big medicine guys wear spots. A successful warrior gets mountain lion skin, or wolf. The lowlifes have to make do with coyote. They're half-wild, worship those Reaper monoliths you see in this part of the country. They ain't after our gear or cargo, just our giblets. They think if they take lives, drink blood, they become as strong as the Reapers. Or turn into them."

Valentine searched the copper-dusted mountains of the Mogollon Rim ahead. The dry air gave the horizon a clarity that seemed to expand his personal patch of earth as it reduced his place in it. He felt rather like one of the valley butterflies, perhaps determinedly unaware of an approaching windshield.

"Will they keep off us?" Valentine asked.

"Depends. Some of the young men might be feeling their oats. Wish I could tell you more. All we got to go on is rumor. No one's lived in Holloweye Valley long enough to do any social studies."

"I didn't see that on the road map."

"It's unofficial, like Checkpoint Circlejerk back there. The valley's not a problem. It's the passes you have to watch. They'll roll a wreck down and try to cause an accident."

"Why Holloweye?"

Salsa probed an ear. "Let's hope we don't find out."

The bikers, skin almost as dark as their faded leathers, reported back as the convoy paused on a long turn looking down into the valley. While they refueled stomachs and tanks from chuck wagon and bowser, Road Chief Lautenberg held a meeting.

Salsa returned and put his crew back in the overwatch vehicle. "We're going to go clear the road while we still have daylight," he told his crew. Swell wiped his palm on his jeans as Salsa described their operation.

"The Jaguars have the road blocked good with wrecks. They ain't manning the barricade, but somebody launched off slingstones at the bikers while they checked for survivors. We're going to go in and cover the wreckers while they clear the road."

"Could they tell how they took out the wrecks?" Zuniga asked.

Salsa shrugged. "Looked like a big road accident, they said. No question, one vehicle blew up. I had dynamite lobbed at me a couple runs back when I was driving the tanker. Maybe they got lucky with a toss. Any more questions?"

"How many dead?" Valentine asked.

"They said it was a dozen at least. They're not even dried out yet."

Zuniga shook his head slowly. Salsa continued: "Yeah. They were about to cut the bodies down when the slingstones hit."

With two motorcycles riding scout, flanking the operation like prowling dogs under the perfect yellow of an Arizona sun, the two wreckers and Salsa's armed 4×4 approached the blockade at a creep. Valentine hung out one door by a safety strap, searching the road for signs of mining. Salsa did the same, from a slightly more conventional position in the passenger window.

The expedition stopped fifty yards from the blockade. Valentine smelled burning tire.

Vultures rose from the wrecks when Zuniga blasted the Rover's horn.

"Okay, Argent, go earn your coin," Salsa said as the vehicles halted.

"Seen-yority," Swell said, swinging the now-uncovered gun to cover the wrecks. "It's got its privileges."

Valentine trotted up the median of the highway with carbine held ready against his shoulder—there was precious little cover on the road itself, and if he had to go to ground, he at least wanted the dry-looking brush in between him and the Jaguars.

The eight bodies were laid out between the wrecks in a pattern that might have been trying to be a flower, or a boat propeller. All were hollow-socketed and opened at the rib cage. Valentine guessed that the heart and liver were missing at least, along with more obvious extractions of eyes, noses, and tongues. Taking a deep breath, he knelt beside one sandy-haired corpse and looked in the nose.

They'd spooned out a good deal of brain as well.

Valentine heard a flutter and whirled, but it was just a crow. The black bird opened its mouth, an angry *Kaww!* contesting the bodies.

Valentine paid it no attention and did a fast search of the trucks and vans. He found three more bodies, similarly picked at but not arranged in any fashion save what was needed for a quick extraction of organ meat.

He heard a chatter of machine-gun fire and the sudden gunning of a motorcycle. He hopped up in a pickup bed—the contents had been stripped as hastily and messily as the bodies—and saw one of the bikers taking off against a running, sun-browned figure. The runner had a bad limp, with blood and dirt caked on his leg.

The biker stopped his bike, lifted an oddly thick rifle,

pumped its action three times, and fired. Valentine saw a thick dart blossom in the back of the runner, who flopped over again.

The biker answered a hoot from one of the wreckers with a wave of his leather cap, and turned his bike back for the road.

Somehow the Jaguar rose again, a thin spear lodged in a grooved thrower. Valentine brought up the Steyr and sighted on the dark blotch of armpit hair under the Jaguar's raised right arm. The gun boomed, startling more crows.

Valentine didn't watch the effect of his shot. Instead he scanned for more threats.

Valentine watched the misthrown spear change trajectory, from straight up to straight down. The biker glanced over his shoulder, turned his bike again, and made for the spot where the Jaguar fell. He raised himself in the saddle and bumped over the body in a figure-eight pattern, making sure this time. Valentine scanned the countryside, wondering if the wounded warrior had been sacrificed to draw the biker into a trap, but no other threats emerged from the brush and cacti.

With the killing that couldn't quite be labeled a skirmish over, Valentine waved the Rover forward, and Salsa gave the okay for the wreckers to come up.

Valentine grabbed a bungee cord and a shovel off a bracket on the back hatch of the Rover. Using the bungee around the ankles, he pulled the bodies one by one off the road, lining them up in the median. When the corpses were lined up, he loosened some soil with the pick end of his worm hook and threw loose dirt over the butchered collection.

Swell rinsed his mouth out with a canteen and spit onto the front windscreen. Zuniga activated the wipers. "You don't mean to bury all those bodies?"

"I do," Valentine said.

The bikers roared up, curious. "Hell, man, the birds and coyotes will take care of them with a lot less sweat," the fat one with the beard said.

Valentine ignored him.

The one who had chased after the Jaguar, a lean, greasy-haired man who looked as though he'd crossed New Mexico dragged by the bike rather than in the saddle, put his bike on its stand. "Coot, be a mensch for once," he growled. "Have a little respect."

The biker slid into the median and took up the pick. "Name's Loring," he said. "Zeb Loring."

"Max Argent," Valentine said. *"Mucho gusto."*

"Aye-yup," Loring said.

"Never met a Zeb before," Valentine said. "That short for Zebulon?"

Loring had his share of scars. His leathers were carefully stitched up, his face much less so. "My father never made it much past Genesis in the Bible. Mom was a rabbi outta New York. It was a compromise."

They moved on to another body. Valentine rolled a rock using his shovel as a lever. "You're a long way from the East."

"Aye-yup. You too, looks like. Those are Kentucky legworm leathers."

"That they are."

"Always thought those beasties were grand. You don't have to feed them gas and oil."

"Ever rode one?" Valentine asked.

"Naw. Too slow. I like to be on something that can outrun those damn golems."

Valentine grunted agreement. "Hey, lookit that," Loring said. He leaned the pickax against his knee and pointed up.

Valentine saw aircraft, in three groups, flying high toward the southwest.

"I bet Denver got hit again. That's the Flying Circus. They range all over the Southwest, set up temporary airfields on old roads."

"Pyp's Flying Circus?" Valentine asked, shading his eyes to take a look at the craft. He guessed they were at above ten thousand feet.

"That's what they're called. I saw a couple of them in

their fancy leathers in a bar in Nogales once. Aye-yup. They're not ones for staying put either."

"What are you going to do when we hit LA?" Valentine asked.

"Celebrate. Then we might head up the valley to wine country. They do a few runs a year over the mountains to the Missouri and Arkansas riverheads. Good money guarding wine, and a flask out of the supply cask really makes dinner an experience." He mumbled a few words as Valentine covered a corpse with a thin layer of dirt. Valentine stood silent.

"I like the old words, don't you?" Loring said.

"Yes. Thanks for the help."

"Mucho gusto," Loring said.

With the wrecks out of the way, and their remaining fuel safely stowed in the tanks and drums of the bikes and wreckers, the vehicles reassembled in the formation they'd used as they approached the blockade. Valentine, sweaty from his exertions and moody because of the bodies, ate a salted hard-boiled egg after carefully washing his hands.

"You feel better?" Salsa asked.

"Pardon?"

Salsa threw his arm over the seat. "You feel better now that those bodies are buried? 'Cause it sure makes no difference to them."

"Nothing in my contract about leaving bodies in the sun," Valentine said.

"Coyotes will probably have them dug up by midnight," Zuniga said.

"What's that?" Swell shouted from the gun.

"Oh, for Kur's dark asshole," Salsa said. He poked his head out the window. "You're at the wheel next—hey!"

Valentine heard it too. A sputtering engine sounded overhead and Valentine marked a twin-engine plane, a dirty-clay color with a red stripe going up the tail like a hockey stick; it spewed white vapor from one engine and faint black puffs from the other as it passed overhead. The engine sounded stronger for a moment and the plane gained altitude, trying for the mountains to the west. Valentine watched as it shrank to a cross in the distance. Then it plunged, leveled off, and disappeared into the valley floor.

"That poor dumb bastard," Salsa said. "He should have set it down in the road by us."

Valentine, meanwhile, searched his map of the Southwest.

"He was trying to make it to his home airfield," Zuniga said.

"Are those the guys with the reward message on the backs of their jackets?" Valentine asked.

"Tempting, isn't it?" Salsa said. "But forget it, the Jaguars will have him by dark."

"How long would it take us to get to where he landed?" Valentine asked.

"I ain't even guesstimating. We're not risking the Rover."

"Then stop, please," Valentine said, feeling light-headed. "I'll go on foot."

"You're nuts," Swell shouted down from the gun.

"Now he can hear," Salsa said. "What about your contract, Argent?"

"I've got the option of breaking it. Please, stop the car."

Zuniga honked and the vehicles slowed, then stopped.

"You don't get paid, then," Salsa said.

"I'd appreciate an extra canteen and some of the freeze-dry," Valentine said.

"Hey, if this is about those bodies, I didn't mean to step on any religious practices. Running my mouth is just how I get to know a man. Nothing to kill yourself over."

Valentine got his gun, sword, and pack and tucked a few extra odds and ends in from the Rover's supplies: freeze-dried veggie packs—about as appetizing as a bathroom mat but full of vitamins—beef sticks, dried fruit. . . .

"Guy's nuts," Swell called to a grizzled mechanic leaning out of a tow truck window to watch. "He's going to go rescue that cloud jumper. Wants the ten grand in gold."

"Big money isn't worth getting dead over, kid," the mechanic advised.

Been a long time since anyone's called me kid, Valentine thought. But the strange clarity that came over him sometimes, the one that infected him when he went into Chicago after Molly, or struck off into the Nebraska sandhills to warn the trekkers against the general, or pushed him to save a wounded Grog who would become his best friend—Valentine felt his eyes go wet at the memory of Ahn-Kha—told him he was doing the right thing.

Sergeant Patel used to talk about a third eye capable of perceiving the invisible. Valentine wondered if there was a third ear, hearing the whispers of guardian angels.

A motorcycle engine blatted and Loring sat his bike next to him as Valentine marked a reference point for the fallen aircraft. The bike growled like a threatening watchdog.

"You're not," Loring said.

"I am. Interested in making a Troy?"

"I'm not parking three butts on my bike for an off-road trip to Neverland."

"I just want you to get me to that airplane."

Loring looked at the sun. "Let's see the color of your gold."

Valentine reached into his belt and palmed one of his coins. He passed it over.

"That thing with the bodies wasn't an act, I hope. If this is some fancy plan to get me out so you can debit my bike—"

Valentine checked the buckles on his pack and the strap fixing his legworm pickax. "I arranged for the plane to go down just so I could get your ride?"

"Right. Sorry. Paranoid is the best way to stay alive when you road it for a living."

"No offense."

"Give my regards to Lautenberg," Valentine told Salsa. "I'll either meet you guys tomorrow when you run the valley or dog southwest."

"You a crusader, Argent, or just greedy?"

"A little of both," Valentine said.

Loring exchanged knuckles with his fellow biker, and edged forward on his seat. "Hang your pack there," he said, indicating a little backrest just above the taillight. "You can put the gun and the giblet prodder on the front rack, if you like."

Quick-release plastic snaps secured the gear there. With that, Valentine climbed on and they were off, back into the once-fertile valley.

Loring gave him a quick lesson on how and when to lean in turns, where to put his feet when they stopped the bike, and what to do in case of attack: "Hug me like an ass bandit. You come off, I'm not turning round."

They stopped once while still on the highway to reconnoiter from a slight hill, and Valentine pointed to where he marked the crash site.

"If you want to take a leak, do it now. It's going to be bumpy for a while," Loring advised.

After a companionable release—Loring loosed a long, satisfied "Aye-yup" along with his bladder—they bumped off into the Arizona dirt, crossing through stands of cacti and waxy succulents.

Loring negotiated the big, woolly bushes and dry washes with a good deal of skill. All they disturbed were rabbit, whose Ping-Pong ball tails bounced away from the bike's noisy exhaust, and roadrunners.

"Practically ringing the dinner bell for the Jaguars, you know," Loring said, at a stop where Valentine mounted a rock to recheck their bearings.

They reached the crash site perhaps two hours after the pilot had set down. Judging from the tire tracks, he'd made a good job of the landing, snapping off a few taller cacti, until the right under-engine landing gear hit a rock. The gear hadn't broken, but it bounced the plane up, and the right wingtip caught and spun it, and once the nose struck it was all over. The rugged frame of the aircraft, though thick with patched bullet holes, had stood up to even the pancake. Wings and tail were still intact.

They made a slow circle of the wreck. Valentine cocked his head to admire the nose art: A girl in an abbreviated red uniform, fighting to keep the front of her skirt down, rode a rocket pointed toward the nose gear. Valentine retrieved his weapons and gear from the bike.

"Wonder if they got him already," Loring said.

"I don't see any tracks." Valentine looked at the upside-down craft. "Anyone in there?"

Loring switched off his motor so Valentine could listen. He saw a pair of bloody fingerprints below one of the windows, upside-down letters reading

MILKMAN

He stuck his head in and looked at the field of gauges and controls. He smelled blood, strong now.

Cargo netting filled the rear of the plane, mostly empty save for a couple of battered crates and strewn duffel bags. He smelled a sweet odor, and traced it to a broken jar of preserved plums in syrup resting against a big water bottle and a mouth tube. An open camera case with a body and a long lens inside rested on the roof. "There are some bags of cargo here. And a camera. You want to check for salvage?"

"Rocket rails," Loring said, still firmly in his saddle, bike pointed for a quick exit.

"Hmmm?" Valentine asked. He pulled the camera case out and inspected the prize. It looked quite valuable.

"On the bottom of the wings. This thing's built to

carry rockets, and they've been fired a lot. Let's get out of here. Let the colab choke out here."

Valentine made a slow circuit of the plane. The ground was rocky and—

Blood on the air.

The pilot's keeping close to his ship, but hiding. Sensible, if his friends come looking for him.

Valentine approached the bike. "He's still in the area," he said quietly.

Loring watched the sun, now touching the mountains. "If you say so. I'm dusting off. You coming?"

"I want to meet this guy," Valentine said.

"Shit. You said there were bags of stuff?"

"Yes."

"Gimme one." Loring unwrapped a bungee cord from his handlebar.

Valentine retrieved an ordinary-looking service duffel. It contained a rolled-up sleeping mat and spare blankets. He watched while Loring took off his leather jacket, zipped it on the upright duffel, then placed it in the saddle behind him. He whipped the bungee around it and fixed it at his belly button.

"From a distance it'll look like we're still riding together. Maybe the Jaguars will chase me instead of hunt you up. Pyp's gold isn't worth your life, Max."

"No," Valentine agreed.

"Hope you make it back to the road, then, Samaritan."

"Ride free," Valentine said, summoning his one piece of biker slang. He handed over the camera case. "Give this to Lautenberg. Maybe you and he can split the proceeds of the sale. A thank-you from me."

"Aye-yup," Loring agreed. "Keep on God's good side." He winked and started up his bike.

Valentine ducked back into the shadow of the plane and watched Loring bump off. He dropped into a crouch, and began to hunt.

Valentine followed his nose uphill, found a telltale drop of blood or two, and finally heard rather wheezy breathing from a thick stand of barrel-shaped cacti. Wild sheep dotted the mountain slopes above, feeding on the grasses in the wind-sheltered washes.

The flier had chosen his vantage well. It offered a good view of the wreck and the mountainside.

Valentine sat down on a flat-topped rock about ten feet away from the cactus and opened a bag of dried fruit, listened to the breathing. He rinsed his mouth out, then extracted a couple of apple chips and crunched them down. "You want some?"

The cactus stand didn't say anything. Whoever was within held his breath.

"This is a nasty patch of ground, flyboy. You're not going to like the natives."

Valentine took a swallow of water.

"On the other hand," Valentine said, "they're going to be happy as hell to meet you. What I can't figure out is what they do with the eyes. Eyes don't keep. Do they eat them as soon as they pull them out, maybe with a little salt like a hard-boiled egg, or do they carry around a jug of brine—"

The cactus stand let out a cough and went silent.

"Option three is me," Valentine said. "I'm just interested in that reward on the back of your jacket. I'm sure you know the wording by heart. It's a win for both of us: You get to be alive, and I get my money."

"Ya-hey," the cactus stand said. A man stood up, a bloody bandage on his hand and a good-sized swelling on his head. He had the blond good looks of an old magazine cover model. Powerful shoulders tested the limits of his jumpsuit, and a brown leather jacket of the type Valentine had last seen outside Dallas was tied around his waist. "You could have said so to begin. Navajo or Apache?"

"Neither," Valentine said. "Max Argent."

"Equality Hornbreed."

Valentine wasn't sure he'd heard correctly.

"First name was good politics," Hornbreed said. He

blew his nose into a silk handkerchief, coughed again. "My genitors were all about good politics."

"Your ribs intact?" Valentine asked.

"It's the pollen. Spring allergies. I can walk all night if I have to. Got a headache that about has me cross-eyed is all."

"I think I've got some aspirin—"

"Took a couple, thanks. Grabbed the medical kit first thing."

"Your friends know you went down?"

He took a handful of dried fruit. "They do. Everyone was low on fuel—end of the leg. Guess no one had the guts to try a setdown to pick me up—strict rules about that, we lose too many ships. The strip we're heading for is just a temp, though, no pickup helicopter. There's a couple parked at Yuma, so I might be on my own until tomorrow."

"Hurt the hand on landing?"

"No. Planted it on some broken glass, otherwise I'd offer you a candied plum. Didn't look when I unhooked. I smelled smoke and was worried I was on fire."

"You armed?"

"Pistol and my flare gun. Want me to turn them over to you?"

He was oddly accommodating.

"Can I look at the offer on the jacket again?"

The wording hadn't changed, nor had the logo of a rattlesnake with dragon wings flying openmouthed toward the viewer. Colorful mission patches and squadron insignia—a hairy pirate face with a classic skull-and-bones cap appealed—decorated the sleeves and pockets.

Valentine joined him in the cacti, saw a blanket spread out with a big water jug, a signaling mirror with a hole in the center, and a fire starter. He uncased his binoculars and made a slow survey of the valley below them from cover. Nothing. Of course, that didn't mean the Jaguars weren't approaching. There was ample cover in the dry washes and brush.

"You picked a good spot." Valentine broke out the preserved chow.

"I've had to set down before. Never flipped my bird, though. I'm sure the squadron's having a good laugh. That's a nice rifle."

"Steyr Scout," Valentine said.

Hornbreed checked his wounded hand. "Hope I don't have to see it in action."

"We've got two options, Equality," Valentine said. "Wait for your friends to show, or try to make it to the interstate you passed over. There's a convoy that'll be passing through at first light tomorrow. We can hitch up with them and drop off at the next crossroads and make for Yuma."

"We'll be easier to pick out if we move. I'm supposed to stay with my ship unless I have to evade."

"The Jaguars—"

"There are Jaguars in this valley? I thought they'd cleared out."

"Change your mind?" Valentine asked.

Hornbreed searched the skies. "No. Generally it's best to wait for help to arrive."

Valentine moved to the other side of the cactus-shrouded enclosure. "I'm not one for waiting. But you know your fliers."

"There are more pilots than there are operational ships. But I'm a wing leader. My pilots will come."

Valentine scanned the ground around the overturned plane again. Was there a new shadow next to the brush in front of the engine?

"I like your confidence," Valentine said.

"Stay put and wait," Hornbreed said. "I was a Youth Vanguard leader up Provo way. Worked my way up from larva to scout ant to warrior-guard. We'd go out on squat clearance, burning old homes and buildings outside of town, finding hidden livestock and fields. One time we came on—sheesh, I don't know what to call it. I guess a pilgrimage. Thousand people or more on foot heading for California, hauling stuff on bicycles and handcarts. Our leader decided to follow 'em, see what they were up to. We just walked up and asked where they were going. They got rounded up, of course, and boy, did we hear it from the Churchmen when they found us dogging the column. They kicked the leader right out of the Vanguard. Worked out for me, though, I was the one who argued that we'd been told to burn down houses and we shouldn't go mixing with dead-feets. Were you in the Vanguard?"

"I grew up off the grid, more or less," Valentine said, still scanning. "I did help teach in a Churchman's one-room schoolhouse." His eyes caught a brief flurry of bouncing brown balls. By the time he got his glasses up and located, the might-bes had vanished into an arroyo.

But the heads were on course for the wreck.

Hornbreed let out a little gasp. "*Huff.* I always fell asleep somewhere between collective rights and mankind's atrocity catechism."

Definite movement at the wreck now. Through field glasses Valentine watched a scout explore.

"Well, the Jaguars are at your wreck," Valentine said.

Hornbreed shrugged.

The scout entered the overturned craft, which tipped a little as his weight changed its center of balance. A minute later he emerged again, eating from the broken jar of plums. With the sun now fully behind the mountains the desert flats turned blue. The clouds above warmed into reds, golds, and pinks and purples.

Valentine decided he could get used to desert-country sunsets, but he kept his attention on the wreck. More Jaguars had shown up and were now tearing the little ship apart, salvaging everything from bits of wire to the seat covers. Hornbreed took one brief look and handed the glasses back. "Savages. I can't watch any more."

A Jaguar in much longer furs, cut about his shoulders like a cape made of animal tails, with a spotted headband around his forehead and furry-trimmed sandals, began a rampage. With a good deal of gesturing toward the mountains behind Valentine he gave his tribesmen a dressing-down, put them in a staggered line like a top sergeant with well-trained recruits, and hustled them away with a glance or two behind.

Valentine couldn't help but turn and look at the darkening peaks behind.

"What do you know about these mountains?" Valentine asked Hornbreed.

"Some farms and ranches on the other side. Pretty well organized, typical Aztlan stuff. There are collar towers below the ridgeline—they're easy to spot from the air."

"Collar towers?"

"Keeps the peons on their ranchos. The collars tighten if they start to stray. Top-quality Korean electronics."

"What about this side?"

"Sheep. Mud pueblos."

Had these mountains turned into a choking, deathly place according to local legend? Then why did the medicine man have to remind his tribesmen?

Hornbreed stretched out, pulled his reflective survival blanket up. "Long, bad day. I'm going to try to sleep off this headache."

"Should we set a watch?"

"You're my rescuer. If anything's going to happen, it'll happen whether we set a watch or not. They outnumber us twenty to two." He blew his nose again. "You wouldn't know it to hear me, but I am a healthy specimen. Just spring air."

Valentine watched the valley until darkness made it impossible, then admired the stars and planets. He hadn't seen them so bright since he'd been at sea in the Caribbean.

The memories that evoked turned him sour and gloomy. He slipped out of the cactus thatch—his old Wolf habit of changing positions after darkness was so deeply ingrained he did it even if it was only a shift of twenty feet or so—and listened. A distant coyote howled in the valley. Others took up the chorus, but none called from the mountains he and Hornbreed rested against.

Too uneasy to really sleep, he dozed, sitting cross-legged with his rifle against his lap, small of his back pressed up against a sun-heated rock. The air had turned cold with astonishing speed, a desert feature he was still getting used to. . . . The moon came up, so bright it looked as though an artist had painted it on the sky with radium.

He heard Hornbreed come out of the cacti, mumble something about *pinching a deuce*. Valentine saw him move off into the bushes, heard him stumble, curse, right himself.

Seemingly moments later, Valentine came fully awake, though he couldn't say why. How long had it been since Hornbreed had stepped behind the bushes?

"Hornbreed?" he said quietly. He raised the gun to his shoulder and came up to one knee.

"Hornbreed?" Louder this time.

The bushes didn't answer.

Valentine touched the sword at his back, tested the slide of the blade in its sheath.

"Hornbreed!" Valentine said, coming up to a crouch.

He advanced, well clear of the bushes.

No sign of the pilot. A white packet shone in the moonlight. Hornbreed had picked a sandy spot for easier burial. Valentine studied Hornbreed's footprints, placed in the expected position to either side of his—well, with a mule deer it would be called "spoor." The white packet was a little cardboard-banded issue of "field hygiene paper" courtesy of High Sierra Paper Products.

No body. No sign of the Jaguars. And no Reaper.

Strange divots stood out in the sand here and there, like little craters. Near-perfect circles. If they were tracks, only an unusually hard-stepping big cat like a mountain lion would make them. But there were no drag marks away from the bootheels and TP.

Ten thousand dollars in gold—and more importantly, a key to the mercenary pilots of Pyp's Flying Circus—had been spirited away without a sound or a cry of distress.

Valentine felt a cold sweat that had nothing to do with the Arizona night. It occurred to him that he'd been meaning to ask Hornbreed why they called him milkman.

Something glittered in the night a few feet away. Valentine knelt, saw loose coins scattered in the rocks and sand. Valentine picked one up, a "five-dollar" piece marked AZT-CON. He'd seen them before, in plastic Baggies holding Texas Quisling prisoners' possessions. He'd been told the coin was good over much of the Southwest and northern Mexico.

Valentine guessed that Hornbreed, literally taken with his pants down, had lost whatever change was rattling around in his pants. At least now he could guess in which direction the mysterious tracks went.

The lack of blood gave him some hope.

As he followed the tracks there were other signs— the creature must have been of some size, at least that of a small tractor. It had snapped off cactus stems in several spots over two meters apart.

It also left an odor, vaguely musty and yet ammoniacal. He traced the source of the smell, an object that looked a little like a hollow-reed thorn, in a vaguely green brown polished-turtle-shell color. Some sticky material coated one end, and Valentine hazarded a guess that it was a quill or spine.

Had a giant Arizona porcupine made off with Hornbreed?

The trail led up into the mountains. The mystery of the Jaguar leader's imprecations against hanging about the wreck had been explained. Anything big enough to approach and then make off with a sizable man in silence was a foe to be feared.

The musty-ammonia smell grew stronger, and Valentine realized that the dark of the mountainside had a darker spot. A cave opening, shaped like one of the little lateen sails he'd seen on fishing boats in the Caribbean. Valentine looked around, got his bearings, and listened to the cave mouth. A bat fluttered somewhere above.

A metallic *clang* sounded from the cave mouth and Valentine went flat, his senses sparking like a downed line. Valentine heard low snorts and growls and watched three Grogs emerge from the cave, heavy sacks across their shoulders. They waited, standing back-to-back, and Valentine felt a fresh chill. A Reaper emerged from the shadows, carrying a long staff that made the robed figure a scarecrow caricature of a desert prophet. It hissed at the Grogs and followed them on a westward-leading path.

The sensible thing to do would be to hotfoot it back to the convoy, leave these mountains crawling with assorted enemies, and let fate have its way with the fatalistic Hornbreed. Duvalier, had she been with him this trip, would no doubt be resting in some hidey-hole with a good view of the interstate, waiting for the roar of truck engines and the rumble of tires.

But dammit, he needed Hornbreed—and the promised reward, provided Flying Circus would be willing to negotiate, not amount, but kind. He slipped off his backpack, extracting a small, tough flashlight with a clip that allowed him to hang it on a pocket or attach it to the underside of his gun. Something in him had to know. He fixed the light to his carbine, coaxing himself into making the attempt by getting his gear ready. If he squatted here much longer, he'd freeze up and come up with more reasons not to try it. . . .

Valentine stepped into the ammonia smell.

A big metal locker, whose door was the source of the clanging sound, he guessed, stood just inside the cave. Electrical cable ran down the top of the cave and into it. The locker was fixed by a simple bolt. Valentine drew it back and opened the locker, smelling Grog sweat.

Long objects like fishing poles rested there, six of them, thick handles fitted into sockets and a battery case where the reel normally stood. Valentine read the pictograms on the poles, saw the electrical insulation. They were like overlong cattle prods. Valentine lifted one up and blue LED bulbs lit up at the end. They offered just enough light for him to see a few feet into the cave, which sloped down precipitously. Someone had tacked down rubber mats to improve the footing.

Valentine guessed what the big red plastic switch at the "reel" end was. He turned it on and touched the end to a rock. A spark like a photo strobe jumped and Valentine smelled ozone. Capacitors whined faintly as they recharged.

Cattle prod.

Valentine slung his rifle and took two from the green-lit sockets, wondered if the Miskatonic had tested electricity on a live Reaper. Of course, had someone suggested they try it on Blake . . .

Movement behind and Valentine whirled.

An arachnophobe's nightmare stood framed by the desert stars, brighter than ever when contrasted with the cave mouth. Shock turned it into a Picasso sketch of limbs and stingers and spines, and Valentine found himself backpedaling, throwing the steel bulk of the locker between himself and the creature, his illuminated prods waving in front of him like drunken fireflies—

It paid him no more attention than it did the locker next to him and clattered down the hole. It had six spiny legs, three to a side, and two "arms"—though perhaps they were vestigial wings, as they swept up and out, folded, and were tipped with a sharp curved point. Its head—Valentine didn't know what else to call the front end—resembled a big tongue more than anything, and held a limp, white-eyed sheep in thousands of mushroomlike organs coating its underside, a carpet of organic Velcro.

Whatever it was, it didn't have a strong "defend the nest" instinct. Valentine wondered if the result would have been different if it weren't already carrying a sheep. Were these some big version of the sand bugs the Kurians used to kill the trekkers' cattle in Nebraska?

Valentine said the kind of prayer typically uttered in atheist-free foxholes and followed it down. It didn't have much of an abdomen—usually the largest segment in a terrestrial insect—just a rutted organ that reminded him a little of an oversized, rotting cucumber. The motion of its legs fascinated him as it negotiated the slope with ease, using the tiniest of projections from the cave wall as steps.

The tricky down shaft lasted only fifteen meters or so. Valentine found himself on an easier-to-negotiate downslope. He wondered where he would hide in the narrow space if another bug showed up, and smelled the bat feces littered about. Maybe the ammonia smell came from bat droppings accidentally picked up here. The cave ceiling came down low enough that Valentine had to crouch.

Red glinted in the dim light of the LEDs on the cattle prods. What Valentine's brain identified as a big rat turned into a little six-legged creeper, shooting out of a crack toward him, wing limbs telegraphing a code he couldn't begin to understand. Valentine put his prod between himself and the explorer and it scurried off.

The cavern opened up, and there was dim electrical lighting ahead, or perhaps an opening to the moon and stars. Valentine found himself crouching in a much larger cavern, curving off into darkness and other chambers like a cow's stomach, lit here and there by panels that gave off a faint yellow glow from behind thick screens.

He scooted out of the low passage, not wanting to block access for the hunter-gatherers. A small horde of the little ratlike creepy-crawlies were massed under a sheep, holding it in their collected top arms, bringing it to the ceiling of the cavern.

Valentine heard—worse yet, felt—a presence overhead. He saw dozens of sacks hanging there, reminding him of a laundry he'd patronized in New Orleans with its rows of canvas bags hanging from the conveyors. Valentine saw a sheep hoof sticking out of one, an emaciated human hand hanging from another. Some of the bags hung from long stems, others shorter, and the scientific bit of Valentine's mind observed that the shape of the sacks turned into a more regular teardrop the closer they got to the floor. Fat, white wormlike creatures fixed their mouths to the lowest-hanging bags and suckled there.

Something vast, glistening, and dark moved among the bags at the ceiling.

Valentine took three cautious steps, careful of where he placed his feet, and found a shriveled teardrop of a bag. It was next to another empty stem, cut neatly off. A faint, sweet corruptive odor came from the bag, but it wasn't the smell that fascinated him—it was the curious, shiny weave of the bag.

He touched it to make sure. Reaper cloth! These creatures produced—wove, even—a rough version of the fabric.

Valentine was tempted to chop off the nearly empty teardrop. But he had to find Hornbreed.

Valentine searched the walls and ceiling, waving the LEDs at the end of his prods, probing corners. He explored deeper into the cave, felt one of the worm things nudge his foot.

He jumped, and came face-to-face with Hornbreed's upturned face. Dozens of the smaller creepy-crawlies were passing the pilot up a living conveyor belt to the ceiling, where the shadowed mass rubbed its limbs against one another expectantly. Sightless eyes looked past him into darkness, but Valentine heard the faint wheeze of Hornbreed's lungs, and drool ran out of the corner of his mouth.

"Sorry, Equality," Valentine said. He reached and struck Hornbreed in the buttock with the cattle prod.

Flash-*tzzap*! The body convulsed, broke away, and fell as its handlers broke contact, or had their pincers torn loose by the muscle spasms. The thud of Horn-breed hitting the cavern floor sent the white larvae humping away.

A rattling like dry bones falling from a crypt crèche, and Valentine looked insectoid death in the not-face. Eyes like gemstones glittered in the reflections of the LEDs on his prods.

"Noogh . . . enoogh . . . havin' a heart attack," Horn-breed bubbled.

The two upper front limbs on the hunter-gatherer struck down and forward. Barbed stingers missed as Valentine dived out of the way, lunging with his prods, but the hunter-gatherer matched him in their dance, keeping the eye clusters toward him. The red tip of the tongue-carrier retreated farther into its forebody.

Valentine lunged for the red mark like a dueling Musketeer, scored a palpable hit. Flash-*tzzap!*

The hunter-gatherer collapsed, legs twitching. Valentine's world whirled as he was jerked off his feet by jointed arms that enfolded him in a firm, irresistible, yet gentle embrace. Twin stingers pinched him at his chest, but couldn't penetrate, emptying themselves uselessly on his leathers. The prod he'd just used fell where his feet had been a second before.

Valentine struck wildly behind with his other prod, convulsed as the current traveled up the hunter-gatherer's limbs and across his chest. Heart stalled, then pounding in shock, he fell to the ground, suddenly at war with his body. None of his limbs seemed to remember how to function.

The hunter-gatherer who'd got him from behind batted at him with one of its legs, but it was just a reaction to the charge. Valentine managed a roll toward Hornbreed.

"What the Kur's this?" Hornbreed gasped, batting weakly at the smaller, rat-sized bugs. Every move brought a wince.

Some of the Christmas tree ornaments above rocked as the roof creature shifted.

Valentine managed to slow his heart, retrieve his rifle. "Can you walk?"

"Lookit my back. It feels like there's about two kilos of flesh ripped out." Hornbreed came to one knee, turning.

Valentine saw a purpurant swelling at Hornbreed's right shoulder blade. He guessed that the welt was the size of a dinner plate.

"You got stung by one of these bastards." Valentine's body was back under control and he felt strangely calm and placid. The bugs weren't so bad, just little machines doing their jobs.

Or very big machines, like the one above . . .

. . . and coming down.

Christ, it's as big as a whale.

Valentine flicked on the gun light, saw ring after ring of arms around a lipless, spiny orifice, a zeppelin of a body behind, long thin arms that couldn't possibly support that mass, froze up until his eye and trigger finger, acting perhaps for their individual preservation against an overwhelmed brain, fired up into it.

It accepted the bullets in silence. A few of the arms around the central orifice stiffened—

Before the cartridge casings even finished their tinny bounces Valentine grabbed Hornbreed by the shoulder, pulled him up and along, when he wasn't moving right got under the pilot's armpit, and half carried him in a stumble toward the exit, carbine in its sling bouncing against his plated leathers. Hornbreed screamed out his agony like a police siren.

Another hunter-gatherer entered, a coyote borne in its tonguelike front appendage, ignoring them and the chaos within. Valentine regretted the dropped prods, grabbed Hornbreed by the collar, and dragged him, shrieking in pain, like a resisting dog, through the low entrance aperture.

A hunter-gatherer's captured limbs darted into the crack, and closed on Hornbreed's leg. Valentine found the carbine's trigger and sent four bullets to the source of the limbs with the serene, observant corner of his mind trying to remember just how many rounds the little minidrum at the bottom of the carbine carried. But the legs let go.

Hornbreed was crying, blubbering to be left in peace, but Valentine got him up the shaft of near-vertical stairs, pushing from behind the whole way. He made it to the locker and retrieved another prod and was tempted to use it on Hornbreed to calm the pilot down. Instead he half carried him out of the cave and to his pack.

The cold night air and open sky acted on Valentine like a refreshing dip in a pool. His limbs tingled and his skin felt delightfully alive.

"My whole friggin' body's throbbing," Hornbreed gasped. "Sears like a hot frying pan. Put a bullet through my head, for Kur's sake."

Valentine retrieved his little razor-edged kidney puncher of a knife from his boot sheath and opened Hornbreed's bulging flight suit, a splotch of red marking the center of the bulge like a misplaced nipple. He tore open the cloth and took a breath at the blister the hunter-gatherer's venom had raised.

"You could be worse. Those things have two stingers. Hold on now."

A lot of liquid was trying to get out. Valentine held the sagging Hornbreed down with his knee and nicked the blister, eliciting a gasp from Hornbreed. Valentine squeezed hot, clear fluid from the wound, then dusted with antibiotic powder.

He gave Hornbreed two pain pills from the first-aid kit. Valentine recognized the odd little hexagonal shapes from his wisdom-teeth extraction courtesy of a Southern Command dentist, and wished he'd gotten morphine instead.

"Doesn't burn so bad," Hornbreed said, catching his breath as Valentine applied butterfly bandages.

They exchanged Valentine's canteen a couple of times. Valentine kept an eye on the cave mouth, wondering when the next hunter-gatherer was due to appear.

"I think we should get going," Valentine said. "Still want to be left to your fate?"

"I want a long, cool drink at the Mezcal," Hornbreed said. "Ice. A whole bagful."

"Better get back to the cactus stand."

About halfway down the mountain it occurred to Valentine that there'd been a yellow rubberized box or two in the locker at the cave mouth that he hadn't investigated. For all he knew, they contained electrical tools, but if the Kurians had some kind of antivenom, that would be the place to store it. But then it might be dosed for those big mountain Grogs. . . .

Bug prod ready against another appearance of a hunter-gatherer, Valentine traced a route that carried them well away from stands of bush and sandy washes (in Nebraska's cattle country he'd once been stung by a smaller creature that could dig, and he still wasn't sure exactly how the beasties hunted).

When they reached the cactus stand Hornbreed collapsed atop his survival blanket. "Enough . . . enough . . . I'm done," he said.

"I want to get farther away from that cave," Valentine said. He stomped hard next to a wandering scorpion, sent it scurrying back into the thorns. "Fifteen minutes, then we'll pick up and move on."

Hornbreed's breath left a moist wing on the reflective surface of the blanket. Valentine decided it was safe to reload, opened a box of shells, and fed them into the magazine. He decided to give Hornbreed a few more minutes and cleaned the barrel.

"C'mon, bud. Up," Valentine said.

Hornbreed moaned. He looked like a deboned fish, sweating and gasping. "Can't. Muscles won't work." He managed to drag an arm under himself.

Valentine sorted through Hornbreed's gear, took medical supplies and water, the flare pistol and signaling mirror. The rest he buried.

Hornbreed was a big man. Valentine could carry him, but he would have to stop and rest frequently, and a few hours would exhaust him utterly. His bad leg started up a preemptive ache at the thought. They'd never make the highway.

A drag might be possible, if—

The wreck!

Valentine felt the flier's pulse, which was regular but fast, picked Hornbreed up in a fireman's carry, and thanked creation that they'd be going downhill. He placed Hornbreed inside the rear cabin of the plane, closed the door, and went back for his pack.

With that done, he looked around the wreck site.

The fuselage was intact—if only one of the rear wings had come off, it would make a good sled.

Doors! The hinges were designed to come apart easily; all you had to do was pull a pin. Even better, a broken piece of landing gear could be used in an improvised wheelbarrow.

He tore up some cargo netting, clipped his light to the higher of the two wings, and went to work, careful to keep the Steyr within reach.

It was in the deep night of predawn by the time he finished. He dragged Hornbreed back out of the aircraft and tried him on the improvised wheelbarrow.

"It works!" Valentine said, though the balance left a lot to be desired. Hornbreed, wheezing and whimpering, managed a nod. Valentine lowered him gently and put the canteen to his lips. "We're out of here, Hornbreed."

It would be a race against the sun.

Valentine never got to test his contraption any further. He caught a whiff of the telltale ammonia smell on the clean night breeze and reached for the Steyr.

The hunter-gatherer rushed out of the night, grasping arms up and ready. Valentine had no idea where the vital spots were, so he settled for sending shot after shot straight down its centerline, trusting that the big-game 7.62mm shells would find something important.

The bug collapsed, flipped forward in a weird imitation of the downed aircraft, continued to twitch with the three legs and the pinioned arm on one side of its body.

Valentine reached for the bug prod, held the rifle at his hip in his right hand and the prod with his left.

The shots roused Hornbreed, though he grasped the flare gun rather than his pistol.

"Most-heeeeee!" a voice shrieked from the darkness. Others took up the chorus. *"Most-heeeee!"*

A fast metallic rattle, either an imitation of a snare drum on some piece of aluminum or an attempt to re-create a rattlesnake's warning, broke out in the desert predawn.

"That can't be good," Hornbreed said, and managed to rise to his feet using the fuselage for support.

"I think I just committed blasphemy," Valentine said.

Something whizzed nearby and the fuselage popped near his ear. Stones!

"Inside," Valentine said, shoving the pilot toward the rear door.

Stones didn't leave a telltale muzzle flash to shoot back at. Valentine fired twice more into the darkness. He helped Hornbreed in, felt a sudden pain as a stone struck him in the leathers just below the shoulder blade. Valentine dived inside.

Stones and thrown spears rattled against the fuselage like a dying hailstorm. More yips and coyote howls broke out around the aircraft, along with a deeper drumming.

The banging grew louder. Voices just outside the fuselage shouted, and the clattering redoubled as the Jaguars banged on the overturned plane with hand weapons.

Valentine checked the lock on the rear cargo door, crept to the missing front door. A shadow loomed outside; Valentine marked a tangle of dirty hair held in place by a broad headband. He fired and the head disappeared.

"Fhway! Fhway! Fhway!" a voice shouted outside from just beneath the pilot's seat.

Valentine smelled woodsmoke. He went to the co-pilot window, saw a figure with a flaming torch, and opened the window, but a hand grabbed the muzzle of his gun. Valentine jerked it back violently, shot through the fuselage at where the grabber must have been standing, then found his torch target was gone.

Hornbreed said something, but his words were lost in the hammering on the fuselage. They might as well have tried to converse on the inside of a giant drum. Valentine smelled more smoke, unsheathed his sword; there was nothing to do but go out the missing door. Otherwise they'd cook.

Hornbreed suddenly opened the door, stuck his flare gun up.

"No," Valentine shouted.

A knife blade stabbed in, glinting on the sudden illumination of the flare. Hornbreed fell back from it. Valentine brought the handy little carbine around and fired through the fuselage again. A hand appeared as one of the Jaguars tried to hoist himself in. Valentine discouraged it by severing a couple of fingers with the sword. He shouldered his gun again.

Thunderous pounding outside—*How the hell are they making that noise?* Then Valentine realized he was hearing the beating rotors of a helicopter.

Tracer lit up the pinkening dawn, bright shards of yellow rain from the sky. The hammering on the fuselage let off and Valentine saw the warriors scatter.

"It's the pickup chopper!" Hornbreed almost shouted. Hope had given him new strength.

Valentine looked outside, saw a big bulbous desert-tan fuselage, a greenhouse of glass at the front, red and green running lights, a uniformed gunner at an over-sized door at the side. Valentine grabbed his clip light and used the signaling switch to blink three times at the craft. Three times again, three times again. They might not know the old Quisling Coastal Marine distress code, but the gunner swerved his crosshairs away from the flipped aircraft.

The faint popping of small-arms fire sounded.

Hornbreed crawled to the rear cabin door and waved. Men tumbled out of the helicopter. Valentine saw another prop plane roar overhead, turning tight circles around the crash site.

Hornbreed waved Valentine out the door. Valentine surrendered his gun, sword, and pack to a corporal. Another soldier, a businesslike submachine gun in his grasp, eyed Valentine. Three soldiers and a medic assisted the noncom, one of them openly gaping at the hunter-gatherer, still twitching at the extremities. Valentine heard one of the soldiers shouting something about a "salvage bird" into a headset.

"Rough night," Hornbreed wheezed at the medic, who helped him out the door and toward a litter. "Forget that. I want to get in the chopper with him."

He held out an arm to Valentine, and accepted a lift. "Max, help me on the bird of paradise. We'll be in Yuma in time for cocktails."

CHAPTER SIX

⚭

*P*yp's *Flying Circus, Yuma, Arizona: The old Colorado River steamboat stop grew up under three flags, Spanish, Mexican, and finally the Stars and Stripes after the territory was acquired in the Gadsden Purchase. Famous after the Civil War mostly for its territorial prison, it became an important military hub and storage center thanks to its dry climate, ideal for testing and storing hardware of various kinds, and the premier Marine Corps pilot training center.*

Under the Aztlan Kur, an association of like-minded Kurians covering northern Mexico and the Southwestern United States called the "Confederation" by the locals, it's still a city that breeds pilots. The more mundane Aztlan Air Carriers shuttle Quisling dignitaries and churchmen from post to post and fly police patrols, but the much more colorful "Flying Circus" of airborne mercenaries, with their distinctive winged-rattlesnake insignia, is what people usually refer to when speaking of the fliers of the Southwest.

In typical Kurian fashion Pyp's Flying Circus is divided into three centers for better control. Most of the fliers and their families live in Yuma, in well-guarded gated communities. Their amenities are so plentiful that it's hard to recognize them as hostages to their good behavior. Airplane storage and maintenance is located at the famous aircraft graveyard at the old Davis-Monthan Air Force Base, now just called "Lucky Field" by the ground staff, thanks to the job security it affords, and "DM" by the fliers. Pyp's operational headquarters is in Tempe, where orders are received from the Kurians and planes are armed and staged for their various missions. No one group of officers, and no one Kurian, really commands the Circus, though all think of their titular figurehead commander as the unit's boss.

There's an air of ringmaster flamboyance to their beloved "Pyp." Patrick Yenez-Powell is the sort of man who stands out in a crowd, not always an advantage that leads to survival in the Kurian Order. With his round-brimmed, black felt Navajo hat, river-guide sandals, gold earring and necklaces, often grease-stained denim flight suit, and elaborately beaded shoulder rig for his ivory-handled peacemaker, he's easy to pick out in a crowd. Though on the ugly side of fifty, he still moves with a spring in his step, and he's hard to follow, as he changes direction the instant he spots anything from flaking paint to litter to a misplaced tool; an adjutant usually carries a bag for such trash that blows across Pyp's transom, which will then be upended on some unfortunate lieutenant's desk.

David Valentine met the mind behind the odd wardrobe and energetic body on a hot April afternoon in Yuma.

The long trip, begun in the noisy vibration of the helicopter, was briefly suspended at a refueling stop at a service strip, where they shoveled down a quick meal of eggs and sausage. After breakfast they were both dusted with some kind of disinfectant/insecticide. Then it was back in the beater until another landing at the sprawling air base in Tucson, where they switched to a tiny, cramped prop plane for the final leg, which left Valentine tired and disoriented. Other than his astonishment over the distance they'd traveled in just a few hours, he also felt nauseous with fatigue.

He wanted cool and darkness when they arrived at Yuma. The soldiers threw their dunnage in a propane-powered flatbed and whisked Hornbreed, Valentine, and the medic with a clipboard full of notes off to a white building with the traditional red cross painted on its roof and walls. Valentine surrendered his weapons again to a pair of desert-camouflaged men with side-arms and blue-banded helmets. Hornbreed whispered into one of the military policemen's ears, but said little else until they reached the triage room, where he refused any attention until the MPs showed up again and looped a laminated ID card around Valentine's neck. Then Hornbreed allowed himself to be put in a wheelchair and taken to an operating room.

Valentine fell asleep on the paper-covered table of an examining room. A thin woman who looked like a hat tree in a lab coat, stethoscope over her shoulder, woke him and checked his eyes, lymph nodes, pulse, and temperature. She asked him how he felt and where he'd traveled in the last month and he answered honestly.

"Drink lots of water," she advised, and turned on the tap in the washbasin. "If you want to get cleaned up, you can use the showers in 'E' corridor—just follow the signs. You can read, right? Wear your ID at all times, even in the shower. There's a staff commissary in that wing too—eat a couple of bananas." She signed a piece of paper and handed it to him. "You're on unlimited rations for three days, so enjoy. Don't skimp on the veggies."

She went to an intercom by the door. "Room three is cleared," she said.

"What about Equality?" Valentine asked.

"Wing Leader Hornbreed's doing fine. He's staying here for observation overnight. Check with the base security by the admitting door and they'll find you a bunk. You'll probably be here until we release the wing leader."

Valentine cleaned himself up using the washbasin, and felt better but still bleary when he presented himself to a potbellied example of base security. They looked him over as though wanting to arrest him on general principles, but eventually informed him that his reward was being arranged.

"Old Pyp's on the way," the corporal explained. "He wants to see you and the wing leader."

Valentine wondered if there was a "Young Pyp," or if the phrase, with its poetic evocation of *Tempus fugit,* indicated some measure of endearment.

"Mind if I grab a meal first?"

"Just don't be long about it," the desk sergeant barked. "He's a busy man and we don't want to be running around looking for you."

The corporal took him to the cafeteria, whistled at the food prescription. "Enjoy. We've been on ration cards for over a year."

Valentine winced. "I know what that's like."

He piled a tray with some dubious-looking meat in gravy, potatoes, fruit, and rice buns. The servers examined his piece of paper at each station, even the woman who poured him a glass of juice.

The corporal settled for a thick slice of bread smeared with "protein paste," and water.

"Hope that tastes better than it looks," Valentine said.

The corporal rolled his eyes. "They say it's refried beans. Tastes like they scraped it off a Dumpster."

"Dig into mine," Valentine said.

"You're a real *guapo* . . . uh, Mr. Argent." He hunched over the table and worked a chunk of Valentine's steak free from bone and gristle.

"Why the food shortage?" Valentine asked.

"Troubles out east," the corporal said, shoveling food and looking over his shoulder. "We just took a bunch of California farmland, thanks to the Circus, but it's taking time to get organized. Headhunters down south are having a tougher time finding peons to work the land. This territory used to be Frolic City—Pyp's Circus brought in a lot of in-kind trade from the Gulag. Now we're fighting to hold our own."

"Here's to better days," Valentine said, swallowing some watery juice.

The corporal removed some gravy with his heel of bread. "If you're looking to set up an establishment somewhere comfy with your reward—"

Valentine picked up his wiped-clean tray. "Haven't thought that far ahead, friend."

Hornbreed was on the telephone when they entered the room. The corporal pulled up a chair outside.

"No," Hornbreed said, wincing a little at the effort. "No. Let's get *Bettie Page* stripped. Put *Tigress* and *Zorro* into reserve, and *Brunhilda* in for a complete overhaul. Let me know the status of *Rockette* as soon as the salvagers bring her in. Yeah, I flipped her. Tell them at least a week for the wing to reorganize. Colorado tore us a new one."

He paused. Then: "Kur! I don't care. We'll lose half the wing if we go into action now. Yes, I'll take the responsibility."

Valentine listened to another call to someone named "Lo," full of many reassurances as to his condition. He went to the window, watched the quiet airfield. Gliders circled far above, featherless hawks on the air currents. Valentine watched a new string of gliders take off, a twin-engine prop with five fiberglass baby planes in tow.

Hornbreed returned the phone to its cradle and rubbed his eyes.

"What are all the gliders for?" Valentine asked.

"Pilot training. You learn most of the principles of flight, and it saves a lot of gas."

"Looks fun," Valentine said, and meant it.

"Just say the word and—"

The corporal's chair in the hallway scraped and Valentine heard him come to his feet. Boots squeaked on the linoleum.

Patrick Yenez-Powell had darkish but freckled skin, a boxer's squashed nose, and ears like a pair of beat-up trash can lids. Valentine didn't know what to make of the variegated uniform. The gold necklace, dungaree overalls, and shoulder holster made him look like a motor-pool inventory guard called away from a good card game, but the round, black felt hat added a serious note.

Valentine envied the sandals, though. They looked cool and comfortable.

"Knock knock," Pyp said. "Got a minute, Horny?" His voice flowed low, musical, and a little sad. If basset hounds could talk, they'd sound like Yenez-Powell.

"Always," Hornbreed said.

Valentine saw a pair of adjutants, male and female so alike that they looked like brother and sister, peering in from the doorway.

Pyp strode in, holding his left arm behind.

"You dumb sonofabitch. I told you *Rockette* wasn't fit to get home. You had to be a hero and make it or go down with the ship."

"Got her in range of the salvage bird," Hornbreed said.

"We'll have to invent a new medal for you—you got all the others. Just park it for now. I brought you a present. Fresh from the Cali Dairy," Pyp said, revealing a big bottle of white liquid Valentine guessed to be milk. "Still a little warm from the cow."

Hornbreed produced one of his little gasps. "*Huff.* Thanks, sir. You're a wonder." He twisted off the cap and tried a swallow.

"Milkman," Valentine said quietly.

"Is this our stray herder?" Pyp asked, turning to Valentine.

"He got me out of a dark hole," Hornbreed said. "Almost punched out doing it."

"Thank you, young man." He offered his hand. "Call me Pyp."

Valentine shook his hand. "Max."

"Good with his gun and cool in a hotbox," Hornbreed said. "We could sure use him."

Valentine shrugged. "I'm flattered, but I'm more interested in the reward."

Pyp sucked air through his teeth. "Sorry to hear that. But don't worry, you'll get it in full."

"Your jackets say the reward is nonnegotiable," Valentine said. "Is that firm?"

Both the pilots exchanged looks and frowns. "Hey, Max—," Hornbreed started.

"Son, most of the fellers who want to haggle don't hand over the pilot first," Pyp said. "You're either dumb or impractical."

"I didn't mean the amount," Valentine said. "I meant the type. Does it have to be gold?"

"What, you want something lighter? We can look into gems," Pyp said.

Valentine held up a hand. "Oh, nothing like that. I was wondering if I could trade the reward for a ride in one of your planes."

This time the pilots exchanged furrowed brows.

"Where you wanna go, Japan?" Pyp said. "You're screwing yourself, son."

"Gold just brings trouble. I've got family on a patch of land up toward Canada. I'd like a ride up there."

Pyp tipped his hat up and forward, scratched his stubbled head. "Easily done. We've got a friendly field in northern Utah."

"Thanks."

"You'll find a little gratitude goes a long way," Pyp said. "We'll put you in the VIP jet if you like."

"Throw in some flying lessons and we'll call it a deal," Valentine said.

"Not sure a man who turns down mint gold should be working a stick and rudder, but we'll oblige," Pyp said. "Horny, you tell Alvarez to arrange some privates."

"I'll take him up myself," Hornbreed said, setting down his almost-empty quart of milk. "The wing's going to be down for a while anyway."

"That's the other thing," Pyp said. "We're going to

have to dummy up for a week or so and make you look operational. There's a purification drive."

"Huff . . ." Hornbreed lost some of his color. "Oh hell."

Valentine wanted to ask what a "purification drive" was, but Hornbreed read his face. "Looks like you haven't spent much time in the Confederation."

"They could show any day," Pyp said.

Hornbreed swung his legs out of the bed, took a deep, wheezy breath. "Get my boots, huh?"

They put Valentine in a comfortable little house in a no-man's-land of fencing that wasn't on the airfield, but rather grew out beside the main gate in a dogleg shape. More houses, a little school with thick bars around it, and some rows of two-story apartments surrounded an empty pool that someone had turned into the world's biggest sandbox for the kids. A driving range/putting green ran in a green carpet out to the fencing. As if to make up for the missing pool, housing management turned a big sprinkler on every afternoon, watering the putting green, and the base kids shrieked as they ran in and out of it.

Runoff fed a vegetable garden, and served as a bird-bath. The birds looked every bit as happy as the kids.

Skinny, shoeless, half-naked kids watched from the other side of the wire, sticking their arms through the fencing and begging food, alternating pleas in Spanish and English.

Valentine took a short joyride his first evening. A young instructor named Starguide offered him the chance to watch a sunset from just beneath the clouds. Valentine gazed down on the rooftops of Yuma, spotted a few antlike vehicles on the wide roads, saw the Colorado and Yuma rivers running muddily beneath, along with the old, perforated border fences and trenches dividing Arizona from Mexico. And of course the sun, turning everything shades of red and copper.

I see why, Dad. But how did you ever give this up?

"Ready to take over?" Starguide asked

Valentine wiped the tears out of his eyes.

"Like with most everything, first time's the best," Starguide said. "Pick a spot on the horizon and keep her level. Don't be afraid—I'm here. Small, gentle movements. You'll just have her for a few minutes—it's getting dark."

Valentine took the controls. The plane waggled a little and settled down.

"You've got good hands for this, Argent," Starguide said.

"I bet you say that to all the boys," Valentine said.

"Dude, don't even joke about it. You don't want a rep as a rainbow chaser. Pilot culture is *muy* macho."

After the exhilaration of a night landing, with the airfield lights changing speed and perspective until they touched down with the softest of bumps, Starguide filled out some paperwork. He then took Valentine toward Yuma on a spring-worn shuttle bus. They stopped well outside of town at a cavernous wooden restaurant, where Hornbreed watched while some musicians set up. A petite, caramel-skinned woman with cheekbones and jawline as sharp as a hunting arrow sat beside Hornbreed, resting her hand on his arm, loving but not overly demonstrative.

"Any news?" Starguide asked.

"No sign of 'em yet," Hornbreed said. "Maybe they'll skip us and concentrate on the out-there."

Starguide didn't say anything, but he didn't have to. His face said "That'll be the day."

Valentine looked around the place. A big U of a room, with pillars where he guessed dividing walls once stood, surrounded the bar. Doors to the kitchen were on one side, to the washrooms on another. A stairway at the side had a blue neon arrow zigzagging up and the legend WILD BLUE YONDER in cloud-scrolled letters.

"Welcome to the Mezcal," Hornbreed said, pulling out a chair at a table with a good view of the band. "Best liquor and music between the LA Slimepits and Austin Holdout. This is my wife, Louisa."

"I am, jusslike, so grateful to you," the caramel-skinned woman said, her voice oddly nasal.

"That's the sound of California class," Hornbreed said. "But she fell for a dashing pilot and joined me in the wasteland."

"Jusslike the movies," Louisa agreed.

Hornbreed gave her a kiss on the temple. A waitress approached them. "Buy you a drink?"

"Whatever you're having."

"It's milk. I don't drink."

"Milk, then," Valentine said.

"Struth, not another one," Starguide said. "Hey, he needs his wings."

Starguide went to the bar and yanked a piece of plastic off a peg. He returned just as the milks and drinks arrived, set it on Valentine's head, and fixed a thin bungee under his chin. It was a kid's toy hat, spray-painted silver, with wings that swept up and back.

A trio in leather jackets, parked at the end of the bar and chatting with a buxom bartender, whistled and raised their glasses to Valentine.

Valentine, Hornbreed, and Starguide clinked glasses. Valentine's milk slopped out a little.

"Why the milk?" Valentine asked.

"My folks were sort of fitness fanatics," Hornbreed said.

Valentine knew better than to inquire further about their health. One never asked about relatives in the Kurian Zone, especially when the past tense was employed. Instead he watched customers stream in. Some pointed to his funny little silver hat, and a pilot or two broke away from their friends and came up to clap him on the back.

"Kick it, Ge-arge," a bandsman with a guitar said. Ge-arge raised his sticks above his head and clacked them together three times, *tchk tchk tchk*—Valentine jumped a little. The sound reminded him of the hunter-gatherers.

A fusion of salsa and Western coursed through the bar.

"Place is gonna be full tonight," Louisa predicted. "Everyone's nervous."

Valentine raised an eyebrow at Hornbreed, who shook his head. A few couples left the bar and began to dance. Valentine recognized one of the pilots from the rescue helicopter, stomping away in elaborately stitched pointed-toe boots.

The band took a quick break. Hornbreed used the silence to tell an abbreviated version of the hunter-gatherers story, attracting a small crowd. "I've seen their tracks, on mule patrol up Goner Ridge," a woman put in. "He's not exaggerating."

Hornbreed left out his injury, and embellished a little, saying Valentine had carried him halfway down a mountain, plinking at bugs the whole way.

When the band started up again they were joined by a zebra-haired singer. She performed in a silver mesh bikini and matching strappy cork-heeled sandals, rattle-snake tattoos winding down each arm and a Chinese ideograph on her back. She'd applied makeup with an airbrush, giving her bright, intense eyes wings like a pit viper's:

> *"Take one take two take three take me*
> *Bled out in an attic so's nobody sees."*

The dancers were limp in one another's arms as they moved, shambling like ravies cases about to keel over. The singer's arms waved hypnotically as she passed the microphone first to one hand, then the other. Valentine looked around, a little shocked at the explicit lyrics, but maybe musicians could sing what no one dared say.

"Hiya, cherry," a female voice twanged in his ear.

A girl in fishnets and feathers, a swan-shaped black bottle nestled under one netted breast, put down a shot glass in front of him. "Jolt of Swan Neck? On the house."

"I'm not drinking," Valentine said.

"He's already at half-staff," Louisa said. "No assistance required."

The woman planted the bottle at the center of the table, put a hand on each of Valentine's shoulders, and did a brief bump and grind. "You wanna go upstairs? Ready, willing, and free of charge."

"No thanks."

"Ah, the follies of youth," Hornbreed said, though Valentine guessed the wing leader had only half a decade on him. "You should take advantage of the newbie's wings. One night only."

"What was the fighting up in Colorado about?" Valentine asked.

"Those jokers are trying to starve us by cutting off the Colorado River. We took out the dams."

"Must have been big bombs."

"No, demolition teams. It was more an airmobile operation. Ever since that fiasco in Fifty we use our own troops on the ground if we have to land anything. Damn Grogs flapped off as soon as things got a little hot."

Valentine wondered if the Kurian Year Fifty "fiasco" was the operation at Love Field in Dallas. His old regiment, the Razors, had been so battered by the aerial pounding, Southern Command had broken it up—but he wasn't about to make Hornbreed feel better by saying so. Odd that he felt more like shaking the man's hand than ever. The aerial assault had been well coordinated and deadly.

"Don't let the rationing fool you," Starguide added. "This is a profound crèche. You never hear a Hisser, unless you're riding a desk at GHQ. We run our own lives. We get—"

A rattlesnake-decorated arm cut him off as the singer wrapped herself around Valentine's back.

"We've got a first timer here tonight, named—"

"Max," Hornbreed supplied.

She hopped up and planted her thong-divided buttocks on the bar table, planting her sandaled foot firmly on Valentine's crotch. Valentine watched her eyeballs rattle around and decided she was a little stoned. "Let's rass it for the Circus' newest hero, Max.

"From the rigs of Catalina
To the shoals of Mississippi
We shall fight for mankind's uplift
To Earth's glorious destiny.

"In our fight for truth and justice
And to keep our conscience clean
We will always follow orders
of the Saviors of Our Dream."

Cheering broke out at the end of the song and Valentine reached up for a kiss, lifting her leg out of the way. He used the leverage to throw her slight body over his shoulder.

"I'm taking her up," he called to the crowd, heading for the stairs.

"Hit that silk hard!" a drunk in the crowd shouted.

"My set's not over, you bastard," the singer yelled, punching him in the small of the back.

Two pipeline-armed men in leather vests, probably bouncers, appeared at the front of the crowd, but no call for assistance came.

He slapped one tan buttock in return. "She'll be back after a brief intermission," Valentine said as he took the first steps, to cheering approval.

He paused at the top of the stairs. A hallway led to a marked washroom and several doors. He tried the nearest door; it wasn't locked.

A big, cushioned wooden lounge chair and a double bed almost filled the little paneled room. Sponge-painted clouds gave the room a nursery feel. He found a light switch. A single bulb in an orange and blue Chinese lantern gave the room a grotto glow. There was a rag rug on the floor, and a pair of towels next to a washbasin and an empty pitcher on a little shelf.

The band had already transitioned into a dance number. Muffled percussion and guitar rose through the floor.

"Classy," Valentine said. He dumped the singer on the bed.

"Fucker!" she protested. "You could ask a—"

"I will," Valentine said. "What's your name?"

She sat up and kicked off her sandals. "Gide. Be careful with my face, okay? Rough stuff will mess up the makeup." She took off the bikini top. "I know it's traditional to keep the pants as a souvenir, but these were—"

"Gide, you can keep them on." Valentine sat in the chair. "I just want to talk."

She flopped back against the wall, extracted a hand-rolled from her hairdo. "What, like dirty?"

"No. One of those songs, the one about the attic, it struck me as odd. Aren't you afraid of saying stuff like that?"

"Got a light?"

"I don't smoke."

"Shit." She felt around under the mattress, peeked under the bed. "They sneak in condoms all the time, but can they leave a match? Dream deferred." She reattached the cigarette, or joint, to a hairpin and put it back in her tangle of hair.

"You wrote that song?"

"Yeah. You hot shits could use a bite of reality. It got a response, you saw."

"What's a purification?" Valentine asked.

Some of the hard edge came off. "It's—it's not my place."

"Please. I'm new here. Call me Max, if you like. I brought in Wing Leader Hornbreed. I'm wondering if I should grab my reward and run while the getting's good."

"You got your gold yet?"

"Working on it. I'm trading most of it for a trip far away."

"Purification's head-count reduction," she said. "Lotta times it makes no sense, who gets chosen."

"Who does it, Churchmen?" Valentine asked.

"Yeah, the church handles it."

"Ever worry that your songs might get you purified?"

"Fuck no. I think they like having me around. They need a place for the zips to let off a little steam. The Mezcal's sort of cathartic."

"Sort of what?" Valentine asked.

"Catharsis. Healthy elimination of emotion. Like a big bawlin' shit into the toilet of life."

"Singer *and* philosopher."

"My old man was a cowhand, but that doesn't mean he was dumb. Always had a book or two tucked away and he read to me a lot. I grew up in the saddle with a rifle instead of a doll. Killed a mountain lion when I was eight."

"If you can shoot, why didn't you join the service?" Valentine studied her tattoos. The snakes were posed differently. The left arm seemed to be striking; the right wrapped itself protectively around her upper arm and watched the world from the soft spot on her forearm.

"I'd be tempted to pull the trigger with the gun pointed the other way. How far away from here are you going?"

"About a thousand miles north."

Her fingers tightened on the stained bedding. "Take me with? I can work off my expenses. Or we can arrange something. I ain't exactly a virgin, but I'm healthy and horny on my own account, not just to keep my job. I'll fuck you like Scheherazade, not some high-mileage brothel cunt."

"I'm tempted just for the conversation."

She tipped back into the bed. "Make fun. Who are you to talk to me like that?"

"I was hoping to figure that out on this trip. How do you survive a purification?"

"No telling what sets them off. But I'd cover that limp if I were you. Life is precarious for the lame and halt. I don't suppose you're a big shot somewhere, and you're just keeping your brass ring hid?"

"No such luck," Valentine said. "How can I get in touch with you?"

"I live above Ling's market in Yuma. I help him stock

after a gig. Then I sleep out the day. But don't be afraid to wake me up, know what I mean?"

"I look forward to the rest of your set."

"Wait," she said, standing. "Undo your hair."

Valentine unwound the thick rubber band that kept his hair out of the way. Gide reached up and ran her metallic-nailed fingers through his hair, tousling it.

"You've got three gray hairs," she said, and kissed him. Her lips traveled down his neck. "Just a little lipstick smear. Someone might wonder why you carried me up here to talk. Though I ought to give you a black eye."

"Thanks for the advice, Gide."

"What about my offer?"

"Under consideration. But if I bring you, it'll be for your trigger finger, not the thousand and one nights."

She blinked. "You've done some reading too."

"Haven't had the time lately." Valentine put his hand flat against the small of her back and gave her lips a quick brush with his own.

"And what was that for? My makeup's already fucked."

"Gratitude. Lone man's dilemma. I was beginning to think all these flyboys were the sane ones and I was the nut."

Valentine took the stairs quietly, noticing on his way down that the crowd had grown. Masses of people and noise made him tense and headachy, so he joined some of the smokers outside. People sat on old car seats and lawn chairs, drinking and smoking and looking at the stars. In the shadows, couples kissed.

Cigarette smoke, stars, and the occasional eager moan turned above Valentine as he stargazed. Were women aware of their strange healing power? He felt the wounds begin to close, but nothing, not Gide, not Blake, not even the satisfaction that would come with a successful assignment, could replace his daughter.

"Never should have made that trip," he said.

"How's that, Max? You regretting popping off into the sage to get me back?" Hornbreed said from behind.

"Didn't see you," Valentine said. "No, different trip, two years ago. Just as soon not talk about it."

"Suit yourself. How'd you like your flight?"

"Loved it, but I still want my reward."

"We're always short planes, but it'll be arranged. You'll go fast and in style. We'll tack on an extra day or two to maintenance and put the fuel use down to testing. Tomorrow I'll set you down with some workbooks—you need to learn a few principles—and then maybe you'll go up in a two-seat glider."

"You worried about some 'purifiers' showing up?"

"I keep my nose clean. Worst thing you can do is get all nervous about it. They see you stammering and sweating, they figure a guilty conscience is showing itself."

"I know what you mean," Valentine said, prickling at Hornbreed's blasé attitude. Did they put something in the water here? Suppose they carted Louisa off?

"They might not even show. The higher-ups are more worried about the food situation. They'll probably concentrate on agro in California and Mexico."

"I'd just as soon get going."

"We're still going to give you a couple thousand in gold, you know. That's got to be arranged for."

Valentine wondered if a stall was on. "How you feeling?"

"Better. Whatever juice the bugs put in me, I think it's about worked its way out. Just sore as hell. You're bunking in our house tonight, by the way. Let's go over to the hospital and sign for your gear. It sits there too long, someone might decide to sell it."

"I'm ready to go."

They took a little Volkswagen ("The Mexicans changed the name for a couple years, but people quit buying them," Hornbreed explained). Hornbreed's house was just shy of some of the estates in Iowa. The imposing, Spanish-style house lacked only the expansive grounds to be a true manor. Instead it sat on a small plot of land in a gated community filled with other equally impressive houses. Louisa gave Valentine a pleasant little room of his own on a central courtyard—its fountain made a pleasing sound—where he could look up at the master suite's second-floor balcony.

He startled awake, reaching for the sword under the pillows, but it was only a pretty Asian teenage girl in an apron bringing morning coffee—real coffee, at that.

"Breakfast in kitchen," she said.

After the strictly portioned meal Hornbreed showed him "the neighborhood." There was a swimming pool, a school, and a small golf course, a private store, and a common garage where the favored families "checked out" vehicles. Hornbreed explained that most of the residents rarely went beyond the gates. Necessities were brought to them.

There was a small playground but only a few children, in simple clothes that looked homemade. They shrieked and chased each other, shouting in a Spanish-English patois that sounded like it had a little Chinese thrown in for flavor. "Staff children," Hornbreed said. "They're really not supposed to be there, but no one complains."

"What about the kids who are supposed to be using it?"

"Most of our kids go to church school, or private academies. Class all morning, sports in the afternoon, and tutoring or apprenticeships at night. Really first-class schooling. Tumlo next door has a daughter already beginning medical training, and she's only fifteen. We got to get to the field. But we're making one more stop. I've got something to show you."

He said no more until they took the Volkswagen out to one of the more remote hangars on the big airfield. Hornbreed maneuvered it around piles of junk, engines hanging from chains, and racks of assorted rusting spares. It was half-junkyard, half-machine-shop, worked by men with overalls and close-cropped hair in their last days.

Hornbreed parked in the shade inside the hangar. A radio hanging from a cord played cheerful NUC choir music as it spun in the dry desert breeze.

"This is sort of a private workshop. The men here aren't paid by the Circus or AAC. The pilots keep them to work on their private craft. Hey, Jimmy."

The man who'd trotted up to get the door liked to chew tobacco. His hands had a fascinating patina; the oil had worked itself into every crevice. He wiped them on a rag before shaking hands with Hornbreed.

"This the bounty man?" Jimmy asked, looking at Valentine's ID card. An aluminum can with a rubber lid hung around his neck.

"Max Argent," Valentine said, extending his hand.

Jimmy didn't shake it. "You got a lift all the way back to Yuma. Sure didn't do much for that gold. I could've done that."

"You didn't face down ten-foot scorpions," Hornbreed said. "He did. Where's the crate, Jimmy? Hope you haven't put it in the same spot as your manners."

"Just speakin' my mind, sir. Pat's just over here."

Jimmy led them past a couple of fixed-gear prop planes and to a little contraption in the bright colors of a yellow jacket that looked like a wheeled two-man bobsled under an oversized beach umbrella missing its fabric. It had a big prop sticking out the back.

"This is a Personal Advanced Aerial Transport. It's an autogyro, Max. Just about my favorite toy for flying out over the dunes. Seats two and some personal cargo. She's a fun little ship, and can run on ordinary high-octane gasoline. Twin rudders. Pretty safe, as long as you watch the weather, and if you stow your gear in to balance the load. Can take off from a cleared field and if the engine conks out, you just rotate back down."

"What works the rotors? All I see is a control mechanism. Or is there an axle hidden in there?"

"Forward velocity. Air resistance keeps the rotors spinning, and they give lift. That's where it's different from a helicopter—you can't hover, and you need takeoff room. Engine's a hundred ten horsepower, and you can engage a driver that works the wheels so it's a motorized tricycle too. There's pretty good ground clearance. This thing was the range model."

"All yours?" Valentine asked.

"No. She's yours now."

Jimmy popped the lid and spit into the aluminum can.

"You're kidding."

"No. It's a thank-you for going into that hole after me. Most men wouldn't have."

"Most men don't like seeing an Archon's ransom disappearing down a big rat hole either."

Hornbreed shrugged. "Maybe. Maybe not."

"Don't know how to thank you," Valentine said.

"I still got my Air Ranger, Argent. You're getting the kiddie toy."

Valentine gave in to his pleasure at the gift. "What are we waiting for? Let's take her up."

"Duty calls. And you've got some workbooks to get through. I'll be checking your math at lunch."

There were anxious faces all over the utilitarian command building and the sound of steel doors opening and shutting as people hurried from office to office.

"They're at the tower now," an airman said.

"That just means they'll be gone by lunch," Hornbreed countered calmly.

Hornbreed's office had pictures of aircraft, glossy pre-'22 images and simpler black-and-whites of younger versions of himself in a neat school uniform and flight suits standing in groups in front of various craft. Manila envelopes and folders were piled on his desk. Assorted pilots were gathered outside, seeking an opportunity to take their planes up. Hornbreed checked off flight card after flight card.

"*Huff.* We'll look busy today, that's for sure."

Hornbreed whistled tunelessly as he got out a clipped

stack of paper titled "Basic Principles of Aviation" and handed it to Valentine. "Grab a pencil off my desk if you like. There's an empty classroom at the end of the hall, if you want somewhere quiet to work, but you should shut the curtains or it'll get hot."

"I'll just grab a chair in here."

"Be my guest."

Valentine dived into equations about lift. Some of them brought back memories of the book-walled little room in Father Max's house. He'd read some about flying in the lonely days after he lost his parents and siblings, suddenly wanting to know about his father only after he was cold in his grave.

Three times Circus personnel popped their heads into the office to tell him about the "purifiers." Each time Hornbreed waved them off.

"They said we lost too many ships in Colorado!" one nervous, pimpled young airman said. "They already took two out of the tower."

"We got the water flowing again," Hornbreed said. "Tell you what, I'm out of copier toner. I'll give you a warrant to run into Yuma and pick up some more. Grab a lunch while you're there, Daw."

"You know Ling's market?" Valentine said as the young man stood first on one foot, then the other, waiting for the purchase order and pass.

"Sure," the kid said.

"You need something?" Hornbreed asked.

"I might take up your milk habit. But give a message to this girl Gide. She lives above Ling's. Tell her Max would like to see her again."

"Max would like to see her again," the kid repeated.

"That oddball?" Hornbreed asked.

"I like the tattoos," Valentine said.

"This I have to hear. Let's take a coffee break."

"While the purifiers are here?" Daw squeaked. Hornbreed passed him the paperwork.

"Why not? Coming, Argent?"

They took some stairs down to a cafeteria, where the

workers were frantically cooking, cleaning, and polishing. Valentine smelled cleanser and wet mops.

"Gide, huh," Hornbreed said, buying them some coffee with his ID. "I don't think she's all there. Though I'll admit what there is of her was expertly assembled."

"I like a challenge," Valentine said.

"If it'll plant you here, then I'm happy. Tumbleweeds have a way of disappearing. You could do a lot worse than the Circus, you know."

"I know," Valentine said, and meant it. He'd seen less comfortable cages.

A hubbub broke out in the hall, and a party entered.

"*Huff.* Oh hell," Hornbreed said. He stood and faced them.

Valentine did likewise, trying not to gape, but it was a strange procession that strode into the cafeteria.

Two teenagers led it, a handsome Hispanic boy and a blond girl with prom-queen hair. They wore impossibly clean white robes that might have been martial arts uniforms had the coats been a little shorter. Neither of the youths could have been over seventeen or eighteen.

Behind them a New Universal Church Youth Vanguard warden carried a big briefcase handcuffed to his wrist.

Then came the muscle. A pair of men in combat vests, burnished pistols holstered low on their thighs, might have been watching him from behind dark sunglasses. It was hard to tell—they kept their noses pointed straight ahead.

Hovering at the edge of the mass was Pyp himself, hatless and complaining. His stray hair gave him a desperate look.

"Wildlife's one of my best radarmen. He lost that arm in action, you know."

"He seemed insolent," the boy said. His voice was that of a man's, but nevertheless a little high-pitched. Sergeant Patel would tell him to "talk like you've got a pair, boy."

"Uh-huh. Or maybe he was just trying to make sure that those planes taking off didn't crash into each other."

"Who's this?" the girl asked, staring at Valentine.

"Follow your heart, Ariel," the warden advised. He opened his briefcase.

"You don't have paper on him," Pyp said. "He brought in the wing leader, here. Saved his life in tribe country."

"No doubt seeking the reward. Greedy," the young man said.

"Is that how you spend your life?" the girl asked. "Chasing money? Flesh for gold?"

"Shut up, Ariel," Hornbreed said. He placed the slightest extra stress on the name, perhaps mocking it. "You don't know what you're talking about."

The teens stood up, almost crackling like charged hair.

The warden shuffled through his folder. He handed a sheet to the young man.

Pyp put himself between the purification team and his wing leader. "You don't let men who bring in our pilots claim their reward in peace, that'll be it for anyone who goes down."

"That's the problem, isn't it? They keep going down," the boy said. "There's sabotage among the mechanics, certainly."

"If we could trade for real spares instead of modifying stuff from the boneyards," Pyp said.

"Do you think you're immune, old man?" Ariel asked. "One word from me and you'll be off with the others. There's more than a whiff of personal corruption about you." She glanced at his feet. "Too lazy to wash your own socks and shine your own shoes?"

Valentine recognized a couple of the phrases from the New Universal Church *Guidon*, while the rest of him was tensing as he evaluated the muscle. How much was show and how much was go?

"You take him and you'll never see three-quarters of the pilots again," Hornbreed said.

The young man consulted the sheet the warden had handed him. "A man who crashed on his last flight might be worried about his own fate."

"Crashed?" Ariel cut in.

"Wipe that sneer off your face or I'll do it for you," Hornbreed said.

"He was trying to get a lame bird back," Pyp said. "I'd ordered the ship destroyed at the forward field, but he insisted he could get it back. He almost did. She's been salvaged and is being repaired now. He's a damn hero."

"This is the real test, Ariel," the warden said.

"He's going," she said, glaring at Hornbreed. One of the security talked into the mini-walkie-talkie clipped to his epaulet.

Hornbreed shook his head, a sad smile on his face. "You'll think about today. Later."

"Lack of humility. Willfulness," the youth said to no one in particular, but the warden checked off ticks on a pad. "Disparagement. What's the phrase? 'Three strikes and you're cut'?"

"Out," Valentine corrected, watching two men, one with a baton in his hand and the other with cuffs and leg-irons, step inside.

"Max, be quiet. Looks like someone else will have to check your equations at lunch." Hornbreed wore the same bland fatalism Valentine had first met in the desert.

Valentine's hand convulsed over the sword hilt that wasn't there. If he angled it just right, he could open both sets of carotid arteries with a single sweep. Make a red mess of the spotless white robes.

Hornbreed turned toward the girl, chuckled. "One day it will be your turn.... I wonder how you'll take the news."

"Our generation will not be tainted," the youth said. Pyp fought with his hands, which were balling up into fists.

"Tell Louisa I'm sorry," Hornbreed said to Pyp as

they shackled him. The wing leader was shaking, just a little. Valentine looked away, embarrassed. Just another Quisling, getting what's coming to him from the blood-greased machine he kept moving, he told himself. "I know she loves that house," Hornbreed said as they led him toward the door, where a woman and two other men waited, chained together. "It's gonna kill her to leave it."

"Let's see how clean that kitchen is," Ariel said, looking past Hornbreed. Did she have a tear in her eye? The kids led the procession away. One of the guards didn't like the look of Valentine, and watched him.

"Argent, wait for me in his office," Pyp said. Valentine listened as they walked toward the kitchen. "Last chance, you two. I'm going to fight to get this commuted to a labor term in California. You resist me on it, and, well, I've got old friends in the church, right up to the Archon. I'll make sure there's a set of eyes on you both every time you draw a breath. You so much as yawn during services . . ."

Valentine hoped for Hornbreed's sake that Pyp could get it done. He returned to the office.

He could still smell Hornbreed's aftershave on the chair. Valentine found the rest of the math impossible.

Pyp didn't return until after 1500, according to the twenty-four-hour clock on the wall. Valentine spent the time looking at the photos around the office, and didn't like what he saw.

"I'm so tired," Pyp said, sinking into Hornbreed's chair.

"Who was that Ariel to Equality?" Valentine asked.

"How'd you work that?"

"There's a picture of them on the shelf next to the running trophy."

Pyp looked up. "I see. She's his sister. He half raised her after their father disappeared. His mother was useless, from what I know about her. I need some food, or I'm going to upchuck."

"I'm not sure that I want to go back to the cafeteria," Valentine said.

"I know," Pyp said. "Let's go down to the ready room. They have a pizza oven."

The ready room was mostly maps on the walls and old books and magazines on the chairs and chipped tables. A shower hissed down a hall that was marked HYGIENE. Comfortable armchairs and recliners were grouped around a somnolent television, where *Noonside Passions* played out the melodrama. Valentine noted that the aging Rebeccah had a new, matronly hairstyle and a church ribbon around her neck. With a better angle Valentine recognized one of the pilots from the rescue helicopter, reading his *Guidon*. Maybe he was resolving to be a better example of mankind's evolution toward the communal spirit. Or maybe he was just memorizing a phrase or two to trot out to the next purifiers.

They found some congealed pizza and warmed it in the oven.

"Want a milk?" Pyp asked. "I'm having one."

"Sure."

They sat. Pyp lifted his carton, held it up until Valentine did likewise. "A good man."

"A good man," Valentine repeated.

The milk didn't do much for the greasy pizza. Both men ate mechanically. Another pilot came in and turned up the volume on *Passions*.

"Crap, a repeat," he said to the reading man, but sat down to watch it anyway.

With some noise cover Valentine finally spoke.

"What the hell was that?"

"Fair question, son," Pyp said, taking some napkins from a metal dispenser and wiping his hands. "It's just how they keep us on our toes. I spent some time researching it, if you want to hear. Pretty clever. You interested in mass psychology?"

"I'll take the short version."

"I think it started in the early years of the Redemption," Pyp said, setting his elbows on the table and leaning close. "In the Southeastern United States the Kurians started using pretty teenage girls as spokespeople every time they opened a new medical center or fair-housing block.

"They find some young folks useful. They're good at picking out an elite, grooming them. Pretty soon the young and the beautiful were acting as spokespeople, passing news, bad usually. Up in the Northeast they were using kids as informers. If they turned in a ring of renegades, saboteurs, terrorists, whatever, the kids got rewarded pretty handsomely, positions in the church and whatnot.

"Practice spread. Down South, where they were having a lot of trouble with the old faiths, they started having the kids of a 'purer generation' rooting out those who didn't have their minds right. Our leaders adopted it. Having a couple kids go around picking out the wild hairs focused the resentment somewheres besides up."

"How do they get the kids to do it?" Valentine asked. "Turning in your own brother, even if he hasn't committed a real crime."

"The real crimes take place up here," Pyp said, tapping his temple. "The kids are actually pretty good at picking out those who have some kind of resentment. Good antennae for picking out those who don't fit in."

"Or maybe less empathy," Valentine said.

"You have kids?"

Valentine shrugged. *Depends on the definition.*

"Me neither," Pyp said. "Not that there haven't been women who've tempted me to settle. No. Some little shit telling his teacher who visits me in my own home at night."

"Why the interest in the purification, then?"

Pyp looked around without moving his head—a skill most older people in the Kurian Zone possessed. He used the shiny side of the napkin dispenser like a rearview mirror. "I was one. One of them. Raised in a church orphanage. I led up the first purification in Aztlan. Mind spotless as an Archon's bedsheets. Zealotry comes easy at that age. They used fine words on us, oh, yes. We were a new generation who'd tear down all the old injustices, the old prejudices, the corruption. But twenty years passed and then it was our turn to be judged corrupt."

Valentine decided to probe: "Ever think about putting your planes in the air and blowing up some of those towers?"

"You're kidding, right? I thought you were a traveling man. You know the teams, I'm sure. We got it better here than ninety percent of the world."

"You're on tight rations."

"Ahh, that'll pass. Same thing happened back during the Lincoln-Grande War. They'll swap a couple hundred square miles and it'll be put right."

"They're having a tough time containing Texas, now that they're linked up with the Ozarks. Suppose Denver throws in with them, or with that fellow up in the far Northwest, what's-his—"

"They'll just drop some new virus on 'em and that'll be the end of it. Now, Argent, listen. You seem bright enough. I know the towers give you the twitch. They do everyone. But that doesn't mean you can't do well in the shade of 'em. Learn a vital skill. Purifications don't come about closer together than six or eight years, and I've got a good chance of getting Hornbreed sprung."

"Seems to me no purifications would be better."

"That kind of operation would take weeks, hundreds and hundreds of sorties. We'd land and get throttled by—"

"So you have thought about it," Valentine said.

Pyp drew back. "Don't think you're going to inform—"

"I'm no rat," Valentine said. "Just heard someone say something about, if given a gun, they'd be tempted to point it in the other direction."

"I've been on Internal Security work groups. Renegade pilots are rare, but it's happened. They have contingencies. I'm sure there are contingencies I don't even know about. I'll tell you this: There are tunnels under this base, under the housing areas. Not sure what's down there. I don't want to find out."

A jet engine rattled the airfield with the noise of its passage.

"They have long memories," Pyp continued. "You do them enough damage, they'll get rid of you one way or another. Even if you flee to the rebels. Assuming you survive touchdown. They chop men like me up, one joint at a time."

Frustrated, Valentine sat back and pushed away the crumbs of the pizza. The man was just as right as he was wrong.

"Anyway," Pyp said. "Pressure's off now. I can arrange your trip north anytime."

"Speaking of valuable skills—I'd like a couple more flying lessons," Valentine said. "Equality gave me an ultralight, I think he called it." *Was that just this morning?* "I'd like to know more about it."

"So you did listen. Good man. I need to get out of here anyway. Think I'll take you up myself."

CHAPTER SEVEN

⚓

Southern Washington, May: Most people think of the Pacific Northwest as a cloudy, rainy woodland, fragrant with the moldy, rotting-pine smell of a temperate rainforest. But beyond the rain-catching Cascades, the eastern plains of Washington have more in common with the high plains of the Midwest than the foggy harbors of salmon fleet and crab boat.

Wolves trot through the open country in the summer, pursuing the prolific western antelope, retreating to the river-hugging woods when winter comes.

The former ranching and orchard country of the dry half of Washington is sparsely inhabited but frequently patrolled for reasons unique to this part of the country. A few Kurian outposts, fed by rail lines running up from Utah and Oregon or in from Idaho, circle their lands with towers like teeth, easily visible from the air thanks to the irrigation technology still in use. But these are the terminal ends, for nothing but one Grog-guarded set of rail and highway line runs up the Pacific coast, thanks to the highly effective, organized guerrilla army under their "Mr. Adler."

The Osprey-style jump jet touched down on an empty stretch of highway, cutting over a high, dry plateau. The Cascades ran in a blue line in the distance, darkening as the sun descended to meet them. Valentine, ears popping in the change of pressure, drank a final pint of milk in memorial to Hornbreed.

It felt like a long flight, and ended with several low passes to find a suitable stretch of road for landing. Valentine had grown used to short training hops in his time with the autogyro, gliders, and small training craft. The jet, a courier craft for high-level Quislings, was plushly appointed beyond anything Valentine had ever experienced and had ample space in the cargo bay for the autogyro, with its rotators folded away. He rode in the cockpit for an hour or two, listening to Starguide's stories of Utah and Nevada.

"That's right, a big chunk of the Salt Lake City folks just disappeared, almost overnight. Some say they all marched up a mountain and killed themselves. Others say they went to another world. I think it's kinda both—Mormons always were weird," he said as they viewed the Great Salt Lake from fifteen thousand feet.

After a refueling stop at a combination armory and coal-processing plant, featuring the first Grogs Valentine had seen since coming West, they took the rest of the hop up to Washington. The jet had enough in its tanks to make it back to Utah.

"I don't believe it. We're out," Gide said. She'd regained the color she'd lost when they hit turbulence leaving Utah.

Much of the past few weeks had been occupied with Gide's "Exit Authority," a polite term for a sheaf of papers representing a series of undercover transactions that allowed her to leave the Confederation. It wasn't difficult for Valentine to convince Pyp that he'd fallen hard for the girl and wanted her up on the family land in Washington. An allied Kurian enclave in northern Utah agreed to buy her, in exchange for three children—one partially deaf and another in a foot brace—who were to be apprenticed to the New Universal Church in Tempe. The Circus arranged for her Utah paperwork to be "misfiled" using some of Valentine's reward.

She stood well clear of the plane now, lost in a heavy military jacket and knee boots, her dark-and-light-pleated hair bound up atop her head like a swirl ice-cream cone.

His pilot instructor, Starguide, helped Valentine take the ultralight from the cargo hold and give it a final flight check.

"What do your people raise, anyway?" Starguide asked, helping Valentine roll out the autogyro from the cargo bay doors.

"Pigs," Valentine said. "There's a catfish hatchery too. That's where spare feed and pig shit goes."

"You must really love him," Starguide hollered over to Gide.

With that, he closed the cargo hatch with a hydraulic whine. "Well, Argent, I still say you might make a good pilot someday. Come back if you get tired of slopping the hogs."

"I just want to be far away from everything," Valentine said.

"The sky doesn't qualify?"

Valentine shrugged, already composing the part of his report about the Flying Circus. Like the sailors on the *Thunderbolt*, at least part of the Circus took to the sky to be free of the Kurians, if only temporarily.

He and Gide stood well clear of the jet as it turned around, plugging their ears against the thunder of its exhaust. Starguide used a more fuel-efficient, traditional takeoff. When the Osprey took its running start back into the brassy late-spring sky, they were alone with the wind.

"We're out," Gide repeated. She hugged him. "Fuckin'-A."

"Feels good, doesn't it?" Valentine asked.

"I'll say. Let's take our clothes off. Like little kids in the sun. I'm so in the mood for a frolic 'n' fuck."

"I think we should get going. That jet might have drawn attention."

She broke contact. "You're a torqued kite, Max."

Valentine considered telling her his real name now, and his destination—though not his purpose. Travel was a lot safer with a companion in case of illness or injury, he rationalized. "How's that?" he asked instead.

"Never taking a run at me. Queer?"

"No."

"Balls blown off?"

"No."

"What, then?"

"Don't have much luck with women," he finally said.

"Just sex, you know. It's healthy. Might get that stick out of your ass."

Valentine opened the autogyro's canopy, revealing the twin seats, the passenger above and behind the pilot. He grabbed the steering-wheel-style stick and turned it so the little ship was pointed down the road, and opened the tool pouch. His nose detected something rotten in the right cargo compartment. Sure enough, Jimmy had left him a dead rat as a going-away present. Valentine extracted it and flung it into the dry, weed-pocked soil beside the road. "Wouldn't work that way with you," Valentine said.

"How's that?"

"I like you."

She stared at him for a moment, her upper lip working back and forth, then tousled his hair. "I know you do. Otherwise you wouldn't have gotten me out."

"I'd like to think I'd still have tried even if I didn't."

"You hide behind a lot of ifs, Max. I know you're a pretty good card player. That's about it."

"Let's change the subject. What's next for you?"

She squatted beside him and lowered her voice, even though there was no one to overhear them but the grasshoppers. "I'm joining up."

"Joining what?"

Her eyes brightened. "The resistance. There's a big army up here, out in the mountains to the west. The flyboys tell me they're tearing assholes out of the KO. I'm gonna join them. I didn't tell you before because . . . because I didn't want you to be an accessory. Just in case they picked me up or something."

"Or in case I was some kind of informer."

She shrugged. "I suppose anything's possible."

"How do you know they'll take you?"

"Can I fire off a couple from your gun?"

"Help me get this thing ready first. I want to be able to take off quickly if we need to."

She helped him stow their gear intelligently enough. "You keeping this thing, or you going to trade it?"

Valentine sat down and tested the simple cable controls. "I'm wondering how easy it'll be to find fuel. I'm more of a horse-and-pack-mule person, most of the time."

"Thought you were a biker, with those leathers."

Load balanced in the little cargo spaces to either side of the chutelike cabin, they were ready to go. "I think it's time to come clean with you, Gide. I'm aiming on the resistance up here too. I just had a few hundred more miles to come."

"Fuckin'-A!"

"If you like, I'll give you a lift to the mountains. Safer for two to travel together."

"You're this gal's knight in shining armor, Max."

"With a motorcycle engine attached to an oversized food processor as a mount."

"So how were you going to get all the way up here without the flyboys?" she asked.

"I've had some experience with ships and boats. Thought I'd get to LA by hiring on with a convoy, then work north up the coast. But an opportunity presented itself, and I always wanted to know more about the Circus."

"Seen them buzzing around?"

"Something like that."

"I'd still like to try that gun. I've only ever shot over open sights since I was little."

Valentine showed her the points of the rifle. "You cock the first with the bolt. Crosshairs are zeroed for one hundred yards."

"Regular 7.62?"

Valentine nodded. She sighted on an old wooden post perhaps seventy yards away, peeping like an owl from a patch of brush next to the road, and fired. They walked over and inspected her shot. She'd almost centered the post.

"Again?"

Valentine decided that ammunition used in practice wasn't really wasted, and he wanted to test the stuff he'd picked up in Yuma anyway.

He fashioned targets by inking a couple of pieces of toilet tissue and fixed them to a tree trunk back toward the autogyro. She was an even better shot than he was at two hundred yards, using the stabilizing built-in bipod.

The only thing they disturbed with the gunfire was the birds.

"I'm convinced," he said.

"The old man sent me to bed hungry if I missed with my bullet," she said. "One shot, meat and all that."

Valentine examined the road. It had been used recently, light trucks by the look of the tread. Someone was taking care of the primary roads out here. He unrolled and studied his map of Washington State.

This could be one of the highways that communicated between the forces in the Cascades and Mount Omega—which wasn't really a mountain, of course. Strange that over all these years the Kurians had never located it. His contact with Southern Command was there. He hoped he'd have reason to visit.

Valentine cleaned and stowed the gun and they climbed into the autogyro. Valentine had flown it tandem before while learning, but never with his food, weapons and accoutrements, blankets and bamboo sleeping mat, and spare clothes aboard.

He worked the throttle and opened the engine all the way up. The autogyro ate highway as it sped up, and finally jumped into the air. Gide let out a gasp.

Valentine brought it up to about a thousand feet.

Flying in an autogyro is noisy and busy. The lift from

the rotors makes it sway and bob like a cork in a choppy water.

"Oh shit. Land again. Land again," Gide gasped.

"Are you—"

A loud retching sound from above and behind answered his question. The smell filled the cabin, half-digested bologna-and-cheese sandwiches giving off a beery odor. Valentine fought his own gorge, rising in sympathy.

Gide cracked a little panel window, letting in even more of the engine's roar. "You can set it down, Max. I think I'd rather walk."

"Give it an hour," Valentine said, watching the falling sun and wondering if he could stand an hour with the vomit smell. "Fix your eyes on the mountains. That's where we're heading."

Twenty minutes of groaning later Valentine spotted a strange bare patch of earth below, a short hike away from a treelined pond. It was too good an opportunity to pass up. He passed low over the cleared oval of ground and sent small, chickenlike birds on short hop-flights.

He landed with a bad bounce.

"Thank Christ," Gide said as they halted.

"Let's clean out the ship," Valentine said. He extracted a collapsed plastic jug and passed it to Gide. "Your spew. You can carry the water."

She looked at the cleared ground, frowning. "What did this? Helicopters?"

"Don't think so. With luck, you'll see tomorrow morning."

Woodpeckers, always up and hard at work even before the roosters cry or the larks rise, woke them. As the sun came up Gide got to see a prairie chicken dance.

The birds, mating in the late northern spring, gathered together at the tramped-down earth and began to jump up and down in front of one another, in wild displays of feathery athleticism.

"Looks like the dance floor at the old Mezcal on a Saturday night," Gide said. "Except no music."

"They're resourceful little birds," Valentine said. "When the snow comes they dive right into a drift and wiggle down deep, making a little igloo. Coyotes and foxes can't smell them under the snow."

"What's an igloo?" Gide asked.

Valentine explained the principle.

"I wonder what the winters are like up here," Valentine said.

"We've got some time to get acclimated. But you don't talk like an Aztlan. Or a Texican, or a Cali, or a Yute. You're hard to place."

"I was born in Minnesota. At least I think I was. I spent my childhood there, anyway."

"That's like Canada, right?"

"Next to it."

Valentine carefully took out his surgical-tube sling, fixed it to his wrist, and put a rounded stone in the leather cup. He sighted on a male at the edge of the fracas, making halfhearted little hops.

"Oh, no, don't spoil their fun," Gide said.

"I don't like to dip into my preserved food unless I have to," Valentine said. "Hickory-and-sage-smoked prairie chicken's good eating."

Valentine knocked the oldster off his feet, scattered dancing chickens as he got up, and ran to finish the job with a quick twist. He bled the bird into a cup and dressed it quickly.

"There goes your invitation to the next church cotillion," Gide said as Valentine dropped it in hot water to soften the feathers for plucking. He lifted the cup. "You're not really going to drink warm blood, are you?"

"Can't afford to waste anything. It's like a multivitamin," Valentine said.

"Give me a sip. Might as well start the mountain-man stuff now." He passed her the cup and she made a face as she sipped. "Fuck, that's rude! Like having a bloody nose."

"Your dad never had you drink blood?"

"We liked our food cooked. Haven't you ever heard of salmonella, Mr. Igloo?"

"Who did the cooking? Your mom?"

Gide worked her upper lip again, this time tightening it against her teeth. "She died having me. There wasn't a midwife or anything, just my dad."

"I'm sorry," Valentine said.

"Kids always get along better with the opposite-sex parent, ever notice that?" she asked.

Valentine accepted the change of subject. "I guess you're right." He'd not had the time to experience it with Amalee. Circumstances had changed.

"I'd better see about that bird. Thought I smelled some wild onions down by the pond. We can have a nice fry-up, then wash while it digests."

Gide kept her food down on the next hop. Valentine argued with himself over what to do with the autogyro. Aircraft of any kind were valuable enough that the guerrillas would probably seize it outright. But on the other hand, it might allow him to make more of an impressive entrance.

He opted for showmanship.

What he guessed to be Mount Rainier loomed in the distance. He passed over valleys under thickening clouds, watching his fuel gauge sink toward E.

Apart from herds of goats, sheep, and cattle, and the attendant fires in the shepherds' bunkhouses, he saw little sign of habitation. But then a good guerrilla army wouldn't advertise its presence.

Then he passed over another town, built around a bridge and its patched-over road in a boomerang-shaped valley, and saw what he suspected was mortar pits in the hill above, looking out over the reduced hills to the east. Camouflage-painted four-wheelers were parked in a line like suckling piglets in front of a redbrick building in town, and there were well-used paddocks behind the line of buildings and what looked like houses converted to stables. He marked freshly sheared sheep.

Best of all, a limp American flag hung from a flag-pole in front of what looked like the town post office. No Quisling force Valentine had ever heard of flew the despised Stars and Stripes, a symbol of racism and greed according to the histories of the New Order.

Valentine swooped around again, enjoying the feel of the tight turn. Men in civilian clothes and uniform were coming out onto the street now to watch the acrobatics.

"Gide," Valentine said, almost shouted. "This looks like the guerrillas. One thing you should know."

"Yeah?" she said, eyes closed, sounding like she was fighting with her stomach again.

"My name's not Max Argent. It's Valentine, David Valentine. I travel under a false name."

"Okay," she burped. "Land, all right?"

Valentine set the gyro down on the other side of the bridge from the town, where the road widened outside the bridge. He engaged the wheel drive and motored toward town. The road was badly pocked, and they bounced a good deal.

Some armed men in timberland camouflage were walking up the road.

"Ma—David, whatever. Open up!" Gide said.

Valentine popped the hatch as he applied the brakes. Gide jumped out and fell to her knees, bringing up a mostly liquid mess.

Valentine jumped out to aid her, but his bad left leg betrayed him and he stumbled. As he caught himself, his foot slipped in a pothole and he felt something in his ankle give. He sprawled.

Gide turned her head, wiped saliva from her mouth.

Valentine rolled over and probed his ankle. *Great, a sprain. So much for showmanship.*

"Here they come," Gide said.

A brown-haired man under a wide-brimmed black hat with yellow cording halted the others about ten yards away. He had a long, thick mustache that covered his upper lip.

"I hope you two have good reason to buzz us like that," he said. "Otherwise, your welcome to Brantley's Bridge will end with you hanging from it."

Valentine sat up. "We're not spies. We're here to join up. Can you put me in touch with a recruiting officer?" He tried to rise, but the ankle hurt too much. He ended up balancing unsteadily on his bad leg.

Gide got to her feet, parked herself under his armpit. "That's right."

"Shit," one of the men behind, a shotgun held professionally but pointed down, commented. "We should just make heroes out of them now. Save a lot of trouble."

"Recruiting officer, huh?" the man with the mustache said. "I don't know that we have any of those. Least not at this depot."

"What do you suggest for recruits, then?"

"You want to die under ol' Adler, we can assist." It began to drizzle. The officer lifted his face to the rain, took off his hat, and wiped his forehead before returning his cover to its place. "First we have to detick you. Then you get questioned. You out of Sea-Tac?"

"No. Opposite direction. We came across the Rockies. The last KZ I was in was the Aztlan Confederation."

"Long trip in that little eggbeater."

"You'll hear the whole story, if you want," Valentine said.

"Tell you what, Mister, we support some garrison militia right here in town. I'm going to hold you here for now, warm and cozy, but we have to keep you to visitors' quarters. We'll turn you over to them and they'll feed you until someone from Pacific Command can get down here. Hope that goes well for you—the alternative isn't pleasant."

After a warm disinfectant shower and a quick physical, the captain put them in a rather moldy house. They had running water, though it was cold. Tallow dips offered smelly light at night, and there were some old books to read.

The windows and door were barred from the outside. Valentine watched off-duty men inspect the autogyro, everything from the still-smelly cockpit to the tail rotor. Valentine's weapons and gear were all locked up in the "armory," what had formerly been the modest post office in the middle of town.

Gide silently fretted. Being locked up, in her experience in the Kurian Zone, meant doom.

"They're just being careful," Valentine said.

Finally a tired-looking young lieutenant driven by a heavyset sergeant with a maimed right hand pulled up in a two-horse carriage and visited the redbrick headquarters building.

In a few moments they emerged, accompanied by the mustachioed Captain Clarke and the militia staff sergeant, who inspected their lodgings daily for signs of damage or mischief.

Clarke knocked and entered without waiting for a response: "You two got a visitor. He'll figure out what the hell to make outta you."

The captain and the militia sergeant waited outside the locked door while the newly arrived lieutenant sat down and opened a folding notebook. He had ink stains on his fingers thanks to a problematic pen, and the frames of his thick glasses looked like they'd originally been intended for a woman.

"My name is Lieutenant Walker. This is Sergeant Coombs. You are . . . ahh, David Valentine, I take it?" he asked, looking through the bottle-bottom lenses.

"Yes," Valentine said.

"So you're Gide. No other name?"

"I've been called lots of names," she said. "But I wouldn't want them written down."

The sergeant assisting licked his lips as he looked at her. She'd found a thick flannel shirt in one of the closets, and pulled her hair back into a tight ponytail, but she still exuded her aggressive sensuality.

"Have you been treated well since you arrived? You can be honest—I report to a whole separate chain of command. Plenty of food? Wash water? Medical care?"

Valentine plucked at the elastic bandage on his ankle. It had healed with its usual alacrity. "They've been generous with everything," Valentine said.

"Good. Place of birth?"

"Boundary Waters, Minnesota," Valentine said.

"Choa Flats, Arizona," Gide supplied.

"Freeborn?"

"Meaning?" Valentine asked.

"Not born into slavery, on an estate or whatever."

"No," Valentine said. " 'Freeborn.' "

"I was born in the Confederation, obviously," Gide said.

"Military experience? Someone must have taught you to fly, David. Should we start with that?"

Valentine put his hands on his knees. "Have to go back a few more years. I first joined Southern Command in May of 2061, when a Wolf patrol came through our area. . . ."

The rest took about twenty minutes. Valentine just skimmed his wanderings after his adoption of Blake.

Lieutenant Walker's pen ran out when Valentine described the bounty he'd claimed. "Damn," he muttered. "Look, ummm, Major Valentine, this is a bit more than I expected. If I can ask you, though, sir, what did you come here to do?"

"I want our side to win," Valentine said. "Your general's fame has crossed the mountains."

"He doesn't claim any rank, actually," Walker said. "Technically, he's still a civilian. But he's kind of like the president to us. Sometimes he's called the Old Man."

"Just say ol' Adler and everyone knows who you're talking about," Sergeant Coombs added.

Walker fiddled with his pen and inkwell. "I'm going to have to refer your case to higher command. Do you want to stay here, or come back with me to my station?"

"If that would save travel time," Valentine said.

"We'll try to accommodate you," Walker said, looking over his shoulder at the sergeant, who straightened up a little in his lean against the wall.

Walker turned up a new page. "Now, Gide, are you going to tell me you sank the Eisenhower Floating Fortress?"

She was looking fixedly at Valentine, as if trying to decide what the symptoms of delusions of grandeur looked like.

"No. I can ride. I can shoot. I'm healthy," she said.

" 'Can shoot' doesn't do it justice," Valentine said.

Walker spent some time questioning Gide, but Valentine could see he was preoccupied. He was a good interrogator, and for all Valentine knew, the thick glasses and cranky pen were props to put people off their guard. He was good at an interrogator's first job, which was just to get people talking by asking questions that were pleasant to answer.

What assistance Sergeant Coombs offered wasn't clear to Valentine. Maybe he just had a good eye for liars.

They broke for lunch, a mutton stew and applesauce. Then the militiamen packed up a box of wax-paper-wrapped sandwiches and thermoses.

"We'll be there by midnight or so if we get moving," Walker said. He wrote out an order sheet for the gyrocopter to be moved, and handed it to the captain.

"You travel at night?" Valentine asked.

"We don't go fast enough so it's dangerous," Walker said.

"I take it the Reapers don't get this far into the mountains, then?"

"No. We give them too much to worry about in the basin. The tower's men are the ones who fear the night. Not us."

Valentine couldn't tell if this was just rear-area bravado, propaganda, or confidence born of experience.

"I don't suppose I can have my carbine back."

"Sergeant Coombs, what do you think?"

"If he's who he says he is, he doesn't need a gun to kill us."

Walker giggled. "The sergeant has a dark streak like the Columbia River. But let me keep the hardware for now. It'll save questions at the stops, as you don't have so much as a militia cap."

Their gear stowed beneath the seats, Valentine helped Gide up into the open carriage, then climbed up himself. It had iron-rimmed wheels and a camouflage-netting top.

"Sorry for the rickety transport," Walker said. "As a lowly lieutenant, I don't rate a gasoline ration for my duties. Our supply line for fossils stretches way up into Canada, and it's not altogether reliable." He took off his glasses and nodded to the sergeant, who set off.

They stopped three times on the journey, twice at checkpoints outside of settlements and once for an exchange of horses. Passwords were swapped and orders and identification examined. The fresh horses made a difference, and they creaked and rattled on the iron rims into an electrically lit military camp a good half hour before the lieutenant's prediction.

Gide sneezed a few times on the ride.

The sign read CAMP DEW, and the town looked to be built around an old high school. There was a hospital just down the highway, and many of the houses had electrical lights.

"Back to civilization," Walker said. "We'll put you in the Lodgepole Motel for now. I'm afraid you'll have to stay under guard."

"For the gal's cold," Sergeant Coombs said, slipping a flattened bottle into Valentine's pocket as he waved over help with the horses and luggage.

Valentine surreptitiously examined the quarter-full

bottle. It was hard to tell the color of the liquid in the dark, but Valentine smelled whiskey.

"Nice of you, Sergeant, but I'm trying temperance until I find my feet here."

"I'm not," Gide said, and Coombs passed her the bottle.

As they got settled in, Walker showed up with a camera and took their pictures, both from the front and in profile. Two more days passed while various orders wandered up and down the chains of command. Gide's face turned red from her cold, or maybe the back-mountain whiskey, and they got sick of washing their clothes and darning socks.

The motel had a water heater that they kept fired up from six until nine in the morning, so Valentine enjoyed hot showers every day. They "exercised" for two hours in the afternoon on a chain-link-fenced basketball court that had replaced the motel's pool, bringing back uncomfortable memories of his time in the Nut. The rest of the time they filled in companionable silence. Though Gide relished stories of his travels and descriptions of the effect Quickwood had on Reapers, Valentine had turned moody and taciturn when not even Walker visited on the second day; he wondered if he'd be sentenced in Washington for crimes committed in Arkansas.

"It's not fun, you know," Valentine said when she asked about the Wolves, and how many women made it into the ranks. "You'll be tired and bored most of the time. Then there's a lot of noise, and you'll look around with your ears ringing and realize half the people you know are dead."

"I don't expect this to be fun," she said. "I just want a chance at them. I'm sick of standing around watching it happen. I can hack it."

"A couple of tattoos don't make you hard," Valentine said, and instantly regretted it.

She crossed her arms and turned away, looked out

at a patch of blue sky through the barred window from the front chairs.

"I'm sorry, Gide."

She studied the street. "Whatever."

"Being cooped up with nothing to do gets on my nerves."

"I've killed a man, you know. Two men," she said.

"Sorry to hear that," Valentine said.

"My dad was drinking a lot as he got older. He got scared of going into towns to get work. Thought they'd pick him up, you know? Finally . . . I'd just turned fifteen. He tried to sell me. For sex, you know, I was a virgin and all. Some rich guy from Tempe and his manservant came for me. The servant washed me up and combed out my hair and told me how I shouldn't be afraid.

"He got sick of me after about a week or so and sent me back to Pa. But I learned the ins and outs of his house, and knew when the servant door in the wall was unlocked. I got me a couple of mean rattlesnakes and chopped off their rattlers. He had this little toilet room with a phone in it. Always went in there first thing in the morning. I cut the wires, broke the bulb, and put them in there.

"The snakes got him, sure enough, and he started hollering. The servant came and put down this big cut-down shotgun to drag him away from the snakes, I suppose so he could shoot them without blowing his master's leg off. I snuck up and got the gun, shot them both in the face. One barrel each.

"Funny thing is, the guy was nice enough. Really loving and gentle with me, and he gave me some kind of pill when it was over that flushed me out, made sure I got my period. The one I wanted to shoot was my father. Maybe not in the face, in the foot or knee or something. I heard later they hauled off the servants, the ones who worked there during the day, and that seemed the most unfair thing of all. A cook, a gardener, and a housekeeper, who all lived miles away and had to take a broken-down old bus even to get there. Up until then everything about the Order was scary, but in this theoretical sense. When I saw it in practice, it changed me more than getting poked by that old guy.

"I ran for Yuma, wanting to get across to Cali, and made it. But I met a nice kid in Yuma, working part-time at the store while he apprenticed at the airfield in electronics. He got purified, though, my first year there."

Valentine waited until he was sure she'd stopped talking. "What happened to your dad?"

"Dunno. I should have gotten a job in town, kept him somewhere out of the way. He wasn't on any sets of official books, I don't think—no one would have looked for him. Stupid old drunk."

"You are tough," Valentine said.

"Only on the outside. Like a bug."

Valentine nodded. "I know what you mean."

A thunderstorm rumbled outside when higher authority called for them. Valentine put on a pair of moleskin trousers they'd given him and his only shirt with a collar, a field turtleneck.

They took them down the road to the echoing halls of the high school, where maybe thirty or forty people worked in classrooms in a school built to hold a thousand. Patched cracks from earthquake damage ran across the floors and up the walls.

It had been a long parade of death since the "turnover" of 2022, when mankind relinquished its throne at the top of the food chain. . . .

Valentine guessed the room they brought them to had been devoted to science. A yellowing periodic table hung on the wall, and all the tables had a thick, black, chemically resistant covering. Cabinets on the wall held binders rather than test tubes and Bunsen burners. A preserved Reaper head sat in a jar on the counter, next to glass-covered trays holding molds of Grog tracks and recovered teeth.

A rather sad-looking elderly man, lost in his green

uniform collar, sat on a stool, resting his back against a whiteboard. Another man, bald with a lightning-bolt-like zigzag tattooed on each temple, wore a smart steely gray uniform. Blued-steel collar tabs and matching arrowheads on his epaulets gleamed like a polished piano top as he stood talking to Walker.

The guard halted Gide outside, offered her a chair.

"She's my aspirant, Walker," Valentine protested as the other guard led him into the office/classroom.

The older man pulled at his ear. "Hmmmm . . . can't say. Can't really say, maybe around the eyes."

"Major Valentine," the bald man said. "My name's Thunderbird. You know Walker, of course, and this is Colonel Kubishev. Colonel Kubishev is semiretired. He came down as a favor to me."

"Sorry, I'm afraid I bunged things up and delayed you a day," Colonel Kubishev said. He had a faint accent. "They asked me to take a look at you. I worked with your father, briefly, in Montana. Calgary Alliance. They asked me about the name and I wanted to see for myself."

None of that meant much. Valentine vaguely remembered the Calgary Alliance being mentioned in War College; it was a short-lived Freehold that collapsed under the Black Summer Famines of the forties.

"I'm honored, sir," Valentine said.

"How is he?"

"He's dead," Valentine said.

"Oh, I am sorry. I am sorry. My wife and I will remember him."

"Thank you, sir."

"You wouldn't know whatever happened to Helen St. Croix, I don't suppose," Kubishev asked.

"He married her," Valentine said. "She's my mother. She died at the same time."

"That's it! He has her hair, exactly," Kubishev said, as though the observation relieved him of a burden. "That is good. That is very good. Died at the same time?"

"Yes."

"I'm glad you were spared."

"I was eleven. Some distance away at the time."

"Major Valentine, I'm sorry to hear that," Thunderbird said. "Were you aware that your Q-file with Southern Command lists your father as J. D. Valentine and your mother as H. Argent?"

"Argent?"

"Yes, the same as that excellent set of fake Oklahoma papers you had."

Valentine stared. "I couldn't say why that's the case. When I filled out my enlistment paperwork I put down the correct names."

"I don't have that—this is just a short version—but it does list parentage and place of birth. Oh, your birthplace is listed as Rapid City, South Dakota. Strangely coincidental error, still."

"Maximilian Argent was a family friend," Valentine said.

"We don't doubt that the man in this file is you," Thunderbird said.

"I'm glad to hear it, ummm . . ."

"Colonel. The insignia for Delta Group is somewhat esoteric. I mean for you to learn it, though. I'd like to have you under my command."

"Delta Group?"

"Lifeweaver Enhanced. Delta is a symbol of change. We're mostly all Bears up here. I'm not sure if it's a regional affinity, or just that we know right where the Fangs are and we don't need Wolves and Cats and whatnot to locate them."

"I've worked with Bears," Valentine said. "If you want me to become one—"

Thunderbird clacked his tongue against the roof of his mouth, thinking. "I don't think I have a slot for you at your former rank. But we might find a job for you and that gizmo you flew in on."

"As you wish," Valentine said. "It'll be good to be back on a team again."

"Then you can satisfy my curiosity, Valentine. Why

did you come all the way here? You could have made yourself useful in Denver, Wyoming, even the Caribbean, and saved yourself a lot of mileage. Why us?"

"You're winning," Valentine said.

"Damn right we are," Walker put in. "And we'll keep winning, as long as the Lord sees fit."

The old man bowed his head, and Valentine saw his lips moving silently.

"We'll give you an orientation later. I want a detailed debriefing first."

They sat down and Walker brought in coffee. For forty-five minutes or so they talked, much more conversational than interrogatory. They were especially interested in his trips to the Caribbean and the exact circumstances of his court-martial and conviction under the Fugitive Law. "Typical," Thunderbird said. "They want victory. Just don't like the color of the coin that'll pay for it." Afterward they took a short break, and Valentine saw Thunderbird pick up the phone.

Later they talked to Gide, and Valentine idled in the hall. Her interview was much shorter.

"Term in the militia," she said. "I guess it's a start for us."

Valentine went back into the classroom, where Thunderbird was on the phone again. "Yeah, that's right. I want everything north of Woodinville Road cleared. They think Redmond's next, but we'll pull back and slide the Action Group north." He looked at Valentine. "Yes?"

"My friend Gide. I was hoping we'd be able to stay together."

"We'll pick this up in ten," Thunderbird said into the phone. He hung it up. "She's a natural. And a woman besides. No room for her with the Bears of Delta Group."

"She and I—"

Tok tok, his tongue sounded. "Something warm to come home to?"

"More like mutual affinity."

"Better check the true-love meter again. She sounds eager to serve, with or without you. If you want a slice of something juicy, Delta Group gets their pick, believe me. Tell you what, I'll get her posted near our operations HQ. She'd just be a short walk away. Fair enough?"

"More than," Valentine said, wondering why his stomach was going sour.

He picked up the phone. "See you on the other side of the mountains, Valentine."

CHAPTER EIGHT

⚓

*F*ort Grizzly, overlooking the outer suburbs of Seattle, Washington: The men call it either "Fort Gristle" or "Fort Drizzly" depending on whether the barrack-room conversation revolves around the food or the weather. Valentine was seeing the Seattle basin in its finest month.

Grizzly is settled on the east-facing slope of a ridge, at an old mine and quarry complex with a network of tunnels dug as though designed to be confusing—which it was. The "rabbit warren" underground works of Fort Grizzly serves as armory, bomb shelter, garage, and warehouse, and, most importantly, staging area for operations against Seattle.

Mining equipment chatters away all day, slowly expanding the works, serving as exercise for men with nothing better to do, adding background noise to all conversations except those in the deeper caves. At night blessed silence reigns, broken by the sounds of training, for the Bears of Fort Grizzly operate under the cover of darkness up and down the western slopes of the Cascades, daring the Reapers to face them when their powers are at their height.

Three-foot-high letters at the entrance tunnels exhort and warn: WE DO OR DIE FOR THE FUTURE; ANYONE CAN BE A HERO; WE'LL HAVE THEIR THANKS AFTER THE VICTORY; PEACE IS FOR GRAVEYARDS.

The warren is surprisingly light and airy. Masonry walls exist in many places, cheerfully painted in soft *greens and yellows. It's comfortably furnished with items taken from old houses; indeed, in some places it seems more like a furniture showroom than a bunker. There is running water in some of the caverns and electricity in all but the blind alleys and undercuts designed to fool intruders. To reach any of the high-priority caves, one has to travel through darkness, then approach checkpoints blinded by spotlights. Almost no amount of shelling would do much but close up a few of the entrances, and an assault on the complex would be akin to bearding a horde of grizzlies in their dens.*

" . . . to never doubt, never surrender, and never relent until our future is our own again," Valentine repeated with Gide, right hand held in the direction of the Stars and Stripes and a totem pole of the faces from assorted monetary denominations that depicted American presidents, left hand next to Gide's atop a black Reaper skull on a wooden pedestal. "I will obey the orders of my lawful superiors until victory, death, or honorable release."

The wording had a tang of blood and iron to Valentine. The oath he'd taken on joining Southern Command, administered very informally by an old Wolf sergeant holding a dog-eared Bible after his first week on the march south from Minnesota, used one similar phrase—"obey the lawful orders of my superiors"—and to Valentine, who turned the words over in his mind afterward, there could be worlds of interpretation separating the two.

He took the oath at Fort Grizzly with Gide, a final sop to their friendship, at the base of the eastern slope of "Grizzly Ridge" with the sun shining above and the pines of the western mountains blue in the sunshine.

"Smallest swearing-in I've ever attended," Thunderbird said, waving a private forward with a black bowling-ball bag for the Reaper skull. "But you're no ordinary recruit." A corporal on Thunderbird's staff named Wilson lit a cigarette and puffed eagerly.

Valentine felt Gide trembling next to him. Didn't Thunderbird recognize that this was an important moment in her life?

"You've done it, Gide," Valentine said. "Congratulations."

"Let's get you both into uniform, now that everything's legal," Thunderbird said. "Recruit Gide, they're expecting you at the fueling depot. You'll get your muster gear there. Get going."

"Salute," Valentine whispered.

"Thank you, sir," she said, saluting. He returned it.

"That entitles you to a drink on me," Valentine said. "Southern Command tradition. I'll call for you as soon as I can."

Tok tok. "This is Pacific Command, Valentine," Thunderbird said. But he smiled as he said it. "But we'll make sure you two keep your date.

"Valentine, let's get you out of that biker getup. Wilson, get Valentine over to the medical center for his capabilities physical, and see if the professor can spare an hour for a quick background lecture."

Valentine shook hands with Gide. She looked brisk and ready for anything, had been quick-witted enough to add the "sir," and she was capable enough. She'd be fine. Why this strange reluctance to let her go?

"My office is K-110, Valentine. The door is always open," Thunderbird said.

Wilson finished his cigarette with a long drag, stubbed the bright red remains out in his palm, and pocketed it. "No smoking in the warren."

"Doesn't that hurt?" Valentine said as he followed Wilson away.

"If it didn't, it wouldn't be much of a trick," Wilson said. "It'll be healed by tomorrow. Privileges of Bearhood."

The physical was more like an athletic contest against a stopwatch than a doctor's evaluation. First they tested day and night visual acuity, then color vision (he had

trouble with reds and greens, as usual). Then they
watched him climb a nearly vertical slope toward a red
demolition flag. He ran laps and they took blood and
had him breathe into a lung volume tube. He was measured for standing vertical jump (eleven feet, well short
of his record of sixteen his first year as a Cat). Then they
ran him through a maze of swinging tennis balls, waving
back and forth at the end of various lengths of string.
He had to roll, jump, and dodge at intervals measured
in split seconds.

"Eighty-five percent," the doctor said as her assistant
turned off the machine that agitated the wooden rigging. "You Cats are something."

"Are there any others here?" Valentine asked, watching her through the mass of waving lines and greenish
balls.

"No. The last one disappeared in the KZ a couple
years ago. There are some Wolves with the forward
observers."

Then Wilson took him to the professor, Delta Group's
archivist and resident historian, a sagging mass of a man
with a neatly trimmed gray beard, who sat in an office
with three humming dehumidifiers and piles of paper
atop piles of file cabinets. After a short lament that he
was forever being called away from the *History of the
Establishment of the Kurian Order,* he briefed Valentine
on Pacific Command's resurgence.

In the last dozen years or so they'd gone from being
a shabby group of guerrillas hiding in the mountains to
the Terrors of the Cascades, thanks to a single man. "Mr.
Adler," now "the Old Man," walked out of the Kurian
Zone, met a patrol under one of the few aggressive
commanders in the "Seahawks" as they styled themselves, said something about his family being killed,
and offered to guide the troops to an unattended depot
where they could get better weapons and explosives,
provided they'd use them on a Quisling named Doorward, who'd betrayed him. Doorward turned out to be
a soldier in the Seattle Order and a recent Ringwinner.

They ambushed him as he pulled into the garage of his mansion, then got away clean.

"He's one of those curious men who can sense when a Reaper's in the neighborhood," the professor explained. Valentine felt a prickle of recognition. Affinity, perhaps.

"Mr. Adler" never put on a uniform, but just directed to target after target. Success swelled their ranks, a Lifeweaver arrived to assist, and soon they were picking off isolated Kurian Towers.

"Same Lifeweaver still with th—us?" Valentine asked.

"Oh yes," the professor said. "He's an odd one, but he can make Bears, sure enough."

Then the "clearing" operations started—"Action Groups" of Bears who hit the Kurian Zone and caused so much damage their targets were unproductive for months or years to come.

"Hard on the poor SOBs under the Kurians. But that's the strength of the constrictor."

The "constrictor," as the professor explained it, was a steadily tightening ring around the Seattle area, denying resources to what had been one of the largest and best-organized Kurian Zones in North America. Now the Seattle KZ was a shadow of its former self, and the awful Chief Kurian at his refuge in the tower that dwarfed even the Space Needle was increasingly isolated. Thanks to the quick-moving and hard-hitting Action Groups, he'd been bereft of several of his key subordinate lords.

"They give up and relocate, if they get a chance. Mr. Adler's got a good sense for when one's getting set to bug out, that's for sure. He nudges them right along."

Valentine got his own room with a private toilet and shower, and eventually learned his way to the cafeteria, gymnasium, laundry, and underground range.

The Bears were a big, bluff collection. Canadians and Native Americans added their own accents and mannerisms. Several had tattoos that read DOER on their upper arms, sometimes pierced by a dripping dagger. They felt more a military machine than the atavistic Bears of Southern Command, but maybe it was because there were so many of them grouped together. They were proud of their position.

"Never thought I'd make it," one told him as they sat and sweated in the gym's wood-walled sauna. "First time out, I thought my heart would burst. But I'm used to it now."

"What have you been up against?" Valentine asked.

"Mostly Seattle Guard types. They run away when an Action Column roars into town. They've seeded the waters with some Grogs—you got to watch it around rivers and so on."

"Big mouths?" Valentine asked. He'd run into them in Chicago.

"We call them Sleekees. That's the noise they make when they're hopping around on land. *Slee-kee, slee-kee,*" he wheezed in imitation.

"What about the Reapers?"

"Not so much. Sure, they'll defend a tower or a hole, if their master's inside. I've heard it's bad going up against a bunker full of those dropedcocks, but Adler's all about Jew-Ginsu. Hit them where they ain't."

Valentine's gyro arrived and after some technicians partially took it apart to learn the design, he started doing practice flights over the backcountry. An overzealous Resistance machine gunner tried to take him down— Valentine dived behind the tree line to avoid the tracers and came home with brush in his landing gear, but refueling gave him a chance to catch up with Gide.

The militia just got issued green caps with yellow safety tape at the back, and the rest of her uniform consisted of a big green field jacket, construction trousers, and some sad-looking sneakers made out of tire tread.

"Someone swiped my boots," she said. "The women have a hell of a time with the footwear. The rifle's a joke. Worn-down barrel."

"Do your duty."

"I do," she said. "Your friends from the Holes have an interesting definition of duty, byways."

"Meaning?"

She shoved her hands in her pockets. "Taking it down pipes or up the chute for the team. It'd be one thing if we were in a bar in town, but I'm just trying to do my job."

Valentine didn't like the sound of that. He'd been in too many Kurian Zones where the soldiers exerted certain "prerogatives."

"Let's go into town. I'll buy you a beer." "Town" was a little row of saloons, a café, and two theaters, one that showed movies on an old presentation projector, and the other with little rooms playing pornography.

"Duty tonight."

"Breakfast at the Coffee Grinder, then."

"Sure. I should tell you, though, I'm asking for a transfer to one of the ranch towns. Being a pump jockey isn't my thing. And I don't like those guys from the Holes. They remind me of the Circus flyboys."

Tuesday nights there were political and social lectures about the miserable lives of those in the Kurian Zone. Valentine hadn't seen anything of the Seattle area, but it must be a hellhole in comparison with some of the most wretched corners of the Caribbean, so black did they paint the picture.

"Their only relief is death," Thunderbird boomed, backing up the mousy little refugee who gave that week's lecture. Foot-high letters painted on the wall under the ceiling read, *Are you a SHIRKER or a DOER?* "We'll pick this up in the conference room in fifteen for those who want to know more. Card tournament tonight, grand prize is a four-day weekend at the next quarter-moon party at the Outlook."

"What's the Outlook?" Valentine asked Thunderbird as the Bears rearranged their folding chairs to make room for the poker tables.

"That's a big resort in the mountains. Beautiful area. Sort of a retreat and conference center for the Free Territory. Sometimes we even get visits from the Old Feds at Mount Omega."

"I thought that was a myth," Valentine said, though he knew differently. The last refuge of the old United States government was part El Dorado, part Camelot, in Freehold urban legendry.

"No, it's real enough. Going there's a bit of a letdown, though. It's not as impressive as it sounds."

The poker tournament got going, a fairly basic game of five-card draw with jokers wild. Each player started out with small stakes, a hundred dollars in chips, and when he accumulated five hundred dollars he could move to the five-hundred-dollar table.

The "grand prize" table required a three-thousand-dollar buy-in. The laurels would go to whoever managed to reach the ten-thousand-dollar mark.

Valentine was lucky—first in betting and then in card strength—for his first two hands and shifted to the five-hundred-dollar table. Other men who'd abandoned the tables made sandwiches and passed out low-grade beer, apple ciders, and "Norridge Cross," a wine from some pocket in the Cascades. Valentine stuck to coffee.

The men at the five-hundred-dollar table were serious players, and Valentine languished there until after midnight, until he got a feel for their respiratory tells. Using the hearing he'd acquired as a Wolf gave him an unfair advantage, he supposed, but a card table knew no law but Hoyle.

He was the last of six seats to join the championship three-thousand-dollar table.

His luck returned the first two hands, thanks to three kings and then a dealt flush. After that promising start, he began to fight a long, slow, losing battle against a Bear named Rafferty, who called him on a bluff. Rafferty's black ringlet hair, long as a pirate's, brushed the felt-covered championship table as he gathered the lost chips.

Thunderbird checked in occasionally to offer a joke and console the losers, and then returned to the bull session in the corner of the conference room.

With a full house Valentine assayed forth, and Rafferty folded. Valentine played the next hand cautiously, and eked out a win with three of a kind, causing two others to drop out. Another Bear demolished all of them the next hand, and then retired to bed, yawning, as a winner in his own mind but unwilling to hang in for the grand prize.

The Bears ate, drank, played, ate, and drank some more. Bear metabolisms could tear through six thousand calories or so a day and still feel underfed.

Card playing provides its own kind of late-night tension, and Valentine gave in to it as the advantage shifted between him and Rafferty, both built up enough so that they could not hurt each other. The other two at the table just played along out of interest.

Valentine drew into a straight, judged Rafferty doubtful, gulped down the last of his second glass of wine, and went all in. Rafferty laid down four of a kind, plus a joker.

"Good night, David," Rafferty said, gathering the chips and draining a tankard of beer. "I'll give your regards to the Outlook." He whipped a thong off his wrist and gathered up his hair, then did the same with his chips.

"I don't know anyone there who can accept them."

Rafferty cocked his head. "Never been?"

"No."

"Oh hell, well, take the prize," he laughed. "You hear that, Thunderbucket? I'm offering up my poor winnings to our newcomer."

"Don't you always get thrown out after half an hour anyway, Riffraff?" Thunderbird called back. "But duly noted."

"Give me a ride in your whirlybird sometime, eh?" Rafferty said.

"Gladly," Valentine replied. "Interested in flight?"

"No. I want to take a crap over downtown Seattle from a whizzing great height."

"Spoken like a patriot," one of the losing Bears commented.

Valentine, with a routine established, felt the days fly by while tension mounted at the warren. Late one afternoon he watched an Action Group set out at the next full moon. Various hidden, revetment-shielded doors opened and belched men and machinery from the depths of the caverns. Armored cars led a long line of pickup trucks towing oversized horse trailers behind, followed by a few military trucks hauling light artillery.

Valentine watched, leaning on the empty mount of a machine-gun nest high on the ridgeline. He'd volunteered to go, but Thunderbird had declined. "It'll be a tough one. We want to start you out on something easier. Besides, I'm setting up something for you and your whirlybird."

So he had to watch.

"Make the poor dumb bastards die for their country!" a legless Bear who manned a communications relay shouted as they passed. His voice boomed over the sound of the engines.

A long arm and hand reached out from the cave mouth and patted him on the back. Long, scraggly hair dripped from it like Spanish moss.

A captive? The Lifeweaver?

Valentine hopped down the shaft leading up to the machine-gun nest, ignoring the iron rungs, and hurried down to the "Gathering Deck," as the extensive level at the valley floor was called. He took a wrong turn, and had to retrace his steps, and arrived at the right cave mouth only as the legless Bear wheeled himself back into the communication center at the cave mouth.

"Excuse me." Valentine fumbled the man's name. He turned and read the man's name tag. "Pop-Tart?"

"Yeeeees?" he said, holding a headset to his ear.

"I was above and saw someone pat you on the shoulder. Funny-looking arm."

"That's the old hairy-ass himself. Came up to see the guys off."

"I've just never met him."

"How'd you rate that uniform?"

"Import from Southern Command."

He put down the headset and looked at the gauges on the master radio relay. "Hairy-ass is the only one we got left. Our others disappeared after the big raid up Interstate Pass in 'sixty-one, where I earned these wheels. He lurks under a blanket of Bears ever since."

One Lifeweaver left. And from the sound of it, even he's not all there.

"Still like to meet him."

"Talk it over with T-bird when he gets back," Pop-Tart advised.

"Hey, Pops," an assistant called from the radio.

" 'Scuse me," Pop-Tart said.

Valentine went down to the reading room to await the Action Group's return.

They came back, almost unscarred. They'd lost one Bear to a booby trap, and another to "overexertion" (Valentine had once heard a story in Arkansas about a Bear dropping dead as he and his teammates worked themselves into a battle frenzy over a Bearfire) and still more suffered wounds and contusions Bear metabolisms would soon overcome. Valentine watched them eat before they even cleaned up.

They were a strangely taciturn bunch. Maybe it was the gloomy climate. A group of Southern Command Bears back from action chattered like magpies, though the conversation usually limited itself to light subjects, like unusual vehicles they'd seen or how much quality toilet paper they'd managed to loot.

Thunderbird, looking drawn, walked among them, passing out candy bars and bags of greasy peanuts.

"New-moon party this weekend," Thunderbird said.

He had a fresh uniform on, but Valentine saw dried blood on his boots. "Have they issued you a dress uniform yet?"

"No."

"I'll make a call."

"What's a PB?" Valentine asked. He'd heard the acronym tossed around as the soldiers talked.

"Punishment Battalion or Brigade. We've got a Brigade, unfortunately. Two combat battalions and a short support."

"What, hard labor, that sort of thing?"

"More like Reaper fodder. They're our first line, out in pickets about three klicks west. Their commander's not a bad sort—they've really shaped up under him. They're criminals. There's some shady types in these mountains, preying on both sides. If they don't like the feel of the noose, they can opt to PB their term. Of course a lot try to desert as soon as they get their bearings. They get shot, of course."

"How did the fighting go?"

"Well. Adler was right, as usual. We caught them pulling back. Got a fair bit of booty—they dropped everything and ran when we showed up."

"I've never seen Bears operate in those numbers before. They're usually used at platoon strength at most where I come from. Accidents."

"They divide up pretty quick when we go into action, cuts down on the chances of two teams attacking each other. We're careful about getting them revved up and pushed into the redline. You'll see. Have a good hurrah up at the Outlook."

"I'd like to bring Gide. She could use a little cheering up."

"You're loyal. I like that. I'll authorize her transport, but she'll have to clear it with her militia duty."

Gide cleared it easily enough. Perhaps Thunderbird made an extra call or two. In any case, they hopped on a horse-wagon train bringing captured scrap for salvage or to be melted down and recast. It was bottom-of-the-barrel stuff, mostly cookware and gardening supplies for civilian use. Hardly worth hauling away.

"How's the transfer coming?" Valentine asked. The dress uniform hadn't shown up after all, so he cleaned and pressed his daily as best as he could.

Gide wore a summer-weight sweater and skirt. "Denied. They want me to spend at least a year," Gide said. "I think it might move along if I fucked old D. B., the militia chaplain. He can arrange about anything."

"Some chaplain," Valentine said.

"Back in Arizona I would have dropped my drawers in a heartbeat. But I don't want it to work that way here."

"Think you made a mistake?"

She rubbed the bottom of her nose. "Shit no. Free air, you know?"

"That's a good way to put it."

"I don't feel like I'm being watched all the time, except maybe through the peepholes in the showers. There's a rumor going around that I've got something exotic tattooed around the ol' chute, and everyone's trying to verify. Just fucked luck. I'll do my year. There's another girl there who isn't too bad—it's better if you've got someone to talk to."

Valentine nodded. She understood, and patted his hand. He squeezed in return.

The Outlook was beautiful under its sickle moon.

It hung out next to, and partly over, a waterfall. Two long blocks of rooms, two stories tall and covered with balconies, looking out over the spill. At the center a great A-framed prow of glass and rough-hewn timber arched like an eagle's head.

The carpeted inside was hunting lodge overlain on luxury hotel. Clean as an operating room, it even smelled like evergreens within. A small army of staff in jet black with immaculate white aprons scuttled around at the edges of the rooms and corridors.

A clerk in a neat, gold-buttoned black shirt and pants admitted them, verifying their presence on an old computer. Valentine tried not to stare. He couldn't imagine Southern Command wasting a functioning computer on a hotel. But then he hadn't spent much time in the higher-class social circles.

The clerk issued them alligator-clip name tags, with first names and designations. Gide's had her name in large letters and VOLUNTEER MILITIA in smaller type below. Valentine's read DAVID/DELTA GROUP.

He tried to decline having a porter carry their small bags, but when the clerk said, "It's his job, sir—he needs it," he relented.

Luckily the scrip he'd won on poker night was accepted at the Outlook. He overtipped the porter as the bags hit the floor of their room.

"King-sized," Gide commented with a smile.

Old beaver traps decorated the walls, and the lights were made to simulate ironmongery holding candlesticks. The candlesticks were topped with small but ordinary-looking bulbs. A painting of a farmhouse surrounded by wildflowers adorned the wall above the dresser; a nude of a strategically disrobed seated woman drinking hot coffee, looking out her window at ice and snow, hung next to the bed by the window. Another sleeping nude hung above the bed.

If it was a brothel, it was the plushest one he'd ever been in.

Valentine checked the view. The waterfall was obscured by a deck from their room, but he had a good view of the river running west. He tried to guess how high it went in the opening minicanyon below the falls in the spring flood, but even with Cat eyes it was hard to judge.

"Cocktails, dinner, dance party," Gide said, reading a schedule on the desk. "Looks like we missed cocktails and part of dinner. Tomorrow: breakfast, exercise, lecture on the glory of heroism, games, cocktails, dinner, party. Sunday: services, brunch, departure."

Valentine despaired at a grease stain on his uniform. He must have brushed against a greasy pot in the wagon. "Let's get cleaned up and eat."

There were two galleries showing movies on the biggest televisions Valentine had ever seen, colors impossibly bold and bright in the dimly lit rooms. A small casino added that special thick, nervous air unique to gambling dens, and some kind of art exhibition was going on in one of the lobbies, well-crafted patriotic pieces that Valentine liked better than the four-color slogan posters of Southern Command.

Attractively dressed women lounged in the bars and in front of a gallery autopiano, ready to talk or dance or be taken back to a room. Valentine watched one military-haircut man in civilian clothes head for the rooms, his hand resting lightly on his companion's buttock. Valentine examined her eyes as they passed. She'd popped or smoked something to get up for the evening.

Valentine suppressed a shudder. He kept expecting the maître d' from the Blue Dome to appear at his elbow.

Gide, now dressed in a borrowed little black dress and heels, eyeliner running up the backs of her legs to simulate stocking seams, tracked down a late-night buffet and they ate.

"I poked my head in the gift shop while you were looking at the pictures," she said. "Nice booze. Perfumes even."

"Bonded whiskey, but they can't get you a decent set of boots."

"Speaking of which, there's a shoe store on the gallery. If you'll loan me thirty bucks, I can sign for the rest. I have to hurry—they close in ten minutes."

Valentine gave her the cash.

He went out on the balcony and enjoyed the summer night, watched the roar of the fountain. He fell into a conversation with another falls gazer, an artist in an ill-fitting sport coat and trousers.

"My piece is called *Hope and Glory*," he said. "I won a new-moon party here with it."

Valentine quietly raked his memory. "The two rising—what are they, angels?"

He seemed pleased that Valentine had remembered. He started talking about the difficulty of getting good paints, when he looked up. "That's Adler. He gave a quick talk at the reception for the artists."

Valentine looked up at the peak of the A-frame. There was a small balcony, hanging over their own, and muted light glowed within. A man stood looking over the edge, his face in shadow thanks to the backlighting. He turned and leaned and Valentine got a better view.

Valentine liked the look of him. Tanned—maybe the altitude of the Outlook helped—and lean but not gaunt, with gray white hair that set off the tan, a father figure in the twilight of middle age stood looking at the western horizon beyond the foothills of the Cascades. He held a lit cigar in his hand.

Late-night diners trickled out of the dining room and joined in the waterfall watching. Gide returned, wearing low black-heeled shoes and real stockings.

Adler set down his cigar on the railing. It rolled and he stopped it with a digit.

"Liquor holding out?" he called down to those below. He had a clear, fast speaking voice, like a radio news announcer.

A few men raised their glasses. A couple applauded.

"I'm here for the night air, not a speech. Enjoy." He lifted his finger and the cigar rolled off the balcony rail. A muttonchopped officer in a black dress uniform grabbed it as it fell.

By the time Muttonchops was showing his trophy to his escort, a blonde who had the body of a seventeen-year-old and the eyes of thirty-five, Adler had vanished indoors.

"He's shy," the artist said. "I like that."

Valentine looked out into the clear night, wondering what the shy military genius had been looking for to the west. Sulfur-colored light painted the distant clouds above Seattle.

"I thought you were going to buy boots," Valentine said as they returned to their room. The bed had been turned down, and the room carried a floral, elegant fragrance.

"I did," she said, pointing to a box. "Socks too, lots of them. Great quality. I picked up a few pairs for Julia. She loaned me this dress I'm not really fitting."

"Who's Julia?" Valentine asked.

"My roomie. She takes a little getting used to—she was born a slave to some Grogs in Oregon. They caught her poking around in a larder and chopped off her nose with a set of tin snips. Though she's always joking about it ... really a lolly person once you get to know her. When she goes out, she wears this silk veil and calls herself 'the Phantom.' The guy gave me a great deal on the shoes, because they were used. You can hardly tell."

Valentine looked at the label in the bottom, something in Italian, as he took off his tunic. It added to the air of fantasy in the lodge.

"Mmmmm, they spritzed the sheets with lavender water," Gide said.

"It's supposed to relax you," Valentine said.

"They had tabs of Horny in the gift shop, can you fuckin' believe it? KZ aphrodisiacs? Here?" She let her two-tone hair fall, though the roots were now coming in an even walnut brown, and flopped back on the bed, her hair spread out like a fan.

Valentine adored her for a moment. Her hard-bitten, tattooed beauty, her profanity, and the military acronym somehow complemented one another. But a moment was all he allowed himself. Much more and his self-control would go.

"I think I might take a walk before I shower," Valentine said.

"Going to buy some Horny?"

"You wish," Valentine said, and winked.

Her upper lip twitched rightward. "I'm not so sure anymore."

The cool, clear air took the lavender out of his nose and replaced it with the mountain smell of pine and cedar. Valentine walked out in front of the resort, where a winding road ended in a dark oil slick of the parking lot. In the distance the green light of the military checkpoint glowed. At one end of the lot by a couple of bright outdoor lights—insects flashed like shooting stars as they whizzed by—a drunken game of pickup basketball proceeded noisily. Valentine watched the players try to dribble with one hand and hold a beer with the other, then turned toward the river.

He caught a little music from the small dance club at one end of the Outlook, but even that was soon drowned out by the quick-flowing river, rushing out of the mountains in a white froth. Some kind of cable contraption hung over the waterfall downstream, a gondola basket providing both a crossing for the river and a unique way to view the spectacular falls. Valentine saw motion across the river, just a sentry out to have a look at him.

He returned to the patio.

Most of the parties had broken up. A few people still smoked, or chatted over hot drinks in the chilly air; Valentine had to remind himself it was June, as in the mountains it felt more like an Arkansas March.

Valentine couldn't shake the feeling that something bad loomed out there, watching the hotel. He turned over in his mind ways he might try to assault the place. There were sentries at the door, and Valentine suspected some kind of security reserve lurked in the basement, as he'd seen uniformed soldiers disappear into the doors marked SERVICE USE ONLY leading down.

Or was he just talking himself into a breakdown? *Not enough stress in this getaway, so you have to bring some along?*

Or are you scared of what's in that king-sized bed?

*   *   *

He undressed and got into bed quietly, the vast bed giving him a margin of error.

She rolled, faced him. "This is different," Gide murmured. "I'm glad you brought me."

"Nice to have a familiar face around," Valentine said.

She took a deep breath, closed her eyes. "Good to be just in bed with a man. Lavender and guy. Someone needs to bottle that."

"What did you mean when you said that you weren't so sure anymore?" Valentine asked, curiosity getting the better of him. Or maybe it was a game he was playing with himself, with her as the prize. Or the other way round.

She thought for a moment. "I used to just be able to . . . turn everything off and enjoy fucking. But I'm starting to know you better. There's a lot of stuff in there I think I like. That weird little smile you wear."

She touched the corner of his mouth.

What the hell.

He reached up, took her wrist, kissed her gently on the back of her hand, then turned it over and kissed the palm. He released it and she reached up to play with his hair.

"Shit, now I've done it," she said. She lunged across the bed as quickly as one of the snakes tattooed on her arms, kissed him.

The rest came in a frenzy of pent-up desire, effervescent as champagne and just as intoxicating.

Valentine woke with a start in the predawn.

Reapers!

He found he was sitting up listening in anxious silence. No . . . the strange cold place on his consciousness wasn't there, wasn't real; it was echoes of memory and nightmare.

"You okay?" Gide murmured.

"Cramp," Valentine lied.

"You're sweating."

"Yeah. I'll be right back."

He washed his face in the bathroom, still listening. Then he went out to the balcony, looked around at the darker-than-ever world under a pinkening sky. He heard someone sweeping on the balcony below, smelled fresh bread, the feminine musk of Gide on him.

He returned to bed and slept hard.

They spent the rest of the weekend mostly in the bedroom, trying something Valentine had never experienced before: room service.

Saturday passed in brilliant sun and wandering clouds, and they restored themselves from bouts of lovemaking with coffees and teas on the balcony, sitting on an old bench with one of the bed pillows cushioning their backs. Gide, like her father in his better days, was also a big reader and they poked through worn, yellow-paged books collected from the hotel's small library together. They dressed for dinner and later discovered a second night together more delectable than the first.

They hitched back west on Sunday, riding in the bed of a king-cab pickup carrying a trio of captains who reminded Valentine of one of the poker hands that brought him up.

Saying good-bye to Gide was hard. But like all such days pried from the routines of war, the brevity made the memories that much sweeter.

Four days later he saw his first action.

"Courier duty," they called it.

Valentine buzzed out over Seattle's waters in the dead night, low and slow as he dared. Any watching Reaper might mistake him at a distance for a fast-moving patrol boat.

They'd modified the exhaust of the PAAT to lower the noise and make its voice resemble the oversized motorcycle it was. Valentine sensed a slight loss of horsepower but it just meant he couldn't do much in the way of fancy climbing turns.

The entrance to Seattle's harbor now had two tall lights marking it, constructed from old radio masts. The north rose up from an island and the other was on the coast. Allegedly some poor bastards made the long climb to the top of each four times a day, keeping watch on the water approaches to the city.

He wondered if they'd mark him as a potential smuggler.

He kept well clear of the southern tower but used it as a waypoint. He picked up a little altitude over the southwestern peninsula, saw the three lights, one blue and two red, laid out in an equilateral triangle.

Two of the lights went out as he passed overhead, leaving only the blue. He banked the autogyro and made his approach.

Heart pounding, he set the craft down on the little field by the signal. He was on a grassy flat next to some manner of drainage canal. Foundations of cleared houses lay under a carpet of weeds, and young pines shielded him from a road. A man left two companions, one with a rifle, the other with a big sporting bow, and ran up to the craft.

Valentine popped the canopy.

"Stop," the man called, crouching.

"Light," Valentine responded.

The stranger hurried up, face concealed behind a scarf and a hat pulled down to his ears. Valentine reached around and took out the duffel bag. Whatever was inside didn't weigh much more than plastic. It rattled vaguely as he handed the sealed case over.

"There you go."

"Tell 'em not to worry, plenty of heroes on this side of the sound." He offered his hand.

They exchanged grips. "I'm sure there are."

He handed over a heavier case that probably contained radio equipment or explosives and the man hurried off.

Valentine checked his map again. His next waypoint was the old Sea-Tac Airport, but he was to keep well

south of it; they had searchlights that could blind him
and guns that could bring him down.

He shut the canopy and gunned the engine. As he
bounced away across the field, the men were already
picking up bicycles and hurrying to meet over the bag.
He marked a little flag and some piled-up dirt at one
end of the field, and rose in the air. A target on a post
flapped in the sea breeze.

They'd met him on a rifle range.

The flashes of gunfire looked like sparks from the air.
They left little ghosts on his retinas for a split second.

Valentine had never seen a battle from the air. The
sporadic gunfire seemed to be coming from spots along
a long, ragged line stretching over perhaps a mile and a
half of ground. They were fighting in what looked like
a residential zone, long lines of what he guessed to be
post-'22 housing—from what he'd heard, a good deal of
the southern areas of the city had suffered badly from
earthquake and volcano damage.

He passed over a street filled with bodies, tightly
packed, around a pair of buses. The Bears must have
caught reinforcements arriving in a deadly ambush to
have the corpses laid in windrows like that. . . .

No wonder the Seattle Guard didn't care to take on
an Action Group.

Valentine's orders were to check in at the Action
Group's field headquarters for the operation. He could
evacuate up to two wounded on the stretcher fittings
added onto either side of the PAAT. It would be a hard
load to fly, because carrying one meant carrying two, or
the unbalanced autogyro would crash on takeoff. He
hoped that if he had to carry two, they'd be of similar
weight, preferably both light.

The Action Group lit the road he was to land on with
headlights from the reserve Armed Truck force. Two
smaller dune-buggy-like craft, one with a recoilless rifle
and the other a heavy machine gun, crouched at the
intersection with the command Hummer pulled into a

half-collapsed brick storefront. An observer and a temporary aerial had a precarious perch at the steeple.

Remember to refuel if you've got wounded. Remember to refuel if you've got wounded.

Of course the high-octane gasoline they were supposed to be carrying with the medical inflammables was probably misplaced.

He puttered the autogyro up to the command vehicle. At the other side of the half-collapsed building, the white medical bus idled, the men sheltering in a doorway.

Valentine popped the canopy and got out, the sweat on the back of his uniform turning cold in the night.

He did see a wounded man, his arm dressed and in a sling, waiting by the command vehicle. Valentine wondered if they'd demand that he be flown out, just to test the system. From the other direction soldiers herded a group of civilians into a dark recreation center, judging from the basketball courts and running track outside. They kept them jogging, despite the age of some of the men, several of whom were gasping for air and supporting themselves on the runner in front.

A sudden burst of gunfire sounded in the distance.

Valentine extracted his carbine and approached the command vehicle. He was waved in by the man with the long night-sighted sniper rifle keeping watch on the road. He found Thunderbird there with some of his subofficers, talking intently to Rafferty with a noncom behind carrying two rifles. Rafferty had his helmet off, showing his ringlets bound up like a hairy handle sticking out of the back of his head.

Behind Thunderbird they'd set up an easel with a carefully drawn map. The radio reports were translated into visual form by putting red slashes over depictions of buildings. Some of the slashes had been turned into an *X*.

Two corporals relayed information over radio to the officers.

"Bravo block cleared, eighty-one."

"Bravo, eighty-one," a lieutenant said in a bit of a singsong, finishing an X on the easel.

The ruined building had once been a hair salon. The man with his arm in a sling tried leaning back and resting his head in a debris-filled washbasin.

"Scouts are reporting traffic on Five-One-Five southbound," one of the radiomen said in a loud but calm voice.

"Rafferty, we'll pick this up tomorrow," Thunderbird said. "You dumb bastard. I told you I'd court-martial you." He turned to the men at the radios, clicking his tongue in thought. "Sound recall to all teams. Delay red column if possible."

"Recall, repeat, recall," the men at the radios echoed.

"Tell the scouts to mine the roads and haul ass," Thunderbird added.

Valentine saw a camouflage-painted pickup truck roar up the road. Two soldiers in back sat in a sea of children. Baby carriers with squalling infants stood in a crash cage.

The sergeant marched Rafferty out. "Rape," the sergeant muttered to Valentine under his breath as he passed.

"Anything for me?" Valentine asked.

Thunderbird looked startled for a second. "Valentine. How was the drop?"

"Completed."

"No, we're good. You can get out of here."

A long rattle of gunfire from across the street dropped Valentine behind cover, but no bullets zipped the headquarters. Valentine saw the athletic building the civilians had been run into alight with the reflection of gun flashes.

The hell? Were they ambushed?

The men at the vehicles guarding the headquarters didn't so much as change the covered arc of their weapons.

"Gamma-Gamma, forty-four," one of the men at the radios said.

"Gamma-Gamma, forty-four," the singsong lieutenant repeated, drawing a big *X* on the map. Valentine blinked.

He'd just put an *X* through the athletic building. Yes, three concrete apartments around it in a U. *Jesus Christ!*

"What kind of op is this?" Valentine asked, knowing, not wanting to know.

"We're clearing this housing complex," Thunderbird said. "Dee Oh Ee Ar."

Valentine heard isolated shots as the executioners in the athletic building finished off the wounded.

"Team Kostwald is loaded and leaving," one of the radiomen said, and an officer made a note on a clipboard.

"Of what?" Valentine asked.

"Destruction of enemy resources," Thunderbird said. "Can't stand to actually see a DOER?"

Enemy resources. "Enemy resour—you mean the population?"

"Without a population to feed on, the Kurians pull out," one of the lieutenants said.

Valentine looked at the *X*s on the map.

"No objections, I hope," Thunderbird said. His subordinate officers tensed, and Valentine saw the man with the busted arm shift his rifle around.

"Objections? Hell yes! For starters—"

Tok tok tok. "Hop off that high horse, *Valentine.* Clearing operations work. Your old man invented 'em, after all."

CHAPTER NINE

―――― φ ――――

*T*he Lifeweavers: *Discussions of the Lifeweavers easily grow heated, especially since they rarely present themselves to conduct their defense.*

The schools of thought—or bull-session opinion—on the Lifeweavers fall into four groups, often blended and shaded into one another at the edges like paints on an artist's palette.

The mystics see the Lifeweavers as divine intervention on humanity's side, or evidence that whenever evil arises, karma will marshal good to the side of the righteous so that the universe might be kept in balance. Thus the Lifeweavers should be considered reverently, and their actions as a form of religious truth. When skeptics point out that raining holy destruction down on the Kurian Towers Sodom-and-Gomorrah-style would save a good deal of effort all around, the conversation usually shifts over to pure religion.

The utilitarians aren't interested in the motivations of the Lifeweavers, only their efficacy in aid of the struggle against Kur. Their opinion of the extraterrestrials rises and falls along with humanity's fortunes in war. They'd prefer a little less anxiety over how the Lifeweavers are using the naked ape, and a little more thought put into how mankind can make better use of the Lifeweavers. Another set of utilitarians calls for some kind of planetwide exodus (along the lines of the improbable story Valentine heard while passing over Utah) where the

Lifeweavers guide mankind to another world that might be made impregnable against the Kurians.

The diplomatists wish to see the Lifeweavers exert themselves less in resisting the Kurians and more in arriving at a solution that would end the fratricide among both species. Visions of some sort of worldwide strike, where mankind nonviolently refuses to aid either side until they solve their differences or take their war elsewhere, make for an attractive flight of Pegasus-winged pigs. But even among the diplomatists, arguments break out when specifics for a peaceful solution are brought up.

The conspiracists come in almost as many flavors as the mystics. Many maintain that the Kurians and Lifeweavers, being of the same species, are simply playing an elaborate game of good cop/bad cop with humanity, to better control them for their own nefarious ends. Others see the Lifeweavers as basically good, but using humans as cannon fodder to fight an ancient war that spilled over onto Earth, to mankind's misfortune.

In Valentine's opinion, the Lifeweaver lurking in the depths of the rabbit warren offered strong evidence that excluded two of the above schools of thought.

Valentine hadn't slept since he set off on his courier flight. *Thirty-six, no, forty hours now,* he corrected himself.

Someone knocked on his door. "Yeah?"

Thunderbird's voice through the steel: "You wanted your interview, you got it."

Valentine wondered if he should shave. No, the sooner the better. Shaving wouldn't make a difference one way or the other. He opened the door.

Thunderbird stood there with two of his bigger Bears.

The enmity that had sprung up between himself and Thunderbird had turned into a wary truce back in the warren. As there was nothing Valentine could do on a battlefield—or a multiblock killing floor, in his mind—

without getting arrested at the very least, he'd followed orders and flown back to Grizzly Ridge. He took the precaution of landing at the fuel depot to refuel, found Gide, and had her guide him up into the hills above the motor pool to a vacant house with an even more vacant garage. She sensed that there was something wrong and asked him about it, but Valentine didn't want to explain, couldn't without following the cowardly urge to flee the Cascades entirely.

But flight wouldn't save any lives but their own.

He trotted back to Grizzly Ridge, explained that his engine was misfiring and being maintained back at the motor service yard. He had written up both a request to see the Lifeweaver and a letter of resignation from Delta Group by the time the column returned. He waited outside Thunderbird's office and told him that unless the request was immediately granted, the resignation would follow.

In all probability he'd resign anyway, but Valentine didn't add that. He needed the interview.

That rated six clucks of Thunderbird's tongue, then an order to return to his quarters and get cleaned up.

Thunderbird walked him to one of the big, gurney-sized two-door elevators that served the medical center. Shielding the control panel with his body, the colonel pressed buttons using both hands.

"I think we got off on the wrong foot," Thunderbird said as the elevator dropped. "I figured you knew about your old man's solution."

Valentine didn't want to ask the question on his mind, and luckily the elevator stopped, and he had a brief reprieve as they met two more Bears at a duty desk in a rough-hewn, unpainted tunnel. Under bare bulbs projecting from boxes linked by a conduit, Thunderbird handed over an order sheet and he and Valentine turned in their IDs. Thunderbird checked his sidearm and they submitted to a pat down and being wanded by a metal detector as one of the Bears spoke into a phone.

A woman in a medical uniform appeared. "He'll see them," she told the Bear at the duty desk.

"Pass nine-nine," the Bear shouted down the hallway.

"Pass nine-nine," a voice shouted back.

The big Bears sat down opposite the duty desk to wait. Thunderbird and Valentine walked down the darkening corridor, following the woman in white, the bulbs becoming less frequent and finally giving out. Valentine spotted an old hunk of armored vehicle crammed into a turn in the tunnel, a turreted gun that looked like a 30mm cannon covering the tunnel back toward the duty desk. Two layers of thick metal cage kept the Bears inside—Valentine guessed there were two, but it was hard to tell—at their station. Valentine saw a portable toilet between the layers of cage.

They turned the corner past the dug-in vehicle and came upon a set of bars worthy of a rhino cage, a small door in a heavy frame offering access to the other side. Valentine heard dripping. The medical officer fought down a yawn, took a key looped around her neck, and put it in a lock at the half door.

They crouched to pass through.

There was another turn ahead, and Valentine felt the space and light around the corner through the transmitted drippings.

"I want to see him alone," Valentine said.

"Don't try anything funny. If the medical staff calls, I'll come in and put an end to you."

"Maybe," Valentine said.

The medical officer looked to Thunderbird, who nodded. "Take him in," he said.

She looked Valentine up and down. "You look tired. Are you okay?"

"Fine."

"Don't be nervous—he's just a bit eccentric. Remember, he's not a human."

"I've met them before," Valentine said.

She took Valentine into a—grotto was the only word

Valentine could use for it. It was warm and humid. Banks of what he guessed were grow lights fed thick ferns, palmettos, rhododendrons, and other plants Valentine hadn't seen since he'd been in the tropics. Off to one side a pool, fed by a sheet of water coming down the wall that most people would call a leak rather than a falls, moved quietly, stirred by some unknown current. The banks of plant boxes and platforms made something of a maze, but the medical officer guided him past the pool and into the center of the plant life.

"What's his name?" Valentine asked.

She led him past a bank of purple flowers. Valentine heard a bee buzz. Something was wrong with that, but he couldn't remember what. "He said we couldn't pronounce it. We just call him 'Sir.' It's quick and easy.

"Don't let his appearance throw you off. Remember, it's just a show," she said, coming to a gauzy tent. She lifted a flap.

"David Valentine to see you, Sir," she said.

Valentine saw a hairy mass and several sheet-covered floor mats within.

"Enter, sojourner," a slightly lisping voice said.

Valentine went into the tent. Enough light from the intense bulbs penetrated the thick white gauze to make him feel as though he were inside some kind of cottony womb.

The creature within made a startling contrast to the whites and pale greens of the sheets covering the mats on the floor. The Lifeweaver looked like a half daemon, half satyr, right down to thick hairy legs hinged like a goat's. Overlong fingers and toes with nails that weren't quite claws displayed delicately painted, mysterious glyphs. Pointed of ear, flat-nosed and slant-eyed, it was barrel-chested but thin-hipped, covered with limp, stringy, dirty hair and the odd bubo about the neck and groin. Valentine couldn't say whether he was faced with a combination of legends or nightmares.

"Sit," it said, with an artful wave of the wrist and overlong fingers. Valentine was reminded of an exhibition he'd once seen after his return from Nebraska where a martial artist showed how to use a war fan. "Cross-legged is best, for your kind." Valentine sat.

It reclined on one of the mats, lounging. "Speak your mind, sojourner."

"Why do you look like that, Sir?"

The medical officer brought in a wide, water-filled bowl. A candle and some flower petals floated within. She set a small stainless steel cup in front of Valentine.

"Suits the profession. Suits of the profession. War, famine, disease, and death. All I've known, watching these thousands of years. It's all that's left of me. I stayed on, you see, though others left after the old battles of your ancestors' time. I stayed and watched, for I loved and admired you. But I'm afraid it's driven me a bit mad."

He smiled, showing brown and green teeth. "Valhalla awaits, if you have the courage and survive your ordeal," Sir said, reaching out with arms that thinned as they extended. Valentine felt the greasy touch of its hands, the prick of its claws, as it cradled his head.

"You will be death, destroyer of worlds," Sir whispered in his ear, despite the fact that his head remained on the other side of the tent.

Valentine broke away from Sir's grasp. "Wait. I think there's a mistake. I'm not here to become a Bear."

The arms pulled back. "Not a Bear?"

"No, I need your help. I'm from Southern Command," Valentine said hurriedly, wondering just how much of this the nurse was hearing.

"A Wolf once, now a Cat, and more in your blood besides," Sir said.

Valentine didn't bother to ask for hows and whys. "They need the help of the *Dau'weem*."

"I never accepted that title. We were right, not backward," Sir said. The shape blurred and returned. "Southern Command, where is that again? Argentina?"

"The Ozarks, Texas, parts of Oklahoma now—"

"Mississippi River, oh yes, of course. Louisiana

Purchase and all that. One of your better specimens, Jefferson, though I've only known him secondhand. I met Washington once. A good man and true. You're not fighting with the Britons again, are you? You've got to settle these squabbles yourselves or you'll never get anywhere as a people. All Rome's fault, of course—if they'd only stayed the course and not become addicted to slavery. It's like an opiate."

Valentine wondered how to drag Sir's mind back out of lost millennia.

"We need your help. I have to get in touch with the other Lifeweavers."

"That can be dangerous," Sir said. "Very dangerous indeed. I can't take that step without revealing myself in the process. Never mind the danger to you."

"I know it's a lot to ask," Valentine said.

"Do you ask?"

"Yes."

"No matter the consequences, the possible harm?"

"I would think that would be your decision. But it's important."

"Not my forte. Not my forte at all. But I'll try."

"Thank you."

Sir slipped out one side of the tent.

Valentine wondered if an all-out assault on Grizzly Ridge would be entirely a bad thing. The medical officer poked her head in. "You got him all stirred up."

"I hope that's all right," Valentine said, wondering if Thunderbird would bust in and start beating him to death with a shovel.

"He needs the activity. He lies around too much, not that we really know what's healthy for his kind. How do you feel? Hot yet? You should have another—"

"I'm fine," Valentine said. "Wait, I think there's been a mistake. I didn't come here for an Invocation."

She blinked. "No?" She knelt and looked in each of his ears, folding his lobes back to peer behind. "That's a relief. But that's all he really does for us. Just a moment." She disappeared.

"Success," Sir said, returning to the tent. He held a small, slightly curled rubber-tree leaf in his hand. Valentine saw a small green stone on the strange presentation leaf. "Took some time to find the right one. Ready?"

"For what?" Valentine said, warily.

"To speak to our kind. You needed to communicate with us, yes?"

"Yes," Valentine said.

"This will do the trick." He passed the leaf to Valentine, waddled around behind, and put his hands on Valentine's shoulders. The hands turned into tentacles, soft grasping veined leaves at the ends. "Just touch it with your fingertips."

Valentine looked at the shard of jade. Some kind of hieroglyph of a bird was carved on the side. "I'm ready, if your ka is," Sir said. "It's quite painless."

Valentine reached down and touched it.

It felt like ordinary jade, cool and smooth.

A roar, hundreds of voices in his head, the static noise of an excited crowd. It overwhelmed him, incendiary butterflies opened their full-spectrum wings in his mind, and he spun around, looking for a way out, but the voices—

He opened his eyes, found he was lying on one of the mats. The medical officer hovered anxiously, Thunderbird behind.

Sir looked at him, eyes narrow and calculating.

"Are you still with us, David Valentine?"

Valentine felt as though he were in another time and space. "I think so. What does that thing do again?"

"It's a touchstone. It opened up your mind."

"Nothing made sense," Valentine said.

"It takes a great mind to comprehend a touchstone on contact. But everything you need to know is—"

The medical officer put a hand to his cheek. "He's hot. Sir, is he entering up as a Bear?"

"No, I simply opened the channels. He shouldn't have the biological resour—wait. . . . Design help us! I forgot. Oh me! Oh me! Your father was a Bear, I believe."

"I think so."

Sir licked his lips with a pustule-coated tongue. "You may have had the talent passed down to you."

The medical officer looked at Thunderbird. "We'd better isolate."

Thunderbird nodded, hurried off out of the grotto. Valentine heard a plant crash to the floor.

"Oh, and he needs calm now more than anything. Oh me, oh me, I've been a fool. Careless! I expect he'll go mad. They said I was useless and they've been proven right again."

"Tell Thunderbird," Valentine said, feeling like he was floating away on a river. "Danger. Sir, you revealed yourself. Don't forget."

"We'll take care of it," the medical officer said. "What's that about?"

"He's confused," Sir said. "He must have thought . . . I had to take my true shape to guide him to the right part of the touchstone, make sure it didn't rush in all at once. I meant the danger was to him, not to me. Oh, this has been bunkum and confusion from the first."

"I'm going to sedate him," the medical officer said. She yanked a big white case from within a stand of ferns and opened it. The needle squirted something on Valentine as she positioned it above his arm. "I doubt it'll last—," Sir said.

"Long enough for him to get on the gurney."

Valentine, disoriented, half-awake, and anxious, didn't even feel the needle going in. . . .

"Don't let him get up. Don't let him up," someone was shouting. A weight pressed on his chest. Valentine saw lightbulbs passing above, one after the other, each leaving a snail trail glowing on his retinas. His heart began to hammer.

Something was in his mouth, he bit down, it snapped, a tooth gave way.

And then a convulsion. Even though he felt that he was lying on his back, someone still managed to clobber him across the small of his back with what felt like a baseball bat. His arms and legs forgot how they worked. He smelled eucalyptus.

"Zap him again!" a voice shouted.

The gurney's wheels chattered as they passed over the uneven surface below. Valentine felt calm and collected, even as his body jumped under another jolt. The world faded away, but whispered to him that it would be back, new and improved.

Madness, fighting in vain against tentacles, bludgeons, ropes, the world had turned crimson and black, shadows surrounded him, baying like a wolf pack. But above and behind it was singing, the most perfect singing he'd ever heard, an angelic choir majestic.

He sang along as he fought until he sagged in exhaustion.

He awoke to find himself in a dark room, his arms bound around his own waist as though he were mummified. No, straitjacket, it was a straitjacket, made out of thick leather. His legs were swathed in some kind of padding and buckled down flat. He sensed he was lying face-up, somewhere underground, but beyond that, he could tell nothing, except that he felt dirty all over, particularly itching and filthy between his legs.

"Hello?" he croaked.

Thirsty. So thirsty.

A presence at his side. He felt a plastic nozzle enter his mouth.

"Get ready to swallow, okay?" a voice said. Gide's, it was Gide.

He nodded, vaguely aware of tubes and wires connected to him. He suspected one of the wires could give him a jolt.

Water, just a tablespoon or two, went in his mouth, and he swallowed. So salty it tasted sweet. They repeated it. Twice.

"Good," the voice said. It wasn't Gide.

Valentine felt a gap in his teeth on the upper left

side. He probed with his tongue, felt a missing tooth, or rather the stump of one. The other felt good and cracked.

The next day—at least they told him it was the next day—he could sit. The tubes were gone, but he still had wires running the length of his body, individual ends attached to forehead, Adam's apple, chest, stomach—a couple more on his back. They hung off the bed and met at a black box.

He had the run of a two-person berth on the hospital floor. It was in the "security" wing—the doors were solid steel, hinged on the outside and closed with what sounded like a heavy bar reinforced by bolts dug into stone beneath the linoleum. The man in civilian clothes sitting opposite, under two painted panels masquerading as windows, didn't have many answers.

His name was Wholmes, and thanks to burned and reconstructed skin, he looked like he'd been freeze-dried and rehydrated. He spelled it as he said it, though Valentine could read it on his ID card.

"How do you feel?" Wholmes asked.

"Better," Valentine said. "I had eggs and oatmeal for breakfast."

"You're on soft foods until those teeth get taken care of. Tomorrow or the next day."

"Has anyone figured out what went wrong?"

"Nicely put?"

"Clearly put."

"You were a pig who wandered into a bacon factory in hopes of speaking with the management. But when a pig visits a bacon plant, there are obvious hazards. Sir doesn't direct or guide or advise this freehold. He's used strictly for creating Bears."

"Who are you, Mr. Wholmes?"

"I help new Bears with their adjustments to transhumanism. You're an interesting case, though, Valentine."

"Why's that?"

"Sir didn't do anything to you. Well, anything much.

To the Lifeweavers, the human body is like a big, locked-up factory with all the switches turned off. How we got that way—well, I'm not going into the various theories. I'll leave that to the philosophers."

Valentine felt a little jolt of recognition; Wholmes talked a little like the general who'd offered him a choice of death or the possibility of eternal life in service of the Kurians.

"Are you feeling all right?" Wholmes asked.

"Yes. Closed factory and all that."

"Now, throughout history a few individuals have managed to turn on bits of their factory on their own, transcending normal human limits, like some of the great athletes or, with mental discipline, astrophysicists and yogis and the odd musician and so on. Some combine the two; I'm told there were martial artists who could do the same sort of tricks you Cats can.

"Now, of course when the Lifeweavers go into the factory and turn on a couple of machines, sometimes it takes the mind a little while to catch up and learn to channel the new outputs. That's where I come in, and were you aware your crystal-spark-snorting mother sucked off drovers in station bars to get her fix?"

"When your old man wasn't beating her to it," Valentine said. "What's the deal?"

"That's the fascinating thing." Wholmes reached under Valentine's bed by the black box and tore off a piece of paper covered with squiggles. "A little stress peak when I questioned humanity's origins. A bigger one, a good deal bigger, when I insulted your mother. Another Bear, fresh from his Invocation, would have jumped out of the bed and started pounding me."

"I take it your job has a comprehensive benefits package."

Wholmes chuckled. "Like you, I'm a fast healer. Plus they learn an important lesson when they calm down, and it sticks, and they become more receptive to my training." He lifted an object that looked like a flashlight held backward, with two small silver prongs. "Besides, a quick jolt calms you down.

"But you, you've been controlling yourself and your reactions since childhood, I'm guessing. You've got straight pipes, so to speak, in the brain-body connection, but you've managed to install a muffler yourself. I wish we knew more of your early childhood."

"I remember fighting a lot with my sister."

"Did you ever hurt her?"

"I—I can't remember exactly. Just kid stuff. She'd start swinging—but since she was littler I had to take it. Mom was always separating us. She'd sing to calm us down." Memories returned vague yet powerful blasts, Mother's leonine bronze face as she held him down, blood on her upper arm. . . . "She'd sing to calm me down."

"Whoa there, Valentine, you're spiking again. And— it's gone. Remarkable. A ramp like that should lead to a redline, and you pull yourself back each time. Your father was—and there's another spike. Perhaps I should leave off your family for a bit."

"What about the—the touchstone?"

Wholmes tapped his thigh with a scar-covered hand. "We don't know."

"Does Sir?"

"Depends on the state of his mind when you speak to him. I understand at one time he was one of the Lifeweavers' leading lights on the study of humanity, followed our civilizations very closely. But he's old now, very old, and he's slipping."

"How did he end up here?"

"In the mess of 2022 he and a few other Lifeweavers revealed themselves to the government. They went to a 'secure area' at Mount Omega, but weren't of much practical help—meaning they couldn't deliver on the magic bullet everyone keeps thinking will get rid of the Kurians."

"There's stuff that helps. Like Quickwood."

"Somebody showed up with a couple seeds of that stuff. I've no idea where it's growing, big secret."

"So did the other Lifeweavers leave?"

"Seems like. I'm told they kept trying to pick up stakes and go elsewhere. They ended up breaking out somehow, oh, about the time I was born. All but Sir, and no one really knows what happened next. The other Lifeweavers had vanished. But I wonder. About the time they disappeared was when we first started hearing about this über-Kurian in Seattle. Some people say they defected."

"Defected?"

"I think it's bunk myself. Adler says he thinks they were captured, and the old King of the Tower used them to increase his power."

Valentine felt exhausted, but he forced a few more words out. "How does he do that?"

"We're still working on figuring out how Bears can grow a new lung back, but not a hand. Ever seen a grown-back Bear limb? Looks kinda like a flipper. Some of the guys have doctors tie the nub off so nothing weird grows back."

Valentine sagged back into his pillow.

"You need some food. I can tell. I'll get someone to bring you a tray."

He saw the dentist, a chattering type who covered all the discomfort with a steady stream of talk. He offered to cap his teeth with ground-down Reaper fangs, a popular option for Delta Group's Bears. One soldier, who had lost his upper lip and a good chunk of gum line, replaced all his uppers with Reaper fangs. Valentine declined.

Nights passed in weirdly vivid dreams, swirling mists that formed into wells and towers only to dissolve a moment later like a sand castle falling to a tide.

"Think I might get a little fresh air today?" he asked Wholmes, who was now dividing his time between Valentine and two fresh Bears in a cell next door. Valentine heard a good deal of screamed profanity, not quite as eloquent as that of the engineering crew on the old *Thunderbolt*, who had practically cursed in iambic pentameter as they overhauled an engine, but a good deal louder.

"It would do you good. Colonel Thunderbird will probably send a couple of men to keep an eye on you."

Valentine was interested to hear a rank used. In Delta Group ranks were for outsiders, rear-zone lurkers, or Pacific Command apparatchiks. Perhaps Wholmes didn't like Thunderbird.

When he went next door Valentine hopped out of bed, tried a few stretches and push-ups. His old leg wound gave him hardly a twinge, though usually a long spell in bed left it more sore than ever when he used it again.

But even that small amount of exercise left him ravenously hungry. He called for food and a nurse gave him a heaping plate of brown rice and dark beer, pushing it through a notch under the door.

He scraped his plate down to the last rice husk, listening to Wholmes encouraging the Bears to calm themselves by mantra. In this case, the old "Itsy-bitsy Spider" song every child picks up somehow or other. Hearing snarly voices talking about spiders traveling up and down waterspouts got him thinking. . . .

Wholmes must have given him an enthusiastic recommendation, because they released him the next day into the charge of a stiff-legged old Bear named Yarborough.

"Machine-gun bullets, both legs," Yarborough said, easing his way down the corridor with a cane carved from Reaper femur.

Yarborough took him up to the Bear cafeteria and watched Valentine consume a vast meal of potato-heavy stew. "Tired. Very tired," Valentine said, wiping up the plate with a heel of warm bread. He was only half paying attention to Yarborough; his mind was on the layout of the elevator, in particular the bumper at gurney level.

"You'll get used to it." Yarborough winced as he rose. "A little exercise helps. Want to throw some pins around?"

"Maybe a walk outside."

Yarborough looked doubtful. "I was nervous as a colt my first time out of doors. You might panic and try to take down a truck."

"I've got it under—"

"Boo!" Yarborough ejaculated, lunging with both hands across the trays.

Valentine found himself six inches backward, heart thudding away, and nonplussed.

"Um . . . grrrrr?" Valentine said back.

They both laughed. "I think Sir's slipping," Yarborough said. "Even a week after my Invocation, I would have been trying to open my head like an M-22 if I were you."

"Can I ask a question, Yarborough?"

"Fire away."

"What happens to the little kids?"

Yarborough's brow came down like a guillotine. "What do you mean?"

"I saw a truck full of little kids, too young for school, babies, pulling out after the last clearing operation. What happens to them?"

"They go to orphanages, poor souls. Some up to Canada, some out East or the other side of Rainier. You know Eagle, right? He came out of one of the orphanages, went in older than most even, ten, I think he said."

Valentine didn't know Eagle, but relaxed. He'd been worried they were used as Reaper bait. Or worse.

"How about that walk?"

"Sure."

The cafeteria was starting to fill up with the lunch crowd. Bears hurried to pile their trays with rice-flour bread and mulligan stew. Thunderbird and an adjutant came walking in as they approached the door.

"Valentine, a new man, I see," Thunderbird said.

"Tired as an old one," Valentine said. "But I'm going to try a walk aboveground, if that's okay."

Thunderbird clucked his tongue. "Sure. Be good for you. Stop by my office when you feel yourself again."

"How about tomorrow instead?" Valentine couldn't say whether he'd ever be himself again, after witnessing Pacific Command's Bears in action.

"Anytime. Door's always open, you'll remember."

Valentine took his walk on the flattened valley floor at the foot of the ridge. He tried balancing on one of the train rails that led to the big unloading station in the tunnellike terminal, though he'd never seen or heard a train come in. The breeze felt good on his face, but clouds screened the sun.

Yarborough watched him from the bench at the headquarters shuttle pickup.

Valentine took a short run about a third of the way up the hill, and Yarborough opened a box marked with the network-phone squiggle. Puffing a little, Valentine reached the halfway mark on the ridge and hurried back down.

His bad leg twinged, but stayed steady on even the steep slope of the warren. He ran to the train-cave mouth, saw a big wire gate inside, and ran back again.

"Good to get some air." Yarborough nodded in agreement.

An engine started up, and Valentine saw a flag-draped coffin inside a black horse-drawn station wagon pull out of one of the tunnels. A big plastic wreath was propped up in the empty, hoodless engine compartment, and the driver steered the horses through a missing windshield, but otherwise the wagon was black and polished right down to the tires, which gleamed and smelled like gun oil. The engine noise came from an honor guard riding behind, rows facing each other on benches in the back of an open pickup.

"One of the new Bears. Poor kid burst his heart,"

Yarborough said, standing up. "Doctors don't catch everything."

Valentine lined himself up next to Yarborough and followed form as he saluted as the station-wagon hearse passed. It was just about the first salute he'd seen since coming to the warren.

"They dye the horses black," Yarborough said after the escort passed, grinding along in bottom gear. "Don't see what difference the color of the horses makes, when you're standing before that Golden Throne getting judged."

"I'm worn through," Valentine said, sitting down.

"Keep drinking water. Lots of water helps," Yarborough advised. "Let's head down."

Yarborough dropped Valentine in his original room, told him that he looked healthy as a horse, then went doubtful as he remembered that the last horses they'd seen had been drawing a hearse.

"I'm going to sleep. If you're supposed to escort me to dinner, give me a break and knock softly," Valentine said.

Valentine hadn't been back since his appointment with Sir. He checked his weapons, which were all still there, along with his ammunition. Someone had picked up his rifle, and accidentally snapped shut both buckles on his pack rather than the one.

He took out his razor-edged boot knife and opened the seam on his mattress, tilted it up, and shook it. He felt around through the hole, came up with his coin belt. More to give himself something to do than out of guilt at the vandalism, he closed up the seam for the second time with needle and thread from his sewing kit. Then he turned out his lights and rested.

The soft knock woke him, but he didn't answer. Yarborough was right, though—he was thirsty. He drank, and whiled away the hours dozing on and off. In the bustle of sentry shift change at eleven p.m. he slipped out the door, gear crammed into an enormous Pacific Command duffel with his bedding peeking out at the top. He went down to the laundry, checked in with the attendant and got tokens for the machine, and put his sheets in. He wandered, grabbed a couple of pieces of fruit from an elegant porcelain bowl resting in the small library on the same floor as the laundry, and returned to put his sheets in the dryer.

Someone else would have to take them out of the dryer.

The attendant didn't notice him extract his duffel from between a couple of machines and exit again. He ducked into the library again and took off his boots.

He went to the elevator bank and was momentarily frustrated when he found it occupied by a couple of bored technicians carrying toolboxes. If they noticed his socks, they didn't say anything. He got off at his own floor and then idled, waited for another. This one was empty.

He punched the button for the second-to-the-top floor, climbed up to the rail, and hung on in the corner using his toes. He opened the service access on the roof, picking the lock with his hairpinlike jimmies, praying that the elevator wouldn't stop on its upward trip.

He tossed the duffel up through the gap and made it to the elevator roof. The rolling gears and cables pulled steadily, their companions to the counterweight on the other side vibrating.

Valentine didn't want the elevator to stop at the top floor; a bell sounded in the corridor whenever the elevator arrived to alert the sentries that someone was coming up.

He climbed to the next level easily enough; rungs were built into the shaft for workmen, firefighting, or a loss of power. Using his gun flashlight, he examined the top-level door, found the trip for the bell. He lifted the latch on the door at the top level, and just cracked the door so he could slip through.

Valentine tucked his stiletto into his sleeve and listened, checking down the corridor toward the machine-gun-post exit. A sentry sat at a junction of rough-hewn tunnels, reading a book.

Nothing to do but bluff. Valentine strode down the corridor. The sentry lowered his book.

"B aerial crapped out," Valentine said. "I'm checking the connection before making a big issue with service." Valentine didn't know if there was such a thing as a B aerial, but it was quite possible the sentry wouldn't either.

The sentry stood, didn't reach for his rifle, but put his hand on his pistol holster. "We need a—"

Valentine jumped, and drove the outer edge of his boot into the sentry's midsection. The breath left the sentry's lungs with a whoosh and Valentine put a foot on his wrist and a knee on his neck, bearing down hard. He dropped his knife out of his sleeve and poked the sentry hard under the chin.

"Last thing I want to do is hurt you, friend," Valentine said. "You make me open up your carotids, it's going to bother me for days."

"Mrfph," the sentry agreed.

Valentine relieved him of his pistol, was happy to see a pair of handcuffs on his belt and a Taser. "Stay flat on your face, spread-eagle. I just got invoked a couple days ago, and I'm twitchy as hell. What's your name?"

"Appleton."

Valentine gave Appleton careful instructions, and in three minutes he was handcuffed and stuck in the big duffel bag, with his bootlaces tied together and threaded through the grommets.

"I'm going to leave your rifle with the handcuff key near the exit. You can work your way out of this pretty easily, I should think."

The sentry was breathing a little steadier now, listening.

"I'm going to be looking around for a while from the exit. Any booby traps I need to know about?"

"No."

"While I'm looking around, if I hear you moving around, I'll come back and taze you.

"Way I see it, you've got two options, Appleton. You

can be a good soldier and work your way out of the bag and ring every alarm in the warren. Someone might ask why you didn't hear the elevator bell, how I caught you unprepared and got the drop on you."

"There are patrols outside," Appleton said. "They shoot on sight, you try going down the west side of the ridge."

"Don't worry about that. Your other option is to ditch the bag and play dumb. I hear alarms going off and they catch me, well, I'm just going to have to tell them I caught you jerking off with your belt around your ankles."

"I wasn't—"

"I know you weren't. But I'm a good liar. Think they'd send you to the Punishment Brigade for that?"

"Don't forget the alarm on the hatch. It's just a switch on the side of the battery," Appleton suggested.

"If I were you, I'd get out of the bag, inch my way down the hall, uncuff myself, and go back to my book. But, then, I'm a deserter."

Valentine remembered the alarm, gave Appleton a little bit of a poser by sliding the handcuff key down the rifle barrel, and cracked the hatch to the air-defense post.

A drizzle that fell like it was too tired to work up into actual rain slicked on his face and hair as he negotiated the warren's slopes, making off down the eastern side.

He marked no activity on the road-rail terminus— the warren might as well have been a graveyard—but that didn't mean eyes weren't watching from doors and sentry posts. Valentine made a long, elbow- and knee-battering crawl to the bottom of the slope. A garbage pit gaped fifty or sixty meters away; one of the more common punishments for minor infractions was a spell either digging new space for garbage or covering up whatever the scavengers—human, rodent, or insect—left.

A dog barked, freezing him, but it was a distant warning from the southwestern side of the ridge.

He rested and waited. Headlights glowed; then engine noise sounded from the road winding down from the western foothills. A motorbike leading a car approached the checkpoint, and Valentine took the opportunity to make a dash for the garbage pit. Half expecting a warning shot if not another bullet through the thigh, he was there by the time the vehicles reached the gate.

On the other side of the garbage pit the woods began. A fence ran through it, patrolled, but it was militia backed up by a few Bears. But the fence was little more than a polite warning, and the patrols were a training exercise, and Valentine had heard stories of paths to sneak out and go into town for a little fun. The tough part was getting out of the warren.

Valentine crept up on Gide's fueling station and motor pool, having gone over another fence. There were a couple of guards at the gate, but the rest of the buildings were locked up tight. Valentine rejoiced in his luck when he saw a woman Gide's size work a crank, pumping fuel from an underground reservoir into a fifty-gallon drum. Then she turned. The woman's profile was a straight horizontal line, flat as a building.

"Julia," he hissed from the shadows.

She stepped away from the pump and reached for her sidearm. "Who's there?"

"David. I'm a friend of Gide's."

"*The* David," she said, reaching for something at her throat. She pulled up a plastic nose and a surgical mask.

Valentine walked up and shook her hand. "You make me sound like a statue."

"Umm . . . sorry? Gide's not on duty until seven."

"Can you get her, please? It's really important."

"Ah, love," she said. "Where are you storing your white horse?"

"It's desert tan, and that's what I needed to see her about."

"Burb," she said, employing the local slang for "be

right back," and went off toward a long building that looked like two separate pre-'22 houses that had been enlarged toward each other until they joined.

She returned alone, as though from a trip to the bathroom. "Meet her in the tomato stands. Far end of the garden."

Valentine found her crouched in the tomato patch under an oversized umbrella. She'd brought a blanket and smelled like freshly applied scent.

"Lousy night for this, you know, it's damp. You could have given—," she said.

"Sorry, it's not that," Valentine said, squatting down beside her, hedged by ripening tomatoes. "I do mean sorry. Gide, I'm getting out of here."

"Huh?" She sat up.

"This place is poison."

"What, sodomy and the lash back in the Holes too? And you an officer and all."

"No. They're fighting . . . they're squeezing the Kurians in Seattle by getting rid of the population. And I mean getting rid of, not relocating."

"Cheezus. Poor bastards."

"I've done what I needed to do here, sorta, and I'm getting away."

"David, you're creeping me out here. Those sheeple are going to get it one way or another. Might as well make sure the towers don't have 'em."

"Don't tell me you knew too?"

"No, you just told me now. But—fuck!—it makes sense. We're what they need, right? Why let the bloodsuckers have what they need?"

Valentine felt his cheeks go hot. "You used to live under them. Your whole life, pretty much."

"Yeah, and I'd rather've been shot or hung or whatever they do than let some fuckin' Hisser get his hook into me."

If she could just see it, see it as it took place . . .

"I'm getting out. I'm going to report to my contact. Maybe . . . maybe change something, I dunno."

"Good luck with that. Me, I'm bucking for the regulars. There's a shooting tournament soon—you can win a monthlong trip up to the wilds for some hunting and training. It's a great way to get noticed." There was an edge to her voice, but she blinked hard, several times.

"Then this is good-bye," Valentine said. He gave her his Steyr. "Maybe this'll help you win the competition."

She cradled the gun, on her knees, the oversized uniform shirt making her look like a beautiful but well-armed garden gnome. "Can't you . . . can't we sleep on it? Maybe it'll look different in the morning. We can talk. You're smart enough to see reason—"

The last thing Valentine wanted to do was kiss her, but he found it happening all on its own. "They'll come looking for me, and yours is the first bed they'll check. If they ask about the gyro, play dumb. I need to steal some high-octane gas off you."

"Let me put my boots back on," she said. A lace broke as she tied it. "Fuck! I'm supposed to be tough. I've been through . . . but you drop your guard just a little bit and it's like you never learned in the first place." She wiped her eyes, buckled her belt. "I'll help you get the cans over the fence."

CHAPTER TEN

⎯⎯⎯⎯ ⟡ ⎯⎯⎯⎯

*M*ount Omega: So many legends have grown up around Mount Omega that even its mention lays a shadow of doubt over any narrative featuring it.

Certain facts are not in dispute. Mount Omega had its genesis in "Fitzhugh's Folly," when the asteroid ZL-624 had its near-Earth encounter. Poor Dr. Donald Fitzhugh— while two other astronomers actually presented the case at the secret government briefing with him, their names weren't quite as euphonious with "folly," so they dropped out of history and the high-level panic surrounding ZL-624's approach. It was predicted to strike early in the second decade of the twenty-first century somewhere between the Mississippi River and the Azores, and Mount Omega was hastily constructed with equipment from the nuclear-waste storage facility in Nevada.

Even after fresh tracking data predicted a near miss, Mount Omega construction continued. It was a massive, well-funded project already under way, employing thousands and thousands of highly paid, security-clearance construction workers and technicians across rural Washington and northern Oregon. An eleven-month, money-is-no-object crash project stretched out into its second decade. Mount Omega eventually worked its way into the defense budget as a secure location for government officials in case of a catastrophic terrorist strike on Washington DC. Work on it never ceased.

Had it ever been finished, it would have been a wonder

of the world. Nuclear power, state-of-the-art hydroponics, air- and water-filtration systems supporting office space and housing larger than the Vatican, the Kremlin, and the Forbidden Palace combined (with the Mall of America thrown in as a cherry on top), from the golf course on the surface to the deepest geothermal heat pump, it would have had space to rival a small city.

But the project was never really completed.

The Kurian onslaught of 2022, with the civilization-shattering mix of seismic activity and the ravies virus, led a skeleton crew of key elected officials, staff, and support personnel to receive their orders to relocate to Mount Omega. As the disaster grew, a stampede to the lifeboat Mount Omega represented began, and only after the shootdown of flight 5X03 did planes cease landing at its little emergency strip of blockaded, reinforced-concrete highway.

And there, guarded by the best the army, navy, air force, and marines had to give under General Roma, they buttoned up.

This narrative will not attempt to answer the question of why the Kurians never attempted to take over Mount Omega. Of course it would have required launching an operation of the scope of the Grog-versus-human battle that took place in Indianapolis now recorded as Congress' Last Stand. There were certainly enough organized Grogs on Oregon's Pacific coast in the years following 2022, after they swept up through Mexico and into California. Perhaps Fort Roma's inarguably passive role in resisting the Kurians led to it being spared. Cynical humor holds that there weren't enough uncompromised human souls buttoned up in the underground refuge to make the game worth the candle, but the fact remains that a number of senators and congressmen indisputably left Mount Omega to make it back to their constituents and share their fate. Only a handful ultimately lent their names and voices to the Kurian Order, and those black names are recorded elsewhere.

Mount Omega was neither a sybaritic paradise where

champagne was lapped from silicone-enhanced cleavage between banquets with Kurian diplomats nor a monastery to Truth, Justice, and the American Way where senators and cabinet officials wore sackcloth and ashes and debated the finer points of federalism by the light of candles, all the while making hand copies of the Constitution and Bill of Rights.

A social scientist or a psychiatrist might make sense of some of the oddities David Valentine saw on his brief visit to Mount Omega, but if any did, their observations aren't easily found. Self-enclosed populations, as Darwin noted on his trip to the Galápagos, lead to a strange selection of attributes. Valentine himself, when asked his opinion of Mount Omega, always shrugged and said, "Three generations of cabin fever."

"That is one darling little helicopter," the corporal said.

Valentine didn't bother with the lecture on the difference between an autogyro and a helicopter.

He'd made Fort Omega in one long, exhausting flight with only a brief stop for refueling and sanitary purposes. The autogyro's stomach-tossing, bobbing motion left him feeling the same way he'd felt when climbing off the old *Thunderbolt* onto dry land—the odd sensation that the ground was swaying.

Mount Omega wasn't on any map; indeed, its "undisclosed location" wasn't even a mountain, more of a sheep-littered ridge on the grounds of an old army training base, a little west of an old, spent nuclear-fuel repository. Valentine simply skimmed the surface until he saw the skeletons of some stripped commercial jets beside a wide patch of concrete highway with a big Day-Glo *X* painted on either end, and then landed and waited for someone to come point a gun at him.

Several someones did, displaying admirable handling of their old, but immaculately maintained, weapons. Of course "old" was a bit of a misnomer, as they looked lighter and of better quality than even the products of the Atlanta Gunworks, with combat zoom sights, lasers, and 20mm integral support cannon. Leather and plastic knee and elbow pads were fixed over outer shells made from old ponchos. Wash-worn uniforms beneath showed signs of heavy patching and repair, but they were still men Valentine would have been proud to line up in front of one of Southern Command's staff inspectors.

They ordered Valentine to lie down on his face, and he complied.

He tried to speak, but they told him to "shut up" until they fixed his hands in what felt like plastic wire, perhaps ripped from one of the airliner carcasses lying by the side of the road.

"Let's have it," a lieutenant said. "Why did you not acknowledge radio signal and land without permission?"

"First, the radio's a piece of crap that's preset to only receive three Quisling frequencies. Second, I'm on Southern Command orders, Hunter comma Cat, precleared to contact civilian authority. I have a verification code that I will supply to anyone with the prefix."

"Shit. Let me get someone from liaison, sir. I'm afraid you have to stay under restraints and guard for now." He gave orders to a messenger, who double-timed off toward one of the grounded planes and disappeared up a nose ladder.

"If it's going to be much of a wait, I need a trip to the john. And I could really use a hot meal." Valentine couldn't remember when he'd last been so hungry, and wondered if Sir had permanently accelerated his metabolism or if he'd adjust in time.

"Understood, sir. We'll have to watch you, though. As to a meal, if you get taken Inside, the food's better than what we can give you out here."

After seeing to his comfort, they started making small talk about the gyro. A five-stripe came out to observe.

Valentine heard bicycle tires and a driving chain. A tall pipe cleaner of a man in civilian clothes, brown wool trousers topped by a khaki shirt, pulled up and removed his helmet and hung it on a hook on his belt. He took a courier bag off the bike's handlebars and trotted up to the soldiers, a holster bobbing at his hip.

"My name's Patterson," the man said, kneeling so his eyes were level with Valentine's.

"Valentine," Valentine replied.

Patterson took out a neatly printed card. "I'm your Professional Military Surrender Resource. I'm completely outside their chain of command, and my only concern is for your behalf. I'm here to see that you get food, medical care, legal representation, and religious or social comfort between now and your release or execution. Do you understand?"

Valentine wondered how the title looked on the paperwork and smiled. "I just need to speak to the liaison officer."

"You should see him do this with Grogs," one of the older waiting soldiers told another, sotto voce. "*Ooks* and bobs his head and rattles beads until they head-butt him."

Patterson ran through a flow chart of questions regarding his treatment. Valentine denied being harmed or humiliated after his surrender.

"Captain Sagamoto is on his way," the lieutenant reported. "He'll verify your credentials and then we'll be done with you. Hope you're telling the truth, because otherwise—"

"Lieutenant, don't terrify the prisoner," Patterson cut in. "I'll have to log that."

"Beg your pardon," the lieutenant said, whether to him or Patterson Valentine couldn't tell. He backed off, and a five-striper nudged him.

"Don't let it bother you, sir. Just a bunch of papers."

Patterson had the lieutenant sign a piece of paper, and while they were so occupied the sergeant knelt down behind Valentine and checked his bonds.

"Inside, ifs they asks you where you comes from, say Canada. Make up some small place nobody's ever heards of like Moose Dick or Fragileoshus," the sergeant whispered.

The sergeant stood up as soon as the officers turned. "Just making sure I could wiggle a finger through," he said to them.

Valentine's ears picked up a faint whine and wheels turning on the landing strip. A golf-cart-like vehicle emerged from between two fuselages and joined the party, parking next to the autogyro. Like Patterson, the driver was on the lean side. His margarine clothes were thin and seemed hardly enough to keep out the dry wind. They reminded Valentine of the hospital gowns he'd seen at Xanadu.

He had faintly Eurasian features and a growth of beard that made him look like a model from one of the old magazines trying to look rugged and fresh off a mountain.

"I'm Captain Sagamoto," he said. He nodded to the lieutenant. "Patterson, I don't think this'll concern you. Can the newcomer and I have a moment?" He squatted down opposite Valentine as the others moved away. Valentine ran through the signs and countersigns he'd memorized back at Nancy's in his head.

"Red to blue?" Sagamoto finally asked, extending his left fist.

"Negative negative negative," Valentine said. "Sorry I can't lock knuckles."

Sagamoto smiled. "I can see that. Prefix two oh nine."

"Suffix V April twenty-seven. I'm here to see Senator Bey from the illustrious state of Oklahoma."

Sagamoto stood. "Lieutenant, he's cleared. I'm going to ask you to use your comset. I'm taking him to the Inside. Patterson, aren't you needed in the marshes? I heard a team of Grogs got captured after the fighting. You pedal hard, you'll be there to make sure they're tucked in tonight and get properly exchanged. Might win you that promotion back to the Inside."

"Barbarians," Patterson said.

The sergeant cut Valentine's bonds and he and the corporal lifted him. Everyone watched Patterson bike away.

"I didn't knows about no fighting in the marshes," the sergeant said.

"I could have heard wrong," Sagamoto said. "You know how rumors fly in there."

It was a fifteen-minute trip to the ridge that sheltered Mount Omega. They drove around a depressed-looking golf course that kept a single hole mowed, plus a putting green. "They cut back and start watering a new hole every couple of months just for variety. Of course even going out to golf is a privilege, Constitution-level officials only."

Sagamoto took his time driving, enjoying the clean, open air and the sunshine. Valentine found it was a relief from the gloom of the Seattle basin too, though hunger still gnawed at him.

The electric car zigzagged around a small, sloping mountain of brush-covered dirt and came to a wide steel door that looked like it was built to keep in King Kong. It was open wide enough to allow two of the little electric golf carts to pass. Part of it was filled with a trestle of closely packed rollers. Men were taking bins of potatoes and onions off of a beat-up farm truck and its companion trailer and sending them rolling down the track. The hundreds of little wheels spun on their bearings as load after load of produce disappeared Inside, sounding like a cave full of angry rattlesnakes.

Sagamoto beeped the friendly-sounding horn on the golf cart twice and passed through the formidable doors. He showed ID to a trio of bored, blue-uniformed police who intercepted them. There seemed to be two ways into the mountain, an express lane for those who lived and worked within, and a serpentine of desks and examining areas. The only other person being processed in the serpentine was a shaggy-looking man with a big netting bag filled with dead pheasant and chickens.

They waved Valentine over to a brightly lit alcove. They let Valentine keep his pistol but put a trigger lock on it.

As they patted him down, Valentine looked down the vast tunnel, big enough for a freight train or a couple of tractor-trailers to pass into the mountain abreast. There were tracks built into the ground, as a matter of fact, and the vegetables were being loaded onto a flatcar.

"What about the damn sword?" the police officer searching Valentine asked as he stood with a thermometer in his mouth while a medical officer checked his blood pressure. "Bells, he's got a knife on him too. You from the bad side of the mountains or what?"

A gray-hair in a wheelchair supervising from a duty desk, an old leather jacket with a CAPITOL POLICE patch draped over his shoulders, glanced at Valentine. "Locker all his gear. Locker, dummies!"

The medical officer stamped his hand with blue dye. After that, they inked his thumb and pressed it on a set of cards. Sagamoto got something stamped at the desk and returned with a temporary ID bearing his name and thumbprint.

By the time the carload of vegetables was on its way into the mountain, Valentine had the slip for his gear in the locker. Two more officials, in black paper clothing that made their skin look even more pale, met him at the next desk.

"General Accounts and Revenue," Sagamoto whispered. Then to the woman: "Visitor, let's get him a card for two days of food."

"What'll that be, an ear tag?" Valentine asked.

The woman at the desk unlocked a big paybox, but the man glared at Valentine. "State of birth, United States designation?"

"I'm Canadian," Valentine said, wondering if he should try to imitate the accents he'd heard on the White Banner Fleet in the Great Lakes.

This made the official even madder. He pushed a yellow card at Valentine and passed over the stub of a dull pencil. "We'll be checking that."

Valentine filled out the yellow card, no easy task with a pencil under an inch long. He gave his correct date of birth and listed his birthplace as "Fat Log, Saskatchewan."

"Two days' visitor rations, six hundred seventy-one dollars," the woman said.

"You must run a hell of a cafeteria," Valentine said. The woman tapped a laminated statement on the desk that showed the daily prices along with various taxes, duties, fees, and environmental-impact charges. He reached for his coin belt.

"Keep it. Guest of Senator Bey," Sagamoto said.

"We'll have to clear it with his office," the GAR man said, reaching for a phone.

"An aide is on his way up," Sagamoto said. "I'll sign and put my sosh." Sagamoto didn't wait for approval; he scrawled a signature on Valentine's yellow card.

"I should tear that up in front of you," the GAR man said.

"Want your bulletproof vest back? You do and I'll have the GAO and the AG on you tonight. You'll be out riding a motorcycle in the boonies, collecting Patriotic War Duties."

"Table it, Barry," the woman said, tearing off a pre-perforated card from the yellow sheet and handing it to Valentine. "Sag here is engaged to a guy on the AG's staff." She stamped it and handed it to Valentine.

The last checkpoint was a velvet-rope serpentine. Sagamoto lifted a latch and they cut through the empty switchback alleys, and came to a pert, attractive woman in a thick blue blazer with a red, white, and blue scarf. Her smile was almost as bright as the sodium floodlights at the top of the tunnel. She checked Valentine's ID.

"Welcome to Mount Omega," she said, handing him a small, dog-eared book held together with a rubber band. "If you have any questions, this guidebook may assist you. Issuing the guidebook is not an implied contract to provide services. Acceptance of the guidebook places you under all the provisions of the Visitor Security Act."

"Take it. Don't worry," Sagamoto said.

Valentine accepted it and the woman recorded his ID number on a clipboard. Her smile brightened by another couple of watts. "Thank you. There is a FAQ and a list of security restrictions in the guidebook. Failure to comply with speech codes on page three will result in loss of Inside privileges. Mount Omega is a discrimination-free zone. Mount Omega is smoke-free since 2024. Mount Omega is proud to be Working for Victory under VO-2011 protocols under the Just Human Rights and the Resistance Acts. For more information on any of these initiatives, consult your selected representative."

Valentine felt air moving, like a fresh breeze outside. The strong air currents indoors weren't exactly disturbing, but they lent an unreality to the cavernous underground.

"We call this level Grand Central," Sagamoto said, pulling Valentine out of the way of a platoon of soldiers with Marine Corps insignia walking toward the entrance, two navy officers in timber stripes trailing behind, one carrying a camera with a long telephoto lens. "Sometimes people come up here just for the chance of seeing a fresh face. Above this level is the atrium, and there are greenhouses that are the next best thing to going outside on your vacation. Getting to be Outside again is a big recruiting incentive for the military, but people generally find out it's not all it's cracked up to be."

"That why you signed up?"

"Wanted to go out and change the world. Felt like it for a while—I was helping refugees relocate."

"Same here," Valentine said.

Sagamoto pulled the string on his paperlike pants and he opened his waistband, as though they were two little boys comparing genitals. Valentine saw a wide plastic tube emerging from a fleshy hole just above his line of pubic hair. "My first battle didn't quite work out the way I thought. Have to stick close to medical care now."

They stepped under a big electronic board, above a guarded alcove with four banks of elevators, where LED lights spelled out activity on different levels. Congress was in session, and various cases were being heard in courts, including the Supreme Court.

"You heard of that butterfly's wings stuff?" Valentine said.

"When there's no lower intestine left to stitch—"

"No, it's this theory—a butterfly flaps its wings in China and you get snow in Virginia. Little, imperceptible events have big repercussions later. Maybe you caused two people to meet out there, and their kid grows up to be the next George Washington."

"I heard that kind of thing from the rehab team. They don't have to wash out colostomy bags—look, Valentine, I'm not challenging. You were trying to be nice." He took a deep breath. "Sure. You never know. At least I tried. I'm still trying, just in a different way. Looks like you've had a near retirement or two yourself."

Valentine opened the guidebook. The map of Mount Omega was a combination of a cross section of the decks of a ship and a subway chart. He tried to find their location on Grand Central.

Sagamoto pulled it out of his hands, snapped the rubber band back on, and shoved it in Valentine's pocket. "That thing's useless. The map makes a lot of sense once you already pretty much know your way around. As for all the rules—just be polite and wait your turn in line, and if the police tell you to do something, do it. Just a second, I'm going to use one of the phones and get in touch with the senator's office.

"As a visitor, you really just need to know about the Mall, the Hill, the Point, and the George. The Mall's just below Grand Central—there are a couple of escalators just ahead there. The Hill's at the end of the Mall—it's an old indoor arena the reps and senators use for Congress. Point is above us—it's pure military. The George is where guests stay—it's also off Grand Central here. Of course there are archives and sewage treatments and waste and workshops and everything we need to keep going, plus the housing levels. The vice president and Speaker and chief justice all get windows and patios. The rest of us make do with twenty minutes in the UV rooms every day." An elevator opened and a small throng emerged. "And I think this is your aide."

A woman with wide eyes and tired hair, but almost glamorous thanks to her choice of scarf and gloves and satchel, broke away from the group leaving the elevator. She had an ID printed on a half-Capitol-dome, half-eagle-wing design, her picture and a thumbprint superimposed.

"Hello, Captain," the aide said. "Good to see you again. Is this our contact?"

Valentine extended a hand: "David Valentine. Southern Command, and lately Pacific Command."

She shook it: "Daphne Trott-Diefenbach, Senator Bey's chief military aide. I bet you're hungry."

More than half the people walking the wide corridor of Grand Central looked hungry to Valentine. "I'm all right."

"Well, I could use a bite. Captain, join us?"

Sagamoto took a step back. "No. I've got to log paperwork on the fresh face here."

"Thank you, Captain," Valentine said.

"Just doing my bit. Ma'am," Sagamoto said, turning.

"Then it's us. I'll take you down to the Mall—it's worth seeing," she said. "Can I call you David, or do you do Dave?"

"Most people just use Val," Valentine said.

"I'm Ducks, then."

"Ducks?"

She jerked her head down the tunnel, and they headed farther in, Valentine unconsciously falling into step. "They used to call me Daffy in school. Daffy Duck sometimes. I liked the Duck bit."

She took him down a worn old escalator. The new

tunnel was even higher and wider than Grand Central. It was arched at the top, like a cathedral, and twin banks of lights shone down on small trees and grass running the length of the Mall. Valentine heard a fountain roaring somewhere. Bars, eateries, shops, movie booths, even a massive gallery piled with used books, lined the Mall. Valentine heard a pounding and hard breathing, looked up, and saw a walkway running above at treetop level, its railing thick with plant boxes. Joggers were running up there.

"I use the pool, myself. Warm as a summer lake, not that I've had a chance to swim in one. Let's break in John Bull's."

Valentine guessed it was an English-style pub, as there was a picture of Winston Churchill he recognized on the wall, and some black-and-whites of Congress being addressed. Behind the bar in a place of honor was a high blue helmet that reminded Valentine of an oversized egg.

"Two fry-ups and two shakes, Walther," she told the barkeep. She led Valentine to a back booth. His strange clothing was drawing stares from the Omegans in their scrublike paper clothing.

"Beer, Ducks?"

"No."

A server wiped their already-clean table and they sat.

"I'm just so eager for news of Outside. Tell me anything and everything," Ducks said.

"Ummm—where should I start?"

"How about Operation Archangel?" she asked.

Valentine took strange comfort in the fact that she'd heard of it. "I didn't see much of it."

"We had—I can't remember exactly how many, but several all-night sessions. Had this whole place buzzing like a beehive. Not that I've seen one."

"Really? Go up to the old airfield. I heard a bunch in the engine housing of one of those big jets."

"I guess they keep bees in some of the agro areas

Outside, but on my vacations I usually just go to the river."

"Why were there all-night sessions? Trying to get other areas to join in?"

"State handles that. No, we were upholding the legality of the operation pending."

"Pending what?"

"Restoration of constitutional civilian authority."

The meal arrived, a couple of fried, sliced tomatoes, a few French fries, and a breaded something about the size of a small sausage. Two big pint glasses came with it, thick with something that looked like a strawberry milk shake.

"Here's to it," Valentine said, lifting a glass. He tried a sip. It tasted like someone had tossed ice and old newspapers into a blender, then added a little syrup.

"Takes some getting used to. I'm told the flavoring is strawberry."

Valentine waited for the "Not that I ever had one," but it never came.

The server was already long gone, arguing at another table that Representative Mowbrarun's credit wouldn't buy a shot of pickling juice.

"What's really in it?"

"Mostly fiber-powdered vitamin supplement. It leaves you feeling full, anyway."

Valentine tried the fried whatever, mostly ground-up bean paste and gristle, he guessed. Ducks went on: "I never get invited to the good parties anymore because I still support the military, as does the senator."

"Who else is going to get rid of the Kurians?"

"Oh, I don't mean the *Resistance*. Everyone supports that, especially Senator Bey. Well, almost. Our military. They're supposed to be out there getting food for us, but a lot of people think they're keeping it for themselves."

"Speaking of the senator—"

"Oh, just a second. We can't talk about him or your operations just yet. I was hoping you might have a valuable or two up in your locker you could donate to the

Winter Harvest fund. Also, Senator Bey has a reelection court date coming up, and lawyers are expensive. Even a small donation will help him win his case and keep supporting the people of Oklahoma in their struggle."

Valentine knew a demand for a bribe when he heard one. At least the fries were tasty, thanks to the salt.

"What's the senator like?"

"He's wonderful. A real American success story out of the good old days, you know? Bunting and John Philip Sousa and all that. A son of one of the tunneling engineers. But he broke out of the father's-footsteps stuff and started standing for selections young. He represented himself at his first selection and the judge was so impressed by his rhetoric, he became a representative from Third District. He caught the eye of the SecDef, and got a position on the Resistance Approbation staff. His press conferences were really something, I think I was nine when—"

"There's a press here?"

"Of course. All the big newspapers still exist—of course they only come out on Tuesdays, which is good news, Fridays, which is bad, and Sundays, which is all analysis. I've got a copy of the *Times* here. . . ."

She extracted a single sheet of folded newsprint. Four "pages" of close-set type under a banner, front-page headline:

PALMETTO-BERGSTROM INVESTIGATION WIDENS

POSSIBLE CABINET INVOLVEMENT

VICE PRESIDENT DECLINES COMMENT

"WILL BLADES CUT HUD STAFFER'S THROAT?"

Valentine scanned a couple of paragraphs. Evidently a judge's clerk named Palmetto was caught sharing a portable walkie-talkie phone with a congressional aide named Bergstrom, violating Separation of Powers practice. The "new evidence" was from the Housing and Urban Development chief of staff, who admitted to Justice Department investigators that he tried to call Bergstrom, got Palmetto, and mentioned that a fresh supply of razor blades had come in.

"What an unwise," Ducks said. "All I can think is she didn't know who Palmetto was. They're just making a meal out of it because right now the VP and Donovan Baltrout are both in Majoritarian. So what about that contribution?"

"This shake is going right through me. I'll be right back," Valentine said. He went to the washroom, festooned with NO SMOKING and WATER NONDRINKABLE signs, took out two of his gold coins—the belt was now well over half-empty—and returned to their booth.

"Okay, I've got—"

"Oh good God, don't give it to me," Ducks said, sliding so far away from him she almost fell out of the booth. "Are you out of your mind? We'll swing by the Fair Politics booth and you'll fill out an envelope, one for Winter Harvest and a separate one for the senator's campaign. You'll have to do a lot of paperwork for the latter. Then they'll give me the envelopes."

"Uh-huh."

"The senator is on the anticorruption committee, you know. We're not going to be caught out."

She put the meal on the senator's account and they went through the paperwork at the busy booths off the Mall, which had an entire section of tunnel devoted to them.

Clusters of people with placards, pamphlets, cups, jugs, and purses filled the hall, swirling around those traveling to and from the booths. "Support Booth-Ramierez!" "Bring America Back needs you!" "Volunteer labor needed for Food for Thought, one free meal per day!" "Stop the Midwestern Senatorial Junta before they stop you!"

Ducks used her satchel like the prow of an icebreaker, holding it in front of her and forcing her way through the throng.

"Unpleasant."

Valentine pressed tightly behind her. People were shoving flyers in his collar, his boot, his empty holster, anything they could reach. They made it to a police officer, who put them in line for the next available federal bursar.

Valentine watched people step up to the glass booths. He'd seen rations doled out at old currency exchanges in the KZ and the setup reminded him of a clean, well-lit version of that. They only had a ten-minute wait, and Valentine's stomach gurgled as it tried to figure out what to do with the pub shake. Valentine extracted folded flyers from his clothing. Most featured drawings of ragged, starving children or trios of heroic-looking soldiers, two healthy supporting a wounded comrade.

Ducks' eyes lit up when she saw the gold coins. She helped him with the paperwork under the bored eye of the woman behind the glass. The bursar gave her a receipt for the Winter Harvest contribution, and the coin for the campaign went into a concealed neck pouch under Ducks' thin clothes.

The rigmarole left Valentine nonplussed. But all the careful record keeping gave the people in here something to do.

"You just made my day, Val," she said, pushing her way through the donation seekers again.

They emerged from the crowd, where another policeman made sure the donation seekers didn't step out into the "sidewalks" and grass of the Mall.

"When can I see the senator?" Valentine asked.

She consulted a clock projecting from the wall ahead. "They're in session for another hour. Want to watch from the senatorial gallery?"

Valentine shrugged. "I could use a shower."

"You can use the one off my unit. Staffers have to share bathrooms, though."

They passed an overlarge team of gardeners taking

care of a set of trees and she took him to another elevator bank. She showed her card to the operator inside, who punched a button for 26 and the elevator descended.

The tunnel level 26 was a good deal rougher, about fourteen feet high and still circular, painted in a cheery soft yellow that had gone dingy, with exposed conduits and pipes running the ceiling. This part was not as well lit; only one light in three even had a bulb. It snaked along in a long bend of about three degrees, Valentine guessed. Seven-foot-high blue cubicle separators closed off by shower curtains divided the tunnel on either side. Some had "roofs"; others were open to the tunnel ceiling.

The cubicle panels were decorated with family pictures, cartoons, even old pictures taken from what Valentine guessed to be calendars.

"This is mine," she said, stopping at a roofless cubicle. Her "door" was a quilt of old materials, mostly faded logos from T-shirts. A Rodgers and Hammerstein *Oklahoma!* poster decorated the outside, a 2016 Broadway production with the cast either rootin' or tootin' energetically in splashy colors. She also had a semifamous black-and-white photo of a tired-looking guerrilla, his back to an old oak, keeping watch while an old man, a woman, and two kids slept in a huddle.

"Hope you live here alone," Valentine said.

"I do, unfortunately. Marrieds and cohabitants get more space—families even get their own toilet. But this is really pretty nice. Downstairs the service staff really just gets a barrack bed with some privacy curtains hanging down. Yeah, the cubicle paneling smells musty, but it absorbs noise like a sponge. I could never sleep in a barrack."

"Consider the criticism withdrawn," Valentine said.

"Let me just grab you a towel and some soap." She ducked into her cube.

It was hard to say which was rougher, the towel or the grainy soap, but Valentine made use of them in the common shower room, a tiled-wall area in a dimple off the main passage. At least the water was deliciously hot. She gave him a tour of the rest of "her" level. They passed other dimples along the way—one had a television and four battered lounge chairs. Valentine was shocked to recognize Kurian Zone programming.

"Actually, their stuff's popular, not that any of us have much to compare it to. We do our own news, of course. Majoritarian news at five and nine, Minoritarian at five thirty and nine thirty. Every now and then they show a movie or a TV series from the Old World, but I don't like to watch those. Shallow, stupid stuff. The real old movies are better. Have you ever seen *Gone with the Wind*?"

"I like it. Don't knock shallow. Any culture that can put that much effort into entertainment about who is dating whom has all the big Maslow-sized problems pretty much solved."

She pointed to an old magazine cover on a staffer's cubicle. "Everyone was so pretty back then. About the only way we look like them is thin. Thin we can do."

They traveled back up in another elevator with a yawning attendant and she took him to the end of the Mall. After another ID check and search they went up another escalator to a sports and meeting arena, a vast open area under reinforcing girders.

The Senate held court from a ring of upholstered club chairs circling a wooden floor with old basketball markings. Little groups of three and four people down on the first level sat together, talking or listening to the senator addressing chambers from a round platform in the center with a podium that slowly rotated. The nonsenatorial watched from the old plastic chairs; every now and then one was missing in the rows, giving the audience area a gap-toothed look compared with the last arena Valentine had been in, the horror show under the Pyramid in Memphis.

The senators had real clothing, it looked like, complete with ties and shined leather shoes.

"One faction in the House wants to set up basketball league play again," Ducks said quietly. "The Senate keeps killing it, says having the Senate break for a game would destroy the dignity of the chamber."

"They're just scared because basketball would draw a bigger crowd," a man a couple of rows behind said.

"Mount Omega can't raise chickens for anything, but we can sure breed cynics," she muttered.

Valentine tried to catch the thread of the speech. The young man kept pausing and saying "hummmm," from beneath a generous overbite.

"McCaffee isn't much of a speaker," Ducks said. "But he is a third-generation senator, and half the Majoritarians owe his family favors."

"So those are senators in the big chairs?" Valentine asked. "They're not thin."

"Privileges of constitutional office."

"I see," Valentine said. "Sounds like he's done."

"New Hampshire is next. Now she can talk."

"Has she ever been to New Hampshire?" Valentine asked.

"Of course not. Senators argue their elections in front of the Supreme Court, so you can be sure she represents their values. She's flinty, tough, practical."

"And married to the head of the Unified Journalism Network," the man from behind said.

"That's Senator Bey there, in the leather chair with the bull horns at the top."

Whatever remained of the miner in the graying body was in the set of the shoulders and head. Senator Bey leaned forward in his chair, chin up and out and fist set on his knee, as if ready to rush the podium and tackle the speaker.

Valentine tried to follow the debate. The "distinguished senator from New Hampshire" was defending the credentials of a new director for the Law College.

"There's a college here?"

"Of a sort. They feed the specialty schools: Military, Law, and Social Support or Revealed Religion, plus a special technical school for the people who keep the juice and water running. Most of the learning is computerized up until tenth grade. Then you get teachers, most of whom are studying at the college at the same time—it's how they pay their tuition. College is tough. I only barely made it. Try going four years on nothing but study naps."

Valentine waited through a vote—the new director was confirmed, and then the Senate ended session for the day with one of the most vaguely worded prayers Valentine had ever heard.

"Sorry it wasn't more interesting," Ducks whispered during the prayer. "Last week we had an impeachment trial. Those are always fun."

"Amen," the man behind said, though whether this was to cap the prayer or not Valentine never learned, for he left a moment later.

Ducks led Valentine through yet another Capitol Police checkpoint, this one with a bank of security camera monitors, but she seemed on friendly terms with all the men there and they made only a cursory check of his ID, and logged him in via computer.

These tunnels were wood paneled, with real door handles separating the garage-sized offices from the carpeted corridor. Soft music played through speakers hidden within the electrical and water conduits. She stopped at a door with a laminated plate that read SENATOR JOHN BEY, SENIOR SENATOR FROM OKLAHOMA, and knocked.

The door opened a crack, and Valentine saw a ferret-like man with a widow's peak. "Ducks."

"Visitor for the senator, Larry."

"Okay, but it has to be fast. He's got a party dinner to attend."

Valentine entered the office, lit by soft bulbs in tasteful lamps. The senator sat in a little chair by a porcelain sink, being shaved by an attendant while another staffer changed his shoes and socks. Valentine thought his face looked careworn.

A bodyguard with a holster bulging under his paper jacket stood in a corner with a good view of the whole room.

Ducks led him to the end of the room and Valentine checked himself in the mirror. "Senator, this is Major David Valentine, Pacific Command by way of Southern Command. Major, this of course is Senator Bey." She turned to the man with the widow's peak. "And this is Larry Decasse, the senator's chief of staff."

"Fourteen and counting," Decasse said. "I could use three more if we could just get the funding."

Valentine remembered hearing that Southern Command's commander in chief, General Phillips, ran his office with the help of two staffers and a communications officer, and had refused the protection of a bodyguard.

"I think I know your name, son. How can I help the Cause and the people I represent?"

"Sir," Valentine said, suddenly unsure about how one addressed a senator, "I've got two reports. One needs to be transmitted to Southern Command." Valentine laid the first document, his one-page report on finding Sir and relaying the message that Southern Command desperately needed Lifeweaver help, down on the desk.

"The second is more for your eyes, though I ask it to go to Southern Command as well. It concerns what can only be called war crimes carried out by Pacific Command."

"War crimes?" the senator asked, and Decasse hurried to the senator's side. "Who? What? We just voted a commendation for Adler for opening a new line to British Columbia."

Mr. A. "It's in the report. They slaughter Kurian populations. That's why Adler is so successful. He murders whole towns."

"It's not slaughter," Decasse said. "They're relocating populations. He's the most effective commander in the Resistance. Very popular on the Hill."

Valentine ignored the chief of staff and stared at the senator. "Call it what you like, it's deliberate murder of civilians. Lot easier to win battles when the other side can't shoot back."

"I don't like this," the senator said. "Staff, give me and the major here a moment of privacy. Yes, you too, Ducks. You're not in trouble—you did your job."

Everyone passed out into the hall, save the senator and the bodyguard. He wiped the rest of the lather from his face and tossed the towel in the sink.

"Major, you think we're insulated here from the world, and about as useful as your grandfather's third nipple. We've got channels of communication all over the country, even a couple of fake ones we let the Kurians listen to going overseas. But for all the folderol, Mount Omega is still wired into the world better than most any other place I can think of. I probably know more about operations in the Cascades than you do."

Valentine felt gut-kicked. "So you approve?"

"If you're asking me if I like it, no, I don't. Do I condone it? Yes. It's a hard truth of this war. We just lost a Freehold in the Balkans and as far as we can tell, the Koreans no longer exist. If it weren't for the Australians, bits of Alaska, and the del Fuegans, the Pacific Rim would be a giant Kurian circle. Southern Command got lucky, but it's about exhausted, and Denver doesn't have electricity anymore. The only victories being won are up in Pacific Command, and he's taking on the toughest, best-organized Kurians west of the Mississippi. Now's not the time for some kind of purge. We do those kind of blood sports here, but nothing that gets said or done in Mount Omega makes a damn bit of difference. I'm under no illusions about matters here. But if we're ever going to win this thing, it'll take leadership from men like Adler. There's even talk of making him commander in chief, if his plan to drive down into California succeeds. We haven't had a president since 'twenty-two."

The gut-kick turned his meal to bile. Bile that had to come up and out.

"Some leadership. Your speech code in the guidebook says that 'no person is to be addressed in a derogatory or demeaning fashion.' But murder is just fine for someone a couple hundred miles away."

Senator Bey's face reddened. "Sure, it's a silly bit of pantomime. But we can afford the niceties of civilization here. The trick is to get the rest of the country back to the point where we can sue each other over passing gas while someone else is speaking. I'm going to paraphrase Lincoln here. The objective is to win the war. If we can win it by killing every last person in a Kurian Zone, I want to win that way. If we can win it without killing anyone, even better. If we can win it by killing some and letting others alone, I'd be for that too."

A strong knock sounded at the door. "Senator!" Decasse's voice sounded. "The Capitol Police are here."

"Now what?"

Valentine suspected he knew what. The bodyguard went to the door.

"Yes?" the bodyguard asked as he opened it.

Valentine heard Decasse's voice: "Turns out Major—"

"We need to take the senator's visitor into custody. He's a deserter from Pacific Command," an authoritative voice said.

The bodyguard turned and looked at the senator. Valentine guessed that some protocol kept police out of the office.

What could he do, unarmed? Take the bodyguard's gun and shoot his way back up through Grand Central?

"I don't suppose Mount Omega has a sanctuary policy somewhere in this?" Valentine asked, lifting the guidebook.

"Too many people here already. There are families of representatives that go hungry at night."

"I'll go quietly," he told the senator.

The senator stood up and patted him on the shoulder. "Sorry, son. I'll make sure the report about your mission gets through. We want Southern Command to know you went out a hero."

CHAPTER ELEVEN

⟡

*P*B *Camp "Sally," July: Valentine had seen dozens of compounds like these in his travels in the Kurian Zone; only the little buildings on the inside varied. Outside it was always the same: two rows of fencing topped with outward-pointing razor wire and a high observation point for the guards. Sometimes the houses were nice little prefabricated mobile homes, in other places drafty shacks where the women and children ran around on bare earth.*

This one, oddly enough, was in an old church-school combination, made of stones as gray as a typical Cascade sky. The watchtower sat in the church steeple, and the fence ran in a great rhombus from the bricked-up side of the school to the old church parking lot, encompassing both the school athletic field and a small park opposite the church doors.

He came to the Sally as a Punishment Brigade convict, having worked his way through the abbreviated Pacific Command military justice system like a grain of sand passing through a worm's tract. Like the metaphoric worm, Pacific Command didn't have much in the way of brains or heart, just nerve ganglia that received Valentine as a deserter (he rode back from Mount Omega in an empty supply truck—heavily caged for transporting valuables east and malefactors west—chained hand and foot and under the watchful eye of a sentry in the cab cage) and processed him by a hearing where he admitted leaving his post without orders with the intent never to return. He gave a fine speech damning Pacific Command from the Bears following orders all the way up to Adler's Resource Denial methodology, but none in the hearing seemed particularly impressed. They convicted him and sentenced him to ten years in the Punishment Brigade. When he asked his lawyer how many men survived that long a term, he got a quiet shake of the head.

They put him to work with some other convicts in a chain gang blacktopping roads and felling trees. When they had 120 convicts together—the additions took roughly six weeks—they gave everyone a hose bath and piled them into a pair of seatless school buses for the trip to Pacific Command Military-Criminal Salvage Training—Sally.

"Okay, you cocksuckers, listen and listen hard!" the top sergeant yelled, standing at the head of the stairs with his back to the church doors. Like Valentine, he had a generous helping of Native blood and wore a mattress-ticking shirt and green camping shorts. Only the jaunty police hat had a military crest, the eagle head of Pacific Command.

Valentine and the others waited in groups of twenty, each under a police corporal. Ever since being hand-cuffed at Mount Omega, he'd given up on hope. He felt like a wrung-out rag, but still had enough intellectual curiosity to wonder what kind of bin he'd be tossed into.

"I'm Sergeant Kugel. You're going to hate me, this place, and every waking minute you spend here. The only way to shorten your stay is to follow orders. You stay here until I decide you're fit to leave, on the bus to the front or in a body bag. Your choice.

"We've got no officers, no la-di-da judge advocates. Just you cocksuckers and your PB training staff and some sentries with scoped thirty-aughts, who'll shoot you down from the wire just for the challenge of a tight grouping."

He took off his pistol belt and hung it on the church door behind him. "I'm going to save everyone a lot of time and mental stress. Any of you cocksuckers feel like taking a shot at me, I'll give you the chance right now. No hard feelings. Anyone swings at me after this big fat kiss of a welcome, I shoot the cocksucker dead and feed his balls to my Doberman. So now's your chance."

He stepped down to the bottom of the church steps and disappeared from Valentine's view, thanks to the rank in front of him. Valentine could see a bit of hat and that was all.

"Well? Well? I haven't had PT today—I could use a good sweat. All right."

Sergeant Kugel trotted back up the stairs and put his gun belt back on.

"You're all standing here because you're useless. You were useless the day the bitch that whelped you squeezed you out, and you're useless now, according to God and Court, which decided you're not even worth the brass a firing squad would expend. We'd float you downriver like shit, except we don't want to give the Reapers the satisfaction. So I'm going to make sure that though you may have been born useless and lived useless, you'll be able to die in a useful manner and following orders for once.

"One last thing. I don't want to hear any talk about how anyone is innocent. That's between you and God above. I don't give a damn, and I hate you all, whether your souls are white as a virgin's sheets or black as the witch king's pits. I'm here to send you out ready to keep the Reapers busy until a Bear team can take them down. There's no sick call, no off duty, and a bullet's the only punishment. We start in five minutes. I'm not going to ask if you all understand. Like the man said, frankly, my dear cocksuckers, I don't give a damn."

Valentine spent forty-nine endless days in the confines of the training school. After two weeks of almost solid physical activity—his only break was the two days he spent in the kitchens under the equally bloody-minded sergeant who ran the laundry and larder—the men began to break down and miss orders, stupefied with exhaustion.

He kept waiting for the pistols to come out, for an execution to set an example to the rest, but they lost only one man, a rapist whom the others called "Short Eyes." Valentine woke one morning and found his bunk empty. His name wasn't called in the morning roll, and nobody asked questions over breakfast. He'd slept at the opposite end of the bunk-littered school gymnasium, and Valentine fought hard to keep from being too much awakened by the inevitable noises of 120 men all sleeping in one room.

He made a few friends. Diaz, who had been caught raiding a Pacific Command depot—according to him, in order to feed his mother and sisters; according to Kugel, he'd been caught with copper wiring and electrical tools. Diaz never seemed to tire, and was always the first to offer a hand to help someone to his feet one more time. Then there was Smooth John Hollows, "Joho," who'd been caught peddling drugs but who had such an easygoing, friendly manner and a sharp sense of humor Valentine couldn't help but like him, or at least look forward to the next quiet quip out of his mouth, and then there was Tuber, a meaty, disproportionate Bear washout who'd lost his temper once too often and killed a man in a brawl.

After the eighteenth day, much of it spent on the broken-up old bleachers on the athletic field, which had been disassembled and turned into an obstacle course, the only way they could make it through their exercises was by teamwork. Pairs and trios of men helped one another up the shimmy poles and over the walls. Valentine divided the twenty-man team into groups of four and shoved them into places as they negotiated the course, then stayed with the slowest team. They'd get a rest break after ten circuits; the faster they got through the circuits, the longer the rest break. "His" platoon finished first.

When the mass could hardly walk without staggering, the sergeants made them crawl through everyone's least favorite stretch of the exercise yard: the mud pit and track circuit. The mud clung until it seemed that every man was carrying an extra thirty pounds for the trot around the edges of the wallow and back to the starting point for another crawl. After Valentine lost count of the circuits, he could rise only with the aid of Diaz and Joho.

"Wish they'd get some quimmies in this mud with us," Joho grunted. "I'd do some fast jackrabbit uh-uh-uh when lil' Keggo isn't looking."

Valentine remembered the shape and bob of Malia's mud-covered breasts, felt his heart break anew. That night drying mud flaked off his hair and into his dinner.

Then, remarkably, the tyrants gave them a day off. They distributed early apples and pamphlets with the history of the Punishment Brigade, its simplified rank structure, and the various sorts of specialty fields.

The Punishment Brigade mostly did high-risk duties: disarming unexploded ordnance, clearing minefields and booby traps, and doing forward signal duty or decoy work (the Kurians had some sort of special missile called a "screamer" they lobbed into the mountains now and then that homed in on radio transmissions), sapping missions, and "river watch."

The last was one of the most dangerous jobs in Pacific Command: guarding the rivers leading up into the mountains. The Kurians employed the fish-frog creatures Valentine had first encountered in Chicago, to guard water-girthed Seattle, and sometimes small teams of the creatures foraged inland. The river-watch teams inspected nets and kept an eye on white water, looking for a glimpse of the pale green bellies and shining goggle eyes of the Big Mouths. At night there was little you could do but keep away from the banks and listen for the *slee-kee, slee-kee* sound of their on-land breathing.

The next weeks were a mix of classroom, lab, and exercise. Everyone paid attention during class, asked questions; anything at all was better than pounding across the athletic field for the ten thousandth time. They were tested daily on their progress.

"Right answers, and I can even read it," Kugel said, handing Valentine back his test on *Eleven Ways to Kill an AV and Crew*. "Where'd you get the thing about hand grenades and electrical tape in the fuel?"

"Southern Command, Sergeant."

"Didn't know you were a habitual deserter, Valentine. Thought Pacific Command was your first. You desert PB and the only direction to go is to the Kurians, where they'll turn you right in to the Reapers."

Valentine looked at the ground.

"Why don't you give us all a big fuckin' shock, follow orders, and see something through for once?"

He passed on.

"What's the thing about electrical tape?" Tuber whispered, as Kugel yelled at some other PB—the involuntary recruits insisted it stood for "poor bastard"—about his handwriting and spelling.

"You pull the pin and wrap some electrical tape around the handle of a grenade. Gasoline dissolves the sticky. The more loops, the longer it takes. Then it blows."

Valentine glanced back at Kugel, who passed out another test and winked. Ten days ago, Kugel would have had him and Tuber jogging around the fence perimeter holding hands for talking among themselves.

The ordnance-disposal training was the worst. They used real shells and demolition charges, with just enough dynamite hidden inside to knock you on your ass with your ears ringing. Worse, you had to work through thick gloves and plastic safety goggles that were more scratch than lens.

Tuber was clumsy, and set off a shell as he and Valentine worked. Valentine expelled a deep breath as he picked himself up, but Tuber went berserk.

"Goddamn goddamn goddamn!" he screamed, spinning, throwing off his gloves, goggles, and helmet like a whirligig expelling sparks.

"You're dead, dummies," Corporal Pope, the bomb expert at the training center, shouted, not that every man in the platoon didn't know.

Tuber charged the corporal. Half the men in the platoon, including Valentine, threw themselves at him. He tossed two men off one arm, sent another reeling with a blow, tossed a fourth through the window.

"Chill, man," Joho squeaked, Tuber's hand gripping at his throat.

Corporal Pope reached for his pistol.

"What the hell's going on in here?" Kugel yelled, poking his head in the door. "Pope, stand down."

Tuber charged at Kugel, hauling Valentine along like a backpack. Valentine couldn't say what happened next, only that he and Tuber went over like a tripped horse, knocking aside tables and classroom stools. He turned and saw Kugel with a club across the back of Tuber's neck.

"PeaBees, hold this cocksucker down!" Kugel grunted. "Pope, get your foot on his neck. Don't let him get leverage!"

Valentine threw himself across the small of Tuber's back. With two men on each limb and Pope bearing down on Tuber's neck, they just managed to keep him facedown on the floor.

Kugel hurried to the classroom slop sink and ran a pitcher of water. He returned and upended it on Tuber's head.

"Tubelow! Tubelow!" Kugel shouted. "Stand down!" Tuber continued to struggle and Kugel took out his pistol.

"No! He's giving," Valentine said, which wasn't quite true, but Valentine straddled the small of Tuber's back, putting himself between Kugel's pistol and the back of Tuber's head for a few seconds. Valentine reached up and caressed Tuber's cheek. "Take it easy, Tube. Take it easy. *Itsy-bitsy spider climbed up the waterspout....*"

Tuber relaxed.

"Fuckin' Bears," Pope said.

They chained Tuber in his bunk for the rest of the afternoon, just in case.

Graduation came, and they were pared down to 105. The 14 rejects, the perpetual screwups who were the kind that got other men killed, were taken away in a barred bus. Some said they were the smart ones; they'd spend the rest of their sentence in a mine or lumber camp. Others said they were being taken off to be quietly hung somewhere. The rest got tiny tattoos on their right biceps, done quick and dirty by the corporals, a little Roman numeral V and 775 beneath.

"You're PeaBees now," Kugel said, addressing them from the front of the church as they sat in the pews. They'd spent the morning cleaning the barrack, hanging up and cleaning the bedding, making everything spotless for the next "class."

"You're moving up to the front. The rest of your training will be in a school that'll make this look like kindergarten, the kind of school where mistakes make you dead. Ready to go make yourselves useful for a change?"

"Yes, Sergeant."

"Seven Seventy-five Company, you're finished here. Go and do right for a change, and maybe someday I'll see you back here."

He rolled up his sleeve and showed a fading blue tattoo: V with some blurry numbers beneath.

More buses came, the same seatless wonders in which the 775 Company rode, hanging on to bars fixed to the roof for dear life, swaying like a single mass in the turns. They were dumped in yet another depot, with the mountains ending to the west and Seattle's tower-dominated horizon blue in the distance. They ate militia sandwiches in an old IHOP. The men looked at the militia women with more hunger than they did their food.

The outnumbered women understood their power and used it kindly, distributing smiles and ignoring some of the bluer catcalls. Valentine smeared some honey on a biscuit and listened to Joho's chatter. The man was as happy as a warbler on a sunny summer day, giving running color commentary every time a militia woman walked by.

An officer in a beat-up old uniform and Windbreaker appeared at the door. He had two shining circles on his collar—Valentine guessed they were buttons or thumbtacks. "Seven Seventy-five Company! My name's Mofrey and we're going to the front. Form platoons on the road, column of two. Don't make me shoot any-one. Punishment for trying to desert PB is summary execution."

Four miles later—Valentine thought he smelled the rotting-plant smell of the bay now and then, faintly on the stronger gusts of wind, but it could have been his imagination—they arrived at an old hotel in the center of a partially demolished office park that served as the headquarters for the Punishment Brigade. A couple of curious NCOs looked them over; then they were brought into a warehouse. Holes in the roof at one end offered the only lighting, and a permanent mold farm on the walls and floor near the gaps the only decor. They were instructed to sit on the cleaner concrete at the other.

"Keep it down, you slugs," a sergeant yelled. "The colonel's gonna admit you to our ranks, God help us."

The warehouse had a little office near the truck bays, and Valentine saw a man circumnavigate some old HVAC equipment to the rail so that he could look down at them. There was something about his easy stance that made him look like a pirate captain watching his crew from a quarterdeck. Valentine blinked, almost unable to believe his eyes.

"Welcome to First Brigade, Seven Seventy-five. You're a different breed of soldiers, and you'll find a different breed of war up here," he said in a loud, clear voice. It was Captain LeHavre, Valentine's old superior in Southern Command's Wolves.

"Anyone doesn't want to fight the Kurians," he continued, "file on over toward the door and go outside. We'll find something else for you to do. It'll involve shovels."

He lost two more men that way. A few more looked longingly at the door, but seemed to feel safer staying with the rest.

"Good. Very good, Seven Seventy-five. Fourteen dumps and two shirkers. Strong bunch." He came down the stairs and joined them on the factory floor. Valentine saw three shining thumbtacks on his collar, arranged in a triangle. He still had his steady green eyes, and his belly was a little more pronounced on the otherwise muscular frame. "Who was born the farthest from Seattle?"

That was easy. A man named Bink held up his hand. He'd been brought up in Nairobi.

"Name's Bink, sir. I was born in Africa."

"You're the new Beefeater. If anyone has a gripe, think they're being treated unfairly, they tell you and you tell me. Understand?"

"Think so, sir," Bink said.

"Only thing I don't want to hear is how you don't belong in the PeaBee because you're innocent. Fate can be cruel sometimes—deal with it or step out that door and cry over a shovelful of shit. Now, platoon leaders: Give me Diaz, Valentine, and Wasilla."

Valentine, having been through the routine before, stepped forward.

LeHavre nodded once at him. "You'll find out sooner or later that Valentine and I knew each other back in the Ozarks. We were Wolves together. I trust him and so can you. But he and the others impressed your drill team back at Sally. Stay in front, you three—the captain's got some pins for you.

"We'll start you off easy here for a couple of weeks. We'll rotate out platoons to train with experienced companies. There's no weekend passes for PeaBees, but we make our own entertainment, usually on Monday and Friday nights. Calisthenics in the morning and then sports. More good news: You've got the rest of the afternoon off. We're going to get cards on all of you and then you'll see the Brigade doc. Be polite to her—she's the only woman in the PeaBees and she'll be cupping your nuts at the end of the exam."

That night Valentine dined alone with Colonel LeHavre in one of the hotel's "extended stay" suites. He hadn't changed much. The brisk, intelligent officer had slowed down a little physically in the intervening decade.

LeHavre, as colonel of the battalion, rated a personal orderly. He still ate the same food as the rest of the men; it was just brought to him and Valentine on a tray.

"Vodka?" LeHavre offered. "The best of the local hooch is called Grand Inquisitor. Made by a bunch of Russians who escaped to Canada from Vladivostok. It's pretty good."

"No, thank you, sir."

"Eat first. Then we'll talk."

They polished off the hot food—smoked ham, applesauce, some dispirited green beans, and honey-glazed biscuits—in silence.

"I miss the fresh veggies from Southern Command," LeHavre said as they finished. "Going to say no to the Grand Inquisitor again? I'm going to put a little in that powder crap that passes for orange juice. Rad, an Orange Wallop please. Privileges of rank."

The servant went to the refrigerator and clinked glasses. He returned with the iced drink.

"We each want to know how the other got here, I guess," LeHavre said.

"They told me you led a party up this way, but you never arrived."

"My report must have been—oh, what's a polite word? Intercepted. You're the junior—let's hear your story first. That way I can enjoy my drink."

Valentine tried to keep the tale short, and concentrated on events from the point when he arrived in Pacific Command.

"It's still a group of warlords here. You know one of them, Thunderbird. There are others. Adler's united them, probably because he gives the appearance of victories."

"What do you mean, appearance?"

"What's he replacing the Kurians with? Nothing. He's just scorching earth in front of him, rather than behind.

"How did you end up in the PeaBees, sir?" Valentine asked.

LeHavre had Rad bring him another flavored vodka. "I'm not a drunk—two's my limit. My story's not all that different from yours. I came up along the coast, out of Grog country in Oregon. I was brought to the Outlook first. Lots of speeches and maps about areas cleared of Kurians. There was another Southern Command liaison there—he'd . . . oh, how would you put it? . . . He'd gone native. Singing Adler's praises. He introduced me to the man himself. I'll confess, even I liked him at first. Quiet, unassuming, but confident. Able to make a decision, suck up a wrong move and move on—you remember, I look for that. Eager to remain a civilian. Yeah, he impressed me enough so I joined. There was no one waiting for me in the Ozarks."

"Not even that little girl, Jill?"

LeHavre massaged his kneecaps. "Wolf duty really catches up to you when you get older. My knees are shot. But Jill would be tickled that you remember. I was told she sorta fell for a young, good-looking Quisling. Yeah, I know. I wish I could have been there to look after her and her mom. But maybe it was the only way she could stay alive. She retreated with them."

"So how did you end up a PeaBee?"

"I saw the results of one of the Action Group sweeps. I suppose I had it better than you—I didn't see the Bears in action, just the results, an old foundation full of bodies. I had to use a pole to figure out how deep they went. Some of them were pretty torn up. Bear bloodlust."

"You blame the Bears?" Valentine asked.

"No, of course not. The Bears are just a better tool for this sort of thing. I know how easily it spins out of control. Again, not just Bears. I heard something about your massacre in Little Rock. You'd been arrested and then escaped, right?"

"Yes," Valentine said.

"Where've you been since? Keeping clear of the Ozarks?"

Valentine decided to tell him. Sooner or later the pain had to work itself to the surface and come out like a splinter. LeHavre was the closest thing he had to a guide in life anymore, and the colonel had lost someone he was more of a father to than Valentine had ever been to Amalee.

"I went back to the Caribbean, really to beach myself there. I'd met a woman there, with the Jamaica pirates. She ended up with a daughter out of it. But in the years I was gone, she took up with another man, both for her own sake and our daughter's. Good man, I shipped with him, and as far as Amalee is concerned, Elian Torres is her father. Malia, her mother, still . . . still feels something for me, but I can't say whether it's love or hate. I've got no business busting up a family. Malia wanted me gone, so I left."

He felt for Malia Carrasca. He'd shown up with Narcisse and Blake—heavily disguised, of course. What woman in her right mind wouldn't balk at such an arrival? It was easier to go than to stay. And after that, the long angry hunt for the killers of Mary Carlson.

"How'd your kid look?"

"Happy," Valentine said. "Little. But God, she can run."

"You did the right thing. I know you've got problems, Valentine, and hurts, but there's a long list of people who'd gladly switch with you."

Valentine had told himself that before, but it helped to have LeHavre say it. Valentine still respected him.

LeHavre took a breath. "Why'd you go down there in the first place? You didn't strike me as the type to give up on the Cause."

"The Cause abandoned me first," Valentine said.

"Whoa, there, Valentine. How can the Cause abandon a man?"

"You said yourself you'd heard about my trial. I ended up a fugitive from the place I'd given up ... everything, everything to defend."

"C'mon, Valentine. You're mixing up people and places with an idea. I asked you this once before: What's making you take up the rifle instead of a tractor wheel or a book or a fishing rod? What's the Cause?"

"Being free of the Kurians," Valentine said.

"There you go. It's an idea, not a person or a place. People, well, people can be awfully little. I've covered a lot of land in my life. There's beauty and ugly, fertile and sterile everywhere. It's ideas that matter. Good ideas, right ideas. Ideas are bigger than any of us. They don't get old, and they sure don't issue orders to get anyone court-martialed. You think I've given up on the Cause?"

"I don't see how you're helping it as much here as you did back home," Valentine said.

"Valentine, I didn't get put here. I volunteered to be an officer in the PeaBees. Remember your first time out on your own? The Red River operation?"

"Distinctly," Valentine said.

"You told me that when you got those folks out, you really felt like you'd accomplished something. Even more than the Reaper you and your Wolves snipped."

Valentine didn't mention his spell in the Coastal Marines, when he was working as a mole in the uniform of a Coastal Marine Quisling, the refugees he'd rounded up . . . canceling whatever karma he'd built getting the Red River families out, or the Carlsons.

"I like PeaBee work. Being the picket line between the Seattle KZ and Pacific Command has its dangers, but there are opportunities too, if you ever heard that Chinese philosophy."

Valentine thought he saw the light beginning to break through the clouds.

"I'm still getting people out and up to Canada, or down into Oregon and east. It's a little trickier—in a way it's like threading the needle between two Kurian Zones—but it can be done. There's a Resistance Network in Seattle, a damn good one. They've got members at some key checkpoints. They get the people to me, and I take it from there. Every once in a while one of my PeaBees really distinguishes himself and then he goes too. There are advantages to being the one who signs the casualty reports. Want to help?"

"Can do, sir."

"My ears must be going too. That voice sounds like my old lieutenant."

Valentine spent the next few months leading his platoon through the different operational assignments as they trained under real conditions. Five veteran PeaBees joined his platoon to help the men learn, but even under their guidance there were losses. A man was electrocuted on a raid against an electrical substation. Even worse, on river watch, three men just disappeared, probably lost to Big Mouths, judging from the crushed plant life leading back to the Snoqualmie River.

But there were rewards to PeaBee work too. Valentine guided dozens of individual families—perhaps a couple of brothers, a wife, and child one time, grandparents with a cluster of grandchildren another, and two sisters with their collective broods—from rendezvous points in the Kurian Zone, then across to the PeaBee positions. From there they were brought to hiding spots, where the PeaBees fed them—who knew what kind of three-card monte shuffle LeHavre's Brigade Supply staff was playing with Pacific Command?

The whole 775 Company was reunited at the end of October, and in their first real operation punched a hole down "Highway 1," clearing mines that allowed a column of Bears, most likely an Action Group, to drive into the Kurian Zone. Valentine wished he'd left a mine or two.

Valentine grew to like their captain, a Canadian named Mofrey, whose grandfather had served with a regiment he called "the Princess Pats." Captain Mofrey still clipped his grandfather's little badge on his steel PeaBee helmet. Every time a Pacific Command regular told him to remove it, he did, only to put it back on as soon as the regulars had passed out of eyesight. All Valentine could learn of his reasons for being in the PeaBees was a conviction for "gross insubordination." Could an affection for an old badge land someone in the PeaBees?

He even saw Gide once or twice, usually on picket duty. She'd made it into the Pacific Command regulars, and they'd trained her as a scout/sniper. She still carried his carbine. The PeaBees were watching the Quisling positions from a railroad culvert in the predawn when they heard the password whispered.

They came just as alert as if they'd heard a rifle bolt being worked, but waited, and then next thing Valentine knew there was Gide, crawling through a plant-choked culvert with a scout in front and a scout behind.

She seemed as astonished as Valentine at the meeting, but for the moment pretended not to know him, and Valentine went along with it.

"Made it right to the edge of downtown," Gide said as they warmed themselves in a basement a hundred meters back from the railroad tracks, Valentine's platoon headquarters. All he could offer them was a hot mush trying to be oatmeal, with a couple of pieces of dried fruit broken into it. "Tough to get there. Water's out, because of the Big Mouths. Bridges are too well guarded."

Valentine was tempted to tell her that some of the bridges were watched by the Resistance, but they didn't cooperate with Pacific Command because of the depredations of the Action Groups.

"Were you just there to look?" Valentine asked.

"We can't discuss operations," one of the other scouts said. "Need to know, you know."

"Except to say girlfriend here is deadly with that gun of hers," the other scout said. "One time a Reaper picked up on our smell or whatever. She killed it with one shot. It just fell over and froze up. Never seen the like."

"Robie!" the senior one warned.

The scout shrugged. "Shit, PeaBees are still Pacific Command. Don't tell me you weren't happy to see the uniform comin' out of that ditch."

"Kinda friendly with the Pee-Pants, aren't you?" the senior said to Gide as she sat next to Valentine, back against the cold concrete brick wall.

Gide took off her helmet. She'd cut her hair almost down to the skin. "I knew him in another life. It's been too long, David. You can get in touch through Ranger Group, if they let you write."

Joho churned rather than stirred the mush on the little camp stove. "I'll do a damn sight more than write if you like. I've got six months' lead in my pencil, wantin' to get out," he muttered.

"Hey, Snakes," Robie piped up. "Whaddya call your gun again? 'Big David'? Any relation? This PeaBee packin' 'Little David' maybe?" The other scout chuckled.

Gide warmed her hands on the hot bowl of mush. "Need to know, guys, need to know. And speaking of secrets—" She turned toward Valentine, unzipped her camouflage Windbreaker, and unbuttoned the top of her uniform shirt. Valentine saw a leather thong around her neck, holding a little modified wallet. She opened it and showed the four remaining Quickwood bullets resting between her breasts.

"I think of them as four little guardian angels," she whispered.

November came in dark and blustery. Up in the mountains they had snow, but on the rim of Seattle's suburbs the brief days and lengthening nights of the season just saw more drizzle, only now it was a little colder and a lot more uncomfortable.

Like a branch snap that starts an avalanche, the next disaster in Valentine's ill-fated trip began with a sound. In this case it was the muffled roar of tires on wet pavement outside another church.

Valentine, Mofrey, and eleven "trustees" of First Platoon were waiting out the wee hours of the morning in the basement of a church that had been converted to a New Universal Church Community Center, but abandoned thanks to its nearness to the war zone. Valentine rested his head against the orange silhouette of a child. A border of colorful kids holding hands ran around the basement wall.

Mofrey always took Valentine on the trips when they were assigned to 775 Company. To the men, Valentine was just an officer who had a good "nose" for the enemy, pulled them back if he felt there was a Reaper in the neighborhood, and usually could be relied on to find a gap in the Quisling positions.

Eight Seattle residents were readying themselves for a run into Free Territory, two parents and their five kids, and an older aunt, the sister to the patriarch. They were divesting themselves of their bright-colored KZ clothing and flimsy galoshes for heavier outdoor work clothes, boots, hats, and jackets for the run to their safe house. Ordinary civilians in the Kurian Zone got only the thinnest kind of outerwear, perhaps to discourage exactly this kind of attempt.

The parents were obedient, the kids wary and asking

questions as soon as they forgot that they'd been told to keep quiet. The Resistance Network member, a pinch-faced woman with nervous eyes, kept flitting back and forth between Mofrey and the family. Once they were properly dressed and fed, they'd cross no-man's-land under the guidance of the short platoon.

"They couldn't tell the kids until they left. Too much chance of letting something slip at what passes for school nowadays," the Network woman explained. "They're confused, naturally."

Valentine watched Joho clown for the kids, but expected he really had eyes for the oldest teen, a well-blossomed young woman with lovely hair who even made the shapeless KZ overalls look good.

Valentine heard the tires outside before the others, found his hand falling to the butt of his wire-stocked assault rifle. The rest of the platoon had to make do with hunting weapons or shotguns, little better than the weapons issued to the militia.

A sound echoed downstairs, an impressive rendition of an alley-cat screech. That was the signal for trouble from Spencer, a PeaBee with a talent for imitative noises, who was keeping watch from the choir balcony.

"I'll go, sir," Valentine said. He signaled two men to their feet and they hurried upstairs. Valentine wondered if his spell in Pacific Command's Punishment Brigade would start and end in a church.

Valentine saw Spencer framed against the balcony window, next to a pane of glass that had been replaced by cardboard and plastic. Valentine went to a different window, saw Pacific Command soldiers—worse, Bears—piling out of a pickup and setting up a clean alley of fire from what had been a bakery.

Valentine hurried down to the basement, waved Mofrey over.

"It's an Action Group," he reported.

"Here? Someone got their wires crossed. LeHavre wouldn't send us into an operation. Better run for it." He lifted off his helmet, ran his fingers through his hair. "Contact One," he said to the Resistance Network woman.

Now the civilians looked alarmed. Picking up on the anxiety, one of the kids began to cry.

She approached. "We've got to get out of here now, and quiet—"

Now wasn't soon enough. The door upstairs crashed, shouts followed.

Mofrey looked around.

"Get them ready," Valentine told the Network woman. He shoved his assault rifle into Joho's hands and hurried back for the stairs.

"Follow me," Mofrey told the First Platoon PeaBees behind him.

"Easy there, Delta Group," Valentine called to two Bears covering the stairs. "There are friendlies down here with Two PeaBee One. Understand?"

He came up and found the Bears lugging in communication equipment. Spencer was under guard, kneeling facing the wall, with his palms on top of his head. Another Bear urinated on an NUC Birth Drive banner. Valentine went to what he guessed to be a platoon headquarters, a radio being set up on the altar with a knot of Bears around it.

A Bear elbowed a lieutenant—Valentine vaguely knew him, Hanley—no, Handley, Valentine read from his Velcro name tag.

"Lieutenant Handley," Valentine said, coming up and saluting. "Reporting the presence of a squad of PeaBees from Second Punishment Battalion here, carrying out salvage operations, plus prisoners."

"We didn't know any of you were in this area," Handley said.

"You're just as much a surprise to us," Valentine said. "With your permission, we'll get out of your hair and get back east." Hopefully Handley was the type who'd gladly accept the offer to have one less worry on a field operation.

Mofrey brought the rest of First Platoon up.

Valentine silently willed him to stand there. He tried to make a little "stop" gesture with his hand. Mofrey saw Spencer, still under guard in the corner, and hurried up.

Mofrey came up the center aisle. "I'm Captain Mofrey. Why's that man under arrest?"

Delta Group wasn't into saluting, and PeaBee troops didn't rate the honor from regulars anyway. "We thought he might be a deserter. Charlie, let him up."

The Bear lifted Spencer to his feet as easily as he would lift a toppled two-year-old.

Valentine heard gunfire a couple of blocks away. Handley checked his watch.

"Spencer, back with the others," Mofrey said. "Lieutenant, I have some civilians in charge. They're my responsibility, and I've no intention of letting you shoot them."

Valentine sagged, glad of the sentiment but gut-punched at how Mofrey went about it. Now the Delta Group lieutenant's decision was framed as a matter of disobeying orders or not, rather than simply seeing a minor headache disappear into the predawn.

"What makes you think you could stop us, PeaBee?" the Bear who'd lifted Spencer to his feet asked.

"They're a technical crew, hydraulics," Valentine lied, desperate to defuse the situation. "We've got a backhoe and a shovel loader we're trying to rebuild—"

"Voorhees, get me Thunderbird," Lieutenant Handley said.

Valentine moved. He chambered a round in the assault rifle, pointed it, not at anyone, but at the field radio. "Don't transmit. I'll disable the radio."

Bears and PeaBees all went for their weapons. Gun muzzles pointed in every direction but up.

"Chill, brothers," Joho called, sighting on the lieutenant. "Nobody's shot yet."

"Valentine, what the hell are you doing? Put that weapon down!" Mofrey said.

"Lieutenant, this could get crazy really fast,"

Valentine said, loudly enough so the church acoustics bounced his voice off the back pews. "I've no intention of hurting your valuable piece of equipment, as long as you let the PeaBees and the civilians walk out of here. Bitch to Thunderbird, bitch to Colonel LeHavre, bitch to Adler himself after we're gone. The alternative is killing all of us and maybe one or two of you. Would you rather spend your debriefing bitching or explaining?"

Reports began to squeak in over the communications system.

"I need to answer these," the radioman said.

"Go ahead," Valentine replied.

"Valentine, you're under arrest," Handley said. "The rest of you, get the hell out of here. Take your prisoners, if they mean that much to you. Torgo, make sure they get out of the kill bottle."

"If you're going to place anyone under arrest, Lieutenant, it should be me," Mofrey said. "I'm in charge of this mission."

"Leave well enough alone, sir," Valentine said. Then to Handley: "I'll surrender my weapon as soon as they're out of here, Lieutenant."

Joho grabbed Mofrey, pulled him back. "Listen to the man. We got daylight coming fast."

When they were gone, Valentine put the gun on the desk and submitted to being patted down and restrained with plastic cording. The stress brought with it a hunger that gnawed at him. Being a Bear meant living with one's appetite as a constant companion.

Bears came and went, but the only one Valentine waited for was goat-bearded Torgo, who returned to report that the PeaBees had left the operations area.

He tried not to listen to the comm chatter. Then he saw a familiar pair of boots step up in front of him.

"Valentine, you're like a bad twenty that keeps showing up in my till," Thunderbird said. "Handley said you were here, but I had to see it for myself. You've done yourself in this time."

"Tell me something, Colonel. How did my father get all this started?"

"You've got more important worries."

Valentine found the courage to beg. "Please."

He clucked his tongue. "Oh, it wasn't here, not in Pacific Command. Kubishev told me about it, actually, never gave me any details. Don't know that you'll get the opportunity to look him up."

"Going to shoot me with the rest of the folks you're murdering?"

"God bless 'em, every one," Thunderbird said. "We'll pick this up in a few hours, Valentine. You'll be traveling, a lot farther than a trip to the nearest brick wall."

They threw him in a truck with a hood over his head, chained hand and foot and nudged by what felt like a shotgun barrel every time he rolled too far away from the side of the bay. But he could still hear. There were babies crying all around.

They traveled at a good speed for what he guessed was a little over two hours. To occupy his mind, he counted minutes and scored them off into hours. Routine soaked up fear like a sponge.

Then they parked and quiet women's voices talked as the babies were passed out of the truck, soothing and cooing over the "poor little things." He was the last to leave.

They kept him blindfolded as someone, a woman by the smell of her, fed him, stripped him out of his uniform, and gave him a quick sponge bath. They let him use the toilet. Then they sat him in a room with a ticking fan, hands and legs cuffed to brackets in an electric-chair-like frame. Valentine kept waiting for them to wire his genitals or fillings, but the silent workers left him alone.

Finally he heard someone enter. "Major Valentine?" a precisely clipped voice asked.

"Yes."

"Do you know my voice?"

"Can't say that I do."

"I'm Adler."

"Now I see why I'm tied down," Valentine said.

"Why's that?"

"So I don't go for your throat."

Adler chuckled. "Three experienced Bears with me."

"Okay, I can't kill you. Are you going to kill me?" Valentine wanted it out in the open, to know.

"Me? No. Another? Quite likely. Unless."

"Unless?"

"You see reason."

"I can't see much in this mask," Valentine said, trying to work it off with his jaw muscles and his cheeks.

"I don't want you to identify this place to the Kurians. We're turning you over to them."

Valentine felt his pulse quicken. "What does 'seeing reason' involve?"

"Forgetting all this ever happened. Rejoining Delta Group. I'll put you in a position where you can fight the good fight. As you see it. You'll hardly even know the Action Groups exist. You can fight the old-fashioned way, the useless way, wading into the enemy with banner unfurled. I have need of skilled officers who can keep the Kurian forces busy. You might be of use with the Big Mouths. They've been destructive as they've grown in familiarity with the waterways around Seattle."

"Let me see your face."

Valentine sensed a mass shift behind him, heard curtains being drawn. The mask came off, and there was the real heart and soul and mind behind Pacific Command.

Adler wore the patient face of a teacher, calm as a death mask, just old enough to be fatherly, just young enough for a spark. He had sad mortician's eyes, but there was a power behind them. Valentine felt the loom of the Bears behind, though what he could accomplish shackled hand and foot . . .

Maybe worst of all, Valentine liked him on sight.

"What did Seattle do to you? You're laying waste to everything he owns."

"I served him. On a whim . . . on a moment of appetite he destroyed my children."

"So now you're killing other people's children?"

"It's better than the alternative. A bullet ends the matter. Having your soul pulled apart, shred by shred, memory by memory, every awful act laughed at, every joy mocked—no one deserves that."

"I've always thought one's soul belonged to God."

"Maybe. Nevertheless, they partake of the distilled experiences of a life. Sip by sip. Stand with me. Or I fear you'll find out."

"How do you know so much about it?"

"He made me watch. He relished every detail. All because of a careless thought against him."

"I am sorry," Valentine said.

"Then you'll rejoin our war?"

"Your war."

For the first time he looked exasperated. "Word games. Fine. My war."

"I pound on the door while your murderers slip through the window."

"Not how I would put it. May I promise you one more thing? When Seattle is destroyed, my war ends. I will retire, disappear, live quietly somewhere. Pacific Command may fight on or hang itself."

Valentine bowed his head. "You've been polite with me, so I won't tell you where you can stick your offer."

"Now it is my turn to feel sorry for you. As to my 'offer,' I doubt it would fit. My staff calls me all sorts of colorful names having to do with anal retentiveness."

They stared at each other.

Valentine broke first: "So we're both too phlegmatic to get angry. Just out of curiosity, what's with the heroism stuff? I missed the chance at a lecture."

"The Action Groups can't get everywhere. We regularly send propaganda deep into Seattle, along with certain painless, lethal pills, encouraging the populace to do the right thing. I understand you even flew some to a very difficult-to-reach area. With luck, many of them will be used. Their names will be added to the hero lists and read out in our broadcasts. I still have a friend or two west of here. But my time is nearly up. I should have liked to bring you to another new-moon party at the Outlook. I believe you attended one before."

"I kept to my room."

"I'm sorry we didn't meet there. Better circumstances might have made our association a happier one.

"Farewell, David Valentine. Your theory about the inviolability of one's soul is about to be tested."

CHAPTER TWELVE

*C*ollection vans: Valentine had seen all varieties of them over the months and years of his trips through the Kurian Zones. He'd seen buses with shuttered windows in Chicago and long yokes for captives to be linked together in Hispaniola. He'd averted his eyes from vans in Wisconsin and armored cars in Louisiana. The principle was always the same, whether they rode on battered old suspensions across snow-dusted old interstates in the Dakotas or were pulled by a team of cart horses along an Alabama backwoods path: Separate those to be taken to the Reapers from the rest of society. Like so much of the Kurian Order, it was a simple mix of deception from the New Order and willful blindness in their subjects. Hide the contents of the stock trucks bound for the slaughterhouse and allow those who might be unlucky enough to see one in operation the comfort of telling themselves a lie.

Valentine had seen more of them than he cared to remember. But that chill November night was the first time he'd been put in the back of one.

They made the switch at midnight on a small, battered bridge over a river. Three Bears, in spiffy uniforms the color of a typical overcast, pulled Valentine out of a concrete bunker and chained him to two other unfortunates, a man in the lead and a woman just in front of him. The man wore thick flannel and was barefoot; the woman stood shivering in militia pants and a T-shirt.

Valentine passed a note to the Bear in charge, a brief farewell to Gide he'd been allowed to pencil, thanking her for their weekend at the Outlook, and asking him to pass his regrets to Colonel LeHavre and Captain Mofrey.

Passing the note was made a little more difficult by the thick leather belt around his waist, and the attachment for the handcuffs around his wrist.

The Bears brought him to the east end of the bridge. Valentine's night-sharp eyes saw a similar party on the other side.

A flashlight waved up and down. One of the Bears waved his horizontally right and left.

"They're ready," an NCO said. "Let's go, dead men."

"And women," the one in front of Valentine added, tiredly.

The man in front sort of lurched forward. "Ahhh! Ahhha!" Valentine heard his handcuff chain rattling against the front fitting at his belt.

"Move it," the Bear at his side ordered.

"My legs!"

"Now they're stopping," a young militia with a volunteer armband said, his eyes pressed to some binoculars.

"You just gotta walk to the other side of the bridge. Nothing's going to happen to you there, not with our guys around," the lead Bear said.

The man wouldn't move. "I will, I will.... I can't, I can't. Can't!" the man stammered.

"Oh, balls," the Bear said. He and another each took an arm and they lifted him.

As they carried him he sputtered something about being really, honestly sorry. Why wouldn't anyone believe him that he was sorry?

At the midpoint of the bridge two prisoners were waiting, one in a bloodstained militia uniform; the other looked like a truck driver thanks to his ball cap with ROLLING COOPERATIVE emblazoned on it.

Quislings and Bears exchanged sets of keys. Valentine noticed that the harnesses were identical. While this was going on, a bottle moved west, a thick roll of newsprint east.

"You shouldn't be doing that, Bongo," a Bear chided his mate.

"I like to read their funnies," the one evidently called Bongo replied. "Don't read nuttin' else."

"Don't or can't?" the chained militia woman asked.

"Shut down, you," the leader of the column warned.

The exchange done, the Bears accepted the two and immediately unlocked them. One of the Bears threw the harnesses across his shoulder, presumably for the next midnight exchange. Valentine listened to the two Bears who'd carried the lead man talk quietly as they walked away.

"The one in the back, ain't he a Bear?"

"Think so. Seen him in the uniform at Fort Drizzle, anyway."

"Do they know that?"

"Like I care."

"Is it just me, or does this side of the river stink?" Valentine asked.

"It shakes in front, shitting himself," a female officer in charge of the Quislings said.

"Better you than me, pard," the man at the back of their file added.

The man at the front, who had perhaps feared a glowering Reaper at the other end of the bridge rather than a group of Quislings, was able to walk the rest of the way. Valentine suspected he had shit himself, as he was shaking something out of his trouser.

"Don't feel too bad," Valentine called to the front. "Those fellas back there do it all the time when they fight."

"Yeah, takes a lot of guts to gun down women and kids," the Quisling at the back said.

They were loaded into an old brown delivery van. Much of the front paneling was missing or cut away, along with the skirting. Whether this was for easier maintenance or a security precaution Valentine couldn't tell, though he knew collection vans were frequently wired with explosives. Duvalier had said something or other along those lines when they saw one in Kansas.

The Quislings rolled the door shut and locked it, leaving them in darkness. Valentine heard the engine start, half hoped for an explosion.

This was it. The last ride. Valentine was a little surprised at how calm he was. It was over, no more worries, cares, regrets about Malia and Amalee. What would Blake turn into, a fallible human capable of empathy, or a cruel, instinct-driven automaton?

He'd had a good run. Duvalier always said Cats never lasted. He'd done more damage than most. If every human piled into a van could just take one enemy to the grave . . .

The blank nothingness that yawned before him, a forever of oblivion, the world spinning along and he'd exist as a memory or a story or one of his many signed reports buried in some archive. He hoped his legs wouldn't fail him at the last—maybe he could stamp on the Reaper's instep—or would his bowels give way?

The militia woman pressed up against Valentine.

"Hey, buddy, can you work your fly?" her voice breathed in the dark.

"Pardon?" he said.

"Let's do it, right now. I can slip out of these pants."

"You're kidding, right?"

"C'mon, hurry."

"No. Thanks, but . . . no," Valentine said.

The truck picked up speed, lurched into a higher gear.

She slid over next to the other man. Valentine tried not to listen as he took her up on the same offer. The bench they sat on squeaked, or maybe it was the wheezy breathing of the man. Valentine smelled her sweaty sex in the confines.

Two distinct thumps as they toppled over into the bed of the van. Now Valentine could hear their chains dragging on the floor. The man groaned and gasped.

Valentine felt her foot touch his. "Offer's still open if you want a turn," she said. He moved his foot away.

"Hey, let me enjoy a moment, huh," the man said.

They exchanged names in the darkness. He was Colin, she Mona.

Fifteen minutes later they arrived.

The van idled, and Valentine heard voices outside. "I'll confirm with Pound," a man's voice said. "Three going in, right?"

"Three, assuming we don't have another fuckin' suicide," the driver said. "They're trade goods, but you never know."

"I wish I had one of those hero pills," Colin said in the darkness.

A bright light blasted into the back of the collection van, giving Valentine one of those instant, diamond-shard headaches a sudden stimulus up his optic nerves seemed to cause. Valentine looked down, saw a name scratched on the wooden seat between his legs.

Bob Barquist Feb 15 68.

Valentine tried to remember where he'd been when Barquist was taking his ride. Probably back in the Ozarks with Ahn-Kha, showing a group of leaders from the Production Resource how to grow heartroot in cold weather, to be eaten or ground up into pig and chicken feed.

He wished there were some way he could have sent one more message to Narcisse—some bit of rhyme to teach Blake—or Malia. Ali even. Would she sigh and say that he hadn't been careful enough?

He felt hands hauling him out of the collection van and they turned the spotlight off.

"I might be pregnant!" Mona said, showing evidence Valentine could only guess at as she pulled up her pants. "You need to take me to a medical center. I might be pregnant!"

They stood at a brick wall. The collection van was

parked at a gate. Old metal letters on a clear stretch of wall read,

ELL VUE B TANI AL GAR ENS

Someone had added an *H* before the ELL.

The gap in the wall, big enough for two buses to pass, was closed by a yellow line of police tape. Inside Valentine saw some old, overgrown buildings. The park looked to be in ruins, but he could still make out old lots and paths.

"You guys got lucky," one of the Quisling guards said. He had flaps on his hat to keep his ears warm, and a short beard. "Only three of yas. Pound-o'-flesh always lets one make it out the other end alive. The way I see it is you've all got a one-in-three chance. Don't clobber each other right off the bat, or we'll give you a dose of bird shot, and then you'll never make it up the other end of Long Trail."

"I want to see a doctor," Mona said.

The Quisling in the hunting hat ignored her. "We use you all because you got that good old mountain-crossing spirit. All you've got to do is get to where them lights are. See it, way over there?" He pointed between two stands of trees.

Valentine saw a pair of red lights on twin poles, like the goalposts on a football field, glowering eyes staring at them across the lush plant life. If they were in fact goalposts, they were a good half mile away, maybe three-quarters of a mile.

"Strip," the Quisling ordered.

Soldiers stepped forward, released their hands so they could pull their shirts off. Valentine felt his skin retreat at the cold night air.

"Please, I could be pregnant. You never do this when someone is pregnant," Mona said.

Colin rocked on his heels. "Shut up, you idiot." He was breathing deeply.

"There's a Reaper in there," Valentine said.

"Good guess," the Quisling said.

Valentine didn't guess. He knew.

"Look at the weird burns on the back of this one. What did they do to you?"

Three Quislings were fiddling with their harnesses while others covered them from an economy hatchback with a machine gun mounted on the hood.

Mona began to cry. "Why can't I see a doctor?"

"Again, don't beat on each other," Hunting Cap said. "When the tape falls you're off to the races."

"No fair, they've got shoes," Colin said.

"No fair, they've got shoes," one of the Quisling soldiers mimicked in a school-yard voice.

"Get the rest of your stuff off. Shoes too."

They complied; what else could they do? Valentine put his arm around Mona, shared body warmth. "I hear it's not so bad. They hypnotize you, like a snake does a bird."

The tape fell and Valentine felt a sharp blow to the side of his knee. Colin had lashed out, and even now was running, the tape whipping free of his thighs as he headed across the overgrown parking lot.

Valentine felt a shove in the back, and he and Mona sprawled on the other side of the wall. Valentine came up to a crouch. The Quislings began to close the gate.

"I might be pregnant. You don't want to lose the baby!" Mona said, clinging to the bars.

A rifle butt came through and struck her in the stomach. She jackknifed, gasping.

Valentine helped her to her feet. "Let's go."

He looked back at the wall. A pair of heads watched them from the other side.

Valentine picked up a rock and sent it whizzing at the heads, but missed.

"Your buddy's already a quarter of the way to them lights!" someone shouted helpfully.

Valentine pulled Mona down the path. It opened up on what he guessed was another parking lot. The grasses and brush had been cleared here, and Valentine saw buildings on the other side.

"Oh my God," Mona said flatly.

Four figures in a line greeted them, like odd, plasti-cized mannequins with their skin removed, feet fixed in concrete. Elaborate layers of muscle made their faces a hideous salmon-colored patchwork. Valentine stepped up to one, realized it was a real corpse, covered in some kind of thick, clear plastic. The first one pointed, Uncle Sam–style.

DON'T BE CHOOSY, read a sign cradled in his arm.

The next one was scratching her head. Her sign was on a sandwich board.

PICK A WAY.

GUESS WRONGLY, said the third, its hands on its hips like an exasperated parent.

The fourth pointed to a little empty cement platform next to the others. RIGHT HERE YOU'LL STAY.

The parking lot trailed away to a path to the left. In the middle were the buildings, and to the right was an-other path heading at a ninety-degree angle away from the twin lights, paralleling the wall.

The left path or the buildings both led more directly to the goalposts.

The buildings would be the most dangerous, but there might be something he could use as a weapon there. Valentine tried to sense the Reaper or Reapers, but he was cold and his knee hurt and Mona was pulling him back toward the gate. "I don't like this game. I'm going to throw rocks at them till they shoot me."

"C'mon," Valentine said, pulling her toward the buildings.

"Let go, you bastard!" she cried, falling to her knees. "You're just bringing me so you can throw me into its arms when you see it, so you can get away."

"Suit yourself," Valentine said, letting go. She ran back to the gate.

He smelled the air, searched the buildings with his ears, heard only a clattering wind-chime noise.

Valentine passed wide around a boarded-up build-ing facing the parking lot and into a courtyard. Doors were welded shut or barred with heavy padlocks. Other closed-off buildings, one marked CAFÉ, surrounded what had once been a nice little garden.

While passing through Wisconsin on his way to Lake Michigan, Valentine and his two fellow Wolves had skirted a big old still-occupied farmhouse where the owner liked to make decorations for his yard. Animals, gnomes, old ladies bending over and showing bright-painted polka-dot underwear, geese with wings that spun in the wind, even old Packer football helmets bobbing on counterweights as the breeze pushed them . . .

The courtyard between the buildings reminded him of that farmer's land.

Somewhere or other Valentine had heard the phrase "bone garden." If there was such a thing in reality rather than a metaphor for a cemetery, this was it.

The wind chimes Valentine heard rattling were human skulls, hollowed out with tibiae suspended within to add to the rattle. Wheels within wheels of plasticized human hands, some holding fans, others carefully cupped to catch the air, spun in the November breeze. Skeletons sat on benches admiring winter-dead flowers; at least here the gardens showed some signs of being maintained. Around a table outside the café, four skeletons held forks and spoons over fresh, reeking piles of entrails.

Part of Valentine was horrified, another taken by the intricacy of the wiring, another grimly followed a mental train of thought about what effect the Kurians were trying to achieve. He'd heard auras could be "flavored" by the emotional state of the victim. Prolonged terror might add some kind of seasoning to the psychic palate.

The tableau even showed a grim sense of humor. A skeleton stood in the classic Hamlet pose, wearing puffy breeches and a nailed-on feathered cap, holding a fresh-looking human head—it certainly stank like a three-day-old remnant.

Hamlet didn't have his sword, but he had a femur.

The tattooed Cat who'd taught Valentine some basics of hand-to-hand combat always made Valentine recite the first rule of unarmed combat: *Arm yourself.*

Or in this case, leg yourself. He wrenched the leg loose, spun and spun and spun it on its wire until the link weakened, then pulled it free. He went to one of the cement benches and broke it off at the knee end, giving himself a sharpened spike.

Several paths led off the courtyard and the buildings. Valentine could see the lights peering at him from across a vast, brushy field, bisected by cover. It was tempting to plunge into the bushes, but he suspected they thickened with what looked like Devil's Foot farther in. Even with a machete and thick clothing, he'd hesitate to hack through spiky Devil's Foot.

He chose one of the paths through the trees, and found it joined the path he'd discarded in order to get at the buildings.

To get to the trees he passed through a vaguely Oriental garden, at least judging from the architecture. The plants had mostly run wild, but there was still a bubbling, attractive-looking fountain.

The water smelled clean.

He reached forward.

A fortunate, foreshortened step saved him. He felt something brush his leg hairs, froze, looked down, saw a length of fishing line passing in front of the fountain. Valentine followed the wire to the trigger, then up to the overhanging trees, saw a big latticework like a spiky flyswatter ready to fall and cripple a hand dipped in the water. It looked flimsy; obviously it wasn't designed to kill, just to injure and cause pain.

Valentine decided to forgo the water, and stepped carefully onto the wooded path, every nerve alert. He willed his eyes into picking up every twig, every branch, every trap that might or might not be along the path.

There'd once been a sign, probably an explanatory map, at the beginning of the tree-flanked path. Now a human skin, face and hair still attached, was stretched between the posts.

DON'T RUN!
YOU'LL JUST DIE TIRED

read the helpful tattooed warning.

The crotches of the trees held human skulls with glowing eyes. Valentine glanced at one as he passed; the "eyes" were golf balls painted with luminous paint. Valentine decided to parallel the path after he found a shallow pit filled with sharpened wooden spikes smelling of fresh blood. Poor Co—

Reaper!

Valentine crouched, tried to lower his lifesign, tried to box up the cold and his sore knee. He gripped the splintered femur in both hands, left steadying it, his right on the ball joint, ready to drive it. . . .

He heard panting and saw Colin running wildly down the path, feet muddy, favoring one leg, but fear driving him through the pain. A cloaked Reaper, its face white-painted with eyes and lips blackened to imitate a skull, thin chest similarly decorated to enhance the ribs, skipped along behind him, raising first one long arm and then the other in a sort of dance.

"and i run and you run and i run and you run . . . ," it sang as it hopped.

Could he catch it unaware?

The Reaper halted, pointed a long black-nailed finger at Valentine. *"you! you wait your turn! gimpy's first!"*

Colin sprawled, tripping on the same hole that had injured him earlier. *"oh, you've tripped. get up, you're not finished yet. run run run little silly man."*

They disappeared toward the buildings, the Reaper harrying its prey like a dog driving a lone sheep.

Valentine angled toward the western wall. Twelve feet of brick, with trees well cut back, was topped with electrified fence.

"Don't even think about it," a megaphoned voice

from the trees called. Valentine searched the timber, saw a hunting blind. "He's busy with the others. If you hurry, you'll make the finish line easy."

Valentine trotted back into the woods.

He ran faster as he saw the two red lights, broke out of the trees and up a long meadowed path, thick with night dew. Valentine saw more lines of fencing, angling toward the finish line. A couple of New Universal Church robed types stood before a candlelit table with food and bottles and a trophy cup.

But there was a cold piece of evil lurking just on the other side of the victory tape.

Valentine sensed a Reaper under the table, alive and pulsing. A final shock for the winner?

He couldn't say why that one little detail bothered him more than the nests of sharpened pungi sticks on the path, or the humiliation of being stripped in front of joking guards. He turned and trotted back along the path toward the buildings.

He found them on the other side of a little wall-less Japanese building, between two gardens filled with stones. The Reaper loomed behind Colin, poking him in the kidneys with a long, black fingernail, urging him toward Mona, crying, holding out one hand as a plea to stop and covering her sex with the other. Valentine could hear the breathy, high-pitched voice.

"*one two three four, i declare a food war. five six seven eight, the winner gets to make the gate.*"

The Reaper jumped and landed next to Mona, who tripped and fell.

"*you can take him. he's out of breath, wounded in the foot! go for his other leg!*"

Colin jumped on her, got his fingers around her throat.

"*now rape her! spread her legs, inside, inside, and i'll let you live.*" It hung over the couple, its cloak drawing a curtain around them. . . .

Valentine flitted between trees, put the cement of the little pagoda between himself and the scene.

"No! No, please! Oh God!" Mona screamed.

Something at the base of his spine woke up and twitched. It ran hot up his back, perched between brain and skull atop his head like a spider.

Valentine hopped up on top of the pagoda, and made the jump with the thoughtless ease of a house cat leaping to a kitchen table. Dirt and clinging plants fell, displaced by his weight, but before they hit the ground he was a gargoyle shape half-hanging from the pagoda roof.

Below, the Reaper opened its jaw and shot its tongue toward Colin's back, teeth following. Colin screamed.

The greenery hit the ground next to the Reaper. It turned its head; eyes followed the trajectory up—

And met Valentine on the way down.

He landed atop the Reaper, driving the femur down toward the great beehivelike organ that sucked down the blood. It reached up, backward-hinging arms moving for him, but Valentine was off it, moving on white-hot instinct, hardly knowing what his body was going to do next.

He swung a stiff-fingered uppercut, felt fingers break through skin, grabbed the Reaper under its hyperextended jaw, fingers closing on bone, dragged it off Colin, who had a gaping, tongue-sized wound in his back. Valentine whipsawed and the Reaper sprawled.

He held its white-painted jaw in his hands.

The Reaper rose, confusion in its eyes as its tongue lolled. Valentine cast the jawbone aside and readied his femur for another strike.

The Reaper turned and ran, but Valentine was after it, a wild predator drawn by flight, got on its back and drove the sharpened femur up through the gap left by the jaw.

Crying, Mona pressed her hands against the wound in Colin's back. Blood came up under her fingers anyway.

As the Reaper collapsed there was another, running from the woodland path in the direction of the goal-posts, its feet a blur, a strange oversized leering jack-o'-lantern mask atop its head. Valentine picked himself up, left the twitching, dying, genetically engineered corpse, and ran toward the new one, ink-smeared bone in his hands. The Reaper slowed, perhaps not used to a man running toward it.

A mindless feral howl sounded from Valentine's throat. His heart seemed to fill his entire chest cavity, its throb rattling his ribs and collarbones. . . .

Some sane corner of his mind hammered out thoughts as fast as letters flew from a quick typist:

You don't know how to fight you great thirsty slug you've forgotten how, send all the puppets you want, you can no more fight than fuck time to face me, product of a warrior race bred and tested in ten thousand years' battle, scarier than any costume, don't run you'll just die tired . . .

The Reaper turned and ran. Its mask slipped, and it blindly plowed into a tree, lurched onward, tearing the mask free to run.

Valentine angled through the trees, yipping like a hound on a hot scent, caught up to it just outside the glowing eyes of the goalposts. It turned at the last second, threw up its arms to ward him off, and Valentine caught it at the knees with a diving tackle, knocking it down, felt claws open wounds in his shoulders as he drove his femur up between its legs. The Reaper didn't have sexual organs, but its skeleton had a gap.

Kill it so they send me another. And another . . . no.

Valentine fought to form words.

"You," he said, straddling the Reaper, feeling stronger than he had ever felt in his life.

He twisted the femur. "You, at the other end. Talk, or I make your puppet into a corn dog."

"ssstop! pleasssse."

Valentine withdrew the femur, and the Reaper lashed out with its free arm. He caught it at the wrist and twisted it until he heard a snap.

"Stop it," Valentine said. It was like talking in a foreign tongue; he had to force himself to make words. "I'll take your toy apart a limb at a time. Then I'll hang your churchmen from the goalposts."

"what do you want? i give you your life, i give the female her life, i give the man his life, just let my servant go."

"Are you Seattle? The head honcho?"

"no, i am but a keeper of—"

"I want to talk to your chief. King. Grand and Exalted Overlord, whatever he calls himself. The one in the big tower."

"he does not deal with your kind directly."

"Then through you. I don't care. Tell him I have an offer."

"what could a human give such as he?"

"Adler. The leader of the resistance."

The Reaper's slit eyes widened. *"impossible!"*

Valentine reached up, got his hand around its windpipe, felt the thick muscles that drove the tongue.

"grraack . . ." Valentine released his grip. *"yes, yes, cease and desist. i contacted, he assents. you shall have your meeting with his representative among the mortal."*

CHAPTER THIRTEEN

*M*outhpieces: *Every Kurian organization depends on layers of intermediaries between the Kurian Lords and their human herds. Seattle is no different.*

All the layers of police, troops, secret police, church investigators, even diplomats to other Kurian Zones, report to one man's office in Seattle, and that man is Maxamom Silas. Impressive looking, with a good eye for clothes, and an even more impressive speaker and judge of character, he's something of a born second-in-command. Some in the know of the ins and outs of Seattle's realm believe him to be more important than the lesser Kurian Lords in the feudal conglomeration, especially with recent desertions of the Kurians supposedly guarding the borders of Seattle's empire.

He has his faults, of course. If an original thought ever entered his head, it got lonely and left. He's also a man who lives very much in the present day. "The past can't be changed and the future has too many variables," he's been known to say.

Maxamom Silas watches over his city from the old Space Needle, overshadowed by the greater Kurian Spire doubling the highest heights of the Seattle skyline, as if contesting Mount Rainier itself. Why he chooses the Space Needle as a location for the meetings of his highest military, industrial, and church leaders might be answered better by psychology than logistics or practicality or even sybaritic comfort—after all, he often weekends at the much more congenial Gates estate. He's earned the view. As a Seattle-born NUC altar boy, he impressed the church hierarchy enough for them to send him East for an education. He returned a bright young graduate of Harvard's Population Management School, not inspired with any particular vision, but crammed with the latest skills and theories.

Silas receives credit for his division of the city into neighborhood-sized "quads"—each ruled by a Kurian. School and work and sports teams encourage quad loyalty. These in turn are gathered into "conferences" where a presiding Kurian clan works out squabbles. In theory, a human need never leave his conference; the whole of his existence is encompassed in the square miles that make up a conference, though he will sometimes travel to another conference to root for a home team in a championship, or listen to a political speech.

Seattle himself oversees the conferences as sort of a supreme judge. His conferences reside in his own massive tower, where they may be more easily watched and controlled. Treachery has been unknown since the great purge of Year Forty, when three leading conference clans were killed in a single deadly night.

It is this simple system that allowed Seattle to expand his realm in the 2050s, owning all the land between the Grogs in Oregon and the thinly inhabited coastline north of Vancouver. From the Kurian point of view, the apparently powerless "quad" role was attractive, for the number of human auras he had to pass up the food chain was strictly limited, and in return he received the military protection of Quisling formations organized at the conference level. While there is some dispute on the matter, Seattle can at least be credited with being the only Kurian overlord who regularly saw his fellow Kurians petition him to be included in his empire.

Until, of course, the advent of Adler and his brutal strategy. Adler would strike in secret, hard and fast, at the quad level of the Kurian Order, harassing and chipping at the vulnerable fringe of Seattle's realm. He avoided every trap laid for him, seeming to know which quads were strongly garrisoned and which were weak.

Even Maxamom Silas had few ideas of how to cope with the crisis. His expertise in security was limited to quelling dissent from within and breaking up organizations like the Resistance Network. After three conferences contributed to a "Guardian Army" that plunged into the mountains, only to dissolve thanks to desertion and harassing attacks from mountain-wise guerrilla bands, no further attempts were made to take the offensive.

But Seattle himself is not without the canniness of a hunted fox. He sent to his subrealm of Vancouver for the "Big Mouth" amphibian Grogs, and used the numerous waterways around Seattle to gird his realm, though a good deal of his productive capacity is now spent feeding Grogs rather than trading with other Kurian Zones for the goods that once made Seattle such a pleasant place to live and breed.

Valentine watched Seattle through the outward-slanting windows of the Space Needle. He tried to imagine what the roads looked like long ago, filled with cars and trucks—the crushed remains of which now formed barriers between Seattle's zones. Now there were just bicyclists and a few motor scooters, making way for smoke-belching army trucks, biofuel buses, and the occasional gleaming SUV.

He'd first relayed the bare bones of a plan to a pair of skeptical military adjutants, but as he spoke they grew more and more interested. Then he spent a day in an apartment on what he guessed was a military base; BELLEVUE CONFERENCE IS THE FIRST WITH THE MOST read a banner hanging over an exercise field that he could just see through his grimy window. Later they told him that he'd need to speak to Chief Executive Silas' Regional Security Work Group. So they gave him soap and a razor, sent a girl in to trim his hair and nails, and gave him an afternoon to present his plan.

They shuttled him to the Space Needle in a motorcycle with a little encapsulated sidecar that reeked of sweat and tobacco. A cold front had parked itself over Seattle, and the normal drizzle had turned to sleet the previous evening and promised to do so even earlier tonight. From the road Valentine got a closer look at the Lord's Tower, as it was called, and didn't care for what he saw.

Five great shafts, laid out like the dots on the "five" on an ordinary craps die, rose straight up in shafts of blue green like a fountain frozen in time. Above the tallest of the city's buildings, the Kurian compartments, as Valentine thought of them, began. They looked like mollusks or barnacles clinging to a pier, rather than the spider-egg-sac orbs he'd seen in the middle of the country. Atop all, like a great mushroom cap, was the dome of Seattle himself. Valentine thought he saw trees up there but could not be sure if the green caps were vegetation or just some odd element of Kurian architecture.

"That must have taken some time to build," Valentine said as they parked beneath the Space Needle and the driver opened his canopy.

The driver shrugged. "My dad knew a guy from the conference who worked on it. Once the foundation went in, they grew the columns. Only steel in there as far as I know is remnants from the scaffolding."

The driver passed Valentine on to one of the military attachés he'd first talked to. They took an elevator up the Space Needle. Some minor earthquake damage had been patched over and painted, but otherwise it still looked fresh from the World's Fair.

Valentine idled in a waiting room, downing a mug of the best coffee he'd had since his last trip to Jamaica. Photographs of post-'22 reconstruction projects and the Victory-5, a super-fuel-efficient observation plane and light bomber produced at the Boeing works, filled the waiting area. A card listed an impressive set of specifications. The plane's lines reminded him a little of the gliders he'd trained on in Yuma, wide flat wings with little stabilizers at the tip, though with a heavier body and push-pull propellers.

He listened to a pair of engineers breaking for coffee, grousing about the state of the sewers. Seattle was only a third as populous as it had been pre-2022, and as the remaining humans no longer produced enough waste to keep the sanitary system working, they were closing off vast sections so as to divert into the still-working parts and narrowing pipes.

"You'd think PVC was gold, they way they stint," one said, sipping his coffee.

"The shit's gold, that's for sure. Energy wants it for the biofuel stills. Fisheries want it for the hatchery. Agriculture needs fertilizer. If they only would let us get a per-gallon rate, we could buy all the tubing we needed from the Oakland Bay Company. But no, 'waste' it remains."

Next trays of food—Valentine smelled fish and roast beef, along with onion and potato—came up the elevator and disappeared into the meeting room.

Valentine wandered to the observation rail while the Quisling leadership ate. A sharp lemony smell filled his nostrils, and Valentine heard a heavy, shuffling step.

He turned. A squared-off man, all right angles and pinstripes, stood on the observation platform, looking at him. He had golden rings on each hand.

Behind him was a big gray Grog, who evidently was the source of the lemony smell. Valentine couldn't remember ever seeing one of the long-armed grays so neatly trimmed and coiffed. It wore a kilt with sewn-in scabbards for weapons, and the butts of two rifles projected from its shoulders. Silver-capped teeth shone against lips greasy with roast beef juice, its tongue discreetly probing for trapped morsels.

"I take it you're Valentine," the man said, stepping up with hand out. He was about Valentine's height, but built a little heavier. "I'm Silas, chief executive around here. Kur commend you." He had what sounded to Valentine like an odd manner of speech, as though all the words were formed in the top of his throat and passed up through his nose as well as his mouth.

"David Valentine. You could get a fair price out of the Louisiana Kurians for me, by the way." The Grog hovered as Valentine shook hands.

"You're not frightened of Grogs, are you? Silvers is well trained," Silas said.

"*U-koos,*" Valentine said to the Grog, lowering his left hand toward the floor and bringing the right to the center of his chest. The greeting was a fairly universal one in St. Louis, but he didn't know if it applied out here.

The Grog slapped his own centerline a few times and hooted. Valentine saw an old white scar on his right breast, sloping down toward the Grog's navel.

"Introductions being over, we've got another hour or so of work after lunch. Sorry to keep you waiting, but we're running late. Then it's going to be all military, and you're first on the agenda. Seattle himself is curious as to what you're going to propose, you know. It would be in your own interest not to disappoint him. If I understand, you're some kind of assassin? You took the measure of two Reapers, unless I'm being misinformed."

"It was me or them. I'm glad Seattle is the forgiving type." Valentine felt shaggy and uneducated in the light of Silas' controlled diction.

"Nobody much likes the Bellevue clan. They trade with the insurgents and word gets around about that little exercise field. Unsettles the herd."

"You're one of the herd yourself, aren't you?"

"One body can always be swapped with another. But talent—that's not so easily discarded. Do you know what these are?" He held out his manicured hands, an NUC-crested brass ring on the left, a plainer one on his right.

"Brass rings."

"Yes. Word of advice, Valentine. Don't believe your own propaganda posters about freedom and all that. There's always been the rulers and the ruled." He tapped the glass in the direction of the city. "The Kurians aren't that different from other rulers throughout history, save for one twist. They want productive births and productive lives, just like all the others. The only thing all this slanging is about is their desire for, when the time comes, productive deaths. Reuse and recycling of strange and mysterious energies otherwise lost to the cosmos."

"If that's what you believe, then I hope I'm around when you go drowsy and forgetful. You going to strip off those rings and volunteer for recycling?"

"I've earned a ripe old age, and I intend for it to be a productive one. Sadly, I've not had time for children yet. Our aphrodisiacs have been certified for ninety-year-olds. But really, I didn't come here to talk about myself or the honorable family name. I wanted to get an idea about you, before plunging into all the hows and whens. I'm a little curious about what you want out of all this."

"Put in your words, I want to stop the unproductive deaths. Adler is slaughtering whole families."

"Both sides are exhausted from all the fighting. The Kurians never thought it would take so long to reorganize us. Every new eruption kills more in a few weeks than the Kurians do in a year. Waste, sheer waste."

An elegant woman in business dress, lovely eyes behind thick glasses, cleared her throat from the hallway.

"Mr. Silas, they're reassembled and await you."

Silvers took a long snootful of the air around the assistant and popped his lips together: *dop dop dop*.

"I look forward to hearing your plans, Valentine. Just don't think you can organize another mutiny here. We're not stupid."

"Never said you were, Silas. Rotten, maybe, but not stupid."

"You're not my idea of an ally either."

"We don't need to respect each other, as long as we cooperate. I'd make a deal with the devil himself to stop Adler's slaughter."

*   *   *

Two and a half hours later Valentine finally got a chance to talk, in the meeting room at the top level of the Space Needle. It rotated with the speed of a minute hand, slowly shifting from city skyline to mountains to the bay.

He stood at one end of a long, slightly curved wooden table, richly lacquered and the color of blood. Papers placed on it seemed to hover above their own shadows. The table could hold twenty-two at a pinch, Valentine guessed, but at the moment only four figures sat at it, Silas at the other end. Lesser operatives sat discreetly at the edges of the room, near phones and computer terminals, but Silas dismissed them for the day, keeping only those seated at the table and his secretary.

And of course Silvers, filling a battered sofa just behind Silas' chair.

"What the hell is a deep amphibious operation?" a general with heavy, burnished steel shoulder boards said. He had the fleshy look of a man who liked to do his generaling after a late breakfast and before cocktail hour.

"Hear him out," a uniformed woman with a raccoon mask of camouflage airbrushed across her eyes said. Her bristle-short haircut made one of Alessa Duvalier's self-administered razor jobs look vulpine. "About time someone talked about going on the offensive. We need more men willing to put their balls on the table, pardon the expression."

"Keep yours behind your zipper, Park," the fleshy general said.

"Let the man answer the question," Silas put in, and the table went silent again. Behind him, the city's skyline glowed in splashes of color, searchlights illuminating the old, empty office buildings as though they were national monuments. Lights dusted the edges of the city, washed down the road.

"I just made up the term," Valentine said. "But it describes what I think your 'Big Mouths' can accomplish, if the field training I received about their habits was correct. I read some news bulletins about their use in Florida deep into the Everglades."

"How many will you need?" a man in thick black wool asked. He had the fishy odor of a man off a long day at a gutting wharf. Valentine couldn't tell if he was in casual military clothes or civilian wear so rugged and severe it could pass for a uniform. His name tag was similar to the general's and that of the woman called Park, a black rectangle with white lettering; his read TROYD.

"I have to see them training to decide that. Do you train them?"

"We do," Troyd said. He kept his hands out of sight under the table, unlike the others, who were making notes or drinking coffee or tea.

"How are you going to get past the river barriers?"

"I know a little about the watch system," Valentine said. "Before my comrades delivered me into your little garden of horrors, I was an officer in the troops that supplied the river sentries. Dangerous work."

"That's why they had PeaBees doing it, no?" Park asked.

"Yes," Valentine said. "I even lost a few men to them in the fall. We never found the bodies."

"They've adjusted their fertility cycle to the salmon runs. Whoever eats the most gets to be female and host the fry. Sometimes they even eat the males, if the males don't swim away quick enough after the mate."

"That's a fucked-up way to do it," the fleshy general said.

Troyd shrugged.

Park snorted. "Make for a quieter world."

Silas cleared his throat. "Let's set comparative biology aside for now. We've learned what you'll need for the job. What do you want in return?"

"Some peace and quiet. A nice little house, maybe on one of those islands outside the bay there. A nice boat, not quite a yacht, but something I can use for travel or fishing. A few servants and a couple women to keep me warm on these clammy nights. But most important, one of those brass rings like you all wear so I get left alone."

"You? Settle with us?" the general asked.

"Not with you. Among you. I'm not going to be welcome back with Pacific Command. I'm under a hanging judgment with Southern Command."

"Brass rings aren't mine to give out. Speaking of which, there's going to be one awarded to our friend Troyd here at the next audience, for his work with the Big Mouths."

"And well deserved," Park said, rapping the table.

"Damn, is that this week?" the general asked, looking at his organizer book. "I may have to beg off—I've got inspections in Tacoma."

Silas kept his gaze on Valentine. "It's a boring ceremony. Speeches mostly, gives the TV station something to broadcast for a few weeks. I might arrange for a short interview. Seattle is most interested in the proposition, and he would be the one to promise a ring."

"I'm not doing it on faith," Valentine said.

"We're not so sure you can do it," the general said.

Valentine shrugged. "I wouldn't expect a ring to be handed out unless I accomplish the mission."

"I'm expected at a wedding banquet for one of my colonels. Can we wrap this up?"

"Hungry for your cake, or your droits?" Park asked.

"Not what you're thinking, Valentine," Silas said. "The maid of honor gets a more active role in military weddings around here, is all."

"Who gives a damn what he thinks?" the general asked. "Are we reporting up here or no?"

Silas nodded to his breathtaking secretary. "I'll call for a vote on the Valentine Proposition, and we'll adjourn." He touched a button on the arm of his chair. "Captain Chu, take Valentine back to the lounge."

"Suppose you vote the proposal down?" Valentine asked.

"You might end up in Seattle's tower anyway, but in considerably less distinction. But don't worry, a part of you will live on as a conversation piece."

Valentine went back to the lounge, smelled the nervousness on Captain Chu. Valentine wondered if the man expected to be stabbed with a stir stick. He felt too tired, too disgusted with himself, to put up much of a fight, even if the vote went against him.

Ten minutes later the door opened and he saw the French cuffs of Silas, a broad smile on his face. But he had Silvers with him rather than the statuesque secretary.

Valentine struggled to look nonchalant.

"The vote ended up unanimous in your favor."

"All four? I figured that general was hedging."

"Three. Friend Troyd sat at the table as a courtesy, but he doesn't have his ring just yet. I decided to seat the minimum for an official meeting of the Security Staff. I imagine the less who know about your project, the better."

"Wise of you," Valentine said.

"I want you to have dinner with me tonight. We'll get you cleaned up and into some decent clothes. When you're out mixing with the other ranks, your cover story is that you're an emissary from Catalina, learning how to handle Big Mouths. You know anything about Catalina?"

"Not really. Island off the California coast is about all."

"Don't worry, no one here's ever been there. Our only contact with them is for oil transactions, and the Energy Staff isn't scheduled to renegotiate for eighteen more months. Just pretend you're wealthy. Oh, and say 'awhoha' now and again."

Valentine rode back to the city in Silas' limousine with his secretary. The trunk of the vehicle had been heavily modified to accommodate Silvers in his own semicupola complete with the first Grog gun Valentine had seen since leaving St. Louis. This one was a piece of craftsmanship, twin barrels each with its own two-thick magazine sloping down at an angle, with a built-in firing shield. Silvers strapped himself into the gun and the seat like the deep-sea fishermen Valentine had seen in the Caribbean.

"That's quite a hogleg your bodyguard totes," Valentine said, looking through the tiny back window at Silver's hair whipping in the wind.

"That little apparatus came off an armored personnel carrier, initially. I think they're . . . ummm."

"Twenty-five millimeter, Thunder City Rangeworks," the secretary supplied.

"Anyway, they cost a lot. Oh, I'm sorry, David Valentine, Luty Loosh. She usually goes by Miss L. Top-quality English import, and almost as hard to get as a Rolls."

"I'll save you some time: Lubey Bush, Lusty Tush, Loosey Flush, Thirsty Lush, and combinations thereof," she said. Valentine detected a little bit of an accent now, and she tended to hit the first syllable of her words hard and sharp, like a determined pianist. Valentine felt like a drawling backcountry scrub compared with these elegant-sounding creatures.

"She was ill-bred enough to make herself so useful I had to keep her around—even after we got tired of each other," Silas said.

They took an off-ramp into the city, passed through a gate in a concrete wall, and pulled up beneath a well-lit turnaround, sheltered by a gold-fringed awning protecting a carpeted path to shining brass-and-glass doors.

"This is my pied-à-terre in the city. Let's get you changed for the better and then talk more over dinner."

"Whatever Silas says," Valentine said.

"I've heard that one before too," Miss L. said.

They rode up in an elevator that made the one in Fran Paoli's building in Xanadu seem like a freight. A little screen in the elevator showed the time, date, and outside temperature as it ticked off names and what Valentine guessed were locations every few seconds:

> Vinson, B. COLTRANE MIL
> Apporimatox, N. TACOMA 18
> Rutig, A. (in transit 5)

Neither of the others paid any attention to the screen, so Valentine ignored it as well.

The elevator opened into what Valentine guessed to be Silas' apartment. It was airy and open, a Prairie-school foyer/living room combination filling two floors. Stairs passed up on either side to doors that Valentine guessed to be bedrooms, and glass filled the wall facing the bay. A patio filled with plants had a second floor to the left side.

"I like a drink after that many circuits in the Needle," Silas said. "You like Scotch, Valentine?"

"You're a brave man, Silas," Valentine said.

"Why's that?"

"You left your bodyguard downstairs. I'm a desperate insurgent. Suppose I went for your throat?"

Miss L. removed her jacket. Valentine saw a soft leather holster strapped under her arm, the shining butt of an automatic inside. "It's loaded with hollow-points," she said.

"Have to admire a woman who brings her own protection."

"I believe in redundancy," Silas said. "Speaking of which, Luty, see if you can find friend Valentine one of my suits from when I'm better about exercising and down ten pounds."

She led Valentine up the carpeted stairs and to a bed-room that had been converted into an oversized closet, complete with three-way mirror. Her heels clacked on the hardwood floors as she walked down the line of jackets.

"I'd like to see you in gray flannel," Miss L. said. "You're too serious for double-breasted. Hmmm, a vest will make you look like a pimp with that hair. We'll stick to a simple cotton shirt. Where are you from, again?"

"Minnesota."

"That's the one east of Wisconsin?"

"West of Wisconsin."

"Ah." She paused until he looked at her. "How old is your mother?"

"I'm sorry?"

"Just wondering if she was Old Regime or not."

"No, she died fairly young."

"I'm truly sorry to hear that. Here, try these. I'll give you some privacy. There's clean socks and underwear in the drawers. I'm sure Mr. Silas won't mind you taking a pair."

They ate off china in a restaurant with a French name filled with blue velvet and gold trim. Miss L. went home for the evening and Silvers took his spot at his master's shoulder. The Grog got his own bench behind a thin curtain and sucked down an entire tureen of soup, softly hooting to himself as the men ate. Valentine had salmon with dill and assorted greens, Silas king crab legs. Silas probed him, not about opinions of the Kurians and those who worked for them, but about music and art and books he'd read.

Over dessert they talked about what kind of sports Valentine enjoyed. Silas apologized for the size of the desserts, enormous slabs of cheesecake slathered in syrupy strawberries. "If I have a weakness, it's for sweets."

"Mind answering a question?" Valentine asked.

"That's foolish to answer before hearing the question."

"Why the VIP treatment?"

"You're not getting the VIP treatment. I am. You're just in the overkill."

"And the questions about jazz versus jug band?"

"Just trying to take the measure of you."

"I appreciate the clothes, but this isn't the life I want. I could never live in the shadow of one of those towers."

Silas laid down his delicate dessert fork. "Do you speak from experience?"

"I've spent years at a stretch in the Kurian Zone."

"Just because you make it sound temporary doesn't change facts on the ground."

"There's no such thing as never. I'm pretty sure some mathematician or other proved that."

Silas put Valentine up in an almost empty apartment in his building, with some apologies that it would be temporary. But it did have a bed and hot water, and it was warm and dry. Valentine looked out at the city through two layers of glass door, both locked and welded shut.

The next day, after a quick rundown on the public transit system from Miss L., they fitted him with a plastic-sheathed metal loop around his ankle. A twitchy technician issued him with an ID card and swiped it through a slot in a black plastic circle the size of a wristwatch face embedded in the loop.

"Okay, Valentine comma D. of the Catalina Island and Baja Principalities. Your TRFID transmitter verifies who you are every time you use the card. Just in case you lose it, it's useless to anyone else." He consulted a screen. "You'll be okay for travel downtown for a couple days. Wow, nice expense account."

"It's not going to electrocute me in the shower, or blow my foot off if I leave Seattle, will it?"

The technician raised his eyes. "Catalina must really suck, if they run it like a work camp."

"No comment," Valentine said.

"Naw, it won't do any of that. Go swimming with it."

He didn't swim, but he spent two days exploring Seattle, staying as far away from the Kurian Tower as he could. It seemed a technology-driven city, and Valentine couldn't understand half of the conversations going on in the cafés. Every other block had a technical college or a medical school, mostly filled with foreign students from Asia. Everyone had an ankle tag, except for a few arty types who wore theirs around their necks, and it was from one of these that Valentine learned the coding system. Black indicated foreign dignitaries.

"Of course upper management has theirs implanted," a youngish longhair cradling a leather-topped wooden drum in a relaxed lounge with the intriguing name "Earworm Café" explained. "Everyone's got to bear the mark of almighty Babylon." He worked on an old computerized music player with a portable light and a set of precision tools.

"Sez the dude who spends every other morning getting CI certification," a girl chided as she cleaned a table and collected discarded mugs. "Double Deck, you'll be wiring IDs to your own family before you know it."

"Go pop out another kid for the churchies, your royal no compromises," the drummer said.

She bared sharpened teeth and Valentine decided to pay his bill. And the boy's.

Back at his apartment he found a note.

"Don't forget audience tomorrow. I had the suit pressed and the shirt cleaned—Luty."

The next day Valentine stood in borrowed clothes under a cheap plastic poncho. Seattle's mighty tower soared above him, making him feel like an ant in the shadow of a redwood.

A vast plaza surrounded the tower, rimmed with decorative columns topped with pensive statues of Reapers that served a more discreet purpose as vehicle barriers. Inside the circle it was paved with red and gray bricks that probably formed some kind of design when seen from on high, perhaps a spiral of some kind. Valentine guessed that at least four square blocks of downtown Seattle had been knocked down to make the expanse.

A strange sort of scaffolding had been set up in front of the tower. Perhaps three stories high on its own, it consisted of two staircases leading up to a long, bridge-like platform, an isosceles triangle aimed at the center column. A television camera was perched halfway up the stairs.

The spectators gathered for the audience consisted of well-dressed functionaries in the front, and a mass of shaggy student types farther back, each of whom received a little paper ticket like a theater admittance. The Seattle Police, in waxy black leather jackets, herded the entire crowd into one narrow mass in front of the scaffolding. Silas went up to the television platform and spoke to the cameraman, who turned his camera out on the crowd. Silas looked through it as well, and the police had the crowd spread out a little at the back, and passed out banners that could be unfurled to hide the lack of numbers.

SEATTLE CITY OF DREAMS AND PROGRESS, read one. PACIFIC COAST BEST AND BRIGHTEST HONORS KUR. Then there was the eternal OUR FUTURE IS BRIGHT AGAIN in phony childish lettering, held up by uniformed Youth Vanguard troops, which Valentine had seen in every political rally he'd attended in the Kurian Zone. Duvalier always said that Youth Vanguard troop rallies were so filled with high-ranking Quisling pederasts and pedophiles that the banners should read *Our cherry is plucked again.*

"Why not just round up more people for the audience?" Valentine asked one of the cops. "That's what we do back home."

"That's what I tell 'em," the cop said. "Just give folks a day off so they can come into the plaza. Give 'em luxury coupons like they give those sweatin' kids. They wanna have their cake and eat it too is all. Can't lose ten lousy hours of work. What they do is give everyone a half day on Fridays so they can go home and watch the speeches rebroadcast."

"That many televisions around? We sure don't have that at home."

"Shit yeah. Back in the good times, before all the fighting with the insurgents, this was a sweet spot."

"Sorry to hear that."

He lowered his voice. "Getting so even a police badge ain't proof against a cull. Like I was—"

A blast of music from the speakers mounted on the scaffolding interrupted him. Valentine wondered if Silas had selected Aaron Copland.

Then a New Universal Church Archon began to speak. He led the audience in a hymn, "Onward Human Progress," and Valentine managed to drone through it; he'd heard it many times before in the Gulf.

Silas' limo pulled up to the scaffolding and he and Troyd got out. Silas, wearing an elegant camel-hair coat that stood out against the dull aluminum of the metal, led Troyd up the stairs, where after a brief introduction as "the skilled xenologist who is doing so much to reverse our recent misfortunes" Troyd walked up a set of railless stairs that seemed impossibly narrow to Valentine. It was tipped with a sort of pulpit, and from there, by leaning on the rail and reaching his hand up, he could just reach a sort of blister on the side of the tower.

Silas spoke, talking about battles recently won that Valentine had never heard of, except for a small skirmish that resulted in a raiding PeaBee company retreating from an old state trooper station. To hear Silas describe it, another Stalingrad had been won.

Troyd passed his hand through a shimmering wall of light and pulled it out, still dripping with what looked like liquid fire. He shook it off and held up his undamaged hand, and the new brass ring on his finger glimmered like Venus on a dark night.

Valentine half listened to the speeches, marking the placement of Reapers. Two stood at the bottom of each stairway.

Troyd descended the stairs more surely, and stepped to the microphones. With the TV camera on him, he gave a brief, halting speech, thanking Seattle for his generosity and leadership, as a banner unfurled from the bottom of the scaffold.

**29 RINGS AWARDED IN OUR SIXTH DECADE
WHAT'S STOPPING YOU FROM GETTING YOURS?**

With Troyd's speech concluded, the Archon stepped to the microphones again. He clutched the railing and sagged for a moment, but Silas helped support him. With that, he raised his head, and with his eyes rolling and cheeks twitching he spoke.

"My children," he said, giving Valentine an odd tingle over the difference in his voice. The Archon sounded a little like a stroke victim who hadn't quite regained the full use of his tongue. "Your Kurian friends and allies have this day placed one of your number among the eagles that soar over this lovely land of ours. He is an example to be followed, for he teaches us the virtue of cooperation and utility. The beings he directs to guard your homes may look fearsome to you, but consider how fearsome they must look to those who threaten our peace. Perhaps then you shall look on their strange faces and beauty. We, your Kurian friends and allies, know you have sacrificed to feed these beings, but who regrets a toe when a leg is saved?

"There are dark forces at the gates of our city, so long a symbol of the heights mankind can reach, with just the tiniest touch of a friendly hand. With these fresh allies beside us, we can look to better days ahead. Belief in victory will lead to work for victory. Work for victory will lead to an affirmation of that belief.

"Too many homes have been darkened by death in the last year. New medicines are even now on their way to church dispensaries to help you dispel whatever fears and doubts you may have. But these have not come cheaply. We must bring the new B-6 into production to meet orders already placed, and certain luxuries will, for a time, become unavailable. Your conferences will provide you with details of our plans to increase output. If we all push together, a very short period of sacrifice will put us back on the road to prosperity and peace. Meet these hardships, not as a burden among burdens, but as a challenge above self! Will you, my family, accept this challenge?"

"Yes," Silas shouted into the microphone. "Yes, yes,

yes," he chanted, and the crowd took it up, perhaps eager for exercise to keep warm in the chill November air. The Youth Vanguard jumped up and down with each "yes."

After a few close-ups of people cheering, and a rowdy student or two lifting her sweater and T-shirt, the TV cameraman left.

Silas came down the stairs, chatting with Troyd.

"Wait for Valentine a moment, won't you, Troyd?" Silas asked. "I believe he's going to accompany you back to your wet little camp. Unless you want to come up and pay your respects in person."

Troyd looked at the ring on his hand, rubbed the skin. "No. I was touched once. That's enough for me."

"Then it's you and me, Valentine," Silas said.

"What, up there?"

"Of course."

"I thought I could just speak to one of the, the . . ."

"We call them avatars."

"One of the avatars," Valentine finished.

"He wants to look at you with his own eyes. All eight of them. Are you coming?"

Valentine nodded, and stepped up onto the scaffold stairs.

The four Reapers came up the stairs with them, boots loud on the metal steps. Valentine saw the TV man blanch as he placed his camera in a padded bag and frantically wound cables as the Reapers passed.

Silas hit a button by the microphones—another worker with a little silver television pin on her collar dismantled the microphones—and the stairs Troyd had used to climb up to the blister lowered and flattened into a narrow walkway, bridging a gap between the tower and the scaffold bridge. Valentine saw a slit open up in the tower wall, saw lips peel back as it widened.

He looked up at the blister in the tower. Some trick of light put six Reaper faces in various oddly shaped shards and panels of glass.

Two Reapers led them inside, ducking to go through

the slit. Silas followed, hands held out a little for balance. Valentine walked the beam uneasily, more thanks to the Reaper following behind than from fear of a misstep.

They lost two of the Reapers at the portal. Valentine couldn't resist turning around and looking. Sure enough, there were lines of triangles like shark teeth, yet off bias like the blades of a ripsaw, deadly yet decorative bumps on the inner side of those lips.

Valentine was relieved to see the inside conforming to human ideas of architecture and design.

"The center tower is separate from the others?"

"At the level humans go to, yeah. People work full-time in here, you know. They use our technology to light the place, keep the air moving. Seattle used to be a popular piece of real estate for them. I learned they evolved in tidal zones when I was out East in Cambridge."

They passed through an inner, curving shaft. Valentine looked up, saw small spiky projections on both sides of the wheel within wheels. There more thread-like projections connected the two layers of structure. It reminded him of a cross section of a bone with the marrow cleaned out. Climbing it would be possible, he imagined, but a long and demanding ascent.

All the corridors curved and wound, so it was difficult to see more than ten meters or so ahead. The Reapers led them to another elevator, in what Valentine guessed to be the center core of the pillar. Silas put his key into the slot and Valentine heard a beep.

"You have to do it too."

Valentine got the same beep and a green light came on over the elevator. The doors opened and they got in, accompanied by the Reapers.

"two for audience, seattle level," a Reaper said to a speaker grid.

Valentine found it interesting that even Reapers had to report in to some central authority. Bureaucracy or security? Weren't these Reapers animated by Seattle himself?

The elevator rose fast enough for Valentine to feel the change in perceived gravity for a moment. Then he concentrated on swallowing to relieve the changes in air pressure.

The elevator opened out on a wide bay. A Reaper in a purple robe, his face hidden by hood and fabric mask, nodded, and Silas led Valentine out of the elevator into the plain, well-lit lobby. Valentine noted that the walls had a metallic sheen, and there were what he supposed were two-way mirrors on each wall.

"Silvers used to wait for me in this room. But he kept getting nervous around the avatars and soiling the corner."

"You feel like you need a bodyguard up here?" Valentine asked.

"You never know. A Grog's like a big, comforting dog sometimes. A dog that can shoot."

The Reaper pointed to a door on the right wall.

"Crap. I hate the tunnel. I was hoping he'd talk to us in the gardens. You're on your own, Valentine."

Silas hurried over to the door, waved at a camera lens—Valentine noted the door had no ID card slot—and it opened. Dim light, such as one might find under fifty or sixty feet of murky water, showed a room beyond.

"Go on. It's safe, until he decides it shouldn't be safe."

"See you," Valentine said.

Valentine passed in, ducking slightly to clear the door, wondering if another elaborate death awaited inside. Funny how even involuntarily one developed a fatalism about that sort of thing. Did they put some psychotropic in the food?

While touring a classroom once in Biloxi as a Coastal Marine, Valentine had to do "community service" in a classroom. The class had a small family of hamsters, and the hamsters had a little plastic warren of connecting tunnels and shafts and rooms. The room he stepped into reminded him of those shafts, save that it was in the shape of a slightly pregnant triangle and surrounded by some kind of liquid.

He thought he could see other shafts and rooms through the liquid, but they might have been decor, or models; the rather cloudy water—if it was indeed water—made it difficult to tell.

Valentine saw dozens of bodies floating in the liquid. Most were in the shape of the octopus-bat creature that Valentine knew to be a Kurian/Lifeweaver form. Wires or lines projected from their extremities and "necks" to a football-sized orb that glowed mysteriously now and then as the forms floated. Something about the slowness of the movements inside made Valentine decide the liquid wasn't, in fact, water.

Others shared the space with the aliens, gentle and predatory. Valentine saw a Grog or two, and humans. An encephalitic fetus, tethered both to mother by umbilical and to its own football, yawned and stretched.

"Do you admire my menagerie?" a voice in his head asked. It was slightly mechanical, and Valentine realized it was from an old battery-operated Ready Reader toy he'd heard Amalee playing with the last time he'd seen her. He'd given it to her when he arrived on Jamaica, and she proudly showed "Uncle David" how good she was with it already, dog and cat and hat and ball prancing, stalking, bouncing, or spinning across the faded screen.

Valentine decided to respond aloud. If he started having conversations with himself, or the Kurian, or maybe that floating fetus, he didn't like his chances of making it out of the tunnel a complete personality again. "Which one are you?"

"All of them. In a way. You have a well-rounded mind for your kind, Vaal-eyen-tine-Dee. Strong extremes of love and hate. I hope you know the narrowness of the balance point on which the scale rests. Oh, here she is. How are you, sweet boy?"

The last was said with his mother's voice. Valentine felt a piece of him fall off. "Don't do that!"

"Do what, you little pail of piss water?" an old drill instructor from the Labor Regiment asked. "Oh, I like him."

What am I here to do again?

"Bargain, I think," LeHavre's voice said. Suddenly he was eleven again, standing in the kitchen above his pantsless mother, blood all over the floor, tomatoes stewing on the stove.

"Oh, that was delicious, thank you," Father Max's voice said. "But my time is limited."

Valentine found himself on his knees in the tunnel, gasping like a fish, his heart pounding. "Stop it! Please!"

"Very well. Why are you wondering if some of these are *Dau'weem*?"

"I have old friends in Southern Command who have vanished."

"I assure you, they are not here," Ready Reader said.

"What is this thing?"

"Are you familiar with your concept of a phased array?"

"No."

"A team of horses, perhaps?"

"Yes, of course."

"It's the same principle. Joined minds able to do what one cannot. It helps me keep tabs on my enemies—and my allies. Which reminds me, which are you?"

"An enemy."

"I admire your candor. Are you here to kill me, Vaal-eyen-tine-Dee?"

"No. I can't imagine how I'd do that."

"You've proven yourself inventive in the past. But you must know your limitations. Watch out for Blake. He'll forget himself someday and kill you, I expect. These constructs have very poor impulse control. Speaking of impulses, you've got strong ones toward my old friend Adler. What kind of a man do you think he is?"

"A madman," Valentine said.

"You're wrong. In any case, he's set me back years. Not that years mean much to me, of course. I shall re-build, better and more carefully, once he's gone. Sooner or later."

"I want to make it sooner."

"You do, of that I'm certain. Your wobbly little scale is quite tipped where he's concerned. I'd like to do it in Silas-Em's life span; he is a talented sort and I shall hate to lose him to age. This new generation thinks the most piddling acts of conformity merit a brass ring. Where is the desire for greatness?"

"Maybe you're breeding it out of them. Herd talk and all that. We've still got it in the Free Territories."

"Dream on, Vaal-eyen-tine-Dee," Duvalier's voice said. "Are you sure you're not mistaking free range for free land?" The voice shifted back to Ready Reader's. "Oh, and now we're tipping back for love again. You're more fun than a good treetop swoop on a breezy day, Vaal-eyen-tine-Dee."

"And my ring?"

"You do want it, after all. And food and a warm wet mouth and poke after poke into delicious juicy pussy and then a steaming hot bath. Are you toying with me, man, channeling the baser urges?"

Valentine kept fantasizing.

"Maybe you're not as interesting as I thought. In any case, I've no doubt you intend to go through with your plan. Your wish is granted. Adler's destruction would be worth eight-count of rings to me. Cross me and you will end up in the tank until your body rots. You can barely comprehend how long that will take."

"Don't forget my island."

"You'll find them cold and rocky after your Carib-bean, but something can be arranged." Light poured into the tunnel. "You may leave now. Good-bye."

One of the human forms jerked as its tether bal-loon changed color. His eyes opened behind his mass of drifting hair and he waved. Valentine saw the eyes widen, and he tore his gaze away and fled back into the receiving room. The man floating in there was the Bear Rafferty.

"You don't look so good, Valentine," Silas said. "Did you see that little girl? Some comedian stuck a—"

"No," Valentine said. "I saw someone I knew, briefly."

"You need some air." He turned to the Reaper. "Can we go into the greenhouse?"

For a moment it seemed as useless as talking to a statue; then their escort Reapers moved to flank the other door. Silas waved Valentine over and it opened.

Valentine smelled fresh, humid air and open space. Above, a crystalline dome diffused and admitted light, whitening the sun a little. A red path covered with a no-slide coating led them up to a little prominence, with a couple of comfortable human lounge chairs before a pool, which flowed over into a waterfall somewhere below.

Staggered was the only word for what Valentine felt. The space was bigger than any stadium he'd ever seen, and filled with a winding archipelago that was half-bayou and half-beachfront.

Red and purple trees topped with bristles of tresslike leaves dropped green vines into the water. Spongy-looking yellow growths clung to the bare trunks of the trees, sending out vast, delicate webs to catch deadfalls from above. Wind swirled around the interior of the dome.

"This is a piece of Ehro, home planet of the *Dau'ar*."

Valentine felt invigorated. "I thought they came from Kur. Someone told me it was a dry, almost lifeless place."

"A castle under siege runs out of even rats eventually. But Ehro is where they evolved, I'm told. That oxygen's nice, isn't it?"

"I wish they'd go back to it."

"They can't, but then you know that, I expect. We're

just a part of a bigger, older war. I worry sometimes that the *Dau'weem* will apply the same strategy to our planet that Adler does to the suburbs."

Something translucent buzzed by on pink wings. "They'd never do that."

"Remember what I told you the other night about nevers? I never wanted the role of interlocutor. I decided to take what they'd hand me and go out East, build an academic ivory town and seal myself into it. But you'd be surprised, once you learn the true history of the world, just what parasites those things that laughably call themselves 'Lifeweavers' are. I've got a book or two I could loan you."

"I've seen the propaganda. Your master's the real parasite. Black bloody leeches. Worse than leeches, leeches at least leave the host alive. The Lifeweavers are interested in conserving life, not devouring it."

"Tell that to Silvers. He says a disease killed most of his people back home. They didn't want the Grogs used to conquer any more worlds."

"Not every plague has a purpose," Valentine said. "Seems just as likely your own masters would use a tactic to get them to quit their lands, force them to hitch up with Kur to find healthy land on another planet."

"Kur hates purposeless death."

"I can agree with you on that."

Silas sighed. "They've accumulated wisdom we can't even guess at in their long years. They're going to guide us up to heights we'd never reach on our own."

"I've had enough of this view. And the heights. I want to go to work."

Silas looked at his heavy gold watch. "Good. You'll start tomorrow."

CHAPTER FOURTEEN

G*rog troops: An easy path to promotion and power for any human with a military background is to volunteer to serve as an Officer of Xeno Forces. High rank and its powers and privileges come quickly to volunteers for the OXFs, but at the cost of a social stigma. Mixing with non-humans leaves OXFs in a strange netherworld, secretly despised by those they fight for and openly by those they fight against.*

Though the rumors of bestial mating rituals and cannibalism are unfounded, and can usually be traced back to Freehold propaganda or melodramatic fictionalizations, there's no denying that OXF attract their share of bad apples. Men who can't win promotion or fit in elsewhere sign up for OXF training, where standards are looser and faults overlooked.

Of all the odd troops OXF have led—or tried to lead—the actions involving Big Mouths evoke the most consistently chilling accounts. Sometimes the only evidence of one of their attacks is a strong fishy odor, bloodstains, and a few bitten-off heads, hands, and feet missed after the seaside scrum and feed. Almost ungovernable, and known to turn on their OXF leaders in victory, defeat, or starvation, they are perhaps the most bloodthirsty Grogs to fight or lead.

Yet it was these dangerous oddities that David Valentine led into one of the most daring actions of his career.

* * *

Valentine stood on the steady deck of the old Japanese factory-fishing ship, renamed the *Redeye Run,* in its permanent Puget Sound moorings in the east passage around Vashon Island and tried not to barf.

He'd smelled rotten fish before. He'd smelled sewage before. If it was possible to mix the two and come up with a third odor worse than the two component parts, the Big Mouths had discovered it in their hovels within the hulk.

He lifted his gaze from the open cargo hatches of the ship and looked at Vashon Island with its herds of sheep. The Big Mouths, when they wanted a change from seafood and crustaceans, had the run of the flat, muddy island and its flocks, stranded there for that purpose.

"Why this heap of junk?" Valentine asked.

"Mostly because the freezers still work," Finn Troyd said. Calling him "Finnegan" was a gilt-edged invitation to a punch in the mouth, and judging from the behavior of the OXFs on the ship, that was the civilized option. "You have to hand it to the Japs—they build industrial equipment to last. We've got a big supply of frozen emergency food. The last thing you want to do is run out of rations when you're handling Big Mouths."

Valentine nodded.

"Ready to go down and meet the gang?"

"I guess I'm dressed for it." Valentine, with the titular rank of captain, didn't bother with "sir's"—no one in the OXFs did.

They both wore old woolen pants and sweaters, covered by a layer of waterproof overalls and thick green plastic boots.

"Grab your S and S and let's go, then."

By "S and S" Troyd meant shotgun and shockstick. The shockstick was almost identical to the ones Valentine had seen and used in the Southwest, save that it had a longer and heavier rubberized handle.

They went down into one of the holds. The side of the ship was punctured below the waterline. Scale and rust gave some color to the old sides, and the barnacles and whelks were making inroads into the water pooled in the bottom of the hold.

The smell was even worse down here thanks to the confined space. Valentine looked around at the staring bright red goggle eyes of the squatting and lounging Big Mouths.

They were hard to describe. Scaled like fish everywhere but the mouth and belly, they had huge triangular heads that tapered off to thin hips, where they were equipped with the long rear legs of a frog, ending in flippers and residual digits—almost useless for gripping, according to Troyd. Short arms, mostly used for climbing out of the water and pivoting on land, had webbed, gripping toes. They had blue green backs and pale, tartar-colored bellies.

The hold echoed with the sound of their breathing, as they sucked air through gill-like openings: *slee-kee, slee-kee.*

They liked to position themselves against an object, an underwater rock or log, with their rear legs folded. They could execute fair-sized leaps even without something to push off, but when properly "sprung" they could cover thirty yards or more in a lightning-flash hop.

Valentine watched a larger Big Mouth come up through a hole in the bottom of the ship and crowd another one out of the way with a few threatening snaps of vertically hinged jaws.

"What keeps her afloat?"

"One of each of the holds, forward and rear, is full of buoyant stuff, and the slop barges to either side are fixed permanently as camels. Marker barrels, Ping-Pong balls, flotation foam from old life jackets and airplane cushions, coconut coir, just about anything guaranteed not to sink. You could rip out the whole bottom of this ship and she wouldn't go down. At least I don't think she would."

Pools of filth rested in the shallow water lapping in the hold.

"They like it dirty down here, don't they?"

Troyd shrugged. "The shit feeds the slime. Little fish and crabs feed off the slime. Bigger fish eat the little fish. The Big Mouths eat the crabs and bigger fish, leading to more shit. It's a regular circle of life."

A Big Mouth splashed around in the filth, wiggling its rear hips and hunching its back. "Lying around, eating, and shitting, that's about all they do when they're not in training."

Valentine noted that the full-grown Big Mouths had stainless steel rings at their forehump between the eyes and in a fleshy taillike growth between the legs.

"What are the rings?" he asked.

"Front one's a towline or tether line. You'll see how those work. Rear is attached to some gonad tissue—that's a control line. About the only way you can direct them is to yank 'em by the balls. But haul too hard on the reins—they'll swing around and try to bite yours off."

Troyd let Valentine absorb that factoid and then continued: "Okay, we've seen lying around and shitting. Let's go look at the eating and training."

They took a flagged motorboat over to a sheltered bay between Maury and Vashon islands. OXF, mostly male but with a few women, stood on little floating platforms heaped with white buckets, or paddled around in sea kayaks, or were pulled about lying on floats Troyd called "boogie boards."

"Hey, Finn, can I borrow your ring?" a man called from a platform. "I'm going into the city this weekend and I could use a little flash."

Troyd laughed. "You'll have to bite it off like that whatsit in the old movie. How are they working?"

"Good. Eager. Donaldson lost one this morning, though—it attacked him. The others already ate it. They didn't get a frenzy going, probably the big breakfasts you're issuing."

"Glad to hear it." Troyd tossed a thermos of coffee to him. "Be nice and share for a change."

"We're going to have to get you a sea suit," Troyd said as they pulled away from the platform. "The water's pretty cold in the bay this time of year."

He pointed to a platform next to the shore. "That's training. You'll learn the hand signals easy enough—there's only sixteen of them. We fire flares when we want them to attack. For the BMs, that is. There's another dozen or so the handlers use to keep in touch with each other."

"What about at night?"

"Same signals, with chemical glow sticks. The BMs actually respond better at night. I think they can see the glow sticks better than they do hands. Same thing with the flares. Just don't pull your flare pistol early—they'll see it and get all idgitated and go nuts because they think it means food."

"I need to know everything about capabilities. Especially speed in water over long distances, and on land."

"On a long haul they average, um, fifteen or twenty miles per hour. That varies depending on currents. They slow down a bit in really cold water too."

"And on land?"

"Land they move along pretty good, a fast walk. But they leave a trail like a mudslide. There's the smell and they lose scales pretty easily, so pretty much any idiot knows when some BMs have been through. When am I going to hear more?"

"What's in the buckets?"

"Positive reinforcement. The BMs go nuts for pork. Dog too, but not so much as a good fatty pig. We give them pigs' feet, snouts, heads, ears, all that stuff, when they do something right. After a successful action we'll usually roast a hog or two to treat everyone."

"I think I read somewhere that physiologically, human flesh is a lot like pig."

"They eat that too. They're always eager to go into action to get a bellyful. You've never seen creatures so eager for a fight. They don't give a damn about casualties either, just means more eating on the way home."

"Any land training going on now?" Valentine asked.

"Yeah, up by those old houses."

"Can we land this thing and take a look?"

"Sure. We'll even show you how to give a couple orders. Just watch your fingers when rewarding. Toss, don't give. These ain't a bunch of backflippin' dolphins."

Valentine spent the next six weeks training with the OXFs. They equipped him with a Chinese SG carbine, reliable enough but not much good beyond fifty yards on autofire or a hundred shooting over open sights. They accepted him as one of their own. OXFs saw a lot of wanderers pass in, decide the work wasn't for them, and pass on again to something easier—like lumberjacking.

He answered a few questions about Catalina Island, and retreated behind the old reliable "That's classified" when probed too deeply, though most of the questions revolved around the weather and the amount of sunshine. He hemmed and hawed during a couple of equivocal probes about needing people with experience handling Big Mouths back on the island.

One of the trainers opined that the Big Mouths wouldn't do well there, as they were cool-water creatures, but another man claimed the eastern shores of Florida were thick with thriving BMs.

He spent his days cold and wet and his nights in his fish-reeking quarters on the *Redeye*, with his hands and arms slathered in lanolin to restore moisture and keep his skin from sliding off the bone. The creatures' odor was all-invasive, all-pervasive, and seemed to be the one thing that quieted his appetite.

As he slept he got the uncomfortable feeling someone was watching his dreams along with him.

Eventually he laid out a detailed plan for Troyd, a route into the mountains that avoided the river-watch stations. It involved a series of upriver journeys and then short overland hikes, always to the north, where a new river would be picked up for a push of a few miles more inland, then another short overland journey. By this long, counterclockwise turn, they could hit the Snoqualmie upriver from the Outlook, unguarded by dams, falls, or nets.

"The BMs can do it. It'll be hell on the men, though. That's a lot of time in some very cold water. We'll need to bring chemical heat."

"How secure is Vashon Island?" Valentine asked.

"No one hangs out there if they know what's good for them."

"Good. I'd like to use that old airfield there. It's about the right size for the target. I was poking around in it the other day to check the interior. With a little fixing here and there, block one door and put in another, we could get the corridors right. We need to rig some lighting and get some interiors. Can you ask Silas about some drywall and some workmen?"

"Jeez, Valentine, these are BMs, not commandos."

"The less left to doubt, the better. Now, the last thing I need is a moon chart—"

While construction went on, Valentine spent his mornings on endurance swims with the Big Mouths. He practiced "driving" paired BMs behind a sea kayak, mile after mile, first up and down the coast of the sound, then up the White River.

Troyd worked out the logistics of the overland part of the raid. The BMs were used to short hauls in tractor-trailers, but the OXFs had to get them worked up to an hour or two.

Valentine agonized over the timetable with the man Troyd decided on as second-in-command, Lieutenant Burlington, another Canadian down from Vancouver. They started making test swims at night, taking forty Big Mouths up the lower end of the White, then camping on the old mudslide damage from Mount Rainier, then spending the day in a lake, then traveling overland a couple of miles more.

"What about getting them back?"

"If they get back, they get back," Burlington said. "They're basically expendable."

That simplified matters. Valentine had a hard time feeling much sympathy for the fish-frogs. At the first sign of injury to a fellow, the others ate it. A military operation deep behind the opposing lines became a good deal more practicable if one didn't have to worry about returning the troops.

"We've got to think about our getting back. I say we go downstream on the Green River. . . ."

On Troyd's recommendation they added a third officer to the team in case illness or injury removed Valentine or Burlington. Holly Nageezi, a tight little bundle of muscle who never seemed to feel the chill of the sound, had been an athlete for, of all things, a women's Roller Derby team. She'd been away from her quad on a night when one of the Action Groups hit, slaughtering every neighbor and friend she had.

Bad luck struck just before the jump-off. They lost three Big Mouths from the ones trained to go into the mock Outlook, when on a trial run in, Valentine forgot and pulled his flare pistol too early as they approached. The BMs became, in Troyd's words, "idgitated," and started attacking one another when he didn't release them right away.

Valentine talked with Burlington about replacing them with Big Mouths from the pool. "Fresh ones would probably just do what all the others do. I think it would be safe to bring them."

"But these have gotten used to going a couple days without feeding. Maybe inexperienced isn't the way to go. They might lead the others astray."

In the end, after talking it over with Troyd, Valentine made the decision to go with just the twenty-seven.

Then Burlington deserted on a dark, late January night, three days before the new-moon weekend. Nobody could say how he had slipped away.

He left a note. Troyd showed it to Valentine but kept it a secret from Nageezi. Burlington had suggested that the whole operation was a one-way trip for the human handlers as well as the Grogs.

Troyd and Valentine informed Nageezi of her rise to second-in-command and she seemed oddly pleased. "Doing's easy. Having someone notice, that's difficult," she said.

They inspected the gear together at a vacant Tacoma dockside warehouse that served as their jumping-off point, and saw that their team of twenty-seven BMs had a heavy breakfast of sheep-with-hooves-removed. Valentine had his carbine, a silenced .22 automatic he'd picked up at the downtown armory, and a heavy diving knife with a built-in wire snip, sharp enough to cut the leather leads between his kayak and the Big Mouths in case of trouble. He oiled everything and placed the guns in waterproof bags.

"Nap?" Nageezi said as the hours counted down to when the trucks would be loaded. She pulled her silenced .45 out of its holster and patted a spot next to her. "We're going to be doing it in the field."

"So get used to it now."

They nodded against each other, but it seemed to Valentine that neither really slept.

Loading the Big Mouths into their covered livestock trucks was comforting in its routine, indistinguishable from the dozens of times they'd done it on long training runs. Valentine rode in the first truck with a pair of experienced drivers, Nageezi in the second. A third truck followed, there in case of mechanical failure, carrying one more meal for the Big Mouths in the form of a heap of dead, mangy dogs. Valentine watched the soldiers in the guard truck sway along—for all the drivers and the guards knew, this was just another training run.

The weather turned nasty at the riverbank, a cold, lashing rain that turned everything dark three hours ahead of schedule. It came down hard enough that Valentine thought it would blow itself out quickly. The Big Mouths hopped into the river eagerly enough.

The drivers of the third truck, anxious at the sight of the snapping jaws, refused to toss the dogs to the waiting Big Mouths until Nageezi drew her automatic and promised the fish-frogs dog or driver.

And with that they were off.

The rain alternating with snow lightened up but never really ceased. It didn't make much difference on the longest river run, that first night. They waited out the day in a backwater of the river, with the Big Mouths either resting or probing the riverbanks for small game and waterfowl.

The first overland trek, almost six miles, went well enough. Valentine and Nageezi hiked what felt mostly uphill on a heavy portage through the woods, following in a trail flattened by the prowling Big Mouths with fiberglass kayak, paddle, and equipment. Anything that didn't involve buckets of ice-cold water being flung in his face seemed like a treat.

He and Nageezi huddled together in the snow as they rested the second day, eating preserved food— appallingly small portions according to Valentine's cold-sharpened appetite—the green and white mountains of the Cascades around them. They warmed their food over chemical heat and pressed close together under a thin survival blanket, recuperating.

The second night's run was a long, churning nightmare of white water as they were pulled by the strong swimming—or hopping, over some of the rapids— upstream. Nageezi had the knack of resting herself and her team in the occasional eddy better than Valentine, and by the time they went back into the water, with fresh chemical heat packs pressed to their feet and the small of their backs, he let Nageezi lead.

The rotten weather carried one advantage: It made observation from the banks almost impossible.

They waited out the third day at a lake on the Green River, with the Big Mouths philosophical about their empty bellies. They'd been trained to have a real gorge after penetrating the fake hotel built up in the airport on the third night. . . .

For the final night's run Nageezi took amphetamines. She offered a pair of white capsules to Valentine.

"Benzedrine?"

"I'm okay," he said.

"Suit yourself," she said, popping the capsules and following them with a swig of water from a big bottle.

Valentine would have just about given a finger for a thermos of Space Needle–quality coffee. He set his kayak in the current and took up the reins from the new team with winter-chilled muscles.

"At least the weather's broke," Nageezi said, smiling. "Seattle stopped the rain."

"That's a bunch of crap," Valentine said, irritated at her chemically enhanced cheer. "They don't control the weather."

"Screw yourself," she said quietly, but Valentine's ears picked it up.

"What's that?"

"Suit yourself."

She's a Quisling. What do you care what she thinks? Because, for one night, you're a Quisling too.

Valentine could live with it. He just hoped the Outlook was filled with Bears fresh from a Resource Denial operation.

The Big Mouths swam excitedly up the Green River. They could already taste the hot pork they expected to be waiting for them. Valentine marked the end of a lake on his map, and broke a chemical light. He signaled for the last portage.

Nageezi took two more bennies at the end of the portage as they slipped into the Snoqualmie, heading downstream at last. Valentine unhooked the reins from his Big Mouth team. He could paddle from here. It would warm him up.

He visualized the bodies strewn in the streets of the housing block, the fearful families in the church, and tried to summon a little of the Bear energy for the final push, but it stubbornly refused to come out of hibernation.

They rounded a bend, shot past a few boarded-up buildings heavy with snow, and there it was. The Outlook.

Valentine paddled his kayak next to hers. "Let's get a little closer." He shook a chemical light and stuck it under the water and repeated a circular signal three times; the red-eyed amphibian behemoths gathered round the kayaks.

They pulled their craft to the edge of the river, beneath a substantial lip of land, Valentine hiding the chemical light in his vest. He checked his knife, and took his guns out of their waterproof plastic sheaths.

"Feel that ring on your finger yet?" Nageezi asked. They anchored their kayaks in the shadow under the earth and rock lip. A paved river path was just on the other side of a set of white-painted warning stones.

"Not just yet. I want to hit the Outlook first."

She checked the safety on her .45, worked the slide. "If I get hit, try not to let them eat me."

"Same here," Valentine said, trying to remember not to reach for the flare gun until all the Big Mouths were out of the water and hopping toward the entrances the way they'd been trained. He adjusted his rifle sling around his neck—the Chinese carbine had a hell of a kick and he wanted it tight against his shoulder....

She peeked over the lip of the riverbank. "You know there's a tradition in the OXFs. If a commander falls, and the second still wins a victory, all the spoils go to him. Or her."

The gun flashed toward him and fired.

Valentine lurched away as the muzzle turned toward him—over a decade of being around guns taught one to keep out of the way of barrels—but even Cat reflexes weren't faster than a bullet. At first he felt a hard thump at the bottom of his right rib cage. Then he discovered he was in the water, bobbing toward the falls, blood warming the interior of his suit.

He saw a Big Mouth turn toward him. Its jaws

opened and Valentine instinctively pulled his feet away, oddly calm.

The last thing he remembered before the jaws engulfed him was Nageezi's face in the dark, as she gestured, lifting a chemical light of her own.

She was smiling.

CHAPTER FIFTEEN

—⚓—

*B*earfire: Ask twenty different Bears to describe the feeling of Bearfire running through their bodies and you will get twenty different answers. Some speak in terms of space and time, everything slowed down and yet compressed. Others describe it mentally, as a determined form of psychosis, where every obstacle, from a minor vexation to a hail of machine-gun fire, is overcome by boundless violence. Most describe physiological changes: heat, euphoria, a terrible driving energy.

Ask the same number of doctors to describe the injuries they've seen Bears survive, fighting on to victory and recovery or toppling only once what's left of their bodies falls apart, and be prepared to have a short book's worth of incredible stories.

This is one of them.

You fucking cunt!

Valentine realized he couldn't breathe or see, and all he felt was a horrible, slimy mess surrounding him, seeping into hairline and nostril, lip and ear hole.

Can't breathe, wet cold panic

And flipped around again, violently jostled.

Wet hot fear

—turning into

White-hot anger.

Valentine wriggled a hand up, closed fingers around the corded knife hilt.

Red!

He lashed out, hand and foot, head and arm. Stabbed hard with the knife handle, punctured, punched through resistance, then with a long backhanded sweep opened up the voluminous gullet of the Big Mouth.

It vomited him out before he could fight his way free, rolled away, stricken and thrashing.

Valentine broke the surface of the hard-flowing river, hurt as he sucked air, found himself bouncing, got his toes pointed downstream, fetched up against a rock, lost it, slid against another, caught it, losing his knife in his desperation to get a grip.

He pulled himself half out of the rushing river, saw a long leg flail as the wounded Big Mouth went over the falls.

He climbed up onto the rock, thought about his wound, reached, and felt the hot wet blood against his palm. The bullet had plowed one long furrow along his rib cage.

You'll live.

She won't.

He jumped to another rock, sucked a deep breath of air, felt pain again, realized his rifle was still bouncing against his chest.

He removed the weapon's final proof against liquid infiltration, a heavy-duty condom over the barrel, and found a stone to crouch where he could watch events at the Outlook.

A stream of sparks cut across the night sky, exploded into red light as a flare wobbled down, blown northeast by the wind.

The parking lot where Valentine had once watched a few drunk figures play basketball was alive with slithering, hopping, humpbacked shapes.

Glowing red goggle eyes fixed on the snow-dusted gables of the Outlook. Warm yellow light shone within, fell in checkerboard patterns on the virgin snow in front of the hotel.

Slee-kee, slee-kee, slee-kee . . .

Mr. Norman Rockwell, meet Mr. Hieronymus Bosch. Mr. Bosch, Mr. Rockwell.

Valentine lifted his gun, chambered the first round in the magazine, sighted on Lieutenant Nageezi. An urge to run at her, grind her face into mush, was suppressed as he straightened up and felt the pain in his side. He lowered the front sight to her thigh as she paused behind a parked truck in the lot, Big Mouths flapping and surging around her.

No, she knows her business. Wait. Get back to the kayak. First-aid kit.

The Big Mouths knew their business too. They divided into three streams of hopping shapes. Leap-gather-hunch-leap-gather-hunch-leap-gather-hunch on their way to the front and side entrances.

Crashes, screams, somehow softened by all the snow. There it was, the mad music of gunfire.

He gained the kayaks and tore open a dressing, pressed it to his wound, found the surgical tape, and went to work.

A Big Mouth made it all the way to the roof of the Outlook in a single leap. Another chased a shadow on a curtain right through the window, crashing through window, frame, screen, and curtain. Valentine heard a squelching noise and blood sprayed on a wall, three quick arterial jets.

A man fled out the front door, uniform coat torn, one shoe off, running into the night toward the parking lot with arms pumping. A Big Mouth flung itself out the door after him, flew over the footprints he'd left in the snow, and fixed its mouth over his head as it landed, folding its prey like a clasp knife.

A soldier ran across the deck, heading for the wire gondola crossing the falls, spraying bullets from a pistol back through the door. Valentine sighted on him, but another shot rang out and Valentine caught sight of Nageezi's features in the shadows of a station wagon parked in the lot.

Gunfire shattered a second-floor window, peppering

the station wagon, deflating a tire, and forcing Nageezi to flatten. Two men hurled themselves from the shattered window, hit the snow rolling, and came up with assault rifles ready. One poured a magazine into the Big Mouth on the lawn, tearing its still-gobbling head to pieces.

They ran for a red full-cab truck. One paused, turned to look up, and waved at something in the broken window as the other made it to the driver's-side door on the truck.

Valentine recognized Thunderbird's features as he turned, bathed in the light of the Outlook.

Adler was at the window now. He hesitated, jumped, fell for what seemed to Valentine an eternity, but landed lightly and with more skill than the Bears.

Nageezi popped up from behind her bullet-stitched car, aiming, but Thunderbird spun and tore her to pieces with a short blast of his assault rifle.

Adler seemed to flow over the snow-covered yard, legs a blur. Thunderbird covered him as he approached the pickup.

Glass exploded and a Big Mouth followed the glittering pieces out onto the lawn, drawn by the motion. Thunderbird put in a new magazine as the creature turned, watching Adler run as the truck came to life, gathered—

And was brought down by a long tongue of muzzle flash from Thunderbird's weapon. He took two steps forward, pumping more bullets into it, flesh flying everywhere in the night.

More screams, more gunfire, a grenade explosion within the Outlook, and the red truck backed out of its spot, Adler slamming the rear passenger door.

Another Big Mouth, having passed all the way through the Outlook only to emerge at the far end of the wraparound porch, liked the look of the truck and covered half the distance to it in a jump. Thunderbird turned, but something went wrong with his gun. He threw it down, pulling a pistol as the jammed weapon hit, and sidestepped for the turning truck.

Now it was Valentine's turn to sight, not at Thunderbird, or Adler, but at the driver of the truck as he reached out to clear ice from the windshield. He flipped the selector to single shot and put three 5.56mm shells through the front windshield into him.

Valentine ducked and changed positions. He came up again to see the truck rolling across the parking lot at the purposeless speed of an unpushed accelerator in drive, turning slightly to follow the path of least resistance downhill.

Thunderbird sprinted for the truck and Valentine fired at him, knocking him down. The Big Mouth liked the look of his fall and pounced.

The truck waggled, then turned, and Valentine saw Adler climbing into the front seat—too late. It bounced over the curb and nosed into the river, doors flying open as it hit.

Valentine splashed, slipped, recovered, and hurried toward the truck before Adler could escape. He saw a shape dive out the door on the opposite side, marveled at Adler's fluid athleticism. Ex-Cat? Valentine jumped up onto the river-walk path and pounded after him, saw Adler slipping and floundering on rocks, arms waving so fast in the light it looked as though there were three of them.

Valentine whipped his rifle behind him on its sling and launched himself into a flying tackle, brought down his quarry in a body blow that felt more like he hit a badly stuffed tackling dummy than a man.

He hauled Adler up by his slippery, oily hair and dug for the eyes, the nostrils, his left hand reaching for the windpipe and finding only cool squishiness.

But the blood was wrong—

"Turn around, Valentine," Colonel Thunderbird said. "I'm putting this right between your eyes. I want to see them empty as the bullet pops the back of your head off."

"Before you pull that trigger," Valentine said, turning and raising his hands, "have a look at this."

Thunderbird's blood-circled eyes widened; the pistol in his hand shook and lowered. Valentine held aloft the leaking, slippery body of a Kurian. Or perhaps a Lifeweaver. Or both. Only the dying mind, twitching as it passed into inferno, glory, or nothingness, could say for sure.

"Is that—"

"A Kurian Lord," Valentine said.

Valentine threw the corpse up at Thunderbird, then hopped into his kayak and started across the river, half expecting a bullet in the back. He chanced a look over his shoulder.

Thunderbird was on his knees, crying.

Two days later Valentine staggered into a motorcycle-cavalry depot in Maple Valley, scribbled a message to be transmitted to Troyd at the *Redeye Run*, and promptly collapsed.

He woke in an ambulance, and paid a brief visit to a hospital, where they found him suffering more from exhaustion and blood loss than any specific injury—though he did carry a recently healed bullet wound—and after feeding him, they sent him back to his old temporary apartment in Silas' building.

Troyd visited him, called him "ring brother" or something just as insipid—Valentine could never remember later—and dropped off a few personal possessions from his berth at the *Redeye Run*.

"Three of your Big Mouths made it back the day before you did. We found two more in Lake Sammamish, but they were making a nuisance of themselves and had to be destroyed."

"Nageezi got it in the parking lot of the hotel," Valentine said.

"I dunno about her," Troyd said. "You know we found one of Burlington's shoes in a bunch of BM shit? I'm thinking she chummed him after getting him to write that desertion note. You're lucky she didn't try to rung-jump over your corpse."

"I guess I am," Valentine replied.

He found he'd suddenly acquired a personal chef and regular visits from Miss L. to ascertain any needs beyond food and sleep. "Does the hero of the hour require anything else?"

"My ring, as soon as I'm feeling up to it."

"Does it mean that much to you?" she asked, looking a little disappointed.

"I went through hell to get it. Cold, angry hell. It's worth it to me."

Even Silas stopped by, with a gift-boxed bottle of brandy to put an edge on his constitution. Valentine suddenly couldn't stand his presence, and pretended to be overcome with yawns. Silas took the hint.

But he found himself leaving his bed, again and again, to look at the downtown skyline and the crystal-capped Kurian Tower. But how?

Once up and around and evidently with plenty of time and money for his recovery, Valentine walked into the student café he'd visited when touring Seattle, but unfortunately didn't see the kid with the drum.

He recognized the girl who'd fought with Double Deck, working behind the counter.

"Young lady," Valentine said. "Double Deck's not around, is he?"

"He's got class. I think he said he had to report to community center later. You might catch up to him there."

"How much are those T-shirts on the wall?"

She raised her eyebrows in surprise. "You don't look like the Earworm Café type. They're twelve dollars, two for twenty."

"I'll take six. But I don't have to walk out the door with them, if you'll just get Double Deck here."

"What do you want with him?"

"Babylon's going to make him an offer of extremely brief, extremely lucrative employment."

"If you're wanting to ditch your tracer for a night or

two, you'll need an excuse." She stuck out a fleshless hip. "If the price is right, I could say you were tied up to me."

Thanks to a dead tracer and a borrowed mountain bike, Valentine made it to the north tip of Lake Sammamish. From there it was a fairly easy run to the borders of the Seattle Kurian Zone.

"We don't know how he kept himself fed," Captain LeHavre said. "There are a couple of theories, mostly flavors of shit whirling off the fan blades."

They spoke inside a sentry checkpoint just outside the headquarters, a little prefabricated set of roof and three walls built like an outhouse and just as cozy. Valentine didn't want his presence known to the men, so he waited until he saw a familiar face and hailed him from cover. He in turn got LeHavre.

"He liked to tour the nurseries a lot, where the babies grabbed in the Action Group raids would be taken. Seems like a crib death or two struck now and then. Some staff got suspicious at an Ellensburg orphanage and they all were 'disappeared.' "

"He had to have some help somewhere."

"There's a Kurian Tower out by the Grand Coulee Dam that might have been visited too. He kept going out that way to survey it with an eye toward taking the power station, but conditions never seemed right for him to give the go-ahead."

"On the inside too."

"I hope most of them took it in the neck at the Outlook."

"There's a witch hunt—maybe it should be called a wizard hunt, at that—going on right now. I hope Pacific Command doesn't fall apart again. Thunderbird and his Bears are all tainted by this."

Interesting as the political fallout was, Valentine's time was limited. "Speaking of Thunderbird's Bears, if you think a successful action would help restore things here, I have an idea or two along those lines. There's a dreary party being planned in my honor and I'd like to see it crashed. But you'll have to get the Resistance Network in Seattle and the Bears to work together. That's going to take a little diplomacy. One more thing. What are the chances of you helping me write a proposal that'll get a scout/sniper named Gide temporarily seconded to the PeaBees?"

"Can do," LeHavre said, and gave one of his dashing pirate-quarterdeck salutes.

Two weeks later, with plenty of notice about the date and time, Valentine stood tall on the field of honor.

Seattle's remade downtown around him, thanks to tricks of optics played on someone standing on the plaza, seemed to be bowing to the Seattle demigod's tower. The strange, clamshell-like growth extending from the central pillars hung in the sky as though suspended by invisible wires, linked to the pillars by joins so narrow they seemed to defy principles of engineering. No cantilevering, no braces, no suspension, assisted the mollusklike housings of Seattle's Kurians.

And above all the rest, a vast jellyfish-like shape, faintly luminescent like dying phosphors, squatted the home of the demigod, challenging even Mount Rainier for dominance of the horizon.

Madness, madness, madness. But Valentine wanted the ring. By blood and thundering rapids, it was his.

Despite the rain, the watching crowds seemed larger than usual.

Silas stood at his side, his elegant camel-hair coat taking the drizzle as if confident that it would be properly dried and pressed after doing its duty.

"Good crowd today, despite the cold. The so-called Radio Free Northwest reported the death of 'one of the leading minds of the Resistance,' " Silas said. "Our broadcasts have been reading locations and numbers of people killed."

"I wonder which epitaph he'd prefer," Valentine asked.

"Every lumberjack and longshoreman's ready to celebrate, it seems. Watch the stairs—they can get icy when it rains in this kind of cold," Silas advised.

"Don't let the echo from the loudspeakers throw you off either," Miss L. said, behind the pair of them. "Just do your speech."

Valentine had rehearsed it twice with Silas the night before. Not much longer than the Gettysburg Address, it would "get the job done," according to the mouthpiece. Valentine checked the words on the little laminated index card one more time.

I stand here, an ordinary man with extraordinary purpose. Today I've been honored with the highest award our saviors can give. But in the end, the sacrifice and struggle that went with winning this ring are meaningless compared to the service Kur has done for us. Kur bestows, with a parental hand that heals more than it hurts, a gift for those with the eyes to see, the new, universal creed that we aspire to: a united human family in harmony with itself and the planet it lives upon, stronger, healthier, happier in our new purpose. Giving up selfishness, I found plenty. Giving up knowledge, I found wisdom. Giving up independence, I found freedom. I thank Kur, not only for myself, but for all mankind.

It had helped him take his mind off the coming ceremony. If he gave the speech he wanted, he would most likely end up looking like a fool for the few brief seconds of his remaining, violently concluded life.

Gears worked and the scaffolding rose and unfolded itself into place, a steel skeleton animated by hidden cables and counterweights. A banner hung from the central walkway.

SEATTLE IS THE FUTURE

At a nudge from Silas, Valentine crossed the plaza. The two Reapers at the bottom of the stairs, dressed in long dark robes like judges and wide-brimmed Pilgrim hats to keep off the rain, parted and pointed with their hands facing the tower up the golden stairs. Valentine wondered if anyone was to be marched up the black stairs. . . . He or she might just earn a reprieve.

If they showed.

Otherwise, he'd have to give Silas' speech. That would be quite a memento for the newsreels. David Valentine, former Resistance hero, praising the Kurians.

Valentine climbed the steps toward the multifaceted blister, saw a Reaper inside, something else, looming behind, like an octopus perched on a leather umbrella.

"Take my ring, David Valentine," the Ready Reader said in his head. Valentine found his hand moving up, passing through the glowing pane at the bottom of the blister.

His hand came back, suffused with light. Drops of rainbow fell from his hands.

Or was it just illusion?

The ring felt real enough, heavy, a little piece of a far-off planet weighing on his hand. He turned, was vaguely aware of cheering, and stepped toward the microphones.

Is a man just a big, talking bag of chemicals? A reputation? An aura?

No skirmish lines of men broke from the surrounding buildings. No trucks roared up the wide avenue from Mercer Island. The Resistance Network had failed, or Pacific Command had, no telling.

Valentine took a deep breath.

"I stand here, an ordinary man with extraordinary purpose. Today I've been honored with the highest award our saviors can give. But in the end—"

Did he catch a glimpse of light on one of the columns at the other end of the plaza?

"But in the end, all Kur offers us is death," Valentine said.

A Reaper at the base of the stairs twitched.

Ka-rack—Valentine heard the shot a split second later.

Another shot, and a Reaper at the base of the right stairs began to run up. It didn't make it a third of the way before it stiffened.

The crowd spread into chaos. Valentine saw men lifting weapons from beneath their heavy coats and ponchos.

It appeared LeHavre had gone one step beyond the plan for guiding the insertion of Pacific Command's forces into Seattle, and had decided to occupy the plaza before seizing it. But, then, his old captain had always been an improviser.

The Bears bellowed and shot into the air, driving the crowd toward the tower with noise and confusion. What it must have looked like to the Kurians above, he could guess—a mass attempt to storm their collective Bastille.

One Reaper stood at the base of the stairs stupidly; perhaps its Kurian had panicked and forgot what it was supposed to be doing. It jerked as a bullet struck, and immediately stiffened.

Score three for the Miskatonic armorer.

Gide missed with the fourth bullet as the Reaper ran for the stairs. Valentine backpedaled, expecting a final, brief struggle, but the Reaper threw itself inside the organic door, which opened and closed like a toad grabbing at a fly.

Below, the riot continued. Police whistles blew, but to little effect, as the Bears fell into teams, pushing panicked spectators out of the way as they streamed for the tower.

Valentine ran down the stairs, heading for Silas, who had hiked his coat up like an old lady lifting her dress to hop a puddle, and was running across the plaza.

Valentine gave chase, heard explosions from outside the column, a scattering of gunfire.

Miss L. separated herself from the crowd, flung

herself on Silas as a police detail opened up with shotguns. As Valentine ran up she drew her pistol from its holster, but instead of aiming for Valentine, she pressed its muzzle to the back of Silas' head.

"Stay down, Sly."

"I need him at the base of the tower," Valentine said.

"Get up, Sly," she ordered.

"You doing this for his own good?" Valentine asked.

They hurried into the center of the four pillars, where the Bears, dressed in variegated civilian attire, now with camouflage vests and hats thrown over them, were prying up cobblestones to make barricades to lie behind.

Valentine saw Thunderbird giving orders, as Bears and PeaBee troops emptied backpack after satchel after bag of dynamite sticks and plastic explosive through holes being made in the concrete with power drills and portable masonry saws.

"We got most of the C-4 in Pacific Command ready to blow, boss," Thunderbird said to Valentine.

"Dunno if it'll bring the whole shebang down," a Bear feeding wire into one of the holes said. "Depends on how strong those supporting towers are."

"How did you get all that past the bomb dogs?" Silas asked.

"The dogs were in the Resistance Network too," Miss L. said.

"Not—not you too?"

" 'Fraid so, Sly."

"This bang better work, or we're going to have a hell of a fight getting out of here," Thunderbird said.

"I'd like to avoid that if I can," Valentine said.

"What's the alternative?" Miss L. asked.

"We'll negotiate," Valentine said. "They've got something we want—those people and Lifeweavers I saw in that tank up there. We've got something they want, an intact tower."

"They won't listen to us," the Bear at the wires said.

"They'll listen to him," Valentine said. "Care to

deliver terms? Not of surrender, just an exchange of hostages."

"What hostages do you have?" Silas asked.

"You, for a start. Maybe they grabbed a few others on the way here. Bridge sentries and such."

"I'm not sure I want to stand in front of Seattle and start naming terms," Silas said.

"Then we'll shoot you and blow the fucker," Thunderbird responded. His hand dropped to his pistol holster.

"I suppose I could try," Silas said.

"Good luck," Valentine said, and meant it. "If it doesn't work out, try and get out of the center tower. You've got fifteen minutes from when you disappear in that tower. Any troops show up on the plaza, we blow it."

Silas gulped, looked up at the towering mushroom cap. "I'll see what I can do."

Valentine watched him ascend the scaffolding, stopping to gape at one of the frozen Reapers. He made it to the door. The organic mouth admitted him.

"Can I stop loading clay into this tower?" one of the Bears on the demo team whispered.

"Sure," Thunderbird said. "Hope this works, Valentine."

Gide returned from her sniper perch, hugged Valentine. "Long time no see."

"Thanks for keeping the Reapers off me."

"They're your fancy bullets. You want the gun back now?"

"I think it's in better hands with you."

Miss L. checked her watch every two minutes, reading the time to Valentine. They heard trucks pulling up on the roads around the plaza.

Then the mouth opened. Rafferty came out, crossed the bridge from the scaffold, carrying a little girl wrapped in a blanket. "They're coming! They're coming! Turn off the bombs!" Rafferty called.

Seven other humans who emerged, rather shakily,

still glistening with the solution they'd been suspended within, must have been favorites to the Pacific Command soldiers. Some of them cheered.

"I don't see any of the Lifeweavers," Valentine said. "Maybe this is a down payment against our leaving."

"Somehow or other, we'll make it back with the real thing," Thunderbird said.

"What is that, a kite?" Gide said, pointing up.

Valentine followed her gaze. Four shapes, reminiscent of jellyfish, drifted, circling down on air currents.

"Creepy-looking things," a Bear commented.

"Depends which side they're on," another said.

"What's that coming down now?" Thunderbird asked.

It was Silas, camel-hair coat flapping in the wind. Gide screamed. Valentine turned away when he hit.

"What was that, a bonus?" a PeaBee asked.

The four Lifeweavers drifted to earth, too exhausted to mask their native form. They couldn't even speak. It didn't stop the Bears from cheering them, nonetheless.

But one figure did not rejoice.

Valentine couldn't say how he crossed the plaza without being noticed. Perhaps he crawled from body to body, hiding among those police killed in the organized riot. But nevertheless Silvers stood over the body of his master. Valentine saw tears wet his eyes, felt his own throat tighten. Even Ahn-Kha wasn't one for tears.

Except once.

The Grog went down on one knee, put a hand against Silas' crushed face, bent down, and listened to the chest. He came away with the side of his face wet with blood.

A deep growl started in his throat. He took a blade out of his kilt and checked the edge with his thumb. For one horrible moment Valentine thought he was going to plunge the blade into his hairy breast, but Silvers made a quick, shallow cut, crossing the angled scar straight up and down, an even longer cut than the old wound. He went down on all fours and hurried to the limo, extracted his twin-barreled cannon from the cupola, and snapped on the harness.

Then he gripped the blade between his teeth and turned for the tower.

As he passed Valentine, he pulled back his lips and one ear flicked up. Valentine, unable to imitate the gesture, thumped his chest three times with his left hand.

Silvers snorted and chambered a round in each barrel. He climbed up the scaffolding, and a loud report echoed as he blew a hole in the door-creature. He worked the bolt on his cannon; then he jumped inside.

"Let's get out of here," Valentine said.

"I'll go talk to the troops outside the plaza," Miss L. said.

"Tell them that anyone who wants to march out with us is welcome," Thunderbird said. "No reprisals. No trials. No more Action Groups. We'll choke Seattle the old-fashioned way, with our bare hands."

CHAPTER SIXTEEN

―――――――― ⚓ ――――――――

*U*nion Rock, Wyoming, July, the fifty-fourth year of the
Kurian Order: David Valentine headed east again on a
road even older than Route 66, escorting two of the four
Lifeweavers rescued—some might say negotiated, others
swindled—out of Seattle. The Oregon Trail had its posts
and stops rearranged, but the old path is still much the
same as it was in the nineteenth century, right down to
form of conveyance, for oxen and horses have no octane
requirements.

Instead of bringing pioneers west, it sees refugees
plodding east and smugglers traveling in both directions.
Like their forefathers of two centuries ago, the parties
travel in groups for safety, guided by experienced mountain men. They travel armed and wary with good cause,
for bandits and grifters hover along its length, and Reapers cover a shocking amount of distance in seven hours
of hard running. All are on the prowl for the vulnerable
and the careless who might be threatened or cajoled out
of valuables, from transport animals to hand-cranked
radios, even if they manage to hang on to their auras.

There's a small Freehold or two along the trail, sometimes filling a mountain valley, or some good ground
in a river basin. Valentine, listening to stories of other
wayfarers along the route, heard talk of a big celebration
that always took place in the Wyoming United Grange
at Union Rock. People from as far away as Denver, the
Nebraska Sandhills, and the Wind River Freehold at-

tended. Picnic tables erupted during the day on land, and fireworks burst overhead at night. News was swapped for news, knitting and quilting for items from the trader stalls, and any number of young people met and married in a whirlwind of celebration. It sounded like the old summer festival in the Boundary Waters, and Valentine delayed his journey a week or two to linger and attend. He could go south easily enough from there, and, he hoped, reach Denver, and Southern Command's liaison, by late July.

They joined up with a bigger train, made up of old automobile chassis pulled by trail oxen. There was already talk of what each party would add to the festivities, making it sound like a potluck dinner with attendance running into the thousands.

Valentine didn't have to get to the Ozarks. The Ozarks came to him. A party of Wolves was in attendance for the Independence Day festivities, recruiting out of a tent thick with tobacco smoke, pecan pies, and Texas chilies and barbecue.

Valentine had seen such displays before, like the welcoming feast on his arrival in Missouri fifteen years ago. *Good God, was it that long ago?* He watched a boy clear a pie tin with two fingers like a bear dipping honey. *Enjoy it, kid. It'll be brown rice and chicken twice a week with the Labor Regiments.*

"Another Sioux, you think?" a sunbaked female sergeant with her stripes inked on her suspenders said to a bronze-skinned youth with a ponytail that dwarfed Valentine's. "Be a good summer for us if he joins. I'm sick of teaching kids how to stretch their canteens."

"Ya hey there, friend," the AmerInd said, approaching. He raised his hand and met Valentine's palm hard enough to loosen a feeding tick, let alone trail dust. "You look like you know how to keep a scope zeroed. Thinking about using it on something bigger than antelope or wild horse?"

The Wolf at the food table hurried around it and into

the crowd. "Bud above, that's Major Valentine! Tell me you ain't David Valentine, off Big Rock Hill and all." Valentine thought it an odd request. The goateed Wolf pushed forward and took off a battered slouch hat. "It's Hornsby, sir. We were in the rear guard on the march to Dallas, when the Razors were guarding the supply train. I helped you fix a bridge."

Valentine was grateful for the name. He extended his hand. "Hornsby. Red River. Good to see you again."

Hornsby made introductions to the recruiting team and guides. "I've got a couple more bodies for Southern Command. You'll want to keep an eye on these two. Meet Oberon and Titania. They're travelers like Father Wolf."

"I'll put us under your orders for the trip back, sir," the sergeant said.

"Actually, I think you're supposed to put me under arrest. But maybe I'll go with you as far as Missouri. I'll have to flake off there."

He'd let Styachowski know where to find him.

"Seen much of the celebration?" the sergeant asked.

"Just got in."

"Take a walk out to Union Rock. It's a sight to see."

Valentine saw the Lifeweavers comfortably installed in the Wolves' covered supply wagon, under constant guard thanks to the alcohol, tobacco, and firearms stored inside.

He wandered through the festival. A hundred or more separate parties seemed to be going on around a central broadway of trader stalls. Bikers congregated on their machines; black belts gave exhibitions of ice breaking for the kids. Ice cream was sold alongside bourbon and tequila. Teetotalers kept a distance from the stalls, and Valentine saw black-coated folk he guessed to be Mennonites, or maybe Amish. Games of baseball and basketball were in full swing on cleared patches of ground with equipment ranging from crude to commercial quality. Lively fiddles and bagpipes competed with accordion and tuba, but the biggest crowd was gathered around a pair of young, shaved-headed black boys creating an astonishingly complex rhythm with plastic produce buckets and drumsticks, with a few cowbells thrown in for gongs. When they finished, a preacher stepped forward and started an energetic sermon. Valentine listened to the mixture of oratory, showmanship, and gospel for a few minutes, then wandered off.

There was the profane keeping a discreet distance from the sacred. A little ways away from the rest of the camp some enterprising prostitutes had set up their tents under a sign advertising GENTLEMEN'S ENTERTAINMENTS, though their camp looked quiet for the moment.

Union Rock would be difficult to miss. It dominated the campsite like an unevenly risen bread loaf. A drum circle in tie-dyed shirts played, and passed around a joint, in its shade while a trio of barefoot girls festooned with beads danced.

There were any number of tourists walking around the rocks or climbing the more accessible parts. Valentine read an old pre-2022 landmark that mentioned this prominence as a popular stop on the westward-traveling Oregon Trail, which visitors often climbed to carve their names.

Someone had been hard at work since. A little path wound around the rock, traveled by families helping their children sound out the letters carved into the rock.

It was rather like a picture gallery, but the frames were shadow boxes, carved a forefinger's depth into the rock. Expertly crafted metal plaques were set into the boxes. Valentine moved down the line, reading with a little tingle running up his spine. The Ten Commandments, the Sermon on the Mount, and the Lord's Prayer, the Magna Carta, the Mayflower Compact, the Declaration of Independence, the Constitution and Bill of Rights, portraits of presidents and the postman Franklin, the Gettysburg Address, and an inaugural speech by Kennedy.

It wasn't limited to politicians. Valentine saw a young

man busy making a rubbing of Shakespeare's *Hamlet* quartos, and Irving Berlin had sheets of music. Robert Frost had a poem about some woods on a snowy evening, and Valentine recognized O. Henry's "Gift of the Magi" in its terse perfection. Someone went to a lot of trouble to reproduce *Whistler's Mother* and a study of a troubled-looking Lincoln in bronze plate.

Above the gallery, in letters big and deep enough to be read from hundreds of feet away, some crammed between others, some in a single line and others in a block of text, there in a glorious hodgepodge stood phrases freshly whitewashed so they might even be read under a bright moon. In fact, the work continued—Valentine saw limber and energetic young boys and girls among the rocks with paint and brushes, cleaning and recoating so the words might gleam under the fireworks. Too many for Valentine to take in all at once, he had to move from quote to quote with care.

"WE MUST HANG TOGETHER OR WE SHALL SURELY HANG SEPARATELY." "GIVE ME LIBERTY OR GIVE ME DEATH." "I HAVE NOT YET BEGUN TO FIGHT." "A HOUSE DIVIDED CANNOT STAND...." "THE ONLY THING WE HAVE TO FEAR IS FEAR ITSELF." "WE SHALL FIGHT THEM ON THE BEACHES AND IN THE FIELDS...." "NO MAN IS AN ISLAND...." "EVIL CAN NEVER SURVIVE, THOUGH IT MAY SEEM TO TRIUMPH. IT IS ONLY A QUESTION OF PATIENCE AND ENDURANCE." "I HAVE A DREAM THAT MY FOUR LITTLE CHILDREN WILL ONE DAY LIVE IN A NATION WHERE THEY WILL NOT BE JUDGED BY THE COLOR OF THEIR SKIN BUT BY THE CONTENT OF THEIR CHARACTER." "DOUBT NOT YOURSELVES, ONLY THE LIES OF TYRANTS WHO HOLD BUT A PROMISE IN ONE HAND AND A WHIP IN THE OTHER." "NO POWER FROM OUR POOR EARTH OR ANY OTHER WORLD CAN STRIKE DOWN THE GOLDEN LADDER BETWEEN YOUR SOUL

AND GOD, WHO IS RIGHTLY CALLED THE ALMIGHTY." "OUR GREAT TEST HAS COME. WE MELTED IN THE HEAT OF DARKNESS AND DISASTER, BUT SHALL REFORM, AN AMALGAM GATHERED IN THE SWORD MOLD, HARDENED LIKE STEEL HAMMERED FROM THE FURNACE."

Valentine circled the rock twice, but kept returning to the Gettysburg Address. Its handful of words renewed him like the free ice water being passed out by the young "scouts" collecting valuables for the extension of the monument.

He had a single gold coin left. He palmed it and tossed it in the old plastic bleach jug as he accepted a hard plastic cup filled from the ice jug. "Please return for reuse," a childish hand had scrawled on the cup's side.

LeHavre was right. He'd made the struggle personal. It wasn't about this or that Kurian, or even some general's ego or his career. Even his family. They were all just caught in the whirlwind, a contest of life and liberty versus tyranny akin to those the men and women who had spoken the words described, even if the stakes were higher.

The Cause wasn't found in Southern Command; it wasn't the Cascades, or even this little band of July Fourth partyers. It was behind barbed wire, in the shadow of the Kurian Towers, in ugly little killing bottles like the Bellevue gardens. In a revolt in the Appalachians, led by a familiar-sounding Golden One.

That's where he'd be too.

He let the clean, cool water pass through his lips and wash him like the baptisms the firebrand preacher was even now attending to at the creek, and read again:

. . . that we here highly resolve that these dead shall not have died in vain—that this nation, under God, shall have a new birth of freedom—and that government of the people, by the people, for the people, shall not perish from the earth.

Read on for a sneak peek at

FALL WITH HONOR

Available from Roc

Stipple Field, Arkansas, October: The skeleton of Southern Command's short-lived Air Force School craws with fresh activity.

There was a time when Southern Command had a substantial fleet of aircraft and helicopters. Accidents and lack of spares has reduced the fleet to a few choppers and long-wearing crop dusters or air shuttles, Frankenstein flyers operating on the parts of dozens of dead ships.

Twenty years ago the airfield, tower, hangars, and office space of Stipple Field had trained younger pilots and mechanics to handle and fix Southern Command's air wing, but with so few craft left, the school only operates for two months in the winter as experienced pilots and mechanics test and give initial training to the few recruits they need.

In the summer, Stipple hosts the cadet games, where promising youngsters compete in marksmanship, riding, and athletic and academic face-offs.

The rest of the year, a few custodial workers keep the place painted, cut back, and lit.

Because the location is remote and easily guarded, low-level conferences between political and military leaders in eastern Arkansas use the facility, mostly to give each side a chance to have grievances heard and smooth over the resulting ruffled feathers over alcohol in the "Flyer's Club."

Kurian spies don't pay much attention to Stipple. Nothing important ever was decided or planned there.

Which is why Colonel "Dots" Lambert chose it as the site for the Highbeam conference.

David Valentine hated Stipple Field's folding metal chairs. And the hangar lights turned the attendees' faces shades of blue, purple, or green, but that didn't bother him like the chairs. There was something exactly wrong about their design for his butt and lower back. Sitting in it for more than an hour made his bad leg ache and his kidneys hurt.

Most days of the Highbeam conference he was in it for six, wearing his rather ill-fitting militia uniform and a fine new pair of fatigue boots, Dallas-made no less, a present from Colonel Pizzaro to replace the ones lost to the Mississippi current—or a Grog scavenger looking for something he could fashion into knee pads.

The hateful chairs were arranged in a square in a big, cold hangar around a map drawn onto the floor in four colors of tape. White for topography, green for Southern Command's routes toward New Orleans, red for known Kurian strongholds and Quisling bases, and yellow for notations.

It was all bullshit. But well thought-out bullshit, in Valentine's opinion. Lambert had probably kept a team of officers working in odd hours planning an operation that wouldn't take place. Maybe it was part of the General Staff training Valentine had once been set to enter.

Lambert did her briefings on whiteboards, which she and her staff worked on for hours each morning and then meticulously washed each night.

The sentries for the conference, all of whom were going on the trip, had every reason to be alert. But Kurian promises of eternal life had found willing ears before. Some maintenance person might figure out a way to get a picture of the map with a micro-digital camera.

The first day of the conference had been spent

mostly in social activities, as officers got to know each other and inevitable late arrivals trickled in—Southern Command's rather rickety infrastructure did well if you arrived within twenty-four hours of the time on your travel orders.

Valentine played cards the first night with a craggy Wolf captain named Moytana. Moytana sported streaks of gray in his long, ropy hair and had once served as a junior lieutenant in LeHavre's old Zulu company, Valentine learned. The Gods of Poker chose not to favor Valentine that night, but Moytana consoled the losers by buying drinks.

He also received, and smoked, a cheroot with an agreeable young staff lieutenant named Pacare. He had a golden, round face, and Valentine thought he'd make a good sun king. Pacare was a communications specialist and told Valentine about the latest mesh that was supposed to keep the juice bugs out of the wiring. Pacare did enough talking for both of them.

Valentine turned in early.

After breakfast, everyone was directed into the hangar. Forty folding chairs, ten to a side, were arranged in a square around the chalked map. Each chair had a name taped to the backrest. Each person stood in front of his or her chair; a few of the regulars stiffly "at ease." A civilian who'd sat stood up again when he realized no one else was sitting.

Everyone waited to take their cue from the general, who stood chatting with some lieutenant colonels.

General Lehman, in charge of Southern Command's eastern approaches, opened the first day of the conference. The general had a famously heavy mustache that covered most of his lips. He was affectionately known back at Rally as "The Big Dipper," as the ends of his mustache visited soups and beverages before his taste buds. He was known as a hearty eater. The moniker might have also referred to his habit of dipping his little silver flea comb in his water glass at the end of the meal.

Valentine's name had been put in the line with support and technical staff, judging from the insignia around him. Opposite him sat Montoya and a couple of his poker-playing Wolves. A lieutenant with a scarred cheek and absent earlobes and who Valentine guessed to be a Bear waited at the far end of the row. Only a Bear would come to a conference wearing a crisp new uniform shirt with sleeves freshly snipped off. A pop-eyed civilian in a natty sportcoat that looked about two sizes too small fidgeted uncomfortably next to the Bear. The fresh sunburn and two-wheeler full of reference binders gave Valentine a guess that a quick look at his ID card confirmed——he was an expert from Miskatonic.

The row of chairs to Valentine's right held General Lehman and the big bugs; to his left, Guard regulars.

The assembly was mostly officers, with a smattering of senior sergeants and neatly dressed civilians seated with the big bugs.

The chair with name "Lambert" taped to it stood empty, as did the one next to it with no name on it. Lambert was present; Valentine had seen her in the hangar office with some other uniforms. She was the closest thing he had to a commander in his ill-defined, ill-starred relationship with Southern Command.

Valentine also recognized one civilian to the other side of Lehman, a well-dressed fixer named Sime. At this distance Valentine couldn't tell if he still used that rich sandalwood soap or not. Valentine had last smelled it when Sime came to visit him in prison, when he was offered up as a sacrificial lamb to doubtful Kansas officials who were considering switching sides and feared reprisals. The Kansas uprising hadn't gone as well as most hoped: The Kurians brought an army all the way from Michigan across the Mississippi and Missouri rivers and smashed the most rebellious territories before Southern Command could get there.

Sime ignored him. Valentine, skin crawling as though trying to make an embarrassed exit, doubted it was out of embarrassment.

Lambert and her group arrived. A man on the hard side of middle age with a loose-skinned face that reminded Valentine of a woeful hound stood next to her at the unmarked chair. He wore a plainly cut black coat, trousers, and leather shoes that made him look like either a Mennonite or a backwoods undertaker. Valentine wondered if he was a Lifeweaver, relatives to the Kurians and mankind's most powerful allies in the war against the Kurians.

"Be seated," Lehman said. Lehman tightened his words before shooting them out of his mouth in little explosions of air, making his mustache ripple like a prodded caterpillar.

Valentine's relationship to the uncomfortable metal chair began well enough. He was glad to sit. Metallic creeks echoed in the empty hangar.

Lehman remained on his feet: "We're present at a historic moment. You've been brought together for an important campaign. What we have come here to plan is no ordinary op. A new Freehold is about to be born. You will all be midwives." The general unbent a little. "Let's just hope it's a live birth.

"Some of you have heard rumors of Highbeam being a move against New Orleans. That's still what it is as far as the various people in your commands who are going to help you organize the men and material are to think. I expect you all to go to sleep every night with a Creole phrasebook next to your bed and maps of swamps and bayous piled on your desk.

"Our true objective is an area in the Appalachians. Some of you may have heard what's happening in West Virginia and eastern Kentucky. A coal miners' revolt has grown into a thriving resistance. Usually uprisings like this are stamped out in a few months, but the fellows running the show there vanish every time the Kurians think they have them trapped. They've got popular support and friends on both sides of the mountains.

"We're going to cross the Mississippi and Kentucky in reinforced brigade strength and offer assistance."

He let that sink in.

Valentine felt a momentary loss of balance. He'd been working out a route of march but had only a couple companies of Wolves and perhaps a contingent of training and technical units in mind when he presented his ideas to Lambert.

Lehman gestured to the big bugs behind him. "And that's it for me. I'm just here to sign and seal the op orders. You all are going to do the planning over the next two weeks. With forty of us I think we can get a little softball going on Wednesdays and Saturdays. I'll handle the rosters and decide who'll be playing and who'll be grilling and baking when. Unless you vote on basketball, that is. My headquarters, barring contingencies, will be located at the old motel just across the road. I've given most of my staff furlough or dispersed them for training. I'll try to get the pool filled so you can use it, if you like. Drop by if you want to sample the liquor and tobacco a general gets."

Valentine's heart warmed at that. It wasn't often you met a general who knew when to get out of the way.

Lambert took over the rest of the introductory briefing. She introduced the big bugs and allowed the other three sides of the squares to present themselves. Valentine was most interested in the first man introduced: Colonel Seng, who would be overall command of the expeditionary brigade. Seng had a flat face; indeed, he looked as though he'd spent some time using it as a battering ram, as it was heavily pocked and built around a big, pursed mouth suggesting he'd been tasting vinegar. After each introduction, Seng's chin dropped and he shifted his eyes to a blank space between his knees.

Seng had a lot to think about. A full regiment of two battalions of Guard regulars would be his responsibility, each with organic light artillery, plus a support battalion with more artillery and anti-armor—or anti-Reaper—weapons. Of course the men and gear couldn't travel without commissary, transport, and medical companies. Another smaller ad-hoc regiment included a full company of Wolves, three Bear teams under the sleeveless lieutenant, and logistics commandos—the scroungers. Seng's headquarters would have engineers, signals, and intelligence staff, and even a meteorologist and an agronomist.

Valentine hoped he had a good chief of staff.

When it came time for Valentine to introduce himself, Lambert nodded at him, giving him the go-ahead to use his real name. Valentine just stood and said: "David Valentine. Last held the rank of major, Hunters and Special Operations."

"I was wondering what a militia corporal was doing here," a civilian sitting next to Sime murmured, showing off the fact that she could read shoulder tabs and stripes. Sime didn't seem to hear her; he was busy refolding his handkerchief.

Some of the regular officers took another look at Valentine. For once, Seng didn't look down. Valentine nodded to Seng as he sat. The chair squeaked and the colonel returned his gaze to that spot between his knees.

"He's attached to my Special Operations Directory," Lambert said.

"Knew he was a SOD," someone in the regulars muttered.

Lambert moved on, beckoning to the woman next to Valentine, a captain with training and indoctrination who smelled faintly of boiled vegetables and butter.

Only one face hadn't been introduced, the person Valentine suspected was a Lifeweaver. If so, he—she—it? was an extraordinary specimen. In Valentine's limited experience they never mixed with so many humans at one time. He suspected they found all the thoughts and moods stressful, or perhaps frightening. The human imagination sometimes wandered into rather dark and nasty corners when not otherwise engaged.

"You've probably all noticed that I skipped someone," Lambert said, stepping forward again to give voice to Valentine's thoughts. "Brother Mark is an expert on the Kurian Zone. He's former New Universal Church with the rank of elector, I believe. He's serving as liaison between Southern Command and the rebels."

Valentine received his second shock of the meeting. An elector was a senior priest with voting privileges that allowed them to set Church policy—for all intents and purposes a bishop, though they were technically below bishops and the all-powerful archons. Most Quislings were expected to obey orders from the Kurians. Churchmen were trained from childhood to love doing so.

"He's also been in the underground longer than I've been alive. He's been serving as our go-between between Southern Command and the guerrilla army."

The sorrowful spaniel in black rose.

"I'm not sure the guerrillas rate a term like 'army' from such professionals," Brother Mark said. "May I call them partisans without offending anyone? Good. The partisan army in the Virginias–Kentucky borderland triangle isn't like the military as you understand it. It is a small cadre of leaders who go from place to place, where they temporarily swell their numbers in order to destroy a specific objective, be it a mine or a tunnel or a garrison house. With the job done the guerrillas return to their homes and remove all telltales of their participation. Still with me?"

Valentine could tell from the exchanged glances and squeaking shifts in weight the officers were uncomfortable being addressed by a churchman. Or maybe it was the patronizing tone.

"There's a potential in that part of the country for a true Freehold. With regular soldiers such as yourselves to handle external threats, the populace could organize its own defense on a county-by-county basis. I'd say the population is six-to-one in favor of the guerrillas, though they've seen enough reprisals to be chary of rising up en masse. Not the best specimens in that part of the country, either physical or mental."

He paused again to let his gaze rove over the room.

He settled his stare on Captain Moytana, who had the thumb of his fist pressed to his mouth as if to keep his lips from opening.

"Yes, we all know what happened when a rising like this was attempted in Kansas. Unlike Kansas, we already have local fighters in place who've lost their fear of the Kurians. This time the rising won't take place until your forces arrive and are integrated with the locals."

Lambert spoke again: "It's not Kansas. The Kurians are holding on to their mines by their fingernails. A couple strikes on key Kurian-held centers, destruction of the local constabulary, and a few Reapers burned out of their basement lairs would greatly further the Cause in North America."

A hand went up, and Lambert nodded.

"That's awfully near Washington," a lieutenant colonel named Jolla with the big bugs said. He was perhaps the oldest man at the briefing other than General Lehman. Campaign ribbons under his name lay in neat rows like a brick wall. "They're tender about that, what with all those Church academies and colleges and such. The Kurians in New York and Philly and Pits would unite."

"The Green Mountains are just as close," Lambert said. "There's a Freehold there. Smaller than ours, but they're managing."

"Can we count on them to take some of the heat off?" a youngish Guard captain named Bloom asked.

"You won't be alone," Brother Mark said. "God sees to that."

Valentine glanced around the assembly. Some eyes were rolling, expecting a mossbacked homily.

"You'll have a friends to the west," Brother Mark said. "The guerrillas are getting help from some of the legworm ranchers in Kentucky. About four years ago the Ordnance—that's the political organization north of the Ohio, for those of you unfamiliar with the area ... as I said, the legworm ranchers have grown restive, especially since the Ordnance began conducting raids into their territory, coming after deserters and guerrillas."

Valentine, who had fled into Kentucky from the Ordnance as something between a guerrilla and a deserter, could tell the assembly didn't like their renegade churchman. The officers were keeping their faces too blank when they listened.

"Some of the troops won't like it," a Guard captain said. "That's a long way from home."

"Their forefathers went ten times as far against lesser evils," Brother Mark said.

This time General Lehman came to his rescue. "Tell 'em what the gals in Kentucky look like, brought up on milk and legworm barbecue. You know that area, Valentine."

"They're pretty enough. Tough too," Valentine said, thinking of Tikka from the Bulletproof. "All that time in the saddle. The backhill bourbon's smooth. Everybody and his cousin has a recipe. Some of the older ones will want to allot out and become whiskey barons."

"Whiskey barons," someone chuckled. "They'll like the sound of that."

NEW IN HARDCOVER
FROM E.E. KNIGHT

FALL WITH HONOR

A Novel of the Vampire Earth

Freedom is on the march as the rebellion against the Kurian
Occupation of Earth takes the offensive. David Valentine has
recruited an ad hoc company of former Quisling soldiers and
puts them through a trial by fire with a successful raid against
an enemy armory. Now, they're ready to join forces with a
guerilla army planning to establish a new freehold in the
Appalachian Mountains.

Valentine knows that a permanent outpost near the East Coast
would provide a strategic victory over the Kurians—and he
believes that only his old friend and ally Ahn-Kha could
possibly be leading the guerillas on such a daring endeavor.
But nothing could prepare Valentine's fighters for what
awaits them at the end of their journey.

S.M. STIRLING

From national bestselling author
S.M. Stirling comes gripping novels of
alternate history

Island in the Sea of Time

Against the Tide of Years

On the Oceans of Eternity

The Peshawar Lancers

Conquistador

Dies the Fire

The Protector's War

A Meeting at Corvallis

The Sunrise Lands

Classic Science Fiction & Fantasy
from
ROC

2001: A SPACE ODYSSEY by Arthur C. Clarke
Based on the screenplay written with Stanley Kubrick, this
novel represents a milestone in the genre.
"The greatest science fiction novel of all time." —*Time*

ROBOT VISIONS by Isaac Asimov
Here are 36 magnificent stories and essays about Asimov's
most beloved creations—Robots. This collection includes
some of his best known and best loved robot stories.

THE FOREST HOUSE by Marion Zimmer Bradley
The stunning prequel to *The Mists of Avalon*, this is
the story of Druidic priestesses who guard their ancient
rites from the encroaching might of Imperial Rome.

BORED OF THE RINGS by The Harvard Lampoon
This hilarious spoof lambastes all the favorite
characters from Tolkien's fantasy trilogy. An instant
cult classic, this is a must read for anyone who has ever
wished to wander the green hills of the shire—and after
almost sixty years in print, it has become a classic itself.

Available wherever books are sold or at
penguin.com

S527

THE ULTIMATE IN
SCIENCE FICTION AND FANTASY!

From magical tales of distant worlds to stories of
technological advances beyond the grasp of man, Penguin has
everything you need to stretch your imagination to its limits.

penguin.com

ACE
Get the latest information on favorites like
William Gibson, T.A. Barron, Brian Jacques,
Ursula K. LeGuin, Sharon Shinn, and Charlaine Harris,
as well as updates on the best new authors.

ROC
Escape with Harry Turtledove, Anne Bishop,
S.M. Stirling, Simon R. Green, Chris Bunch, Jim Butcher,
E.E. Knight, and many others—plus news on the
latest and hottest in science fiction and fantasy.

DAW
Mercedes Lackey, Kristen Britain, Tanya Huff,
Tad Williams, C.J. Cherryh, and many more—
DAW has something to satisfy the cravings of any
science fiction and fantasy lover.
Also visit dawbooks.com.

*Get the best of science fiction and fantasy
at your fingertips!*